The Defendant

Romaine Brook, award-winning actress. On the witness stand—beautiful and unafraid, an inspiration to wronged women everywhere—she turned in her crowning performance.

The Judge

Cliff Rhodes, one of America's most celebrated men on the bench. He concealed a personal secret every bit as shattering as the true identity of Marc Sterne's killer.

The Victim

Marc Sterne, the spoiled son. Strong drugs and beautiful women were his life's passion—and his final undoing.

The Hollywood Wife

Audrey Sterne, the woman who had it all. Married to one of the most prominent men on earth, living a golden life, she had special interests to protect in the case of her murdered stepson.

The Detective

Alonzo Fahey, the private investigator. Hired by Romaine's attorney, he was to probe her shadowed past and perhaps save the case. Never in his wildest dreams did he imagine a truth so shocking—or so dangerous...

Also by David Cudlip

COMPRADOR

STRANGERS IN BLOOD

DAVID CUDLIP

A Warner Communications Company

WARNER BOOKS EDITION

Cover design by Jackie Merri Meyer
Cover photo by Palma Kolansky
Stylist: Nancy Sarnoff; make-up by AKIRA; leather by WESTBAY; gloves by LACRASIA

Warner Books, Inc.
666 Fifth Avenue
New York, N.Y. 10103

 A Warner Communications Company

Printed in the United States of America

First Printing: October, 1986

10 9 8 7 6 5 4 3 2 1

For
Mary Duque and Bob Frank

"Injustice is relatively easy to bear; what stings is justice."

H.L. Mencken

Author's Note

Mencken said it deftly; and I may not have said it so deftly when writing the courtroom scenes of this story. We've so many thousands of trial-gunners in this land that any of them might have chosen a different defense for Romaine Brook. But writers, like lawyers, are known to take liberties when heavy temptation strikes at us.

So I simply gave in and did it my way.

D.R.C.

Prologue

. . . As excerpted from a midwestern newspaper, an update on The People of the State of California vs. Romaine Brook.

(Los Angeles)—Tempers flared again yesterday as Assistant Attorney General Lloyd Pritter produced a threatening letter written by Romaine Brook, who stands accused of murdering Marc Sterne last November. This is the most damning evidence yet offered during the trial.

Along with a series of allegedly sordid photos taken of Ms. Brook—seen only by the judge, the jury and the lawyers for both sides—the letter and a hypodermic syringe constitute the state's main evidence to date.

It is the syringe, however, that seems to intrigue most onlookers at this trial. No fingerprints were found on it, a fact that led to Ms. Brook's indictment. She was the only person known to be at his family's home in exclusive Malibu Pointe, where and when Marc Sterne died from an overdose of drugs.

The state claims Ms. Brook not only administered the lethal dose, but also attempted to remove herself as a suspect by wiping her prints from the syringe after injecting the victim. The state's theory is that young Sterne had no reason to wipe away his own fingerprints, even if contemplating suicide, which so far is not an issue in the trial.

At least, it is reasoned, his prints should have appeared on the syringe. As there were none, a homicide presumably took place.

"She killed him," said Lloyd Pritter, the lead prosecutor, in his opening remarks six weeks ago, "and she tried to wipe away the traces of her deed. Her grave mistake."

Raye Wheeler, counsel for the young actress, objected strongly to the manner in which the letter was introduced by the prosecution yesterday. Their words heated, both lawyers were finally silenced by the threat of a contempt ruling from the bench.

Outside, it is hot in this city. But here, inside this jammed courtroom, it seems to be getting even hotter for Ms. Brook, whose supporting role in *Tonight or Never* won her wide acclaim last year and an Academy Award nomination as well.

Yet Ms. Brook seems cool and aloof, almost oblivious. She is charged with the first-degree murder of the scion of one of California's wealthiest families. A family, ironically, that controls Parthenon Studios, where *Tonight or Never*, one of the leading box office draws of all time, was produced.

Now in its seventh week, the trial continues to grip the nation's attention. So much so that Cliff Rhodes, the presiding Superior Court Judge, found it necessary to sequester the jury in the downtown Biltmore Hotel. There, under guard, the jurors are isolated from the sea of ink and heavy television coverage that have floodlighted the trial.

Off to a slow start, the trial has lately picked up pace. Local observers credit this to Judge Rhodes who, until assuming his judicial robes two years ago, ranked as one of the West Coast's finest trial lawyers, and has in fact been called by some here "the Dance-Master" for his gifted defense of former clients. Until coming on the bench, Judge Rhodes was a senior officer of the International Academy of Trial Lawyers; only a month ago he was nominated to the Supreme Court of California, this state's highest tribunal.

To date, the defense seems to be waiting its turn. As one local wag put it, "If this were a prize fight, they would've called it by now."

Still, Ms. Brook's defense counsel, though showing his age, is an experienced veteran of courtroom battles. Wheeler surprised the prosecution at the trial's opening when, after lightly cross-examining Mrs. Julio Sterne, stepmother to the deceased Marc Sterne and one of the state's leadoff witnesses, he reserved the right to recall her to the stand...

PART I

Chapter One

Day fifty-two.

You could walk the entire China coast in less time, Rhodes was thinking, or make a dozen trips to the moon. He sighed inwardly. Part of his silent sigh was aimed at the woman on the witness stand.

Rhodes's cat sense told him she was fibbing. A lie, even. Everyone hid something—past sins, a fault, a wrong against another. Something. Still, the truth could ruin people as fast as a lie, sometimes faster. What was she hiding?

Cliff Rhodes moved. His leg was nearly asleep. He leaned forward, waiting.

"On the night Marc Sterne met his death, you saw Romaine Brook. Correct?" Raye Wheeler asked his witness.

"That's right."

"And do you remember what time that was?"

"Around ten at night."

"Why do you say it was that hour?"

"Because the evening news was on television when she came to my apartment."

"You watch that news show every night?" asked Wheeler, who leaned over suddenly from an angry cough, as if someone had unexpectedly punched his neck.

Waiting for him to recover, the woman said, "I watch it most nights."

"All right. Let's say it was ten o'clock or so at night. Miss Brook comes home. Tell us what you saw or recalled. Was there anything unusual?"

"Nothing. She just stopped by my apartment. We talked and she asked for a glass of milk."

"Milk?"

"She likes milk with egg in it."

"Did she appear strange? As if she'd just come from the scene of a murder?"

Pritter struggled to his feet, waving one thick arm. "Objection! He's not only leading the witness, he's asking for a conclusion that—"

"Sustained," said Rhodes. He shook his head, smiling wanly. "You'll have to fix that question," he said to Wheeler.

He nodded, turning to the witness again. Drawing two or three deep breaths, he patted his mouth with a blue hanky pulled from his back pocket. Then he bowed with mock courtesy to Lloyd Pritter, the heavy gun sent in to add firepower to the state's case.

"How did Miss Brook appear to you that night?" Wheeler continued.

"Just fine."

"No noticeable marks? No rips in her dress? No bruises?"

"To me, she looked fresh as next Friday."

"Did she tell you where she'd been?"

"No."

"Did you ask?"

"No."

"Did Miss Brook look as if she was running away from the police? Or from a murder?"

"Objection." Getting up, Pritter knocked against the table and a sheaf of papers flew across the floor. An aide bent over to pick them up.

Two or three of the front row press rose halfway out of their seats. Stretching, gazing down on the spilled papers, they were hoping see the notorious photos of Romaine Brook.

"Up to the bench, please," Rhodes said, motioning both attorneys forward. He waited. "C'mon. You both know better. Do it the right way."

Crossing glances, the attorneys ambled away, each in a perfect contrast to the other: Pritter, large and slope bellied, his face full of blood pressure; Wheeler, features haggard and worn, his suit drooping badly around his thin, brittle frame.

"And how would you describe Miss Brook's moral character?" asked Wheeler, changing his tack.

"Wonderful. Just look at her," said the witness—as some of the jurors did for the hundredth time that day. "She is thoughtful, kind, terribly honest."

"Ever known Miss Brook to do anything immoral? Break a law, anything of that sort?"

"Well, I paid a parking ticket for her once when she was out of town."

A quick volley of laughs came from somewhere among the spectators.

"Thank you . . . Your witness," said Raye Wheeler, turning away.

"A moment, may I?" requested Pritter. He looked straight up at Rhodes in asking for a pause before his cross-examination.

"All right. How much time?" Rhodes replied.

"A minute or so. No more."

"You have it."

Pritter shifted around in his chair. Motioning his two colleagues closer, he cupped one hand to the side of his mouth to muffle his bull-lunged voice. The juror nearest to Pritter peered intently at him, as if trying to lip-read him.

A trial where time seemed to tiptoe, occasionally run, then all too suddenly stop in a freeze-frame. But in murder trials you never hurried the clock. You slow it down to expose every fact worth pinning down to get at half-truths, to let the jury hear everything so they could sift what was important. You were doubly careful of every statement, every exhibit. You let the whole wheel of evidence turn and turn again until it wore out.

That was Rhodes's formula. Murder trials depressed him. He'd done too much killing with his own hands. Done away with nameless foes in war and, now that he looked at them, done away with a long row of juries too.

Catching Pritter's eye, Rhodes pointed at the clock. The

attorney made a quick gesture, asking for just a few moments more.

Once more, this day and every day, the courtroom was filled to capacity. Bodies cramped together, bodies eager to see what lurid sparks might fly. And the press in the front rows, scribbling notes, waiting avidly for a fresh headline.

Go away, play with someone else today, Rhodes implored them silently as he ran a thumb under his collar in a futile attempt to let some air in under his robe. He sweated uncomfortably in the stuffy courtroom.

A faint rustling from the witness stand made Rhodes look over at the woman in the chair. She was fortyish, he guessed. Robustly healthy, the strong arms ending in curiously delicate hands that were clasped on her lap.

Wheeler had cruised her smoothly across the finer sides to Romaine Brook's character, and had smiled after finishing with her. But he looked old, haggard, as if all the invisible worries of the world were tied to his back. Ill, often coughing in deep spasms. Rhodes knew the lawyer's lungs were in sad shape: emphysema, a hard go for anyone, but fatal for a man who made his living with his mouth. Still, it might win him sympathy with the jurors. God knew he needed it, the way the trial was going for his client. Rhodes was fond of the older man. Very fond.

Wheeler with his young celebrity, the fated Academy Award nominee. Acting pretty nicely here too, Rhodes thought, for someone with a murder-one rap as her very shadow.

Her posture made her seem taller. She was tall, but the way she sat, so erectly, imparted a regal line to her body. An alert, intelligent face, one that fell short of beautiful but with very clean planes and more alluring than most. Moneybones is how they called that look in the film game.

A strange pull there. A main presence, as if she were touching you when she was actually all the way across the room. Tawny hair rolling to her shoulders, direct and doelike eyes, wide mouth, high breasts and legs for making a bishop jump.

Young, but how innocent?

Pornographic photos of her were now in evidence. Naked, with the mouth of another woman hanging on her breast, hands of a man or men fondling her. Hard to believe it was the same young woman sitting there so demurely. Innocent? Somehow those photos gave off a vague feeling of resistance. Eyes always closed, lips tight, jaw hard along its firm lines. Ecstasy? Or was she trying to fight?

Rhodes wondered.

Pritter came up to the witness stand, placing one meaty paw on the railing, a smile frozen on his face and a scowl knitting his black eyebrows together.

The woman raised her chin slightly, and inched forward in her chair.

Rhodes guessed that Pritter would plow up the earlier testimony and reveal the small lie. But he was way off.

"We're going to go over a few things, if you don't mind," Pritter began, his voice booming like a drill sergeant's.

"Oh, I don't mind."

"You said earlier that you've known the defendant for two years."

"Yes, that's right. Two years and two months now."

"And first met her," Pritter said, "when she rented a room in your boardinghouse?"

"It's not a *boarding*house! I lease out three small apartments in my triplex to young women from the School of Drama at the university." She spoke with wounded pride.

"Very well . . . Miss Brook rented from you from the time of two years ago. Is that correct?"

"Yes."

"And so now you know her quite well?"

"I get to know all my girls quite well."

"My girls? What do you mean by *my girls*?"

"My guests. I don't accept just anybody, you know."

"So I'm told." Pritter looked over at the jury and slowly repeated, "Yes, that's what I'm told."

Rhodes saw Raye Wheeler come halfway out of his seat. His hand went up and down, but then he sank back into his chair. Coughing again, shaking his head, choking. The young lawyer next to Wheeler rubbed the older man's back. Romaine Brook turned away and for the first time in weeks Rhodes saw a deep, pleading look on her face. Frightened, Rhodes thought, as Pritter went to work on the witness once more.

"Are you familiar with the film Miss Brook appeared in? Her second one, I believe—"

"Yes. Marvelous, wasn't she?"

"Do you have any idea what she was paid for appearing in it?"

"Objection!" Wheeler's young assistant nearly catapulted out of his chair. Rhodes cut him off. "Sustained. Where're you taking us, counselor?" he asked Pritter.

"I'm going to impeach the earlier testimony of this witness, your Honor. It needs airing, we think."

"Get to it, please."

At the word "impeach," uttered so forcibly by Pritter, the woman in the witness stand blushed. Her eyes narrowed. As Pritter watched them go very cold, his neck squeezed down into his shoulders the way a pit bull does before attacking.

"Madam," he said, "how much rent did Miss Brook pay to stay in your triplex? Monthly rent?"

"Five hundred dollars. Same as the others."

"Why does she stay there?"

"She likes it and told me so. Many times . . . There's a waiting list."

"No doubt it's wonderful," Pritter agreed. "But Miss Brook could afford her own home somewhere. More privacy, a garden, perhaps a pool—"

"I wouldn't know. I'm not her accountant."

"But you were something else, weren't you?"

The woman looked up vacantly. "What do you mean?"

"What I mean is that occasionally Miss Brook spent her nights in your room. Isn't that correct?"

"Not really."

"Never?"

"Sometimes I'd rehearse her lines with her if she had a class the next day. I enjoyed it."

"Enjoyed what? Her spending the whole night with you in your room?"

"I beg your pardon."

"Did Miss Brook ever stay the night with you in *your* bedroom?"

"Sometimes she might have fallen asleep. She worked so hard and—"

"How many times?"

"I don't know exactly."

"More than ten?"

"I can't remember," said the woman slowly.

"Twenty?"

The woman shrugged. She swiveled her head to look up at Rhodes, who told her she must answer the question.

"Possibly ten times, I can't remember . . . Sometimes she was lonely and she would stay. And we would talk the way women do when they're alone."

"That's all?"

"Yes, of course."

"Now, isn't it a fact that you are involved in the Women's Gay Liberation movement here in Los Angeles?"

"Yes, I am. No law against it either."

"Your privilege naturally," Pritter said as he scanned the jurors for a reaction. "But you testified only minutes ago as to the good character of Miss Brook . . . And now you want us to believe your statements were made in good faith. Were objective and not tainted by more intimate and personal feelings. She is presumably paid well for her film appearances. She didn't have to live with you and I suggest she did because on the ten or more nights she spent in *your* bedroom something else was going on—"

"Objection! Objection!" Raye Wheeler could hardly get it out, waving a frail arm furiously.

"You, you're a lying bastard," shouted the woman.

Hurriedly Pritter threw his deep voice across to the jury. "And it was something other than rehearsals, wasn't it, unless they've got a new name for it."

The woman's mouth opened, closed, flopped open again. She glared at Pritter, paling visibly. Then her eyes fluttered, rolling upward into white disks. She tilted, in sections, tumbling forward onto the floor in a heap. She went down so fast and hard her blue skirt twisted up over her hips.

The jury craned like storks, as if on cue, with their stunned faces glued to the unconscious woman.

What they saw, what everyone up close saw, was a large blue and red rosette tattooed on her upper thigh. Very near her shaved and exposed sex.

The room shuddered nervously. People milled around in

the aisles as reporters tried to elbow their way through. A bailiff knelt by the witness, tugging her skirt down, then patted her face gently.

Rhodes waved another bailiff over. "Clear it out. Everyone. Get the jury out of here, and tell Pritter to be in my chambers in five minutes . . . Hear me?"

Goddamn it anyway, Rhodes swore to himself.

As another yell echoed from somewhere out in the throng of pushing spectators, Rhodes glanced around quickly. He saw Raye Wheeler and his assistant, the gawky young lawyer, hovering around a quite composed Romaine Brook who seemed, oddly, to smile.

The witness sat up slowly. Rhodes guessed she would be all right. He left as he saw the last of the jurors ushered out.

Back in his chambers, he pulled off his robe and draped it on the wooden tree next to his work desk. Leaning on it, his balled fists supporting his weight, is how Macklin Price found him as she came in with a glass of iced tea.

"What happened out there? Everybody buzzin' again out in the office."

Rhodes looked away, then at her. "Pritter cooled Wheeler's witness right to the floor. She actually fainted."

"Gawd, really? I heard all the commotion. Everyone did."

"Yes, really."

"Well, don't blame me."

Moving closer, Macklin Price saw that Rhodes's shirt was wet and his unruly sun streaked hair was mussed again. Little tufts curled over the back of his collar. Time for a haircut. She handed him the tea and he played half of it down in one long gulp.

"What's in this?"

"Jose Cuervo, the Golden. Figured you might need one," Macklin replied.

"You're an everything with ribbons." He flashed her an easy smile.

"You know me, God's chosen child . . . You want your messages? A stack of 'em. One from the governor's office—urgent as diarrhea."

"Later. Pritter's due in here any minute."

"Can I listen in?"

"Sorry."

Hearing a knock, they both turned to see Pritter looming at the open door. Rhodes looked coldly at him. Pritter wore a gray suit cut by some tailor of sufficient genius to almost hide his massive width, but the clever stitching couldn't hide a double chin, nor the rolls of excess flesh on the back of his neck.

"Interrupting anything?" Pritter asked.

"No. Come on in," Rhodes said, and then to Macklin: "This won't take long. I'll be with you in a few minutes."

The door closed as Pritter asked, "Is it sit or stand today?"

Rhodes pointed toward a leather sofa, and heard the cushions squawk as Pritter dropped his freight there.

"I'm close to lowering on you, Lloyd. I thought you ought to know . . . You've seen all the dance floor you're going to get around here," said Rhodes. He sat down at his desk, lighting a cigar at the same time.

"Frosty in here, isn't it?"

"And slippery too."

"Are we informal today, or what?"

"Informal?"

"Can we talk plainly?"

"I can certainly, and you're going to listen—"

"Good then—"

"No, not so good," Rhodes stopped him.

"Look, I can't help who they put on as witnesses. If they can't come up with better than lesbians, then that's Wheeler's worry," Pritter complained.

"We've got a powder keg smoking here—"

"God Jesus! She doesn't even put on underwear. In a courthouse, even."

"That doesn't give you the right to—"

"I came down on her because that's my job. You know it is."

"You can impeach any testimony, I agree. But this is the third time you've bulldozed the jury." Rhodes floated a stream of smoke over his desk. "You tried to jam the jury and the record with slurs you knew Raye Wheeler would've objected to. I would have sustained him, too."

"I didn't hear any objection from Wheeler."

"He never had a decent chance. That's why."

"You know how it is out there. You've been in it a hundred times. I get excited—"

"You're getting me excited. Notice?"

Cigar smoke hazed Pritter's face. He waved it away only to find one more billow coming at him.

"You pulled that stunt for the last time. You're trying to slant the jury with what comes damn close to slander," Rhodes said.

"I've got a right to go after Wheeler's witnesses . . . Besides, I may have a few of my own to tell about the lovey-dovey that went on between Brook and that—"

"You've got witnesses who'll actually testify that way?" Rhodes asked, surprised.

"I said I *may*."

"*May* isn't good enough. You alleged homosexual acts between the defendant and the witness. You tried to slam it into the jury's ears before Raye Wheeler could react and I could act."

"Well, Wheeler ought to sharpen up. Not my fault, is it? I've got the clear right to demolish any defense witness's statements. Of all people, you should—"

"You're accusing witnesses of things that don't matter here. You're playing to the prejudices of the jury and sucking up to the press, too."

Pritter shifted. The davenport creaked as he handed away more cigar smoke.

"Putting on a medicine show out there, aren't you?" continued Rhodes. "Hell you will. Not in my courtroom."

"You gag ordered us with the press. Now you want to gag me when I cross-examine."

"Not quite."

"Then what?"

"Have you got someone lined up who knows there was some sort of affair going on between those two women? Have you?"

"We're looking into it."

"You think you can show, absolutely show, the woman was involved with Romaine Brook?"

"I . . . I don't know for sure." Pritter faltered.

"Here's what's for sure then. Tomorrow I'm going to strike your statements from the record." Rhodes picked up a yellow pencil, snapping it in half easily between two fingers. "And I'm probably going to remind the press again of their forgotten duty *not* to publish crap trumped up by the prosecutor... You know what you're going to do, Pritter?"

"I can't even imagine."

"You'll apologize to the witness and the jury."

"Hell, I will. You can't do that." Pritter pried himself off the couch and lunged toward the desk, then stopped abruptly as if a knife had pinked his belly. "I can file a complaint with the whole Superior Court, too."

"Sure you can. But not before I shut the book on you and throw it away."

"Stretching it, aren't you?"

"I'm going to stretch the record back into shape. You're going to help by apologizing."

"Supposing I produce a witness who knows what was going on?"

"I'll want the name first thing tomorrow."

Pritter glowered. "Is that it?"

Rhodes nodded as Pritter spun around, heading for the door. He thought of how the press would play up the fracas. A witness fainting under duress, a witness who was damn near jay-bird naked. And the jury. Seven women on that jury. Pritter must know they wouldn't be overjoyed with his sort of hammering at one of their own. Still, those same women were unlikely to forget the tattooed thigh of that witness, who had probably nose-dived her way onto tomorrow's front page.

Another knock on the door signaled in one of the bailiffs. A lanky man, stony faced, with a strong nose and cropped black hair, he came looking for guidance.

The jury was about to leave for the Biltmore, he told Rhodes. Tonight was one of their nights out for dinner, and a private room had been reserved in a Chinatown restaurant. All right? *Yes, fine.* The hotel manager agreed to open up the health club at 6 A.M. as a special favor. But it'll cost. Was there enough money? *Somehow, yes. Just see to it they don't get near the newspaper stand.* Then the little bomb: some of the male jurors, said the bailiff, are up to some light housekeeping with two of the women—the redhead and the rangy brunette with the horn-rims. *That's your department, you handle it*. But it's six weeks now, these things happen, and there's no rule to go by. They're all cooped up at the end of one floor. *I know*. We can't exactly stop it, your honor. *No one ever could, and I can't issue chastity belts either*.

The bailiff left no wiser, despising his baby-sitting chores with this locked-up jury. After a few weeks, it seemed to them that they had become the real prisoners. Surly, they sounded out with every imaginable complaint; threatened to get sick, quit; wanted to see their own worlds again. "What's happening out there, for chrissakes!" "Hey bailiff, this steak, I wouldn't sole your goddamn shoe with it." "What breed of donkey did they strain this vodka through?" "My dog gets washed with better soap..."

Everything.

The sky threatened to pour wet lead and mirror pools of water dotted the sidewalks. A knot of people crowded against the front doors, waiting for the drizzle to let up. Lloyd Pritter turned sideways and pushed his way through.

Apologize to the jury? He fumed. The press would jump all over him, and the thought of it doubled his rage. Just when he had the newspapers hooked too; the trial was nearly sewn up, all but put away.

Out on his feet, ready to kiss the canvas, the great Raye Wheeler wasn't even smart enough to know when to quit. Probably made ten million in his time. Now it's my time, Pritter thought. That was the word floating over from Oldes & Farnham. "Win this one, Lloyd boy, and we've got a cushy office waiting for you. A hundred and fifty thousand sound about right for starters? You've labored in the public vineyard long enough, eh?"

Weight. Strength. Julio Sterne's strength, the nice smooth force of money talking in green-papered words through Sterne's personal lawyers. But the high lamas of Oldes & Farnham wouldn't be so pleased if he had to apologize before the entire courtroom. He'd have to figure out how to duck that one before court opened tomorrow.

* * *

"Lawdy-dawdy," Macklin Price sang out. "No panties I hear, and all barbered up like—"

"C'mon, Macklin, just let me have the messages." Rhodes extended his hand.

"I'll read them... Here's one from the great Alonzo Fahey wanting to know if you're on for poker Thursday night." She flipped to the next pink slip, batting her eyes comically. "Fritzi called, needs to talk to you." Then she scowled. "And I already told you about the governor's office."

"Call Fahey, tell him I'll see him Thursday."

"And Fritzi?"

"I'll do her myself."

"You'd better," Macklin advised. "She sounds like what you'd call *neglected*."

Rhodes raised his eyes. "She say that?"

"She didn't have to. She's a smiler but there *ain't* no tinkle-bell in that voice today."

Rhodes rolled his lower lip under his front teeth. Send flowers? A present? Screw it, he was busy handling the hottest murder trial in years, dividing himself like an amoeba. She'd have to be patient.

"You need a haircut."

"Schedule me somewhere," he replied absently.

"I can do it for you."

"Even better, if you wouldn't mind."

"I wouldn't mind."

Rhodes missed the caring look in Macklin's face as he flipped through some papers on his desk. Forms he needed to complete before his nomination to the State Supreme Court could move forward. You'd think you were replacing God for the amount of information they requested. Taxes. Financial holdings. Security clearances, if any. Mother, father, spouse, children. Nothing for dogs or cats, but all about your homes and schools, all of them. Record and disposition of any arrests. Military service and rank. Your whole life neatly marked in small squares.

"What did the governor's office want?" he asked, looking up. "When this stuff will be ready?"

"Didn't say. They want you to call back though. His assistant."

"Okay. Let's handle them first."

Macklin nodded and looked down at her notepad. "There're those speech dates. B'nai Brith and Town Hall Meeting. What about those?"

"Tell 'em thanks, but not while the trial is on. Draft them a letter and let me have a look at it."

"And you lecture tonight at the law school," she reminded him.

"I know."

"I could call and cancel."

"You'd ruin the only fun I can count on this week. Besides, it's a new class."

"Sure. I'll get the calls going."

He watched her move off. A gazelle of a woman, with a café au lait complexion, she rolled as smoothly as a ball-bearing when she walked. He had defended her sister against charges of running a call-girl operation in Hollywood. Gotten the sister off, too, but not in time to collect his fee before she had waltzed off to Rome. Macklin had offered to pay if he halved the fee and agreed to employ her. She was so talented he had canceled the debt after two months. They had worked together amiably for ten years, singing over victories, cursing the defeats. She ran half of his life, kept him even with his calendar, out of harm's way, and tried to keep the bureaucracy of law and order off his back.

A light blinked on his phone console. The governor's office.

He spoke to a smooth-voiced man up in Sacramento. A man who was the Macklin Price for the governor, and a man who handled the larger errands. They were getting to understand each other. But this was the third time he had called about the trial: "The Sternes were good friends to the governor," the assistant reminded Rhodes, who needed no reminding. "The trial must move swiftly; the press reports looked promising, didn't they?"

Counting to five, then to ten, Rhodes was still furious when he got there. "Tell the governor, for me, to stay away from it."

"Sure. Heh, heh!" said the assistant. "I don't think you want it said quite that way, though."

"What way is that?"

"Quite so, well, stridently."

"I'd like it said about as stridently as you can say it."

"Look here, Judge. It's the governor who is nominating you to the high court and—"

"And I'm grateful," Rhodes said. "But this trial doesn't need any more kibitzers."

"I resent that. I really do." The voice was suddenly chilly.

"Drop the heat then, and we'll both feel better."

"There's no pressure at all from this end. I merely make an occasional comment from time to time."

"Three times," Rhodes said. "That's not what I call so occasional."

"I'll tell the governor. I'm sure he'll want to know."

Rhodes decided to back off, and floated a small apology. "This thing is full of booby traps, you know. The Sternes seem to be kissing the press up to a white heat, and it's nothing the governor should mix into. For his own good."

"The governor," said the assistant, "does not forget his friends either."

"Are you one of them?"

A pause. "I don't think that's fun—"

"Neither do I. Not funny at all. So let's forget this whole conversation."

"Perhaps."

"I'll get on with your forms."

"And the trial, Judge. Let's not forget the trial."

Rhodes slipped the phone onto its cradle, then pressed his fingertips to his cheekbones where blood was heating his skin. He tried to stall his temper before it ruled him. Had he screwed it for good now? He wanted that high bench appointment badly. The top rung. Criminal lawyers were rarely named to the Supreme Court. Other lawyers, of course, but not a pit man, not a trial gunner who freed people the public wanted hung or jailed or both.

Criminal lawyers, as he had been, were barely tolerated in some parts of society. Sort of half-breed outcasts with dirty hands. Mothers never wanted you in close range of their daughters. You went to church, if you went, at night. But when trouble came, it was so very different. You were this year's hero. Then you were clean and wonderful and very civic.

Rhodes quit thinking about it.

He hated getting pushed. And he resented the very hell out of the Sternes sending messages at him this way. Right through the governor's office no less. Incredible. Didn't they know the jury is the only real judge in a murder trial? What the hell could he do anyway? Plenty, he supposed, now that it crossed his mind. But he chose to ignore that dangerous voice.

He barely knew Julio Sterne, the film impressario, and had never met the dead son, Marc. But he knew Audrey Sterne as surely as if she were an everyday echo in his life. That blue warm of a candle's flame in her; a body that went from fire to wildfire faster than any he'd ever known.

But that was so long ago. And perhaps she'd changed.

Quite a social animal, though, and she probably knew all the kings and queens of everywhere. The latest rage in fashions, the best hairdressers, when to show up for the season in London or Paris. He had seen her only a few times in the past twenty years. The last time right out there in his own courtroom on the day she'd come to tell about finding her stepson's body. One of the state's leadoff witnesses.

To see her again, this way, and so close, had jolted him. Got him going again, made him remember things he thought were washed away, gone out to sea somewhere. Newer feelings that shouldn't begin when the old ones weren't even dust yet.

An hour later, he left to lecture at the law school. He was still thinking of Audrey Sterne, and why Raye Wheeler wanted to recall her to the witness stand again. Be interesting to see what that old magician had up his sleeve the next time out. Weeks ago, Wheeler had barely sparred with her. A featherweight bout.

In the deserted corridor Rhodes's footsteps tapped on the sleek marble floors. Small echoes, from his heels, not at all like the other echoes from a past that never remained buried for anyone. But only slept for a time and then, waking, froze you with a nightmare.

Chapter Two

Romaine Brook pushed the tray away. More starchy food. Enough starch, she thought, to run the laundry here in the county detention center. She almost gagged at the sight of it.

Standing up, she yawned, went over to her bed and lay down.

Try not to think of why you're here. Don't think about that night when the world emptied itself of Marc. Still, it all comes back, in darkness and light. A horror story they wouldn't dare put on film.

Not about a Sterne anyway. Me, yes, but never a Sterne.

All that pulls me through this horrid mess is the wonderful feeling that I'm acting a new part. That it goes on. But the script is lost. The director is on a binge somewhere. Yet the money doesn't run out and so they're still shooting.

Keep my eyes as much as possible on the jury. They are the lens intently focused on me. The judge is interesting, he's my producer. Soft-tough, sometimes sloppy, pretty cool though. Curiously casual when the courtroom goes crazy. One of those steady faces with deep lonely eyes. Where did he get that scar over his left eyebrow?

All those gawkers at the trial, and it's all I can do to ignore the press. A year ago, after Tonight or Never *was released, I was their golden girl. The whole world was my friend. Now I'm the princess who turned into a toad.*

Pritter is the frog-lizard. Which reptile he is depends on which day. Hopping his fat ass around and tormenting me with his forked tongue. Me, his one winged fly. I see Pritter and I know what Shakespeare meant in Henry VI: "The first thing we do, let's kill all the lawyers."

For loathing, after what he did to my landlady. I did stay with her at times. She was the mother I can barely remember. Made love together? What a laugh!

God, I'm only twenty-two and my career is so much faded confetti now. Shit is more like it, but Raye Wheeler has told me to clean up my act till he puts me on the stand . . . if he ever puts me on the stand. He will. He has to. I'll make him.

By the time I'm through, they'll think they're seeing Joan of Arc at the stake again. I can act.

Poor old Raye. His face is white as salt and he can hardly breathe. Goes through three hankies every morning. Drops pills like a junkie. But he was the only name lawyer who would take me. Owns me. I'll be paying him off for the next century.

Men get all the breaks. They never seem to learn what it's like for women. Just use you. My father—God rot him, too, wherever he is—was no better than Marc Sterne. Have to play men like harps. You must, to survive. Why does it take so long to learn that?

A rapping at the bars of her cell brought her back to where she was and wasn't. To the lumpy mattress, stained sink, cold floor, and toilet that rarely flushed.

The matron wanted the tray back. Romaine stirred herself, swinging her legs off the bed, as she'd done for several months.

Hang on, she told herself. It can't get any worse. Not this week anyway.

Chapter Three

Usually thirty or so students attended. This evening there were more, and all of them were new. Rhodes never gave lectures. He simply met several times with those wanting to talk shop, plenty of give-and-take. A free look around the corner for some; for others the itchy feeling there were better ways to draw your pay in life than by defending criminals.

"The way of a good trial lawyer," Rhodes was saying, "is the same that makes for a really good crook. You need to think like a thief sometimes. Otherwise you never know if your client is pulling your chain."

"Be a crook yourself?" asked a young woman. She sat midway up in the small auditorium.

"C'mon. I never said that."

"Even so, a lot of people think criminal lawyers are the grubs of the law."

"What do you care what they think?"

"I don't want to be a grub."

"Well, if you're the kind that would really go sailing when the jury comes in voting your way, then maybe you'll like it." Rhodes shrugged. "Otherwise, do something else."

"You think we're too easy on criminals here in the United States?" another asked him.

"Outside of Russia," said Rhodes, "we've got the stiffest conviction rate in the world."

"I don't believe it."

"Look it up."

Another query. "What did you mean when you said only poets should write laws?"

"Where'd you see that?"
"In a back issue of the *Law Review*."
"I was just making a point, I guess."
"But what point?"
"Laws are too hard to understand," Rhodes said. "You can't expect people to respect what they can't understand."
"What's the answer?" asked the same student.
"I don't know. But it's worth working on. The Ten Commandments are on one page, and they've stood for a couple thousand years. No changes. Everyone knows the score."
He beckoned to a heavy-faced young man, a few rows higher up. "This one's off the wall," said the student.
"Go ahead."
"You think it's unethical for lawyers to sleep with their clients?"
Rhodes smiled slowly. Guffaws crisscrossed the room. Every session produced at least one bell ringer, part of a game the students cooked up.
"Up to you," he said. "But that's how you get arrested for bravery."
"How often does all the truth come out in a criminal trial?" asked someone else.
"Rarely," he said. "No more often, I suppose, than it does in a marriage or a divorce. A trial is a dispute. No one tells all he or she knows."
"You think that's right?"
"I think that's life."
Rhodes felt himself growing tense and tired. He had skipped lunch, trying to catch up on some personal mail. And he hadn't slept well the night before, thinking about her again.
"Just a couple more, okay?" he said. "Then I gotta go." He nodded at a student who circled one raised finger in the air.
"Why did you quit practicing and go on the bench?"
"I wonder myself sometimes."
"But you quit."
He shrugged. "Maybe I burned out."
"Don't you miss all the publicity?" he persisted. "I mean, you were the Dance-Master and everything. So don't you miss all that?"

Rhodes blushed slightly. "No. I'm getting more press than I want right now"—and went on quickly—"and, I want to leave you with a little problem. . . . Discuss it next week . . . Ready?" He waited until he saw enough faces nod agreement.

"All right," he said. "If I hit you with a pipe and break your arm, that's assault and battery. You press charges, and the law's coming after me now. But what if I say I love you, when I don't and when you want me to? I don't even have to touch you to murder your heart and soul. But you can't really press charges, can you? Why not? And what causes more damage—a broken arm or a busted heart? For next week, so think on it."

Up next to a pillar in one of the highest rows, a fuzzy-haired man waved furiously. "On your current trial, Judge?" He stood up in the light of the auditorium.

"Yes?"

"You under any political pressure there?"

Rhodes had seen this man before. Wearing a three-piece business suit, he seemed older than the other students. Rhodes tried to get a fix on the man's face.

"Do I know you from somewhere?" he asked.

"I've been to your court."

"Have you? In what capacity?"

"I substitute once in a while for the regular guy from the *Times*."

Now he remembered. The reporter leaned against the pillar and stared at Rhodes expectantly. Some of the students swiveled in their seats aiming sour looks at the gatecrasher. A few hisses sounded.

"Got to take off," Rhodes said. "See you next week . . . Be careful which professors you *don't* kiss."

Walking away from the lectern, he went through a door to the faculty room. Usually he would stay longer, answer whatever he could, loving the fun. Always trying to find out if there was any real talent coming up. Someone with a fleet brain, healthy ego, an idealist, an aggressor.

But he was exhausted, and dinner awaited him at home. He was slightly miffed by the reporter sneaking in, but it would give the students something to talk about. He loved the school, and he came there gratis. A small enough service for a place that had saved his sanity after Vietnam had nearly rolled him into a ball.

Gravel crunched under the old Bentley's tires as Rhodes pulled into his driveway. He pushed a dash button, watched the light flood out from under the lifting door, then drove in and sat there. His hands remained on the wheel as he thought about the reporter's question.

Political pressure on the trial? Maybe. Meddling? Yes. Was a signal coming down from Sacramento? Get the actress convicted, or you can forget about your Supreme Court appointment.

The governor owed him.

Rhodes had campaigned hard for the man. Made the effort when his reputation as a trial lawyer was at its peak, and when he was known just about everywhere in the state. With the timing nearly perfect, he'd pulled some votes and raised buckets of money in a very tight race.

But this was Julio Sterne country, too. A very big tuna in these parts. Not just the kingpin of a film studio, but one of the top industrialists in the state. A man who had lost his only son.

Blood for blood. The trial was beginning to smell like a hot brake, thought Rhodes as he lifted his foot off the one in the Bentley. The state didn't have that strong a case against the girl. They must know that in Sacramento. Maybe Sterne knew it as well, and that's why all the not so velvety pressure was coming down.

Leaving the garage, he lingered on the flagstone walkway to catch the cooling breeze. On the higher ledges of Bel Air the soft night air drifting in from the ocean would clear his head. Perhaps it would clear his doubts, too.

He came to the door and fished in his pocket for the key. An overhead light cast his shadow against the white brick of the house. Suddenly the door flew open, startling him. He jerked sideways, then saw Consuelo Ramirez, his housekeeper, the front of her white apron wound nervously around her plump brown hands. Small and dark, her graying hair seemed even grayer in the half-light, and the brown eyes a size larger now in her round Mexican face.

"Now what you do?" she asked opaquely. "You come in quick."

He grinned. "I come in, get a drink and have your dinner. What's the *comida* tonight?"

Consuelo stood in the foyer as Rhodes stepped in, licking her lips nervously.

"What's the matter? You hear from your ghost or something?"

"You not hear? On tee-veeah every few minutes."

"What is?"

"The *abogado*, your friend. He get sick, they say, and go to hospital."

"Who?"

"The . . . man . . ." her words stumbled ". . . the one who fight for girl . . . Wheela—"

"Raye Wheeler?"

"*Si!* Him, your friend," she repeated.

"Christ Jesus!"

Consuelo tapped her head, her belly, and both sagging breasts twice, making the sign of the cross, praying up her saints to forgive Rhodes for his oaths.

Throwing his briefcase on a bench, he bolted for the phone in the library. Calling the local CBS station, he identified himself to the news desk and asked which hospital had admitted Raye Wheeler.

Cedars-Sinai.

Dialing again, he was put through to a floor nurse whose rundown on Wheeler's condition was as clipped as her sharp tone. He asked for Wheeler's doctor, who was unavailable. Rhodes left a request for a call-back, any hour.

He tried another call to Macklin Price, who didn't answer. Another one to his law clerk, to whom he gave instructions as fast as he could reel them off. Then to the Biltmore and the bailiff there, telling him to advise the jurors of a pending trial delay. *And, no, there wasn't time now to discuss any more complaints.* Finally, the call to Pritter who seemed almost enthusiastic. Rhodes guessed it was because the prosecutor wouldn't have to stand up and make his apologies after all.

Calling around had taken up most of an hour. Consuelo brought his dinner, setting it on a small table: soup, enchilladas gummy with crabmeat and cheese, a pot of steaming coffee. He snatched a few bites, drank all the coffee, and waited for the phone to ring.

He thought, thought again, and became certain the defense would ask for a delay. Days possibly.

Rhodes swore. He played his nerves off with a cigar, and paced the room. He spent more time in the library than in any other room in the house. Some of his best memories were locked up there. Shelves halfway up one wall held leather scrapbooks with clippings of court fights he'd won, and some he'd lost, too. Macklin had kept them as dutifully as an archivist. His trombone, in a crocodile case, leaned up against one corner.

The walls were painted in Ferarri-red lacquer that shone in the subdued light of brass table lamps. A fun room, bright and cheerful, banked with deep padded couches and chairs covered in three hues of Brazilian leather.

The room meant comfort, where he could do as he damn well pleased. Read his favorite poets—Blake and Tennyson and Burns; study up on some little known point of law; drink with his pals; and dream of court battles he would never fight and of loves he would never touch or know.

But no poetry tonight. Still mired in heavy thought, he opened the French doors and went out on the terrace.

Burke? Was that the name of Wheeler's assistant? Just a rookie who looked as fragile as a hummingbird. A clumsy looking boy with a ripe girlish mouth. Pritter would blow him away. If a new lawyer were called in, a delay could roll into weeks.

As the hours ticked by, he waited for the doctor's call. Then he prayed, once and silently, for Raye Wheeler, who had taught him so much about the finer art of getting juries to see only white, when the truth was made of so many colors.

Audrey Sterne was saying goodbye to the last of the guests in Malibu Pointe. Not the sort of guests who were socially close, but just a handful of volunteers who offered to help her with the Motion Picture Relief Fund ball. They'd come for coffee and cake after dinner to discuss some last minute details.

The table layouts. The flower arrangements. Graphics for the souvenir program. A change for the soup course because avocados were so pricey this year. All the last minute naggers had to be settled.

This upcoming Friday, she would accompany Julio to Masquers for dinner with the other studio chieftains. She would be ready for them, have her end of the planning buttoned down perfectly.

She went back inside. At the end of the mirrored front hallway she walked a few steps to a drawing room rarely used except for nights like this one.

Kardas was cleaning up the cups and saucers and plates. An image that she knew so well. Black hair, thick and beautiful. High Magyar cheekbones and a complexion most women slaved for. Dark eyes that followed her like a dog's. Her houseman but her husband's valet.

"Ferenc," she said, stopping at the door, "this can all wait until tomorrow."

"I do it now. Very easy."

"Suit yourself. But I'm going up."

"Perhaps later?"

"Later what?" But she knew.

Ference Kardas looked at her brazenly. He looked at her in a way that no woman ever mistakes, not even once. Folding his arms across his white linen butler's jacket, he said: "Later, I come to you. He's away for two more days. Why waste them?"

"Julio's apt to come home"—and Audrey caught herself—"it's over, Ferenc. Totally over. We made a stupid mistake."

"But you must think how happy we were for—"

"Over. Please get that absolutely straight. Will you turn out the lights?"

Without waiting for his answer, as there was none, she left the room, her ash-blond hair swinging against her stiffening shoulders.

Ferenc Kardas stood quietly, musing to himself. So much she didn't know. Probably nothing at all of the arrangement he had with her husband. To keep her content, pleased, served, especially when Julio Sterne was away on his everlasting business trips.

A good thing, a necessary thing, thought Kardas as he stacked more Limoges china on a silver service tray. This was a good life. A very good life before Marc Sterne died. Profitable. Warm in bed with her, too, in this lush glass palace by the ocean.

No, she knew nothing. But it wouldn't do to press her, not now. Better to keep a watch on her.

He owed the old man. Kardas had owed him ever since Julio Sterne had found him—an ex-captain in the Hungarian army, a refugee who had crossed illegally into America from Canada. An actor with some skill but with no movie parts for that small skill to earn a living on. Sterne had taken him on as a valet, and paid him more to double as a houseman after his marriage to Audrey.

He was very grateful to Julio Sterne. But now Kardas wanted the wife again, the leggy blonde with that face. It was all right with the old man, but no longer with the old man's wife.

Something had to be done.

Soon.

Chapter Four

Arriving at Cedars-Sinai, Rhodes chased through a maze of corridors, saw the doctor, then was sent to Raye Wheeler's room. It was the fifth day after the trial had once again become a snail.

His usual rule was to stay clear of hospitals. After spending months in two of them in the Philippines and Texas, any reminder of those days still made his spine wiggle. He wouldn't have done this for most lawyers. But Raye Wheeler was someone very special, easy to rate, both as a friend and as one of the finest legal minds Rhodes had ever known.

Bending closer, he could see webs upon webs of tiny lines in Raye Wheeler's sunken face, as if a hairnet had been pressed into the grayish skin.

"Raye," he was saying, "they may not put you on the cover of *Sports Illustrated* next week, but you'll be out of here before we know it."

A quivering smile from Raye Wheeler, who could make a good guess how he looked. Like a skeleton. But he was too weak to banter now.

"They only gave me a few minutes, Raye . . . Anything I can do for you? Look in on your house, anything like that?"

"Taken care of," murmured Wheeler. One bony hand gestured on the sheets. Its veins stood out, greenish, like the larger one pulsing near his ear. "No good at all. Me like this, with everything up in the air." Wheeler began to wheeze, his lips chattering together as his head rose a few inches.

"Easy now. Let me do the talking. I've got to convene the court again pretty soon," Rhodes said. "That's partly why I'm here, Raye. Can't hold it up much longer as long as your client is represented in court. They say your boy Tommy Burke is going to stand in."

Wheeler nodded.

"Looks to me like he's still got diaper rash . . . Pritter, you know?"

"S'alright. Has to start somewhere, doesn't he? You did and I did."

"You're not thinking of calling in someone else?"

From the back of Wheeler's mouth a sound came like two drumsticks clicking together. "No mon-money. Took the case for a song."

Rhodes sat back. "Well, I didn't know. Do what I can to help, but I have to keep things from drifting."

"Need help, too."

"It's not over yet."

Wheeler's eyes glinted, sharp as two needles. "Can you get Fahey to help us?"

"Fahey? Why him?"

"S'good, that's why. I need that beserker for a few days. He begged off once. Too busy."

"You want more investigating done? Late in the day for that, isn't it?"

Wheeler could barely shake his head. "Some loose ends. Couldn't get to them all and look at me now."

"Sure, I can try talking to Fahey, or send him to see Burke. But that's all I can do."

"Talk to him. I need him."

"Okay, I'll ask . . . Anything I should know about?"

"She's adopted. See if he can find her family. Fahey's good at—"

"For money help? For that?"

Wheeler nodded weakly again. "Unless you can get us public investigators."

"I can't, Raye. Your client doesn't qualify."

"She's broke."

"Sorry, but no go."

Wheeler's head fell away and his chest seemed to flatten. His head lifted off the pillow once more as he sucked air before expelling a sob. Pink foam oozed from his mouth.

Rhodes reached swiftly up to a small console dangling at the head of the bed. He pressed the button for the nurse three times. To the side, on a cabinet, he saw a kidney-shaped steel dish full of gauze pads. Taking one, he patted away the stringy drool on Wheeler's chin.

"Stay down and don't talk, Raye. Everything'll be fine."

Looks like a ghost, Rhodes thought, held together only by loose wires. A battered warrior struggling for another swipe at the world, yet one unable to answer the call anymore. Wheeler's hands shook, a shoulder twitched, and then he passed out with a hollow moan.

The nurse came in. "You rang?" she asked.

"He's coughing up. I don't know how to help—"

"I think you should leave now." Going to the bed, she straightened the covers and smoothed back a scarf of white hair from Wheeler's forehead.

"How can I find out how he's getting on?" Rhodes asked. "The doctors here are almost unreachable."

"Call the desk on this floor," the nurse replied without shifting her gaze off Wheeler.

Rhodes leaned over and opened a briefcase. He pulled out a bottle of Jack Daniel's Black, walked over and placed it on a windowsill. The nurse looked up, a frown galloping across her face, and her lips seemed to disappear instantly. Hand on hip, she waited for him to leave.

"Guests, you know," Rhodes said haplessly.

"He can't have anything like that." She pulled on the chromed arm of an oxygen tent, draping the plastic hood over Wheeler's face.

"He'll like knowing it's here, believe me."

"I'd like knowing that you're out that door this very minute," snapped the nurse.

"Sure. On my way. He was head of the varsity, you know. Take the best care of—"

"We always do our best." She dismissed him, annoyed.

Rhodes walked slowly to the elevator, pausing to look at several framed prints on the pastel walls. One was a Picasso copy, another a Cyrik, further down a Matisse. The place could pass for a good hotel, was famous, had the best and hired the best, and took care of half the Hollywood clan.

And none of them were more colorful than Raye Wheeler in his time. There weren't half a dozen lawyers alive who could quarry rock alongside the man.

Grim lipped, Rhodes waited for the elevator, certain that Wheeler would never go into the pit again. The pressure would be too great. He'd never withstand it in his condition.

Rhodes remembered back to a time when he had been just a beginner trying to unravel the mysteries of the courts: who the stricter judges were; where the real talent was in the D.A.'s office; how to butter up the court clerks who seemed to run his whole world. He had nearly starved learning his way around. Who needed a Vietnam vet to solve their legal problems anyway? No one, that's who.

And then one day the widow of a police officer had asked him to defend her daughter on an embezzlement charge.

Against the odds he had won. He had caught Raye Wheeler's benevolent eye, and Wheeler threw a few smaller cases his way. More wins. Then the older lawyer had asked him to help out at fifty bucks an hour in some really important cases, carefully watching him. Cuffing him with sharp words when mistakes were made, but showing him the craft: how to read a jury, how *not* to cross-examine, how to learn a judge and play to the judge's style of thinking.

How to talk soft with nails in your words. Where to set the traps.

Rhodes reached the street. His eyes stung, thinking about it. He wanted to offer his hand to an old friend. Both hands if he could. But this time other kinds of hands were needed.

He would try to persuade Fahey to take a look around for Wheeler. This trial was getting so much attention that Rhodes was ready to bend over backward. He had to.

He had thrown his last big trial out of court. And the press had bared their fangs and chewed him to pieces.

Child molesters, a ring of them, the worst dregs, but he'd pitched the case because the police had come by their evidence illegally. Stolen it almost. Rhodes could still hear the public outcry—mothers had called, fathers too, railing and cursing at him. The police were praised, naturally.

He needed a good, tight, fair trial now, and he'd like to go up to the Supreme Court knowing he'd done his best.

He had the power to appoint investigators to help either the defense or the prosecution. But Romaine Brook wasn't on welfare, so it was never as easy as it sounded. Still, asking Fahey to help was perfectly okay. Really a pretty small thing, Rhodes thought, for he'd already locked up the jury and gagged the lawyers so they wouldn't try their case in the news media. He could do many things as a judge, especially in a murder trial.

Nothing wrong in asking, so he would ask the Irisher, who was also a good friend of Raye Wheeler's. A dinner with Alonzo Fahey would be good for a laugh at least. And Rhodes needed one of those, too. He didn't know it would be his last one for a long time.

At the Jonathan Club in downtown Los Angeles, Lloyd Pritter helped himself to his third smoked trout. He had already put away a large fruit salad and a small loaf of sourdough bread spread thickly with butter. Eating lightly, on a diet, he basked in a leisurely day off from court.

After lunch he planned to get a haircut, see his tailor, then find out about a mortgage for a new condominium he was planning to buy.

He was about to loosen his belt buckle when his waiter hurried over to advise him of a phone call waiting for him in one of the cubicles down the hall. Pritter told the waiter not to clear the table, and charged off. It was his boss, the Attorney General, the state government's highest ranking lawyer.

"Going to be a long holdup over this Wheeler thing?" Pritter was asked.

"A few days probably."

"How's it look?"

"No different than last week. Fish is tight on the hook," replied Pritter, thinking of the trout awaiting his return.

"Who's going to take over for Wheeler?"

"Some junior who's been helping him. Burke. No one ever heard of him before."

"Well, okay then. Keep your foot down on it."

"Don't worry. We got it wrapped and ribboned. The least she'll get is hard time."

"You been in touch with Sterne lately?"

"Some. Mostly his lawyers over at Oldes & Farnham."

"And their view is?"

"Same as ours."

"There's real interest up here, if you know what I mean."

Pritter became petulant. "I've been hearing about *that* for months now."

"Just so nobody forgets."

Hanging up, the Attorney General called the governor's assistant, filled him in, and then offered a suggestion: "Drop a little weight on his head," he said. "Give him something to stay awake on. Why not hold his appointment up?"

Chapter Five

Tommy Burke came over this morning. They'll delay my trial at least a week so I can rot here some more. Tommy is sweet. Thin as a vanilla bean, pink as a baby. He stuttered when he asked if I would allow him to take over my defense—now that dear old Raye is down.

There's no more money to hire a new gladiator. Made that clear. So it's Tommy now and God help me.

He brought some newspapers and the Hollywood trades. So far I've counted fifty-nine articles on the trial in the Los Angeles papers alone. Made Time *magazine three times and twice in* Newsweek. *Mostly sly innuendo.*

That letter. Tommy is worried about it. God, how I wish I hadn't lost my head and sent it to Marc, that prince of all bastards. Nasty as I could write one, and Pritter waved it in front of the courtroom like it was my white flag of surrender.

Raye Wheeler told me before the trial began that it's always a contest for truth. I tried not to laugh. No one can stand the sound of truth. Hollywood truth is the biggest illusion since the Resurrection or something. Celluloid truth. Takes one lit match to make it disappear.

The truth about Bastard will never be known. Too slimy. They'll never get it out of me. If I tried, they'd twist me into a liar, and send me up for sure. I have no real proof anyway.

Pritter has it all screwy. I never knew about those disgusting photos. But I know where they were taken and why. Pritter thinks I was threatening Marc Sterne about them. That I trashed him out of revenge.

The letter was only to get my money back. Fifteen thousand I loaned him like an idiot from my last payment for Tonight or Never. *And then the other money for a screenplay idea that Parthenon bought from us. My idea, the whole thing. Bastard goes and puts his name on it. Collects the whole thirty-five thousand in front money we were supposed to split.*

I got taken. But who can I tell that to. They'd for sure think I had a motive to get him. Me versus the Sternes is a joke.

Tommy Burke doesn't know what I've got cooked up on my abortion angle. That'll take care of those awful photos. I can out-act anyone in the courtroom. I'll have to.

Chapter Six

Curtains of rain fell over Los Angeles all the next day, the sky guzzly, unable to wring itself dry. Streets flooded to the curbs. Traffic crawled along like armies of wounded caterpillars.

Rhodes drove impatiently. Spotting an opening, he ripped the wheel over, and sped his chocolate colored Bentley up an off ramp. The going was somewhat easier on the side streets. Half an hour later he had slugged his way across Sunset Boulevard, out beyond Brentwood, then finally to Lost Canyon Road.

A good car the Bentley. Tired at the seams but still steady and he liked its comfort and depended on its strength.

The windshield fogged. He wiped it with one hand as he braked twice, fishtailing on mudwash oozing off the hills. After nearly missing the stone pillars marking the driveway up to Masquers, he skidded more on the way up. Leaving the keys with the doorman, he took the steps two at a time until he reached the double oak doors.

Just past seven in the evening.

Behind a front desk sat Ginty Jellicoe, working his way through a racing form. A friendly man, once ranked sixth among the best light-heavyweights, his face had a battered look. One ear was half folded from all the hitting it had taken in the ring. That was Ginty's left ear, as he'd always been a mark for a fast right hook. A couple of his front teeth were whiter than the others. He had been at Masquers for ten years, keeping the riffraff out, and he ran a small betting book on the side. Ginty was also the man to see for a ride home, if you'd been trying to set any new records at the bar.

Marking his place with a pencil, he rose to greet Rhodes. "You been a stranger, Judge. Wet out there, huh?" He flicked a few drops off Rhodes's shoulder.

"Like someone pushed the whole Pacific our way. Your horse come in today?"

"Things are swell," evaded Ginty Jellicoe with a grin that threw his jaw over to one side. "There's an underpriced filly in the fourth tomorrow at Hollywood Park. Looks real good on form. Like some of her action?"

"Only on your side of the sheet."

"Judge, I just give with a little advice here and there. Customer service is all."

"It's okay by me, Ginty. I never issue warrants when it rains."

They laughed.

"Six-to-one, and that girl is wire-to-wire," Ginty urged.

Never yet had he hooked Rhodes into a bet. Talking to him openly about the ponies gave the impression they did some wagering together. The word got around, even if untrue, and that was good for business. Rhodes let him get away with it because Ginty did him small favors and asked no questions.

"Tell you what, Ginty. I'll give you six-to-one the filly doesn't hit the wire first. How's that?"

Ginty lifted eyebrows bumpy with scar tissue. "That ain't good for anyone's reputation, Judge. You gotta know that."

Rhodes laughed again, then asked, "Fritzi around?"

"In her office. I'll ring in for you." Ginty reached for the desk phone.

"No, no, don't bother her. I'll be in the bar."

"She comes out, I'll give her the word first thing."

"Good luck on the filly."

Across the red carpeted lobby, past the coat check, Rhodes stopped at the cigar counter. He asked for a few Honduran Panatella 6's. By the side of the counter a Dow Jones broad-tape clacked away with news flashes from around the world, and he paused to scan the tape.

He saw her then. She stood just inside the curved opening to the bar. Moving a step, he could see Julio Sterne too, and Barry Diller of Twentieth-Century, and then the heads of Paramount, MGM and Columbia. Studio moguls. He supposed the women standing around were their wives.

He wished he had not seen her. But he kept looking right at her as if she were some optical magnet.

Polite waves a few times at a distance were all they had managed since she had come back to California. But then they traveled in very different lanes. She had lived in London for years, married there to some earl or lord until a messy divorce had dropped an axe on that one. Twin boys. He remembered reading about them in the papers when she had married Julio Sterne several years back.

Polite waves except on the day when she appeared in his court. Merely some very polite words then, as she took the stand and stopped his heart, all in one moment. A helpless feeling. Like giving in to a bad habit, and he knew he ought to know better—a lot better by now.

He took his cigars, signing for them. When he turned again Audrey Sterne was so close he could touch her. The sultry tint of a Damascus rose under her skin, swept back ash-blond hair falling to her shoulders, a mouth he could never forget. Nor the eyes glinting gray and green, and sparkling so you thought they were hooked up to a private battery. A thirty year old face on a forty-three year old neck, and still very nice scenery in any land. He knew women who would trade teeth to look like Audrey Sterne for only one night.

"Cliff," she said. "Well, how nice to see you."

"You look lovely, Audrey."

"Thanks, really."

"Having dinner?"

"Beastly night to be out," she said. "Yes, it's a get-together for the Motion Picture Relief. Julio is chairman this year."

"Busy man, I hear."

Rhodes thought about his recent dust-up with the governor's assistant. How Sterne was busy backstage, putting heat on the trial. Or was he?

"I'd invite you for a drink with us," said Audrey, "but I suppose that wouldn't look right, would it?"

"No, I don't think so. But thanks anyway."

Still looking at her, remembering, he nearly failed to see her husband.

Audrey had braved it out, coming up to him, wanting terribly to find out if she were nervy enough. Showing no telltale signs of the small but growing battle brewing inside her. She was sure she had overcome her fright, and was proud of herself.

"You'll pardon us, we're going in to dinner now," said Julio Sterne, more like an order than a suggestion.

"Yes, of course," Audrey spoke softly. "Darling, you know Judge Rhodes, I'm sure." Her fingers fluttered nervously to her throat. A diamond, big enough to skate on, shone brightly on her finger.

"We've met once or twice before, haven't we?" said Sterne tersely. He gave Rhodes a tight smile, a smile made by a plastic surgeon.

Rhodes nodded. "Nothing to do with the trial, Mr. Sterne, but I'm terribly sorry about your son. I've never had an opportunity to say so."

"Thank you. No one is sorrier than me."

"Naturally," said Rhodes, distinctly uncomfortable now.

Sterne slid his hand under Audrey's elbow, guiding her away. Tall, much older, but ramrod straight, he had an aquiline nose and face. A full head of white hair that streaked its wings over his ears. Supposedly a tough operator and he looked it. He certainly seemed to know how to keep a towrope on his wife.

Rhodes watched Audrey disappear, amazed at how the feel of her still lingered. A surprising feeling like salty and hot mouth blood after an unexpected blow. The heat of her nearness had dazed him.

The crowd in the bar wore everything from business suits to tailored denims. Rhodes went around to the far side, where it was still too crowded for him.

Two women he was mixed up with under the roof of one restaurant. Lovely. Almost like shooting yourself in the head, he thought.

Shaped like a bow, the bar had an overhead bridge of stained glass that ran its full length, and under the bridge were racks of upside-down snifter glasses, the only kind used at Masquers. At the back beveled mirrors were separated by six hand carved figurines of satyrs and maidens. A quick look into those mirrors and you saw double the number of people actually there; triple if you hung around long enough to have yourself a real outing.

Two old-timers, black men wearing red waistcoats and black bow ties, made the drinks. They had been there as long as Rhodes could remember, and were one of Masquers' many traditions. He liked it here, the very good bar, the waiters, the rhythm, an atmosphere that appealed to women and men.

Rhodes asked for a double José Cuervo Gold, no ice, from a nearby waiter. The drink was in his hand within a minute. Wonderful service—you paid for it—but it was the best anywhere. He stopped to say hello to some people he knew, and then went over to the baby grand, where he sometimes swapped one-liners with Sweetpear Porter, a musician from Memphis with the bluest of blood in his musical veins.

And watched, fascinated, as Sweetpear's fingers moved like fast mice up and down the keyboard. Beautiful Gershwin stuff. Once in a while for fun, they played together, by themselves, but Rhodes never kidded himself. Sweetpear was in another class, a natural, and did it by ear alone.

Rhodes ran some of the drink into the back of his throat. Partial to José Cuervo Gold whenever his drinking hour came, he saluted Mexico for ever thinking it up. Tonic for banging nerves, and when they banged, a couple of deep conversations with good old José usually cooled him off. When turning forty, he had upped his daily cigar ration to three and lowered the Cuervo intake to no more than four ounces. Which usually meant one high octane drink from sundown to sundown.

Tonight would be an exception: for Fahey, ex-police officer, a four star dreamer, and now an eminent chaser of lost or stolen art. Damn good at it, too.

Going over to sit by the fireplace, Rhodes soon heard Fritzi's laugh roll across the room. Then he felt lips brush his ear as he inhaled the exotic fragrance of her perfume.

He stood up, and she sat down.

"So where've you been?"

"Waiting here to see if you smell as good as you look. And you do."

"I mean for the last week, lug."

"Looking for my lover," Rhodes said.

"The one you lost?"

"The very same, kiddo."

"She's upset in the extreme, I hear."

"And she's always so beautiful that way."

"You ought to be arrested or something," said Fritzi Jagoda. "You know that?"

She seemed put out, but he knew she was only womaning him. "You always arrest me, especially the way you walk," he told her.

"And you're getting very unreliable."

"All the way busy, too."

"You're not forgiven. You look tired, and I've missed the hell out of you, Cliff."

Rhodes sat down again. His hand was on her knee, and his eyes never swerved from hers. She smiled finally, but he knew she would rub more scolding into him for a day or so.

"Seen Raye?" she asked. "How is he?"

"The doc says the emphysema is bad, and there're other pulmonary complications. A mild stroke maybe." Rhodes blinked the wet from his eyes.

"Oh God, really? You know what?" Fritzi's face lit up. "I'll send his food over. Be a lot better than that hospital fodder."

"Better call first. I think they've got him on the tubes."

"Well, I'll find out. What happens for you now?"

"Monkey-wrenched again. Have to delay the trial for another week or so."

"Doesn't sound like he'll be up by then."

"I doubt if he'll be up in a month. But we have to keep going. Got a locked up jury for one thing."

"That poor girl too," Fritzi said. "She must be ready to smash down the walls. It's been months now, hasn't it? I think anyone would go crazy in all that time. I would anyway, I'd be a wreck and worse."

"About five months to be more exact," Rhodes said, hoisting his drink. He looked up briefly over the fireplace to a Frank Tenney Johnson painting of a lone cowboy nighthawking his herd on some lone prairie. A painting he greatly admired, it reminded him of his younger days in Montana.

"You think she did it? I don't believe it somehow."

"I can't talk about that, Fritzi."

"I feel sorry for her anyway. Are you going to break training and come over tonight?" asked Fritzi pointedly.

"Soon as dinner with Alonzo is over, I'm there. And you're shameless," he said, reaching for her hand again.

"Well, I'm liberated now, along with the rest of the girls. I can ask for it."

"You care to shout that around in here? Maybe write it on the wall a few times."

"Owner's privilege. You can say anything you want in your own joint, can't you?" She smiled back at him, having her fun.

Fritzi's gaze swept over the bar. Her eyes became intent and far off. She looked back at Cliff again, her mouth taut, a blush flaring on her cheeks.

A raucous shout rang across the room. It was loud enough to startle a waiter, who was pushing a silver cart laden with smoked salmon by their table.

"Look at her, will you," Fritzi said in a low voice.

"By the bar?"

"The one getting fresh with Robert De Niro. Six months behind on her bill . . . the nerve of some people." Her eyes narrowed again.

A woman wearing a safari jacket with matching pants had her arms looped around the famous actor. A wide-brimmed bush hat with a leopard band partly shadowed her tanned face.

"Looks like she's having fun anyway," said Rhodes.

"On my nickel too. I'm going to *fun* her the hell out of here."

"Easy, sweetheart. Maybe she went to Kenya and just forgot."

Fritzi was already off her chair, and she blew him a kiss as she moved away. She possessed what Rhodes liked to think of as a mellow figure: a well slung front, haunchy at the hips, flat bellied, and lovely long legs. She moved well. He liked watching how her midnight dark hair shone like the surface of stilled water.

Those were only her assets for show. The interior qualities, the ones you had to learn about, gave her a glow and a natural pulling power that touched almost everyone who knew her. A woman in balance, he thought, very much in tune with her world.

Other women, as far as Rhodes could tell, rarely seemed threatened by Fritzi. They liked her, as men did, and the few times he noticed any bitchery directed her way, she had either ignored it or foiled it with her easy laugh.

Theirs was an affair that had traveled safely for several years now. Arguments? Awkward moments? Plenty of both, but they had never sloped off the way so many affairs do, and at times he wondered why. His work was necessarily of the day, hers of the night. As a judge, he had to run his life with at least mild restraint, while Fritzi adored the romp of an active social calendar. Her nature begged for attention; his needed air and freedom to thrive.

She knew how to confuse him, though, and he let her, helplessly sometimes, as she swayed him into the ways of her love.

Yet something was changing now. Changing fast, too, and it upset him—another woman strumming on his strings. The tune was beginning to get inside him, beginning to torment him again, whenever he listened too closely.

Rhodes looked at the drinking crowd by the bar, and then across the room, in walked Alonzo Fahey. Rhodes got up, glad to send his mind elsewhere, and went over to intercept him.

Fahey threaded his way through the tables. He waved openly at everyone he had never met nor seen before, and paused to talk with two women he knew very well.

A fascinating man to watch in action, and Rhodes would lay money his friend could take nearly any woman here, waltz her outside into the rain, and somehow persuade her the wet drops falling on her cheeks were secret jewels sent directly from eternity.

Lean and deceptively strong, Fahey had earned a shattered elbow one night when chasing a crook. The man had suddenly swung around, pulled a gun, and almost put some daylight through Fahey who had plowed on, knocking the gunman over and breaking his neck. Cited for valor by the police chief, Fahey was given a medal, but that all happened before his other trouble with the Police Commission.

"Boyo, h'lo there. A bit late, we are. Traffic end by fucking end the whole way. Had a drink for me, have you?" said Alonzo Fahey coming up, a smile bright as a new penny.

"One with Fritzi."

They shook hands.

"God, will you look at all the gash in here tonight," said Fahey. A low whistle sung through his teeth.

"You're married. Off limits."

"No one's that married, Rhodes-ey boy, no one."

"C'mon, I'll buy you some of that sewage you drink."

"I mean, Jesus," said Fahey, as if hard of hearing, "all we'd have to do is kick a few husbands out to the alley, and there's enough here to last us till Easter."

Fahey stood there, absorbing the view. Women adored him. Tossed their garters and fell like cut timber for his dark Irish looks, and the small miracle of palaver he spun so shamelessly. "Can't believe a word of him," they would say as they begged for more. He had a gift for giving women a sense of place. Put them up on a very high billboard, and like kittens they would lap up the warm milk of his flattery. When Fahey was off the scene for a time—Fritzi had once told Rhodes—some of the women who frequented Masquers became uneasy. Started talking a little too loud and fretting. They missed their confidant who knew so many of their secrets.

"C'mon. Let's go," Rhodes urged, sensing that Fahey was on the roam tonight.

"See the one in uniform there. With the big melons?"

"Yeah, I see."

The playgirl in the safari rig was back on station at the bar.

"I could go stamp her parking ticket while you're slopping yourself at dinner."

"You know who she is?"

"I'm going to find out, Cliff." Fahey started his move.

Rhodes grabbed a handful of his sleeve. "Listen, that babe is trouble. Probably spreading the bug around. She's with De Niro anyway."

"She looks to me like she needs a savior. A face like that ought to be on a holy card."

"The hell with it. I'll see you later."

"Jesus, relax. A true son of a bitch you were to marry me off so young."

"You had it coming."

Fahey rocked back and forth on his heels. A woman down the bar, next to the one wearing safari, kept eyeing him. He smiled back, winking, then his fingers suddenly locked into fists. "I'm starved. I could take a whole cow down, honest," he side-mouthed to Rhodes.

In the main dining room a maitre d' greeted Rhodes politely, and tried to hide his dismay at Fahey's outlandish garb. Tonight he was gussied up in a gray lodencloth jacket with a green velvet collar, yellow corduroy slacks, a white ruffled shirt, and a red bolo tie. Rhodes was so used to the wild combinations that he hardly noticed them anymore. The maitre d' showed them to a small private room.

They passed an hour eating and catching up. Rhodes asked about Fahey's wife, Wanda, then of the darker side of the art market. He learned little of Wanda but heard a lot about Fahey's theory that all the hot art worth real money was ending up in the Vatican's vaults or private Arabian collections. Business was soft; all the good second story pros were either lying low or in the slammer.

"Ought to let some of them out, Cliff, or I'll starve this year... And you know we've some friends who're buffed off we canceled out on the poker tonight," Fahey added in a new swerve of thought.

"Couldn't be helped." Rhodes leaned across the table and poured more red Cabernet in Fahey's wineglass. "I know another friend who could use some help from you, if you can spare the time . . . On the Brook trial."

"And what would that be? Raye Wheeler already asked me once and—"

"I know. But he's sick and he's asking for help."

"Been away from that line of country for a while."

"You did plenty of it when we were together."

"Other years and other star clocks, friend." But the centers of Fahey's eyes began to glint.

"Could you give them a few days? I told Raye I'd ask you."

"What's it to you?"

Rhodes shrugged. "It's a murder-one trial as I'm sure you know. Nothing beats a fair one."

"Something specific?"

"Not that I know of. I went in to see how Raye was getting along, and he asked me to ask you. Could hardly refuse him."

Fahey ignored the wine. He chugged occasionally on a Bushmills whiskey. The true holy water, he called it. A steady drinker, Fahey managed to keep an unending flow of the stuff near to hand.

"You want me to poke around for you. That it?"

"No, not for me," Rhodes said. "I'd like you to think about going to see a young lawyer, name of Burke. He's at Raye Wheeler's office."

"They're in a spot."

Rhodes nodded. "Don't you read the papers?"

"Not if I can help it. Wanda does. A regular dustpan for news, she is . . . Last time Raye called, they couldn't pay anything. All on the come-line," said Fahey.

"They're short on money, I guess. Expensive, this kind of a trial."

"What've they really got on that girl?"

With his thumb moving from one finger to the next, Rhodes ticked off the evidence against Romaine Brook:

"A tantrum letter that doesn't sound so good if you read

it a certain way. Some lurid photos that may or may not be relevant. She was definitely there the night Sterne was killed; two gate-guards confirm it. The big thing is the hypodermic syringe. No fingerprints on it, and that is pretty hard to figure when you think about it."

Fahey pondered a moment. His eyes wandered off to the far end of the room. Screwed into the dark green wall there, a brass plaque with black letters on it read: FOR BOYS ONLY. A momento from Fritzi, who had personally fixed up the room for the stag poker games held there every other Thursday night.

"Not so bad a case for the state," he said, eyeing Rhodes again.

"Pretty political, Alonzo. Someone's worried."

"The family, you mean?"

"Maybe."

"Is this a *what*, a lover's quarrel? A fuck from the closet?"

"I don't know. We haven't heard her side of it yet. And may never. Depends on whether she testifies or not."

"Money? Photos for blackmail? Reverse blackmail?"

"Possibly."

"Or she didn't do it at all. Snow White getting her ass stung?"

"I don't know," Rhodes said.

"So why do you care?" asked Fahey cynically.

"Of course, I care." Rhodes stiffened. "This thing is a damn potboiler. She deserves a square shake, at least. If she loses, it'll go up on appeal, and I don't especially want to get reversed on any errors I made."

"You mean you don't want to look silly if you're up there on that Supreme Court?"

Rhodes admitted, "Who would?"

"I told the wife we'd go down to Cabo San Lucas for a week of the marlin," said Fahey. "Getting cranky again she is, I'll tell you for free."

"Can you delay it?"

"Have to tickle her up. Let you know tomorrow, that be good enough?"

Rhodes saw a mixture of pity and disdain now in Fahey's razor-blue eyes. Everything was there of the man, and yet nothing. The bloodhound in him, the quixotic nature, the big exuberant heart, the remorse. But loyal, always watching for you and that side of yourself you could never see.

"Like another?" Rhodes raised his glass.

"Had my barrel of wine for tonight." Fahey looked pensive. "But I've got the hell of an idea to tell you."

"Go ahead, I'm listening," Rhodes said. He got up, heading for the small bar on the other side of the dining table. Splashing some Cuervo into a tumbler, he studied a painting of a nude reclining on a pile of tasseled burgundy rugs. He hadn't seen this one before. One of Fritzi's latest touches, he guessed. Very nice.

"You listening, are you?"

"I am, Alonzo. Both ears at the ready."

"Then look at me."

"In a minute. Go ahead."

Rhodes had a pretty shrewd idea of what was coming. An old refrain by now, and he tuned out slightly while viewing the nude's turban gleaming with rubies. Slave bracelets adorned her ankles and wrists. A baby ocelot nestled against one breast, its tiny pink tongue licking close to the nipple.

"Why do you need to go up there?" Fahey was asking. "I mean, Christ, Sacramento is a bean pot. Have they an airport yet?"

Fahey was talking of an earlier time when they had worked together, and Fahey had run the three-man investigation team in Rhodes's offices. A time when there were some big wins, and they would celebrate wildly at full throttle. They had it all coming their way. A roomy floor of offices up on Sunset Boulevard, a private dining room run by a Chinese, a jacuzzi and sauna, a well-stocked bar, and streams of troubled visitors. Cops up on charges, politicians under indictment, bankers caught with their hands in the wrong drawer. Reporters hanging around, nosing under every rug for a story. Clients from everywhere, mumbling with fear. And at night, sometimes for several nights, after a long-hit in the court, they would dent every good watering hole in town. Go to Doney's and trombone for a few sets. Dine ten or fifteen strong at Chasen's over two thousand dollar dinners. Call up the girls, then take them to Puerta Vallarta,

New York, Hong Kong, who cared? They were young, on top of the heap, tough and ready. Very ready in those days.

"We could do it again, Cliff. You'll die in one of those black robes. That's why they're black. For sinners and priests and fucking death."

"For priests in your church," Rhodes reminded him.

"Who are the worst! Six of them just got caught for keeping a young girl. Barely fourteen, the kid is, and they started on her."

"I want to try it up there for a while, Alonzo," Rhodes said patiently.

"Why, man? Do what you were born for." Fahey's voice was much closer now. "Throwing it all away. Why?"

"You know how many lawyers with a name like mine ever made it up to the Supreme Court?"

"Nor do I give a shit."

"Not one. That's how many."

"You looking for Christmas in July again? Trying to put two suns in the sky when only one fits."

Sighing, Rhodes sipped his drink, tired of explaining himself, tired of people on his back, even his friend Fahey.

"Jesus, Alonzo, let up will you?"

"Don't *Jesus* me. I get enough of that on Sundays when Wanda drags me to her pew. Quit running is what I say."

"What's there to run from?" Rhodes still stared at the painting.

"Yourself."

Fahey now stood very close, his face moist and his breath warming Rhodes's cheek.

"I'm not fast enough to run from myself," said Rhodes, turning to face Fahey. "Let's go home."

"You said after a couple of years we'd be back together again."

"I know. But I've got some ideas I want to try out, and the high court is the place to go."

"Cat crap."

"So let's go," said Rhodes wearily.

"You're afraid to fight again. Pillar of jello is what you—"

"Alonzo. I'm me. And all I want for me is to be the best I can. Now what in hell is the matter with that?"

"You were already the best."

"*Were* is right on the mark. C'mon, let's adios."

Fahey stalled. Inspired by a crasher of an idea, he wanted to float it by Rhodes. It had popped right out of the side of his brain in the shower one morning, delighting him. He plunged ahead, as if what they'd just been discussing was a lost fragment of history.

"And there's the new regiment to provision," he said out of nowhere. "Takes time to organize one. Be busier than ever."

"A regiment?"

"For you and me, we can have it."

"You don't say." Rhodes knew it was coming for sure.

"A whole gorgeous regiment. Ours. Think of it, Cliff."

"Not tonight, thanks. Call me when it goes overseas."

Pain gathered around Alonzo Fahey's mouth. Black curls had tumbled across his forehead. "Okay," he said. "You want to be the general? You can be the general."

"Regiments only go as high as colonels."

"This one is different. Better than the Queen's own . . . Jesus! She never even sent me a birthday card this year, the old hag."

Fahey's whole face glistened. Excitement poured from his eyes like they were reflectors for the Milky Way. He had a whole sales pitch ready, with no logic to it, but based on the most sacred notions.

Of how the unions had gone sour. Crooked police commissioners. Churches filching from the poor and the weak. Politicians passing off their lies. What was needed was a true regiment of crusaders to protect the public. One with the best camp followers and a squad of brain surgeons to keep them fit; first-line troops chosen from the ranks of Olympic athletes; every man mounted on an Appaloosa; Russian bat boys to slop the latrines.

"Listen, Jesus, Cliff," Fahey went on. "We can bivouac up in the vineyards of Napa Valley. Wine by the fires at night with the women. Cut down on the expenses." Fahey stopped suddenly, breathing as if he'd made a strong finish after a ten mile run.

"Who're we fighting, Alonzo?"

"There's always someone. Turks. Koreans. Boat people. Clean the city up before they run us out."

"Maybe you better have one platoon just for lawyers. You'll need them."

"You get them for us, Cliff."

"That's exactly out of the question, amigo."

"Got the uniform picked out. Beautiful thing. Women'll love it. Saw one like it at the Vatican once."

"Stole one, you mean."

"It's on loan."

"Some loan."

"Needed it. They've a regiment in Philadelphia. Got another for the rich eggs on Park Avenue in New York. Th' fucks a matter with us?"

"Nothing. Send me a regimental tie and I'll wear it to the hanging."

"You don't care at all, do you?"

"About you I do."

"Look into it, will you? Imagine the fun. Get the White House permit or whatever it is we need."

"Can't be done, Alonzo." Rhodes started to laugh.

"Hell, I can't. If Lafayette did it, goddamn it, so can I." Fahey teetered back on a diagonal line, his face aglow, as he looked down the alley of his mind toward some new adventure.

"C'mon, Lafayette, we gotta get out of here," Rhodes said.

He thought he heard Fahey behind him, but it was only the noise of his sitting down again. When he reached the door he saw Fahey gripping the neck of a Bushmills bottle, pouring a steady stream into the bull's-eye of a large tumbler.

True Fahey, he thought, who played at blindman's bluff to tame a world he found so very frightening.

Sacked by the Police Commission for telling the truth too loudly about corruption rife in the department. And, lest it ever be forgotten, for shacking up with one commissioner's wife while designated only to look after internal affairs—those lower and higher sins of the police.

Charged with unbecoming conduct, and for all the hell he constantly raised, Fahey had been suspended without pay. Rhodes had agreed to defend him for nothing. He was simply interested in meeting Fahey who was fast becoming a legend in police circles. But at the special hearing the Commission convened, he wouldn't even get a chance to put up a fight. Fahey took care of everything himself in one of the greatest performances Rhodes had ever witnessed.

There came Fahey, undaunted on that day, to stalk those wise men who dared to judge him. Confessing them, it almost seemed. Barraging them with nervy questions about delicate items conveniently buried under the dust of the past.

And at the end of it, Fahey coolly reminding the Commissioners that yes indeed, he was their internal-affairs officer. "That poor wife," he had shouted, "was criminally neglected." She had craved an affair. Approved it was, too, by the Holy Church. On that point, Fahey said he had checked and double-checked with his own conscience and a few priests who must remain nameless. And because he was an internal-affairs specialist, who else was better qualified to look after the affairs of the Commissioners's wives? "Fahey, gentlemen, that's the only *who* in this falling temple. Yes?"

They had wanted to crucify him. But the Commission had agreed to drop all charges if he would only shut up. About everything. And Fahey knew a gift whether it was wrapped in tinsel or not.

"See you later, pal," Rhodes said, shaking his reverie away.

"Hold on, and I'll find us some nice tarts," promised Fahey, for he was night people.

"Already got my bed, thanks."

Fahey held a finger out as if he were pointing a gun, one aimed at Rhodes's thoughts of a moment ago. An eyebrow arched up.

"Your trial?" he said.

"Yes."

"Somebody's made a mistake, you think?"

"You mean the prosecution?"

Fahey's head lifted in a theatrical pose, then dropped suddenly.

"Unlikely to admit it now, if they did," Rhodes said. "Too late for that."

"I'll ring you up soon. Get a leaf reading from the gypsy first thing in the morn."

"No, not me. Call that guy Burke. S'long, Alonzo."

Rhodes closed the door. He'd done what he could for Raye Wheeler, and friend or not, he didn't care to get into whoever the gypsy was with Fahey. Be there half the night listening to that one, and he promised Fritzi he'd come by. She hadn't been kidding about it either.

A simple thing. A favor for a sick man who was a friend to them both. Only a small request, but for five people at Masquers on that evening the backwash had already begun to rise.

Chapter Seven

The evening air was quiet enough, but aloft a wind pushed thunderheads south into a blacker sky. Rhodes stood on Fritzi Jagoda's front lawn, listening to the dark, and looking down over the hills to the silent traffic. The car lights at that distance fused into long strings of electric spaghetti. So many people still on the move at that hour, and then remembered he was a good five miles from his own house. He smiled and went up to the door.

Even before walking into her bedroom, Rhodes caught the fragrance of flowers. They were everywhere. Red roses down the length of a side table; yellow blossoms next to a chaise longue; white chrysanthemums piled up in vases on the fireplace mantel. The colors of the flowers matched the chintz drapes hanging down from the high ceilings.

"You sure do this place up right," said Rhodes admiringly.

"Heaven, isn't it?"

"Just right for you."

"Us."

"Right, us."

"The gardens are really fabulous now. I thought the rain would spoil them, but it didn't." She put her book on the bedside table.

"Rain's on the run."

Rhodes moved next to her, sprawling across her bed, and his hand wandered across her lush breasts. Leaning closer until their noses met, then their mouths, they kissed deeply, smoothing each other out.

When he broke away, Rhodes whispered, "I'll change. Be right back."

"Do. I'll brush your teeth later."

"But with what brush?"

"Ah, the clowner tonight." Fritzi made a face, then giggled.

Rhodes changed into a red flannel robe he kept there along with a few suits, some shirts and ties. They were handy on the mornings after he stayed over and, pressed for time, was unable to get by his own home. Coming back, he switched off the light on his side of the bed. He waited for her to do the same.

"Come on," said Fritzi.

"Flip the light."

"Undo your robe, then I will."

"This is silly."

"You're the silly," said Fritzi.

"Head games are what I can do without right now."

"Really? I was sort of looking forward to one. The other kind."

Rhodes's smile left before it arrived. Peeling off the robe, burning a little inside, he slid under the covers. Fritzi snapped out her light, then snuggled close.

"I don't know why it bothers you," she said, "after all this time. I mean we've been in the shower, the pool, God knows where, and you—"

"Innate modesty. I'm really one of Fahey's priests. I just pretend to be a public servant."

"Wouldn't it be easier just to face up to it . . . Look at all the women with mastectomies. People with no arms or legs—"

"Let's leave it, please. Write me an essay sometime on how to go to bed."

"Why not just face it."

"You know what?" Rhodes lifted his head from the pillow. "Fahey and you must be reading from the same song sheet. You sending notes to each other?"

"Not about this."

"That's nice."

"You're really in a great mood, aren't you?"

"I'm okay."

"Just a little black and blue inside, where we can't see it and kiss it," Fritzi kidded him.

Nothing from Rhodes. A breath was all, a hard exhale.

"Sometimes," said Fritzi, "I think you use your cock as an excuse for everything."

"I really don't need this now. Okay?"

"You know what?"

"I'm fast learning without knowing."

"You can't stand it when you're not the best at everything you do. Isn't that right?"

Rhodes's outflung hand grazed the mahogany headboard of the bed. The noise startled Fritzi. She laughed, low and throaty. "Easy. Don't go violent on me."

"Are you sore because I've been tied up and scarce all week?"

"And don't even call me. I'm supposed to do what? Wait and worry? Look for you on TV? Do it with the cat when I get lonely?"

"How, for Christ, can you get lonely? You're surrounded by mobs every night."

"Never mind, if you have to ask."

She was about to touch him and show by her touch that it didn't matter. That it never really had mattered to her, only to him. But an invisible wall had descended from somewhere. She took his last remarks as a rebuff when in her own mind all she had tried to convey again was that he shouldn't be so sensitive.

Because he was disfigured there didn't bother her at all. Surprised her at first, but she'd known and loved him for three years. They all but lived together.

What upset her was his failure all last week to call and

find out how she was, what she was up to, doing. Taking her for granted, and she wouldn't, by God, take that from any man. A call took five minutes. Less.

Down came his arm, sliding across her belly. His legs entwined with hers and he started to play. She began to feel better though more tense now that her nipples tightened. Fritzi felt herself rise when, later, his mouth searched her thighs. She held him very hard with both hands, and could feel the small scar ridges on his upper shoulders.

Much as she tried to excite him she couldn't, and she tried everything but finally gave up. "You're tired, baby," she soothed.

"Sorry," he said, making an effort not to think of Audrey Sterne.

"We've got all night, and then some."

They moved apart and Fritzi shook out the covers and spread them evenly. Shallow breathing, a stirring of limbs against the sheets, a breeze from the opened window lapping at the drapes was all they heard.

Rhodes bit the inside of his lower lip. His neck swelled and his skin began to feel like wet rubber. He should apologize but the words died in the back of his throat, then sank away.

Cong.

He still wanted to maim every one of the black shirted bastards. But they hadn't asked him to come there, had they? There were penalties, weren't there, for trespassing on other men's lands?

His thoughts drifted back to the Army captain, a psychiatrist, who nursed his mind after the surgeons had fixed him up with half a new *pico*. "Any size and shape you want," they had told him, full of good cheer and humor. Rhodes had hit one of them so hard that he broke his own thumb.

The captain, who had been so nice, older and a healer, had tutored him, even in bed, to believe he was still a man and not a freak. He remembered her.

And still remembered the clunking sound of the grenade. How it bounced down the dirt path inside the cave where he had lived for months in Laos. So fast, a bursting flash, a whop of thunder that knocked him flat, splitting him apart.

It was always easier, he knew, to blame the Cong when he didn't work right in bed now that Audrey Sterne invaded his mind all the time. And asking himself what Fritzi really meant to him anymore. He shouldn't be here with her; the worst kind of cheating.

Rhodes tried to shove the thought of Audrey away. But it went stubborn on him and refused to budge.

Fritzi rolled away to her side of the bed. She had known other nights like this one, forty or fifty perhaps, and they always seemed to happen when she needed him most, and when her natural urges were pitched up so high.

Another of those soft killings that go on in the soul. Worse, she thought, than angry words. You could always take those back, but how could you take back the sex you were supposed to have but never had when you wanted it most? A little killing that stayed buried in you until some unlikely moment when your dam burst and you started spilling out awful things to the man you loved.

Fritzi sensed him trembling. She knew he wasn't crying. He never cried and she rated that as a flaw in anyone. She began rubbing his back lightly, surprised at the wet there on the smooth cords of standing muscle. He was barely a foot away, but it seemed like the width of the Grand Canyon.

Sex and the male ego. God, she thought, there will never be a solution to that one.

At Cedars-Sinai, Raye Wheeler made a small round hole with his mouth, sucking hard for air. A feeble effort, though, because no power came from his lungs anymore. His inflamed throat and bronchial tubes were partly blocked, so pulling for the air always hurt him. Sometimes it felt as though the air had first passed through a furnace, then was forced down his throat.

But he didn't want the oxygen tent again. It frightened him, looking through those plastic tent windows. Made him think of an aquarium: that he was a fish out of water, gulping and flapping for breath.

It was over. What was the matter with that? Seventy-one years of the best times a man could hope to have. But now the vents were all worn out and there were no spares to fix them.

Once more he pulled hard. The scorch he felt dried his eyes. A vicious pain.

For a very long minute the struggle lasted before his sight blotted out, and he thought he was gargling with stones. Strange images came and suddenly disappeared. He saw a shadow wave at him, and when the shadow came closer, it seemed to take the shape of Romaine Brook. Laughing at him, shaking herself, and as naked as she'd been in those photos that bothered him so much.

He tried to shout out a warning. But no one heard anything. Not the nurses down the hall; not Tommy Burke, who had no idea of Wheeler's game plan for winning the case; and not Rhodes who was soon to climb a cross.

But his plan, and everything else he hadn't gotten around to doing in his life, died right along with him.

Crossing town the next morning, thinking of Fritzi, Rhodes stopped on a whim at a pet shop. He sent her a pair of plump lovebirds in a large gilded cage as a peace offering.

As he left the shop he paused and took stock of the Bentley. One front fender was rusting and a door had a jagged crease marring the chocolate finish. Tires looked as if they were run down at the heels, too. Time for a fix-up, but he had promised himself to get the car over to a garage for over a month.

He drove away, came to a stoplight, and turned on the radio for some music. What he heard was a news bulletin announcing Raye Wheeler's death. Memories whispered, hundreds of them, all at once. His shock only jumbled them up more. Behind him a horn blared, then another as he blocked the intersection, thinking of what life would be like without his friend. The world was poorer now by one champion.

He drove on.

People like Raye rarely came more than once in your life, like a desperate love, or having children, or fighting in strange lands, or getting your hands on some real money.

His thoughts traveled to Romaine Brook. Was there anything he should be doing for her? She might be safer where she is now than any other else she'd be in her life if they find her guilty.

And the jury locked up at the Biltmore. They would find out about Raye Wheeler soon enough and probably go into a red lather at more delays. Rhodes knew he would have to calm them down somehow.

Chapter Eight

Later that afternoon, at the dock in front of the Sterne house, Ferenc Kardas unhitched a line and helped guide the *Paloma* out of her slip. The cabin cruiser slid out smooth and straight, churning up the barest froth of wake as she eased away.

Thirty yards from the dock, Julio Sterne swung the boat around and headed out to sea, waving at Kardas.

Ferenc saw no sign of Audrey. She was probably below, fixing drinks or getting the cold supper ready.

An evening cruise, California style, for those who could get away from work midweek. On Mondays and Fridays nobody went to work in Malibu Pointe as far as he could tell. That's what phones were for. Or the executive assistants who were ferried by limousine through the gates with papers to be signed, read, even ripped up.

Kardas's dark eyes flashed. Nice. He intended getting a bigger slice of that life for himself. He had part of it—a small suite of rooms over a five-car garage at the house; sixty thousand dollars on deposit in different banks; and for a time there an old man's wife.

He climbed to the house. Thirty-two steps, the same number he had climbed on the night they had found Marc Sterne's sprawled body—eyes white and unseeing, one hand barely covering his genitals, the other near a hypodermic.

And with Audrey Sterne looking over Kardas's shoulder, choking back a scream.

A bad way to die. But then, thought Ferenc, are there any good ones? He hurried. While the Sternes were out boating, he had three hours to get in touch with some of the other butlers and housemen on the Pointe. His pushers.

Already he had lost Marc Sterne. If he didn't come up with a top quality source soon, he would lose the rest of his market. Now the other side of the business would be shot to hell if he wasn't quick to move.

He fed the noses and arteries of some very rich people: a life insurance tycoon, actors, the number-three rock-and-roller on the charts, and a dozen lesser lights. Quiet action, with a turnover of about twenty thousand dollars a week if he hustled.

But Ferenc Kardas was out of silver dust, and had been unable to connect to the right source for more ever since the kid spent himself. Too good a thing to give up, and it worried him. He had already lost thousands on one missing bag of Colombian that Marc Sterne never delivered. Some of the other butlers and housemen had chipped in for the buy. Growling, they wanted either their money back or more brain powder, and they wanted it very soon.

Two of them had cornered him a few nights before as he walked on the beach. They called him names that were only used by the politest society of Malibu Pointe. They hadn't been fooling around either.

Fahey stopped and checked a street number. It was the right place, but he looked twice anyway. Tijuana North. The building was an old-timer, still sturdy but tired looking, on the corner of Broadway near the law courts. Once this had been the most fashionable office area in the downtown of the city. But then Little Tokyo edged closer, Chinatown crept in, finally a swarm of Latinos made it their own camping ground. If you stopped to listen as Fahey did, the sounds of the streets were embroidered with a dozen tongues.

He couldn't begin to guess why a lawyer of Raye Wheeler's rank had stayed on when so many others had left years ago. Maybe, thought Fahey, it was plain sentiment, or the proximity to the courts, and maybe it was only a dose of superstition—that if old Raye had left, his luck would've left with him.

In the front of the lobby a computer dating service promised bliss for twenty bucks a throw; a money changing cage; and on a whitewashed window a tattered poster advertised a week in Acapulco for two hundred dollars, air fare included.

Fahey rang the elevator. Overcoming a nibble of fear, he stepped in as the rickety gate closed, and prayed for the first time all year.

Coming through the door of Wheeler's office, he was eyed suspiciously by an elderly woman, who gave him a look hard enough to scratch a match on. She stopped tapping the keys of a typewriter to ask him what he wanted. When he told her, she sent him on his way with a few curt directions. Manners. He would show her about manners later.

Perched on a stepladder, his head buried in a law book, Tommy Burke failed to see Fahey at first. The room was a small library with a high ceiling, shelves that sagged under the weight of books, dark paneling, and the musty smell of a cellar.

Fahey tapped his knuckles on a square of the paneling. Burke looked down, startled as a feeding deer.

"I'm Fahey. At your service. And you're younger than I thought."

"Twenty-eight."

"Barely off the breast, then."

"I'm afraid you're wrong there . . . By the way, can you show me your ticket?" asked Tommy politely. He marked a page with a piece of string.

Fahey reached for his billfold and then showed a photostat of his license. Burke handed it back, saying, "You look different in this picture."

"I got older. Hung around too many lawyers."

"You don't like lawyers, Mr. Fahey?"

"Eighty thousand of 'em in this state. That's a lot of troublemakers. Call me Alonzo, incidentally."

"I'm Tommy."

"I know. Irish. What part?"

"County Sligo. Two generations back."

"Sligo, eh? Not like Donegal, but passable."

As they talked, Fahey began to absorb the younger man. He looked like a growthy colt, all the bones sticking out in the obvious places. A puckery mouth, a long and freckled face with a pale glow of blood under the skin. By his left eye a purple birthmark stood out like a shirt button.

"You think my shoes are funny," Tommy Burke said, watching Fahey look him over.

"Boots, aren't they? Climbing boots."

"Everybody jokes about them." Tommy Burke's mouth turned into a sheepish grin.

"You a climber?"

"I have weak ankles. Grew too fast, and the boots hold me up better."

"You up to talking about this trial?"

"Sure. We can talk right here."

"You can maybe. But my neck is going stiff looking up at you."

"Oh, sorry." Burke's voice, already high, crept a note higher. The knob in his slender neck bobbed twice.

He came down off the ladder, legs and arms working as if they were each getting a different brain message. Burke was double-jointed. He began to remind Fahey of a stick figure in a comic strip drawn with a sharp pen almost out of ink.

Still, Fahey could feel for the young lawyer. A natural cripple, born that way, and Fahey thought of his own shot-up elbow. He understood.

"So what made you change your mind?"

"About this case?" Fahey asked.

Burke nodded. He was a full head taller than Fahey, who measured six feet without shoes.

"When Raye Wheeler first asked me, I couldn't do it. I was busy on something else."

"I thought you didn't do trial investigations anymore."

"I haven't for a while . . . I'm an art man now," said Fahey with mock pomposity.

"Now you're ready again?"

"Help you if I can. I liked Raye."

"Everyone did."

"And you're in charge of the whole bus now. Is that it? No one else coming in?"

"Just me. You're looking at it. Besides, we're short of money."

"I was afraid I'd hear that again."

"Then I'll be seeing you."

Fahey rubbed his eyes before they wandered up to the ceiling. He was there only because of Rhodes and he doubted whether Burke knew anything about it. He had called Burke yesterday and told him he could spare one week and not a day more. That the trial looked interesting.

"Look," said Fahey, "I'll trust you. Up to you . . . I'll do it on the cuff."

"No way I can guarantee you anything." Burke shook his head vigorously until copper colored ringlets spilled to his eyebrows.

"Then I'm free to walk whenever I want. Right?"

"Yes."

"So how do you get paid, if that's not too nosy?"

"When we win, Romaine'll pay us."

"So, let's get on with it," Fahey urged.

"Any place special you want to start?"

Fahey yawned. Then he told Burke what it was he'd like to know about Romaine Brook. What did Burke think of her? How she answered questions. Where she grew up. Her discernible habits. A score of things, all adding up to—who is Romaine Brook?

Fahey asked for everything they had linking the young actress to the crime—the sheriff's confidential reports, other police records, the coroner's findings—all the data the state had collected and by law must turn over to the defense.

"Like to meet her myself. Soon as you can arrange it," Fahey requested.

"That's easy. Tomorrow? After the funeral?"

"Good. But I want to look at those evidence files first."

"That it?"

"I'll need to see those photos," added Fahey in an afterthought. "You've got copies?"

"Yes," said Tommy, frowning.

"Lots of skin, eh?"

"I suppose. But you don't need those pictures."

"I do if you need me, boyo. We either work this thing together or I go home. You tell me."

Tommy shrugged, then quickly turned away so Fahey couldn't see how upset he was. Those photos gave him nightmares. She wasn't like that; she was beautiful, dreamy, a wonder. Marc Sterne had tried to stain her. It drove Burke crazy thinking about what a camera had done to Romaine.

They walked down a hall to a small room between Wheeler's office and the one Tommy used, and Fahey said it was just what he had in mind. "Quarters fit for an admiral. Exactly adequate. Better than I've ever had before," he lied very pleasantly.

Burke lingered, looking uneasy. Fahey wondered if the young lawyer had to shave that translucent baby skin.

"You going to work tonight? Here?"

"A few hours anyway." Fahey closed the desk drawer he'd been exploring. "Learn my way through your files."

"Want to join me for dinner later?"

"Sure. Is it on the client?"

"Afraid not."

"Let's skip Chasen's then. Fuck, Burke, you running a Red Cross here or what?"

"She'll pay. We'll just have to wait for it. Till she gets working again."

Fahey's grin disappeared. "Supposing she gets the iron bars, or worse?"

"I don't think about it," said Tommy, his voice high again.

"I was right. You're young, all right, young as next New Year's."

If Tommy was insulted or miffed, he hid his feelings. He was trying to get a feel for Alonzo Fahey. He knew the man carried a solid reputation as an investigator. But he looked so off-center, so impulsive. What kind of a man wore an electric blue shirt and a scarlet bow tie?

Tommy started for the door, then hesitated and spun around on one spindly leg. "I know you worked with Judge Rhodes at one time. Raye told me so."

"Raye was right."

"What's he really like?"

Fahey itched the stubble on his cheek, a darkening shadow going clear up to his sideburns. The blue-black of the windows behind him and his shirt made him look sinister. Now he squinted, and he looked slightly dangerous.

Burke waited for a reply.

"A minor poet," said Fahey after a moment. "Fights filthy, a dirty one, bad as a woman. Seen him do it."

"You mean with his hands or something?"

"Oh, Jay-sus no. With his ghost. He fights with his ghost and it *ain't* fair, is it now?"

Tommy tilted his head, looking slightly dazed, and the coppery curls danced on his forehead again. Heading out the door without another word, he went back to his law books. If he was worried about the sobriety of the detective, he was doubly concerned for himself. He had hardly slept the night before, he had been so nervous standing up in front of all those people, about the way he looked, his voice.

Would they laugh at him?

Fahey had called out of nowhere, offering help. A man who talked like a lunatic. But Tommy would clutch at any hand offered now.

Three hours passed as if they were one. Tommy led Fahey to a noisy Mexican cantina around the corner from the office. They sat in a booth in the back, away from the mariachi music blaring out of the sound system.

Fahey ordered a Bushmills and was told they didn't stock it. He asked for another brand and got the same answer, so he settled for a margarita with extra limes. "And for pure love of Christ turn down the music."

Chasen's tomorrow, Fahey decided, and fuck the expense. He would take it out of the wife's dress money.

"Las Infantas," he said a few minutes later over the green of his margarita. "What is it, a sacrament?" The thought had come like a rifle shot from an unknown direction. "I saw it in your files."

"It's where Romaine was put up for adoption," Tommy said. "A foundling home run by a religious order."

"Adopted? Does she know it?"

"Yes, she does. Would you go up there one day soon?"

"What for?"

"Before the trial actually began, Raye tried to track down Romaine's natural parents. To see if they might be willing to help her financially. But Las Infantas wouldn't give us the time of day. We sort of dropped it then. Ran out of time. And who knows where her parents are anyway."

"Places like that are usually pretty touchy," Fahey said. "Doubt if I could help you on that one."

"Worth a try. Maybe if someone went to see them, told them what a spot we're in. The expenses just keep climbing."

"Tell me about her. Start on Romaine, and let's see how far we get," said Fahey, his outrageous bow tie skewed at an acute angle.

Burke began.

But Fahey was thinking about the photos he had seen an hour before. Romaine Brook's body, naked and quite aristocratic, he decided. Its whole length exposed on a dozen prints of film. A healthy looker who belonged in a soapsuds ad. Another woman's hands, holding a dildo, showed up in some of the photos and at least one pair of male hands was also in attendance. In one shot there was even a dog.

The photos were of good quality—an impression that disturbed Fahey—but it was the look on the actress's face that mystified him. He couldn't tell whether she was asleep or on a sexual moonray ride.

Alonzo Fahey, sleuth of all he surveyed, would be bothered again in a very few moments. He listened raptly as Burke outlined the twists and turns of Romaine Brook's young but eventful life.

Of how she had been adopted from Las Infantas by Josephine and Chatham Brook. The mother had died of double pneumonia when Romaine was only ten.

"And the father, where's he gone to?" asked Fahey.

"Went out for a beer one night," Burke advised. "He was last heard from in Morocco or someplace. Turned Arab, I guess."

"Abandoned the kid? Who was he?"

British, an immigrant. Arranged and composed music for movie soundtracks.

"How'd she get along?"

The family had lived in Encino. A tract home, fully mortgaged and sold to pay debts. Romaine was taken in by her high school principal and his wife. She lived with them for three years.

"And then?"

She competed for and won a scholarship at the School

of Drama. She had a small part in another movie before getting the break with her role in *Tonight or Never*.

A slant, a trail—Fahey wanted a feel of her background. What her life was made of.

From the way Tommy Burke talked, Fahey was fairly sure the lawyer had fallen for her. Eager of expression, a slight blush in his cheeks, his high quick voice. The signs of a suffering lover were scribbled all over his face. Fahey wondered again who had taken those photos.

"You think she's innocent?"

"I know she has to be," Tommy answered.

"Where the hell's dinner?"

"They are a little slow here."

Fahey pushed himself up from the booth, throwing a few crumpled bills on the table.

"Where're you going?"

"I teach higher gods the alphabet at this hour. Makes up for cases with short fees."

"Can you drive me over to Raye's funeral tomorrow?"

"Can't you drive, crissakes?"

"I never learned. Never could afford a car either," said Tommy Burke, making it sound like a high recommendation.

"Jesus, man, this is Los Angeles . . . I don't know." Fahey started to leave.

"Don't know what?"

"Anything," said Fahey. "How do you get around?"

"The bus."

Fahey turned and went down the bar. He'd go to Masquers, where he had credit, and order a decent whiskey and a dinner to go with it. Chat with the girls. He needed time to think, and a solid cup or two of Bushmills would help. Get out of this whole quirky thing right now, he told himself. Pauper's work. Still, he'd hang with it for a few days. Give him an excuse to get out from under the wife's stamping feet.

Chapter Nine

A half-light misted the corridor. The few people they passed seemed remote and furtive in this tomb for the living. Fahey didn't like the faint carbolic smell. And the clop of their heels on the cement floor sounded too deadening and cold to him, especially after the funeral.

When they'd entered the building, Burke had passed through a screening gate immediately, but Fahey, the newcomer, was asked to step aside. A quick frisking by the desk guard uncovered a silver flask in his hip pocket. Told he could pick it up when he left, Fahey, grossly insulted, had shouted at the guard. He stunned her even more with the way he had dressed for Raye Wheeler's burial earlier that morning: a green suit, a candy-striped shirt, with a tie, loud as a siren, that changed colors with the light. On one lapel an odd looking medal hung from a daring red ribbon.

They had come to a stop. Fahey gripped his black beret in one hand, tight as his mouth.

Their uniformed escort unlocked a door, then showed them to a small room for visitors that was as lifeless as a moonscape. The walls were dingy and one small barred window gave little light over a wide metal table with four steel folding chairs around it.

Alonzo Fahey felt trapped. It was much too somber for his liking, and his face showed the strain as he paced around. He sailed a joke over to Burke, who was arranging a legal pad and pencils on the table.

The door opened again. She seemed to glide in almost noiselessly, a spirit passing through the wall. She wore a sort of loose drab gray shift; the hem touching her knees;

sandals of black leather opened at the toes. Tommy Burke scrambled up, nearly knocking a chair over and, flustered, turned to see Fahey advancing like a prophet with arms spread wide.

"Hi, Tommy," she said softly.

"Hello, Romaine . . . This is Alonzo Fahey."

"A new lawyer?"

"No," Tommy said. "A sort of specialist, who used to be with the police here."

"There's no money for any more of you, Tommy. You have to believe me."

Taken with the silk of her voice, Fahey was also impressed by her welcoming smile. And he noted her calm manner, her clean and scrubbed looks.

"We'll worry about the money part later," said Tommy.

"Gifts," said Fahey to no one in particular. "Get up a church collection for the cause. Burke and I may rob a chapel or two tonight. The stars are just right, and we're here to finish the plans."

Romaine giggled.

"You'll get to know him. It takes a while," Tommy said, mildly exasperated.

She extended a cool and pale hand to Fahey, who continued to regard her silently. He held it for a moment, surprised at her strong grip. Even in the ratty shift she looked appealing—a golden madonna, he thought, and took a deep breath as she smiled at him.

"Tonight or Never," he said. "A great one. Should've won the Oscar. You *was* robbed."

"Oh! You saw it?"

"No. But now I will," Fahey replied. He moved with her, as consort to the princess, sat her next to Burke, then took a chair for himself across the table.

"Alonzo here is an investigator," Burke began. "He's going to help us and run around and check on some things."

"What sort of things?" asked Romaine.

"Here and there," Fahey said evenly. "Just test the wind a bit. Nothing much, then again . . ."

"He's got some questions," said Tommy. "Things you might've discussed with Raye."

"Poor Raye. I don't know what more can happen." Romaine's eyes, brown and steady, seemed to cloud over. Fahey saw a faint blush on her neck. He was tempted to lean over and feel its warmth. "You've got to get me out of this hole, Tommy. God, I just can't stand it anymore," she said in a misery edging toward despair.

"You're almost home," said Burke, even as doubt journeyed across his face. "You've got to be patient a while longer."

Romaine snatched a quick glance at Fahey. He seemed strong and hard as a dock worker, she thought. And very flirty with his sudden eyes.

"You hurt your arm somehow?" she asked him.

"A lot of nights ago."

"I'm sorry. Excuse me for—"

"S'allright. I'm used to the damn thing by now." Fahey had been massaging his elbow. Tender there today, and he wondered if it would rain again tonight. "Now then, let me advise you what I can and can't do for you." After briefly telling her what the law allowed a private investigator to do, he wanted to hear a few things from her. "Absolutely straight, straight and clear for my own ears. It might give me a feel for something. Make me hear what you don't even intend to say."

This last remark caused a stir of alarm in Romaine. What did he mean? She started to speak but her mind raced everywhere.

"Okay?" asked Fahey.

"Yes. Naturally I'll answer anything."

"Good." Fahey's eyes narrowed. "You want me to take a stab at finding your father?"

"No, thank you."

"Why?"

"He ran out years ago. Somewhere . . . North Africa I heard. I don't ever want him near me."

"You're sure?"

"Perfectly."

"Maybe he can help you with money," Fahey pressed.

"I want nothing to do with him." Romaine was vehement. "Nothing."

Fahey waited, but she had turned her head away. He had obviously touched a frayed nerve.

He went on, "There're notes in the files saying that you claimed Marc Sterne was into drugs."

Romaine nodded.

"He spent time in some rehabilitation center? A private one?"

"I think about three months," Romaine said. "It was before I knew him."

"Did he talk about it?"

"Never. Well, hardly ever."

"So if he got eased off the drugs, why do you say he was on them again?"

"How he died for one thing."

"What else?"

"He dealed. He dealed to a lot of people in the industry—"

"You mean the film business?"

"Yes," said Romaine. "And the recording companies too. He knew all those people. All kinds of them."

"You ever see him peddling anything?"

"At a few parties we went to. He would disappear, and I'd go looking for him."

"Lot of cash?"

Romaine shrugged. "I guess so. But he was always short. His father kept him on a tight salary."

"How tight?"

"Seventy-five thousand, I think."

"What's so tight about seventy-five thou?"

"In the world he lived in? Are you kidding, Mr. Fahey?"

"Alonzo. I'm Alonzo for now. Don't go formal on me or I'll up my rates."

"Alonzo," she repeated, smiling slightly.

"So he was a pusher? Heroin, cocaine, all that?"

She nodded again.

"Where'd he keep it?"

"I don't know."

"Were you fucking this guy? Hot and heavy, were you?"

A flying pencil hit Fahey in the chest. He looked across the table to an enraged Tommy Burke, whose mouth opened and closed, a sort of strangled sound coming out.

"Where the hell do you get off talking like that to her?" asked Burke when he regained himself.

"It's all right, Tommy," said Romaine. She touched his knee with her hand. "I don't mind."

"Look, you want a tea party, then I'm not your man. I gotta find out what was happening, that's all," Fahey stated, then continued: "You don't know where he kept his merchandise? Or who he bought from?"

Romaine hesitated. She knew the answer she would give; she just didn't want to give it too easily.

"I'm not exactly sure where he kept it," she said after a pause. "And I've no idea who he bought it from."

"Okay. Where do you think he stashed it?"

"Somewhere in the living room of his apartment. Near a long couch there. When he needed some he'd always send me out of the room, and when he let me back in, one section of the couch or sometimes the lamp was out of place."

Fahey jotted some notes, then made a rough sketch of a sectional couch. As he drew, he asked Burke: "Place was searched, right?"

"And sealed afterward. It still is. That's where they found the letter Romaine wrote."

"The photos were there, too?" Fahey asked.

Romaine averted her eyes as Tommy replied, "Yes, with the letter."

Fahey laid down the pencil. Bothered suddenly by a rush of prickly heat, he rubbed his nose and the side of his mouth. The girl, he had only shaken her hand, no more, and yet she was seizing him somehow. He eyed her. "Are you into drugs?"

"Never."

"You sure?"

"I swear," Romaine protested. "Please believe me when I tell you something."

"I will. But I'm also trying to make sure of things. Can you tell me how you met Marc?"

"I already told Raye Wheeler once."

"But he's not with us anymore," reminded Fahey. "We are, so please tell us."

Romaine knew she must be very careful. She got up from her chair and walked slowly to a corner of the room. Fahey gazed at her, admiring what he could see of her legs.

"Give me a minute, and I'll tell you," Romaine said. It

was the same, almost, as remembering lines from a script. She turned and faced them.

Nothing ever excited me more than getting the supporting role in Tonight or Never. *Like I'd died and gone to heaven. The cast and crew were great. My part was fabulous, the lines terrific, everything.*

His stepmother introduced us one day at a lunch she gave. Marc Sterne in the flesh: Assistant Producer, and he was assigned to my film. Wow!

He had this deep voice. Musical. It was as if I had opened my eyes for the very first time, and then looked and looked again at all this man. He was tall, with a great body, and periwinkle eyes, and dark wavy hair.

And then every day when we were shooting, a small wicker basket arrived in my dressing room. One pink rose. One split of Moet. Even on location in New York the same thing. I went crazy. I was so flattered. And his manners were perfect, always. Did I have everything I needed? Was my hotel room all right? Little things, nice things.

We went everywhere together: Beverly Hills parties, had our own special table at Ma Maison. I was dizzy and felt so beautiful, so alive. Even the gossip columns called me "a radiant Cinderella."

A couple of months or so after the shooting ended, things started to change. At first I sort of ignored it. But then I discovered another side of Marc when he took me to those parties with dope and coke and lots of stuff I never even heard of before. He'd leave me at odd times for five or ten minutes. No one seemed to bat an eyelash, and that's when I learned he was dealing and I got mad.

Then things smoothed out again. The charm oozed, flowers arrived, no more crazy antics. He asked me for lunch one day at the studio commissary. Half the big brass stopped by our table. Everything but the band rolled out. Marc had been given his own film project to produce.

I was offered the lead. His father had approved a substantial increase in my fee, too, and I wanted the money. It was still a small budget movie, but that didn't bother me at all.

I was really excited again. But that's the last I ever heard of the film. Never saw the script and neither did my agent.

Romaine stood serenely in the corner. Her hands were laced together, resting in front of her shift, and her remembering eyes shone so brightly that Fahey's shone with them.

One moment she seemed twelve years old, the next thirty. Fahey had watched her happen, and he knew she was taunting him with her now-you-see-it, now-you-don't magic.

Maybe Romaine really is a star, he thought. I mean, Christ, here we are in a cement cell. She's got little more than a shirt on, and yet she can still make you believe you're somewhere else with her. Her face interested him. It hadn't fully set and she was too young for worry lines. He wondered how she'd look ten years down the line. Or if she'd even be around to tempt people with powers that were so extraordinary and strange for a person her age to have. Or any age.

"You want to tell me about the photos," Fahey suggested.

"I never knew about them."

"How come?"

"I was drugged and—"

"You said you didn't take drugs."

"I don't," Romaine said defensively. "Please don't try to confuse my words either . . . I was slipped drugs in a drink, I'm pretty sure."

"Where?"

"Palm Springs."

"Would you tell me—" Fahey broke off, glancing over at Burke. "You heard this?" he asked. Burke shook his head. "You tell this to Wheeler?" he asked Romaine.

"Yes."

"But he didn't tell you," Fahey said to Burke.

"No. Remember I was just researching and that sort of thing before Raye died."

Fahey danced a fingernail along his upper teeth, then frowned. "Can we hear about it? The photo session? That same nice way."

"There wasn't any *session*. Not on my part. But it all happened in Palm Springs."

"Please go ahead," said Tommy, his voice canary-high.

Romaine still stood in the corner, very straight though easily. Fahey swore on saints who never existed that she had an actual aura about her. Perhaps it was only a fragment of light from the barred window playing a trick on her very blond hair. But somehow he didn't think so. She was different—one of those who could make a Pope squirm. He listened raptly as Romaine, her eyes closed, began to talk.

We drove down early, the sun just rising, and I remember we were going to make up. He promised there'd be no more drugs. We went up some road that overlooked a canyon and came to a curved house so low it seemed almost hidden against the rocks. It was still cool outside and I remember seeing steam rise from the swimming pool. It was a really nice place. It belonged to his parents.

Marc lied to me. He told me his parents were coming later, but they never did.

A couple came out from the house. Mexicans. They were young and very good looking.

We swam and sunned and swam some more. I was in a bikini, and Marc took pictures of me with his Leica.

By afternoon I was lazing around, enjoying myself. We were having a nice time. Marc made me a white wine and soda. At first, I guess I thought I was dizzy from all the sun. But then I saw colors, every color of the rainbow swirling together. Crazy. And then nothing.

I don't remember the rest. I don't even remember where the big dog came from that was in those awful pictures. I mentioned the Mexican couple. I think they were in the pictures, doing those filthy things.

The trip back to Los Angeles was a total blur. It must have been the day after, I guess, but I don't really know. I was drugged so deep and I never take drugs so whatever it was must've really knocked me out.

I woke up in Marc's apartment in Hollywood. He was gone and had left a note saying he was at the studio.

My breasts and neck were covered with splotches. I could hardly get up. I stumbled into the bathroom, sat down, and found blood dripping, but from the wrong place.

All I could think of, when I could think at all, were those times when my father went after me. Came slinking into my bed late at night and forced himself up my back. Exploding in me. Telling me in drunken grumbles that this is how little girls learned about it. The smell of whiskey in my ears, in my hair, made me sick.

When I cried, he would muffle me with his hand. I thought I would suffocate. God, how he hurt me and shamed me. I hated him. Oh, you have to understand, both of you. They were using me like my father did, and I was so afraid and felt so dirty.

Romaine opened her eyes, an empty look on her face. Tommy Burke had noticed that, though dry, her eyes seemed full with fear, and she had trembled as she spoke. Rage welled up in him at her terrible, ugly story. He wanted to lash out with his fists, his feet, anything, at Marc Sterne and Romaine's father—wherever the bastard was now. He recalled how Raye Wheeler had said, "The girl had been through plenty." But nothing more.

He yanked himself off the chair, wanting to sweep his arms around her. But she moved, tugging at her shift, and came back to the table before he could touch her.

Fahey sat still, numbed. He picked up his pencil again and doodled. A raped angel, he thought, and drew a double halo.

"Pritter know any of this?" he asked Burke.

"How could he?"

"You never mentioned this to anyone except Wheeler?" Fahey asked Romaine.

"I could never," Romaine said, her voice faltering again.

A pause then, as they gathered their separate thoughts, until Tommy Burke finally said, "Can't use any of it in the trial either. Sure as toot the jury would think Romaine was out for revenge."

"I just want to forget," Romaine said aimlessly.

"We're going to have to put you on the stand, Romaine," Tommy said. "You know that, don't you? You'll just have to deny, deny and deny you had anything to do with Marc Sterne's death."

"One thing I haven't heard," Fahey said, dropping his pencil. He met Romaine's bewildered look with a hard one of his own. "Why, after all this, did you ever see the guy again? Go out to Malibu . . . I'd think you'd never want anything to do with him."

"I already told Raye."

"Told him what?" Tommy asked, leaning forward.

"The money."

"What money?" Tommy said.

"Marc owed me money that I loaned him. And other money from a story treatment we sold to Parthenon. I told Raye all this . . ."

"That right?" Fahey asked, looking at Burke.

"I suppose," said Tommy. "Raye never told me everything."

"I swear," Romaine said.

A plausible lie.

It was the first of three she'd already planned in her cell during those long and monotonous hours with all the time in the world to think them out. Seamless, perfect lies. She'd act her way through the whole grim charade, scene by scene, if she had to. No one would ever catch on, and Romaine scanned Fahey and Burke to see how her story played so far. So far they were biting.

"How much money are we talking about?" Fahey wondered aloud.

"Fifteen thousand."

"He borrowed that?"

"Yes," Romaine said evenly. "My last paycheck from the film, and he owed me a share of the story money besides."

"He was broke?"

"Nearly always. He spent money like no one I ever knew."

Fahey blew a low whistle under his breath. "Can't use that in the trial either, can you, old son?"

"Not a chance," Burke agreed.

"You see," Romaine said, "I went out to Malibu to see his parents. I was going to ask them to talk to Marc and help me get my money back."

"You called them?" asked Fahey.

"Before. A day or two, I think, and asked if I could come out."

"And spoke to whom?"

"Ferenc. The houseman."

"He testified, right? Was that in there? In the transcript?"

Burke said no, it wasn't. That Wheeler might have decided not to press that angle. Pritter might pounce on it eagerly, opening the way for a money motive as a reason for the murder.

"I didn't kill him . . . I didn't, didn't! Can't you believe me?" Romaine wailed. She buried her face in her hands.

Fahey examined the ceiling. His thoughts hopped everywhere on the gray blackboard up there. He tried catching them in his suspicious mind. But whenever he reached out to hold one steady, it seemed to sprint off with the speed of light.

Burke intervened. "Romaine, they said you could come out to Malibu? The Sternes?"

"Oh yes, Tommy. Ferenc asked Mr. Sterne, and then told me it was fine," said Romaine, with her second maiming of the truth that afternoon. She was afraid these new men in her life couldn't protect her. She would have to do it all by herself.

No one talked for a moment. Romaine's eyes seemed so intimate, so searching and eager and playful that Fahey had to blink several times to keep his gaze steady on her.

"Be wanting to take a look up there at that Hollywood apartment," he said to Burke. "What do we need? An order from Rhodes?"

"Or I can ask Pritter. He'll have to know anyway."

"What good does that do?" Romaine asked.

"Maybe some. Maybe none," Fahey replied absently. "Look around, check the pipes. I don't know."

"You wanted to ask about those water sounds," reminded Burke.

Fahey looked at Romaine. "You know what a sheriff's confidential report is?"

"Not really."

"It's what they write up when they make an investigation."

Romaine nodded.

"The night Marc Sterne died the neighbors questioned by the sheriff said they heard sounds out on the water . . . Did you hear anything like that?"

"Yes," Romaine said. "I heard something. The grumble sound of a motor. A boat, I suppose."

Fahey smiled, then smacked the table. "For how long did you hear those sounds?"

"I don't remember," said Romaine.

Fahey liked that answer. It rang true. No one could remember something like that, not in a time of stress months before. He was beginning to trust her.

"The Sternes' boat, you think?"

"Maybe. I don't know. All I know is Mr. and Mrs. Sterne were out on the boat. With Ferenc Kardas, the houseman."

"You didn't see their boat at the dock when you arrived?"

"I didn't look either," Romaine said. "But if I'd known they'd be out on the boat, I'd never have gone to the house that night."

Fahey looked confused, but he'd get back to it some other time, when he knew more.

"Tommy," she pleaded, "you're going to help me, aren't you? You just have to. I can't stay here." Her eyes clouded again.

"You've got to hold on," Burke said. "Pritter has to prove everything. And the jury's got to believe him."

"Or me."

"Or you. Right. I'll be coming back. We'll go over everything, again and again, and you won't have to worry about anything."

"Oh, thanks, Tommy, thanks. I adore you for it."

Burke blushed the blush of a man ready to scale any rampart ever built or imagined. The sound of her vibrant and steady voice rang in his ears before it was swallowed up by his heart.

"You, too, Alonzo. I know you'll help me," Romaine said.

She reached out and squeezed both their hands. Innocence washed her face as Fahey thought he saw her aura once more. He looked down at the double halo he had doodled on the pad. He knew he was back in the pond, back in the murder trial business again.

For the raped angel.

On the way out, Fahey retrieved his pocket flask. Jiggling it a few times, he accused the woman guard of nipping from it. Burke, taller and more confident now that Romaine Brook "adored him," pulled him out the door.

"You're all the way crazy," he told Fahey.

"The bitch. You see the hair on her lip? Ought to shave for chrissakes."

"Look, I have to stay on even terms with those people."

"Kick her in the ass is what you ought to do. You wear the boots for it."

"You're funny, Alonzo. But you're nuts, too."

"Let's go for a drink. One for old Raye."

"Sorry, but I've got to get back to the office."

"Some girl, that one." Fahey watched for Burke's reaction. "Ought to put her on Austrian television. Has the right looks."

"Romaine?"

"Sure Romaine. Who the fuck else? Got some class, she has. You see how she looks when she talks? Like she's got a private vision of Jesus in her soul."

"Trouble class. She's the head of that class, I'd say."

But Fahey's mind was elsewhere. Burke had to turn down an offer to visit one of Fahey's favorite gin mills where they raced turtles on afternoons of odd numbered days. And of girls. Fahey was full of excitement as he talked about his great gypsy whore, a spectacular find. She knew things. Where to look for stolen art. Told the future, she did, with her tea leaves, and she read from secret star charts written in ancient Bulgarian. Weighed two hundred pounds, solid as a rock, with one ebony eye and one of amber. "Going to put her in charge of the Regiment's Intelligence Section." Fahey stopped suddenly, pulling on Tommy's arm. "Gave me this medal," Fahey said proudly, pointing to the obsolete Turkish medal dangling on his lapel. "Wear it to remember the fallen like Raye."

Tommy stepped away as soon as he could. He told Fahey that he needed a leash, or at least a straitjacket.

Fahey grinned as he savored a swig from his flask—his "emergency supply" he was calling it today. He pointed across the way to a bunch of boys tossing a football around, and then pleaded with Tommy to find a store that sold red berets. A bloody winter was coming up, and Fahey was going to lend himself to a new regiment rumored to be stationed one county to the west.

"A grand outfit, Tommy. With a perfect battle record,"

he added. "And you know what? Listen, they're all mounted, the regiment is, on camels with silken saddles. Think of it."

"I better not."

"Oh, Tommy, laugh for chrissakes. It's only one life, so fly your heart, man. It's all God's joke on us, so let's play one back." Fahey looked at him with mock scorn, then jumped to a newer thought. "You keep an extra gun anywhere?" Fahey asked him.

"A gun?"

"A Luger or a Colt, either one. Not sure I know where mine is anymore."

"I don't keep guns."

"Too bad. I'll have to knock over a cop on the way to the gypsy's."

"Alonzo, I swear I don't understand you half the time."

"Doesn't matter, does it? Life is mostly smoke signals. The Commanches made the best ones. Got it down to a fine art."

Grabbing him again in a powerful one arm hug, he kissed Tommy on his birthmark. Flustered, Burke pulled away, wiping his cheek, and hurried off, hoping no one had seen them.

Fahey needed his credentials for tomorrow, when he would call on the nuns at Las Infantas. Instinct said he should borrow a rosary, charm God's virgins, vacant of all the men meant for them. Must do it, he thought, get to her real parents, touch them up for the green needed to save their locked-up angel. Money for everyone—even the gypsy. He owed her for last month's frolics and her other lessons in that freezing bathtub.

Stopping at the corner, Tommy Burke looked back, then down the street for Fahey. At first he couldn't see any sign of him. Then, hearing shrieks, he saw Fahey, football in hand, with a circle of kids gathered around him.

Fahey seemed to step back from the huddle, and suddenly Burke saw a blur of legs, then the football itself gaining altitude, shooting up through the air like a frightened hawk.

Tommy smiled. He'd never met anyone in all his life who behaved like Fahey.

That night Fritzi stayed over at Rhodes's house. She liked his bed, custom-made, space enough for three.

Monday, a breather for her, with Masquers closed so the staff could take the day off. She and Rhodes nestled together as he praised her belly mink or whispered that she was his pasture of joy, the most fabulous of sexual orchards, fruits unknown to anyone else in any time of history.

Fritzi laughed him along.

Falling between the cushions of her thighs, he made her moan, but failed to keep up with her. She tossed and turned, and later tried to make him promise that he'd see a doctor.

But he had no doubts about his physical well-being. He could run four miles easily, and swim up to a hundred laps if he pushed himself hard enough.

Rhodes was certain his sex life could work again. If he ever got honest with himself, said a voice deep in his soul.

A soul turning to stoneware. He slept with Fritzi Jagoda, but any lovemaking, such as it was, was with Audrey Sterne in his private world. And right then he didn't think a lot of that world so he tried not to think about any of it at all.

But that didn't work any better than it had the other times. He was slowly killing Fritzi off inside himself. He knew it, and it made him sick.

One sapper's grenade from one of those runty Cong girls and me their prisoner and half my cock missing till the Army sewed me a new one six, no, seven months later. About the time when I no longer thought I'd ever see Audrey again. Or any other woman.

And Fritzi, my sweetest, luscious one, wants me to see a doctor. She means a shrink. Already seen my quota of medics and I don't like people tinkering with my head. What's up there is me. When I get done breathing, no one has to put up with me anymore.

Who was it from the newspapers who once called me the "Dance-Master?" One of those screwy names that stuck somehow. Danced plenty, real hard, burning myself into a cinder.

Couldn't fight there anymore either. But I started sleeping like a state secret again until two months ago.

Then her again. Audrey. Unfair somehow, and I'm tired of fighting and don't need to fight her out of myself again.

Not when Fritzi, who is world class goods, is beside me and how can everything get so loused up?

In her third floor cell Romaine Brook fretted her way in and out of sleep, struggling with her loneliness. The best way, she found, was to run some lines from plays she had memorized. Plays where she was always the heroine. Either that or rub up her newest ideas for outwitting her enemies.

In Hollywood they say there is no manna. They're oh so right. What rains down from Hollywood is spit-on dreams. "Trust me." You hear that one a lot. It's the local code for "Let's open your veins and see how much comes out."

Going up against that family, all that power and money, and I was getting so close to it, too. They were worried sick I might marry him. I could've, too, with a little more time.

That Fahey, him I've got to watch. But how? He sees into me, I can tell he does.

Chapter Ten

Soft and easy air from the soft and fruity groves of San Timoteo. Fahey had already made one quick and early tour of the small coastal valley. It had changed little since he'd last been there: a haven for the rich who wanted to dally at ranching.

After breakfast at a country inn, he called to say he'd arrived. The same standoffish voice at the other end gave him directions. But he could tell the voice was not very thrilled about his visit.

Still, it was a new day, not to be wasted, and he would find some way to make it sing its song. He had already envisioned the regiment there, in that valley. Hills and gullies and stream beds everywhere. Perfect terrain for field exercises. Clear air, great for the trumpeters to blow their notes, carry a mile at least.

A town with a nice clean evergreen smell to it. Probably *too* clean, Fahey thought, as he left the inn for another stroll down the main street of San Timoteo. Hushed as a cathedral at midnight, and having an ear for such things, he knew it for what it was: the sort of quiet that could always be arranged by old and very heavy money. Though it was barely nine in the morning, he counted eight Mercedes station wagons and four Rolls Royces parked along the stone curbs, some in front of white hitching posts. A nice touch, those hitching posts, and Fahey liked them. He was tempted to spit on the spotless walks just to see if an alarm would go off somewhere.

He ambled over to where he had parked his Buick near the local tavern. His silver flask needed refilling. He had some time to give away, and he'd find out about flowers, then check his appearance again.

He wore church clothes today. A blue tie against a pale blue shirt tucked into his dark blue suit. Had even brushed the suit carefully that morning. Around his waist as a sort of belt he had folded and tied a pink head-scarf belonging to his wife.

In the bar he sat on a cowhide stool, having an early one along with another cup of coffee. The bartender remarked on the pink of Fahey's belt and the hip holster with the .38 poking out of it. Deep in thought, readying himself, Fahey merely said, "I'm having my last drink for a while. Been sent orders on short notice to report for training to a regiment up this way. A Vatican outfit. Amphibious troops. Getting rid of the Swiss Guards over there . . ." The bartender backed away when Fahey asked where he could buy flowers at that hour.

He tarried in the tavern for an hour, then left to find the florist before driving out a back road. Cloudy with dust, the road was shadowed by great hanging willows that almost hid the hills all in feather with daffodils.

Fahey had expected a quite different set-up, when he pulled up to a front gate.

A defunct brewery. Through the bent bars of the padlocked gate, he saw the main building—low slung, decayed walls, a patchy slate roof and thick oaks towering against the bluish stone facade. A marl driveway full of deep ruts and potholes led straight up to the building.

Wonderful, he thought. Be perfect for a headquarters, but the idea of a brewery still held a certain appeal. Perhaps the good sisters would sell on generous terms: a payout, say, of forty years at a Christian rate of interest. How does one apply for a license to brew rare ales? Rhodes might know and Fahey made a mental note to ask him.

He warmed up with a fighting ballad the gypsy had taught him one day when they'd been in the sauna sweating it out. Suddenly he let out a deep buffalo bellow aimed through the gates at a hunched over figure at the driveway's end.

Shaking the gate, he saw the figure rise and shuffle his way closer. Fahey went back to his convertible and slid a long green florist's box off the back seat.

Peace offerings.

A dark-skinned man drew nearer. He had a flat and unlucky face with no teeth visible when he opened his mouth to speak. A groundskeeper, Fahey guessed, spotting the clods of dirt on the man's overalls.

"I'm Fahey," he said calmly. "They expect me."

"Señor?"

"An appointment. Me . . . Sister Marius."

"Si. You please move your car, señor?"

"How about you watching it for me? Don't drive it over that tank course either," said Fahey, pointing to the rutted driveway.

"I busy, señor. You must move your own car."

"Speak Italian?"

"No, señor."

"Parlez-vous Français?"

The man shook his head.

"Russian? You must speak Russian fr'chrissakes, it's Monday today."

A droopy-eyed look crossed the Mexican's face. All he could think about was the gun on Fahey's hip, and the smell of liquor on close, shouting breath.

Fahey rattled the gate again. "I important, little man.

Come straight from the Vatican... Office of Lost Souls, you wonderful little mother." He shifted the flower box and opened his jacket far enough so the groundskeeper could see the gun better, then pulled a tenner from his pocket, handing it through the gate. "Here. Now open the fucking gate, son, or I come over the wall for you."

A hundred yards later, Fahey looked into colorless eyes on the other side of a Judas window. He stated his business again. The Judas window closed with the raspy sound made by old and warped wood.

A bolt slid back and the large oak door of Las Infantas yawned open. He was allowed in by a young fresh-faced woman, a postulant, he would later learn, about to vow her life to God forever.

He was asked to sit. With the green box on his lap, Fahey let his eyes roam the foyer. He could have his office right here, he thought, and keep the keys to the brewery. Greet the important customers, chase away the bill collectors and Treasury agents.

Up high, the ceiling was cross-braced with heavy aged timbers. A rose window was cut into one wall, and an intricately carved choir screen, like a balcony, stood out on the opposite wall. He could use it to deliver pep talks to the good nuns who would sell his brews. They sold for God, why not for Fahey's Heavenly Ales? Put them on a special commission and excuse them from their Lenten fasts.

His busy mind tinkered with two or three sales slogans until the postulant returned to guide him into the deeper mysteries of this sanctuary. Walking along, he noted stone walls of irregularly cut granite. Can't be another like it anywhere, he decided, as he followed the musical sway of the postulant's chaste hips. Somewhere around her fifth sway he knew she would be just right to conduct tours for the paying public.

Make a fortune. Can't miss if God smiles on this place of very cold bedsheets.

Brimming with enthusiasm, he handed the two dozen roses to Sister Marius in her small office. She thanked him politely and remarked on the pink ones. Sixtyish, he guessed, and a bit rotund under the flowing blue habit that almost concealed her black lace-up boots. Skin the color of rose pearl, hardly lined at all, and dark eyes glowing like lasers out of the gray shadows. Lot of woman there.

Fahey feigned with: "Quite a gardener you've got here. A linguist, eh?"

"I hardly think so. Pedro's been with us for years. He barely speaks English."

"Caught a trace of Russian there under the Spanish. Rare combination, you know. Not the same lip muscles."

"You're a linguist, Mr. Fahey?"

"Gaelic. But I've a few minor languages like French and German."

"I see." Sister Marius sniffed daintily. "Are you drinking so early today, Mr. Fahey?"

"Doctor insists on it. Touch of insomnia . . . Say, Sister, have you ever thought of selling Las Infantas? For a worthy purpose, of course."

"Why, never, Mr. Fahey. It's our home."

"But it's no longer a foundling home."

"Not for some years, that's true. They changed the laws and we didn't have the money to change with them."

"Sodders," murmured Fahey.

"Beg your pardon?"

"Plodders. Fools in government, you know. Ruin us."

"Well, we've managed all the same. But we miss our little ones . . . Now, Mr. Fahey, I'm afraid you'll have to tell me your business. We don't allow visitors on the premises very often and—"

"Surely." Fahey's smile competed with the sun. "You won't sell it? The place, I mean?"

"Where would we go? Of course not, Mr. Fahey. Why would you want it anyhow?"

Fahey crossed his legs. His coat slipped open. "A restaurant is what I had in mind. Country inn. Religious lore and that sort of thing. Be nice, wouldn't it?"

"This is consecrated ground." Sister Marius saw Fahey's gun as she was meant to. "You're here, I believe, on some confidential matter. Isn't that what you phoned about?"

"Ah, yes. Glad you reminded me. One of your own, I gather. The Brook girl."

"And how may we help?" the Marius voice sharpening now.

"She was adopted from Las Infantas?"

"That's quite correct."

"I'm told her adoptive parents are either dead or missing," Fahey said. "We're trying to locate her real parents . . . And we knew you'd want to help."

"Excuse me, but who is the *we* you refer to?"

"Thought I explained. Sorry. I'm working for Romaine Brook's defense counsel."

"Well, Mr. Fahey, that may be so. But I wouldn't have any way of knowing that, would I?"

Fahey pulled out a breast wallet. As he opened it, one side dangled down to reveal an honorary sheriff's badge brightly scrolled in gilt and silver. A jeweler friend had embossed the shield with a few extra touches, engraving it with an illegal badge number as well. He slipped out a letter written by Tommy Burke and handed it over to Sister Marius.

As she reached for it, the cowl of her sleeve slipped back to reveal an Ace bandage wrapped around her elbow. For arthritis, Fahey supposed. She moved stiffly at times, yet her serene face never betrayed the slightest grimace.

Sister Marius read the letter. Then she looked up, saying, "Well, that's all very interesting. Yes, quite interesting. But I still don't see how we can assist."

"Maybe you could help us with a few answers. Then I'm off like the fair wind. Besides, you don't want a subpoena and all that foolishness." Having made his opening gambit, he took the letter back.

"I wouldn't expect anything like that. A subpoena, you said?"

"A real nuisance, those are. You'll be hiring lawyers and all the rest of it," Fahey went on, explaining that he was new to the case. He understood that Raye Wheeler had requested information from Las Infantas on the identity and whereabouts, if known, of Romaine Brook's biological parents. Wheeler had gotten nowhere. And now at the eleventh hour, Fahey was pleased to make the same inquiry again.

"The defense, you see, needs money to defray costs. Perhaps her real parents, if they could be contacted, might help. No obligation naturally. Yet," Fahey conceded, "worth a try, isn't it?"

As he talked, Fahey noticed a faint swinging, up and down, of one of Sister Marius's feet. Suddenly it stopped. She was uneasy about something, he was sure of it. He had trained himself to observe such things.

"Mr. Fahey," she said when he'd finished, "the information you seek is held in the strictest of confidence. I'm sure you can appreciate why—"

"I think, Sister, begging your pardon, those laws have changed somewhat."

"But the policies of Las Infantas haven't," she stated adamantly.

"I got it. You don't want to help us. Such a shame... You want that poor young woman on your conscience... Not really, Sister Marius, do you?"

"I'm very sorry."

"Well, then." Fahey stood up. He adjusted the pink head scarf around his waist, and saw her staring at it. "I'll tell the lawyer and you might be expecting that subpoena any day now. I was hoping we could make it easy on everyone."

"Please, Mr. Fahey. You must understand a few things. Romaine Brook was born out of wedlock. I was here, and I remember the circumstances well enough..."

Fahey sat down again.

"...and the mother of Romaine Brook was herself a young woman at the time. From a very prominent family, who were deeply upset about the situation. Often it's the best thing," persuaded Sister Marius, "to let these regrettable incidents sleep. Naturally, we would like to help Romaine Brook. We're a Christian community. But we must also respect the wishes of others."

Fahey remained quiet. He looked around the almost scruffy room, absorbing some of the religious objects: a crucifix surrounded by a wreath of palm fronds; a glass case enclosing a carved Madonna; a missal with a tattered leather cover resting on a small table. Then he regarded Sister Marius again, with her earnest face that seemed to fear nothing and know everything.

"You see," he said, "it's a trial about murder. Her lawyer has to fight hard as he can for her. Go to any lengths."

"Well, I'm sure you're wrong about one thing, Mr. Fahey."

"Please tell me, Sister." He smiled at her.

"I don't think any judge would approve a subpoena if it meant stirring up the past for innocent people."

"Who's so innocent?" Fahey said. "I'm pretty sure this judge, and I know him, would do whatever's fair . . . As I say, it's all about murder, isn't it?"

"Supposing we no longer have the records?"

"Won't make any difference. You were here, you said. So they'll just subpoena you. Probably bring you to court."

Alarm tightened Sister Marius's face. She'd never expected anything like this to happen. Las Infantas was indebted for those donations, very needed ones, it received on condition they kept to a strict silence about Romaine Brook.

"Suppose, Mr. Fahey," suggested Sister Marius, after dueling with her conscience, "that we compromised?"

"I'd love it. Wonderful." A ray of hope in his voice.

"Then suppose I contact the, er, mother and ask if she'd like to help in some way . . . That is, if I can contact her at all," Sister Marius hedged. "I can call you later. Perhaps you'll leave me the letter?"

He handed her Burke's letter again. "That'd be fine. Glad you'll cooperate."

"And there'll be no subpoena?"

"Won't be necessary, if you'll help us."

"That's not quite what I said."

"Let's just see what happens, Sister. I'm not the one trying the case. Lawyers, you know. They're liable to do anything."

With those words Fahey thought he saw Sister Marius's mouth close up, and her voice, so even and clear before, became ragged. Her silver crucifix shifted places on her bosom.

"I'd like to know for certain," she insisted.

"You can have the subpoena or not. But why go to all that trouble? All you have to do is lead us to the parents."

"We are not the ones making trouble," Sister Marius said firmly.

"Remember, I'm trying to help the girl. I'm on the same side as her, and she's the angel of this very hour."

"These matters are very, very confidential," repeated Sister Marius. "Surely you understand that innocent people have a right to privacy and—"

"You keep saying *innocent.* I don't know how innocent they are, Sister. They had babies, without the sacrament of marriage, but then there are worse things."

"That was a long time ago."

"Help us, then we'll help you by going away." Fahey pressed her, throwing down his bluff. He unwound from his chair, slightly frustrated. But then he hadn't expected much either.

"Mr. Fahey, I've no right to be personal, but are you a Catholic?"

"Sometimes."

"Sometimes? Does that mean you are uncertain of your faith?"

"When I'm in a bad corner, I'm very certain of it. You see, Sister, I've been searching for a long time. Whenever I get close, I get run over."

"Run over? By what?"

"By me."

She shook her head. The man was trifling with her, and she almost resented it. Where, she wondered, had he ever come across such an odd looking belt? And why a gun for heaven's sake?

Fahey was warming to the Sister, but it was time to leave. She had a nice tough way about her, the sort of quiet authority that reminded him of a blackjack tapping on glass. She probably had a lot to deal with—a crowd of women, her nuns, and no men around to keep them down. Must be very hard, and he wished he had her job.

"You've been most kind, Sister Marius," he told her as he buttoned his jacket. The knot in the head scarf still showed.

"Oh, not at all."

"And you'll let me know if you ever want to sell out here?"

"You're really quite foolish to keep bringing that up."

"Must cost the sky to keep it up."

"Oh, we manage."

They left her office and walked to the large foyer with

the vaulted ceiling. Sister Marius unbolted the huge oak door and held it open.

"You know," Fahey said with his goodbyes, "if you weren't already spoken for, I know a place we could go for a great dinner, champagne and all."

"I really think it's time you left us."

Bolting the door once more, Sister Marius leaned back against it, making a silent list of her troubles. Another mortgage payment to meet, new habits for the nuns who had resewn their frayed garments several times, medical bills, broken plumbing to repair.

Now this, a threat of a subpoena, and more trouble was a certainty. Sister Marius knew she would have to make a call. An urgent call.

But dear Lord, she thought, what will happen to Romaine Brook? Guilt pressed its frown on her round and usually serene face.

A brassy hot twilight burned around Fahey as he reached the outskirts of Los Angeles. The top was down, and the congested air smarted his eyes and dried his throat. He took a deep pull from his emergency reserves. Stopping for gas fifty miles back, he had tried to call Tommy Burke but found out the lawyer was over at the detention center again. He had tried the judge's chambers, kidded around some with Macklin Price, then learned Rhodes had left for the day.

Fahey grunted to himself. Las Infantas seemed a blind alley. But the Sister had spoken of a prominent family. Maybe there was money, but then plenty of prominent families found it touch and go with their banks. Have to see. He could use a yard or two of cash soon, for he had never saved a *sou* in his life. Weighed a man down was his theory.

In Bel Air an hour later he parked in the driveway, off to one side, and saw the Bentley in the garage. Fahey heard a low melodic sound, partly muted, as he circled the house.

Rhodes was standing on the terrace, one foot up on the stone balustrade, filling the air with notes; a tape recorder played the background sounds of a piano and a snare drum. The music came together, full and smooth, then stopped abruptly when Fahey clapped his hands.

"Scaring the owls again. The Humane Society'll be after you."

"H'lo, Alonzo."

"And yourself. Thought I'd try you here. Mackey-girl said you were splitting up the payoffs with the other judges."

"That's right. Everybody made plenty today . . . I just got home. C'mon up."

Rhodes rested his trombone on a chair. Flicking off the tape recorder, he dipped into his shirt pocket for a Honduran cigar.

"Like one?" he asked.

"Can't. Ruins my taste for what's good for me."

Rhodes looked out over the lawn. "Sun's across the trees, Alonzo. Feels like a—"

"Thought you'd never ask. Have to do something about your manners, old son."

"You just got here," Rhodes said, a little uneasily. "What're you wearing? That pink thing—"

"Need a new color image. An experiment of mine. The women have it all over us on color . . . Can't let 'em have everything, can we?"

"Why not?" Rhodes smiled. "Hells bells, they got *everything* else you seem to want."

"Only when they're lying down."

"I'll never quote you, Alonzo, I promise. You want the usual? Bushmills?"

Fahey nodded. He removed his sunglasses. Seeing the look on Rhodes's face, he decided to explain himself.

"I know you told me to stay scarce until this work for Burke is over. I couldn't get him earlier on the phone. He's with the girl, or was anyway. I'm trying to find out if we got the okay to look around Marc Sterne's apartment." Fahey stepped onto the terrace.

"Burke called me about it. I told Pritter to call the sheriff and take care of it."

"Good. I'll get over there tomorrow then."

Rhodes saw some redness in the rims of Fahey's eyes and knew he'd been drinking already. "You want a short one or the long kind?"

"Long. Why walk when you can stagger is what I say."

Pausing to light his cigar, Rhodes exhaled and saw Fahey dissolve for a moment under the white gauze of the smoke.

"Found a lovely little tavern today up by San Timoteo. Nice lay-by. Bartender needs disciplining, but we ought to buy it. Be just the place—"

"What's in San Timoteo? A girl?"

Fahey repeated, more or less, the wisp of what he had learned as they passed through a terrace door into the red walled library.

Going to the bar, Rhodes asked a little testily: "What's with that gun you're wearing, Alonzo?"

"Not loaded, so don't worry."

"See that it stays that way. Hope you've got a license for—"

"Don't go up in flames, Cliff. It's just for dress, when I need it."

"With a nun?"

"Anyone. In my game you use whatever you can. As you know . . . What're you today? The first Bishop of Christ or someone?"

A pause, as both men tried to avoid an argument.

"Well, Romaine Brook's birth, or her parents, have nothing to do with nothing," said Rhodes after thinking over what Fahey had related.

"Except maybe money."

"Yes, maybe that."

"Would your court ever issue a subpoena to help find out who the real parents were?"

"Have to think about it. I doubt it, though." Rhodes began to fix the drinks.

"Well, the nun may come across without one. I bluffed her a bit, told her you'd issue a subpoena if it came to that."

"That was really very good of you, Alonzo. Maybe you'd like to take over the trial, too."

"Jesus, aren't you the one. Who'n hell asked me to come into this thing anyway?"

Rhodes stirred ice into Fahey's drink. "You're right, I did. But you can't go throwing subpoenas around." He handed the drink over.

"You look all in, you know that?" Rhodes seemed drawn, tight, and without his usual color.

"Sleeping funny. Don't know why. Raye's funeral got to me, I guess. Anyway, cheers."

Their tumblers clinked together.

Politely but definitely he would get rid of Fahey. Find some lame excuse. Any other time and he'd gladly ask him to stay for dinner. Call his wife, Wanda, and have her come as well and laugh over past times when he and Fahey had been closer than two crossed fingers. But now it was different. And it was not such a hot idea for Fahey, while working for the defense, to be dropping by the house.

They gabbed a while. After one more rendezvous with the bar, Alonzo Fahey went home.

Rhodes put the trombone away, went to his desk, shut off the phone, and then removed a sheaf of papers from one drawer. He could put in a few hours now. With time to whittle away for a change, he would work harder on a pet project: his ideas to improve the state's criminal justice system.

Streamline it, fix it up. A year ago he'd gotten the governor's go ahead to draft proposals for the Legislature. California was different than most other states; a place in constant flux, a country apart it often seemed.

More rapes, murders, scams, embezzlements. The courts jammed to their gills. Cases awaiting trial for four and five years. Witnesses died, so did felons. Innocent people were caught in a time trap waiting their turn, facing a rising river of legal bills and no way to dam the flood.

If you were in money, you could hunt the law down—instead of the other way around—by hiring the best guns.

Rhodes knew all about it. He'd played on the course many times, been in the fray as a hired shooter himself. And for big money.

Delay trials. Get yourself a battery of top researchers. Engage experts to confuse the facts. Appeal and appeal again if you don't like the first one. Baffle the judge, blind the jury, screw the public conscience silly. With enough money you could show how Christmas day was illegal.

Money was an infection in the system. Rhodes found that out when learning his way up. Others had already learned it, so fast and so well, from the wise scripture of the streets.

Wrong way. A good way to cave in the ribs of fair law, but the wrong way for sure to build anything worthwhile.

So Rhodes stayed with it. He sketched out his ideas, devising what he thought would be a better path. And one day, up on the high court, he would try to persuade others that the law was basically good but needed a newer engine to make it work better. A hard sell to make, and he would need the backing of the big court to have any chance at all.

He had no illusions as to how many of the lawyers he knew would take to his ideas. Cost them fat fees, and sometimes he could already feel the burn of rope they would braid for his neck.

Lost in thought as he looked down at the pale cone of light shining across his scrawl, he heard Consuelo Ramirez waddle in. Scolding him, twice in the same breath, for putting off his dinner so long. Telling him then of the phone call he should answer.

He picked up the phone at his desk, remembering that he'd shut if off earlier so he could work quietly. The voice surprised him, so nice at first, pleading a moment later, then begging—but not with a beggar's words.

Chapter Eleven

Checking the number on the stone wall, Audrey turned into the driveway. With hardly more noise than a butterfly, her white Jaguar coasted to a stop.

Looking into the vanity mirror, she tried to calm her nerves. Nerves that had refused to quiet, nerves that had kept her awake for nights. She thought she'd collapse from exhaustion, or the waking fright whittling away at her.

Lipstick was fine, she saw while primping her ash-blond

hair. Outside the car she smoothed down her peach colored dress and slid her hand through the straps of an alligator handbag dyed to match her dress.

She was tempted to jump back in the Jag. But she'd come this far already. She prayed it would never go past him, and that he wouldn't do anything foolish, and would understand what it was costing her to come to his home.

She walked on, giving his house the once-over: the slate gray roof; grape ivy climbing the white brick walls; red geraniums in window boxes; a black front door set back into a high turret that ended in a crown above the roof line.

About to press the bell, she was startled as the door to her latest hell opened suddenly.

"Heard you pull in," said Cliff Rhodes, his voice forcing its way through a grin. "You always look so marvelous, Audrey."

Returning his grin with a smile you could hang laundry on, she said, "Oh, Cliff, yes, thanks. I guess I'm fine anyway." She sighed softly.

"Come in, please." He backed away and gestured her forward. "Right straight ahead. We'll sit on the terrace; it's nice out there today."

Her eyes roamed the high hallway with its winding staircase and a banister of polished teak. "Your house is lovely, Cliff. Very, very nice."

That mouth for breaking your heart, slightly drawn up at one corner so that it always seemed as if an invisible cigarette dangled there. You were mine once, he thought.

Audrey paused by an antique table. Guiding one finger along its inlaid design of tulip wood, she asked, "Sheraton period?"

"I think so."

"Neat."

He stood there waiting, not knowing what to make of her visit. She had sounded so urgent, so hurried, on the phone the other night, but right now she looked as cool as mountain mint.

On the terrace Audrey arranged herself on a chaise-longue, and Rhodes leaned against the stone railing a few paces away so he could see her better. They talked away, gauging each other, attempting the impossible task of sifting through twenty-odd years. Easy questions, then vague ones, and vague answers to go with them. She told him of her twin boys by her previous marriage to a lord of the realm. "My London incident," she termed it. The boys were attending Eton and often visited California on their summer holidays. A proper British arrangement, but she missed them madly all the same.

Then, almost deftly, Audrey shifted gears. "A strange way for us to come together again, isn't it?"

"You mean the trial."

"Yes. You running the trial and everything. That's quite strange, I feel."

"Unfortunately, it is. It's even stranger than you might think."

Rhodes told her how the trial had been assigned to him almost by fluke. His calendar had opened up when two cases he'd been hearing were settled by plea bargains. And the judge, originally slated to hear the charges against Romaine Brook, had been in an auto accident. So the trial fell into Rhodes's lap by sheer chance.

Audrey turned her face at the sound of Consuelo Ramirez shuffling across the terrace. Rhodes introduced them, and Consuelo smiled politely and very gravely. "Ees all right for eating soon, señor?" she asked.

"Anytime. Audrey?" Rhodes looked at her.

"Would you mind if we wait for a . . . No, let's go ahead," she answered, changing her mind.

"I open wine now?" asked Consuelo.

"Muy bien."

As Consuelo padded away, Audrey went on: "Where were we?" She sighed once more. "Julio was devastated when Marc was killed. Bitter, God! He barely talked to anyone for weeks."

"You could hardly blame him. But I don't think we can talk about the trial, Audrey."

"I'm afraid we have to."

"That's all but against the law. So I'm afraid we can't. That's one of the rules."

"Tell me, Cliff," she said, "what would you say if I told you I needed help. Badly needed it."

"I'd say I'd give it to you if I can. But not on the trial, if that's why you came here."

"Well, that's why I came." Audrey tossed her head back. "And what would you say if I told you you might need the most help of all."

The way she said it shook him. Across the terrace Consuelo fussed with the dishes; hearing the clatter, he smiled and motioned to Audrey.

They sat at an umbrella-table to a first course of gazpacho soup. To their side the green neck of a bottle poked its nose out of a silver wine cooler. A spray of roses lifted their faces from a crystal vase near Audrey.

He would wait her out. Rhodes wondered if this were some new ploy, some new game of pressure. Julio Sterne working an angle, an angle dealing with Rhodes's pending appointment to the High Court. A political shot? Something else?

Her spoon poised, Audrey said: "You remember, Cliff, when you were leaving for Vietnam? When I took off from school for a week, and we went up to Pebble Beach?"

"Sure, I remember." He'd never forgotten.

Audrey sipped from her spoon. "I don't know where to begin."

"Start anywhere."

"You don't know it, were never told, but I . . . well, I got pregnant. Had a daughter, *we* had a daughter, I should say. That's who Romaine Brook is . . . our daughter."

There, she'd said it, straight out, and Audrey was relieved to find out her bones weren't flying apart.

The first thing leaving Rhodes was his spoon dropping into the soup bowl. The blood inside his head seemed to rush to his feet. The tiny creases around his eyes went smooth, his eyes shut, and his mouth became thin as a matchstick. When he peeled open his eyes they flared wide with surprise.

Like millions of other men faced with a claim of paternity, his instant reaction was: it must be someone else's, not mine. He'd seen Romaine Brook's birthday in the trial records somewhere. He tried to recall it, furiously. But his memory blanked on him now as surely as if a hammer had come down on his skull.

"You don't believe me?" Audrey asked.

Rhodes shook his head. "What can I say? You've got the drop on me."

"She was born in the night," said Audrey as she began to work out all the arithmetic for Rhodes. Their week in Pebble Beach together before he left for Vietnam, the birth nine months later, the twenty-two years in between. Bing, bing, bing, like an adding machine tape counting up an overdue loan.

Searching his face as she talked, Audrey could tell he was busy trying to tack down the edges of his flapping nerves. "I'm sorry to have to tell you now, after all this time. But you had to know," she said sadly, worriedly.

Confused, and listing inside, he somehow knew—if only by her manner in telling him so evenly and dourfully—that he'd just been severely wounded by the bullet of truth.

"Why now?" he asked hoarsely.

"Because something happened three days ago, Cliff. At Las Infantas, that's where Romaine was sent for adoption . . . Someone went there and threatened a subpoena, or whatever, to find out who her real parents are. That's why I called you. If it ever came out . . ."

But he heard no more. His mind thrashed around again. Fahey, of course. Oh, my Christ! How could it be! There'd be no subpoena. He'd all but told Fahey so.

"Audrey, there'll be no subpoena."

"But I don't know those things. A nun at Las Infantas called me, really shaken up, and told me one was coming. I had to see you, Cliff. My name is on the original birth record."

"And mine?"

Audrey nodded into Rhodes's face that fell everywhere at the news.

"Why in hell didn't you tell me? A long time ago, I mean. Or before the trial began at least?" His words poured hot and Rhodes tried to stop himself from drowning in more waves of disbelief.

"A long time ago I couldn't find you," Audrey said woodenly, and began to tell him of that wretched stretch in her life.

Of how, discovering she was pregnant, she finally broke

down and told her mother, who wasted about ten minutes before telling Audrey's father. Their rage was volcanic. Abortion was against the law then, and it wouldn't've made a whit of difference anyway. As Rhodes knew, her family were devout Catholics.

"They tried to locate you in Vietnam," she told him, "but the Army wouldn't say where you were. For months and months they stonewalled us. Said you were missing, possibly dead. How was I to know? I really crashed. I was nearly disowned, and my parents forced me to put the baby up for adoption. At Las Infantas, where my father gave free medical care to the nuns . . . I couldn't tell you. I couldn't find you. I loved you, Cliff, but I couldn't find you anywhere. I was sure you were dead because they wouldn't tell us anything.

"So I was sent to England, and a year later I married, trying to blot out the pain and misery and missing you. I thought I'd put it all behind me. But found I couldn't do that either."

Audrey stopped.

My daughter? Rhodes thought. This woman lost to me, and then my daughter, because of that goddamn war?

"Who else knows about us?" he asked solemnly. "That we're the parents."

"Me. You now. Of course, Sister Marius at Las Infantas. That's everyone."

"Not your husband?"

"That would be the final bell for me," Audrey said. "Marc was his only child. If he ever knew it was my daughter—" she stopped abruptly. It was too horrible, too unbelievable to even try talking about.

"Your parents, but they're dead?"

"Yes."

"That's everyone, you're sure of it?"

"Everyone, Cliff."

Was the loop really closed? Maybe, maybe not. His brain thrummed away. He was still spinning on air, the rule of gravity somehow thrown aside for him today.

"Audrey, how did you ever find her? What happened?" Rhodes's face deepened again.

"I hate to even think. At one time I cared very much.

But now I have much less trouble working that feeling off. I just don't know what to feel."

"Tell me." Rhodes poured some wine. The bottle almost slipped from his moist, fumbling fingers before he caught it.

She began.

It wasn't at all what he'd heard Audrey explain in court on the day she'd come to blister Romaine. These were backstage scenes, the shifting of them, and the raising of a dark curtain to reveal a hidden past.

Of how after eighteen years she'd divorced Lord Robert Hubbard-Hewes, a famous London theatrical producer. They had come to the end of their arguing over his constant affairs with every actress in England and places beyond. She met Julio in Surrey at a weekend houseparty, and one thing led to another until they decided to marry. But the British courts insisted her twins be allowed to finish their schooling in England.

After she and Julio had come back to California, she found herself missing the boys unbearably. She had always wanted a daughter, though at Julio's age that was awkward, if not impossible.

But Audrey knew where to go looking for her own daughter.

She befriended Sister Marius at Las Infantas. Gave money, gave quite a lot of it, and in return she learned the identity of Romaine's adoptive parents. Waited for a time, setting a plan, then hired Pinkerton's to finish the search.

A month went by. One day the news came. Romaine Brook was a student at the School of Drama at the same university "where you and I first met, Cliff," Audrey said poignantly.

She went on, explaining how she had persuaded Julio to make a heavy donation in the name of Parthenon Studios to the school. She attended the acting classes occasionally as a welcomed observer, and they were flattered—and said so—to have her there. Weeks went by. She began to make casual inquiries, as a veil, about three of the drama students, then two of them, finally just one—Romaine, her daughter. Who would never, if Audrey could help it, learn of the fact.

The rest was easy. She had invited Romaine to lunches

at the nicer restaurants. They were seen, occasionally with Julio, at Sunday polo matches or the glitzier tennis tournaments, at dinners and parties in Beverly Hills and Malibu where Audrey arranged for Romaine to be added to the guest lists.

Other nights Romaine, all sweetness and lace, came for dinner at the Malibu Pointe house. In time, Audrey, who had no particular feel for acting talent, saw what the teachers and coaches knew all along. Romaine had the makings. "One of the rare ones," they said, "born to the stageboards."

"I was so proud of her. And I began to quietly back a few small productions so she could appear at the Santa Monica Playhouse," Audrey went on. "Audiences loved her. The reviews were often excellent, and then came the inquiries from Broadway producers and Hollywood studios.

"I wanted to showcase her, though I never told her I was an angel, an investor. I had her meet society, the real kind and the Hollywood kind. It was lots of fun at first. She bowled people over with that deadly charm."

Audrey's voice faltered and she stared out at the hills out beyond the terrace. Rhodes watched as she struggled to control her emotions.

"I wanted to look out for her, help her, give her a future," Audrey said with tears in her eyes. "My own daughter, still and always a stranger. I came to love her, then fear her, and now I often feel hatred for my own child." Audrey shook her head as tears spilled down her cheeks. "But that came much, much later."

She wiped her eyes. "When Julio approved Romaine's role in *Tonight or Never*, everything seemed to change. Practically overnight. Somehow the sunshine Romaine turned into black clouds. Overnight, Cliff, she became moody, tricky, sly, even more of a stranger. I thought *I* was going crazy. Her behavior was outrageous and she manipulated shamelessly.

"My mistake was failing to put a flat stop to Romaine's chase after Marc. I was the one who had introduced them. Before I knew it, a casual friendship blossomed into a raging affair. Talk of marriage, of a new world, of love everlasting, you know what I mean. . . .

". . . and Marc Sterne had to have her. I nearly died twice every day just thinking about it."

He was all bright and starlight in Julio's eyes, and if Marc wanted Romaine, what could or should she say? But on the business of marriage, Julio smartened up; there was a lot to think about, he agreed—and not the smallest of those soft rumbles was fifty million dollars or so in Sterne money that needed guarding.

"It was all a big boomerang," Audrey confessed, "and I could never bring myself to explain the truth to Julio. Not before and certainly not after Marc died. It was one of those times when you *never never* can be wholly truthful. There's no sane way I could explain to my husband that his only child, his son, was killed by my daughter that he never knew was my daughter.

"And after that I couldn't believe she was my daughter either. It's been impossible to believe. The whole mess."

Rhodes was silent. He let her tale seep down into his memory, admiring Audrey for telling him, knowing it couldn't be easy. And not knowing how much was shaved off to make her side so clean and goody.

He was in stiff trouble. That much was deeply etched into another part of his memory by now.

"I'm so sorry, Cliff," said Audrey, breaking the silence. "But my life is so filled with torture that the idea of a subpoena nearly drove me nutty. I don't think you can understand what it's been like, and will be like, for me."

"I'm still trying to touch earth. I can't get used to the idea of a daughter yet."

"You haven't eaten anything."

"Not sure I could hold it down either."

"Me neither."

Another pause took hold.

"A lost letter finally got delivered, didn't it?" he said, shaking his head. "My God."

"Somehow I can't read it anymore. I tried once."

"You can't send it back either."

"I can and I must."

"You came here because some nun thought I'd subpoena her records?"

"Yes. She was frightened. She knew it would all come out, ravaging us and stunning everyone else."

"A damn subpoena." Rhodes went blank, shaking his head again aimlessly.

"How was anyone to know, Cliff? I came here to ask you to stop it. For your own good as well as mine."

Rhodes was still pale from the strength it took to keep his insides together. "What's she really like, anyway? Romaine."

"Not what she seems. I just told you, I thought."

"Tell me more."

"Well, you see her every day, don't you?"

"See her, yes, that's right. I've never talked to her though. Never yet heard her utter a word."

"Go see her movie." Audrey shifted in her chair. She saw Rhodes looking at her well-sunned legs. "What's she like? I don't know. I have a daughter and no idea who she is at all. I don't think *she* really knows." Audrey rubbed one eye, looking off to nowhere. "A shark," she continued in an empty voice. "You think she's so naive. So innocent and vulnerable. Even I was fooled. She's got scalpels for teeth. Being around her when she was smothering Marc, I got so afraid I never turned my back."

"Dangerous, you mean? C'mon, Audrey."

"Lethal. A sorceress."

Almost amused, Rhodes tried a smile. But his mood changed quickly when he took another look at Audrey's face. As if suddenly frostbitten, two white patches appeared on either side of her mouth.

"She stole something from me," Audrey said. "Something dear and damn valuable too."

"Stole what?"

"An emerald bracelet. A Bulgari from Rome that Julio gave me for our anniversary."

"Are you sure?"

"I couldn't prove it. I just know, that's all."

"Then you shouldn't accuse her."

"Oh please, Cliff. I'm just a woman, not a lawyer or a cop. I just feel, then know . . . And Romaine knows I know."

"But why would she steal from you?"

Audrey told him of the time when they were off on the

Paloma together, Julio, herself, Marc and Romaine. They had gone swimming one afternoon in a small cove on Catalina Island. Romaine had often admired the bracelet. Audrey had taken it off while changing into her bathing suit in one of the cabins, and left it on a table. Forgetting all about it until later, on the way back to Malibu, she couldn't find it anywhere. Searched every nook of the boat. But the bracelet was missing and Audrey could hardly accuse anyone there of stealing it.

"I just know," Audrey said after thinking and talking about it again. "There're things you simply know. She's full of guile. I don't know who she is. And she's a thief, damnit all."

"Not a helluva lot to go on," Rhodes observed drily.

"Oh, she was always so clever. Afterward she said she saw me go in swimming with it on. Tried to warn me, even."

"Maybe you did."

"I get careless sometimes. But not that careless . . . Julio was furious. It cost a bomb. All matched ten-carat stones and my initial in diamonds on the clasp."

"Hope you were insured at least."

"That's why Julio was so angry. It wasn't. He thinks I'm careless too . . ."

"Ah."

"I can't bear to even think about it," said Audrey, tears in her eyes again. "I don't know what to do. I'd like to wring her damn neck, but she's still my daughter. *Our* daughter. So how am I supposed to feel?"

Rhodes had been nursing his wine. He put his glass down on the table. Thinking desperately, he tried to pin the problem together so Audrey would be sure to grasp all of its collapsing sides.

"If I stay in the trial and Romaine is found innocent, and then later I'm discovered to be her father, it'll seem like I put the fix in somehow . . . but if I stay on and they find out, I'll be disbarred for sure. I could even get jail for judicial misconduct."

"I didn't realize it could be that bad."

Rhodes looked right at her now. "And if I leave the trial, Audrey, there'll be all hell to pay. I'd have to explain why, you see, and come up with a damn good reason. And once they find out I'm the father, the newspapers are sure to find out you're the mother."

"They'd never get it out of Sister Marius."

"Are you up to taking that chance?"

Audrey thought a moment. "No, I guess I'm not." All at once her face went tragic, hectic, teary. "God, what'll we do? Oh, Cliff, help me, please help me."

"I don't know what we can do. This trial's cost a million bucks already. If it's a mistrial, they'll hang us. Me, at least." And there would go the Supreme Court appointment, he thought. All his work down the chute.

"Cliff?"

"Yes."

"The lawyer who died, Wheeler, the one who said he might recall me?"

"Yes."

"You've got to get me out of that."

"It's all up to them. The defense."

"You must. You're the judge."

"I cannot. There's no way. You're already sworn as a witness."

"She killed Marc. You must know that, don't you?"

"That's for the jury to say."

"Help me, you said you would. You said it, Cliff."

"Not that, I didn't say."

She stood and he stood with her. She ran to him and clung with both arms locked around his neck. He thought every organ he owned had moved a foot.

"Audrey," he murmured in her ear. "Try to hold up. You're the kind who can. Who must."

She sobbed in muffled words. "I can't stand it anymore. Julio or Ferenc, the whole mess . . . S'breaking me apart."

He didn't pay any attention to her mention of Ferenc Kardas. His thoughts were a mile down the line. On Audrey, then on Romaine, and a full ladle of thoughts about himself. They held together for a time, very close. Consuelo came out the terrace door and quickly went right back through it.

Audrey pulled away, saying she had to leave. She needed to be alone. He saw her out to her car, where she seemed to go limp. He hugged her again, assuring her, telling her he'd think of something. Twenty-three years jammed into less than two hours was all he could grapple with now.

He could remember their week in Pebble Beach as easily as his own street address. Nor was nine months hard to add up after that glorious, flesh-sodden time there. Romaine was born just about the time the Cong had collared him in the mountains of Laos.

Another truth gnawed at him later, after she'd gone. There would never be another blood daughter for him, nor a son either, and he would give plenty right now for just one of them.

What kind of man wouldn't fight for his child? He could beat Pritter hands down, if only he were down there with Burke instead of being up on the bench. The thought drummed and drummed again. And who was Romaine? How much of her was of him? Was she a murderer, a thief? And those photos. How did Marc Sterne come to possess those? What had really happened?

For sure, something had happened at the Sterne house on the night of Marc Sterne's death. Rhodes began to wonder if anyone really knew the truth—or was telling it if they did.

A quarrel took place deep inside him, anguish slugging it out in there with his confusion. Had Marc Sterne abused Romaine? She looked as innocent as a nursery rhyme. Your looks, how you really look, always meant a lot in a murder trial—to a jury, the press, and often the public.

Across the terrace he heard Consuelo clearing off the table, muttering, giving him a jumble of hell for ignoring the lunch she slaved over all morning.

Why not bail out? Tell the world he had a swell sleep-in years ago with a beautiful girl. A billion-to-one shot had turned up. Sorry. Next case, please. Let someone else handle this one. Call God in, if you can.

A scandal. The press would soar into a frenzy, nail them both to the post. Goodbye to his Supreme Court appointment. Goodbye to Audrey's exalted image. Goodbye to the next several years. Rhodes had one of those funny feelings that whatever was going to happen had already happened. And what of Romaine?

Chapter Twelve

Fahey waited.

By a short slope of road, Upper Alta Street cut into one of the smaller Hollywood hills. The road curved at its bottom and ended at an apartment house that was a copy of a hundred other places up there: bleached tiled roofs, stucco walls, pseudo-Spanish in style. The top of the road, where he waited, met with a longer street lined with houses and a row of magnolia trees.

By his watch it was 10:17. He leaned casually against one fender of his Buick, glancing at his scribbled notes; the ones penciled at the detention center when he and Burke had seen the girl.

She had told him how Marc Sterne always sent her from the room whenever he went digging for his drugs. A strange maneuver, Fahey thought, his instinct for solving the unknown rapping away.

A black and white car nosed over the rise of the street. Fahey put his notepad away as the car drew up to the curb.

Scrambling out the car door, a man hurried over, almost at a half trot. He had a tough leathery face like a baseball mitt used for too many seasons. He wore an off-white suit, a very white shirt, and a thin black knit tie.

"Hello," he said, "I'm Redd Cullis."

Fahey shook hands. Cullis was tapered and wiry, with steady but quick eyes. Skin as black as a domino and the white suit crisp as an altar cloth.

"How'd you come up with Red for a name? Someone colorblind?"

Cullis chuckled softly. "R-E-D-D. Everyone asks . . . And you're the one, aren't you."

"*One* of the what?"

"The guy who got busted off the Commissioner's staff. For donging his wife, I heard. That story still travels."

"Wonderful woman. Great ears."

"Ears?"

"Could hear your heart a whole county away."

"Wasn't she Miss California once? What I heard anyway," said Cullis, his eyes covering Fahey like a searchlight.

"She's Miss Tahiti now. Ran off to there with a priest I knew. Abyssinian, I think. You're a lieutenant, right?"

"Three more years to go. Then me and my brother in the haberdash business."

"I can see."

"You come down and see us. Get you all rated out on real friendly terms."

"You make uniforms? Pale blue with red flashes on the collar. Crossed keys, like the Vatican has, sewn on the front pockets . . ."

"You gonna be a doorman? Shit, no, we don't make uniforms. No uniforms for me for five, count 'em, five years."

"Been a loo-ey that long, eh?"

"S'right. Change their luck, I said. Get yourself a sharp black man. Redd Cullis reportin' in for his gold bars, I told 'em."

"You really did all that, eh?"

"I did, Fahey. And I didn't have the Commissioner's office come down on me neither . . . So tell me, what's a dude like you do all day long?"

"Make babies. Black ones, when they let me."

Fahey smiled as they started down the curved road to the apartment house, Cullis moving like a scat-back. He reached the manager's ground level door ahead of Fahey, who never hurried unless something notorious was about to happen. Cullis knocked on a bright brass plate with the name: A. Noor, Manager.

When the door opened, a frumpish woman came outside. She seemed to sag everywhere, with heavy jowls and jet-black hair gathered in a bun pierced by an ivory needle.

Her dark features said that she came from somewhere out of the Middle East.

The woman knew Cullis, and she smiled at him, but when he introduced her to Fahey she frowned. Fahey slipped out a different wallet this time, palming it in one hand behind his leg.

"I've still got a key," Cullis was explaining to the woman.

"No-e-noah," the woman protected. "I let in, is bett-or."

The woman closed her door as Cullis led the way up a small flight of stairs. When Cullis's back was turned, Fahey flipped open his wallet so the woman could see his bogus sheriff's badge. She dropped him a scowl, and he privileged her with a smooth smile. Better to seem harmless, thought Fahey. Later he would need her; if not quite as a friend, at least not as a bitchy old harridan.

A musty smell greeted them in Marc Sterne's apartment. A nasty closed-in odor from brown and withered plants hanging over the sides of their clay pots. Cullis switched on the lights. Fahey stifled his surprise as he moved over to a wrought-iron railing and looked down into a sunken living room. Behind him the woman fussed about, and she sounded to him like a camel driver who'd missed too many caravans.

"Don't you air this place out?" Cullis asked her.

"I see sign you put there. Bad luck for me," she said indignantly, and pointed to the open door with its sheriff's seal, advising of the legal penalties for entering the apartment without lawful permission. "When you take that down for me? I loose-a money every week."

Cullis sent her off. "Some place, ain't it?" he asked Fahey.

Other than a few scattered pieces of white furniture, everything was cast in shades of lavender. The walls were painted in winter lilac; the carpet almost the same hue; the long, closed drapes were of a bluish purple. The entire ceiling was paved with smoked glass and, in the corner of the room, white pedestals supported fake Grecian statuary.

"This a cathouse," asked Fahey, "or an upstairs massage parlor?" He blew one of his low whistles.

"You like it, huh?"

"I never . . . You've been here before, of course."

"Oh, yeah. A few of my men swept it the day after our Malibu station started their investigation."

"When exactly was that, Lieutenant?"

"When the Sterne boy went down. They went right at it that night out in Malibu. Next day we got asked to look this place over, then seal it up."

"That letter and those photos, where'd—"

"Right here. Dresser drawer in his bedroom."

"You see them?"

Cullis laughed. "Yeah. Everyone here did. Some piece, ain't she?"

Fahey didn't answer. He still looked around, getting a feel for the place to store in his mind. Whenever he thought of the photos, his sympathy begged for Tommy Burke, who seemed to be heels-over for Romaine Brook.

He noticed the position of the long white couch, the chairs at either end, the side tables, and the white floor lamps that arched up and curved over on top like the necks of two swans.

According to Romaine Brook, somewhere in there was where Marc Sterne had stashed his powder-bank.

"Can we see the rest of it?" Fahey asked.

"Right this way," said Cullis, hovering close by.

"You know anything about Marc Sterne and his drug dealing?"

"Let's take you where you want to go," said Cullis evasively, turning away.

They went through a small kitchen, where Fahey opened and closed some drawers. The refrigerator held a dozen cans of Budweiser, a cut of moldering cheese, and a carton of spoiled fruit juice. It smelled like an unwashed dog kennel. After a look at the dining room they came out to a hall with bedrooms at either end.

Cullis still dogged Fahey, never leaving his side.

Marc Sterne's bedroom was a smaller version of the purple living room, only this time the color was brown, with more of the smoked glass on the ceiling.

"Liked his glass, didn't he?"

"Awful lookin', ain't it?" Cullis said.

"Wonder what the Noor lady gets for it?"

"You ain't gonna tell me you'd want to have this—"

"I was wondering if she took anything off the top of his narc deals. Ever ask her?" Fahey waited, listening very closely for Cullis's reaction.

"You seem mighty fixed on that business."

"Aren't you, Lieutenant? The kid was a dealer. Maybe he forgot to pay the wrong man once."

"And that means?"

"Could mean anything, couldn't it?"

Cullis spread his mouth slightly. He seemed ready to speak, but he only scratched behind his ear somewhere, as if puzzled about the way his day was going.

"Couldn't it?" Fahey repeated.

"You tell me."

"I might."

Fahey walked over to a floor model TV set. He picked up a few video cassettes, read their titles, and replaced them on the video cassette player. Porno films. He opened two closets and found forty or more suits, racks of every style of shoe, and several shelves piled high with sweaters. Some of the sweaters still had price tags and most of them were cashmere knits.

Out in the hallway again, Cullis asked: "You lookin' for anything special?"

"Know anything special, do you?"

"Nothing that isn't in our reports, Fahey."

"Maybe you missed something."

"Like what?"

"Who Marc Sterne really *is* or *was*. How he lived, functioned, fucked, shaved, who he stole from . . . His brainwork, all those things."

"We combed this place out all the way."

"And found photos and a letter."

"I told you that once."

"What I'm interested in is what you haven't told me. Or anyone else."

Even in the semi-darkened hallway, Fahey could see the lieutenant's face grow stronger. His eyes widened and looked yellowish in the faint light.

"Just a goddamn minute," Cullis said softly, then louder, "I don't have to take shit from you."

"You might have to take it from the lawyer I'm working

with. Wears mountain boots. Might put one of 'em up your tail pipe."

"What're you gettin' at?"

"That there's more than what's in your reports. Always is, and you know more and you're keeping it under your hat you don't wear."

"You're goin' way out of line, Fahey."

"Am I? You want to be in the regiment, you better get your eyes checked."

"What in hell does that—"

But Fahey had already pushed by him. He had to shake Cullis somehow. Get out of range for a moment so that he could leave something behind. Something he'd come back for. He whipped around suddenly, knowing Cullis would probably bump into him.

"Any closer," Fahey said, "and you could share my socks."

"Or fix your mouth for you," he answered, coming even closer.

"Get your hands off me, Cullis."

The man was so close Fahey could smell his breath. Like any other breath, neither sweet nor sour, just a man's mouth smell. But too close for Fahey's liking, and he knew the lieutenant was ragging him on purpose.

On the way back to the living room Fahey felt for his pen. He plunked himself down on the long white sofa, opened his notepad and scribbled a few lines of nothing. A moment later, to divert Cullis's attention, Fahey slid open a drawer in one of the side tables. A stainless steel table knife rattled around and he picked it up.

Cullis's eyes followed the knife. With his other hand, the hidden one, Fahey shoved his notebook down between the cushions, then he dropped the knife back in the drawer.

"You know Tommy Burke?" he asked, and made a ceremony of clipping his pen inside his coat.

"What you been writin' down?"

"My maid's address in Moscow. She's due for a demotion." He held his breath, hoping Cullis had missed his maneuver.

"You're a real smartass. No wonder they ran your butt outta the Commissioner's office."

"Did me a favor, too." Fahey clasped his hands over one

knee. "You know I read all those confidential reports put together by the Malibu sheriff. Then some others by the Attorney General's crowd . . . and nothing on Marc Sterne's dope traffic. It sort of tickled my curiosity, Cullis."

"Easy to answer, too. Wasn't the point of our investigation."

"Usually, though, there's a small section about any past brushes with—"

"Ain't nothin' on Marc Sterne. No record. Not even with the Los Angeles police."

"Maybe no record, Cullis, but how about information? Street rumors, informers, that kind of *record.*"

Cullis shrugged. "I stay away from the narc detail. I wouldn't know."

"Would your memory get better if Burke threw you up on the stand? Tear you up a bit. Put a spot of blood on your teeth?"

"Who in hell'd'ya think you are, coming at me this way?"

A clam-mouth. Obviously Cullis had been told to cooperate, but vaguely, then offer nothing more. Fahey decided to push him hard, just once, to see what would happen.

"Tommy Burke, that's the girl's lawyer. I really came here to get a gander at you so I could tell Burke."

"Tell him what?"

"How you'd come across when he puts you on the stand. Starts frying your black ass for you."

"They ain't gonna call me."

"Sure they are, Lieutenant. Burke will want to find out a few things. Like why your Malibu people and then you—the Hollywood sheriff—got stepped on. Wasn't that what happened? The State Bureau of Investigation came in, looked at your crummy work and threw you all to hell out of their way."

Fahey had started a fuse burning. Cullis was too black to show a blush. But his neck seemed to widen over his white shirt, and he cleared his throat twice before his eyes began showing more white than brown.

"Political shit," said Cullis eventually. "A big case, big folks, those Sternes, and the State people insisted on—"

"Like Jesus clearing out the temple, eh? Rolled you right over and out."

"State always has precedence."

"Sure, and they can shut things up more easily. Or forget they saw or heard something. . . . So Burke may want you, Cullis."

"They don't need me, goddamn you. I'm looking after this apartment till it's over and that's it." So easy and sure of himself until a few minutes ago, now Cullis's face wobbled slightly.

"Save yourself a long day downtown and tell me what you know," Fahey said.

In the round brown irises of Cullis's eyes a warning light appeared; it stayed there for a long moment until a few blinks washed it away.

"We got a real small narcotics squad at our station. Most of that work's handled by LAPD . . . We help out, naturally. Got to . . . So you'd best try them."

"Maybe I will. But you're the one who's here, aren't you?"

"I could come down on you, Fahey." Cullis simmered noticeably.

"Personally or officially?"

"Both ways."

Tread gently, Fahey advised his more aggressive side. Look at Cullis, then away. Keep your voice of all voices casual, not one decibel louder than necessary.

"Been a lovely morning, hasn't it?" Fahey began to rise from the couch, careful not to push the pillows down.

"I really don't know that much," Cullis protested.

Fahey sank back.

He guessed correctly that Cullis, like Sister Marius before him, shared a fear of becoming involved in a murder trial. Trials were the great breeding grounds for making people dumb with fright. You could so easily be made a fool of, be kissed by trouble when the cold wind of an even colder lawyer blew your story apart, and the press decided you were fair game for a mauling. Better to shut up. And if they wouldn't let you shut up, then say as little as possible.

Fahey waited for Cullis to begin again. He wanted to wet his drying throat with a pull from his flask, but fought the urge down. Cullis might use it against him somehow.

"There's always talk going around," Cullis said, turning

his face slightly so that his line of vision came diagonally. "Lot of it's just shit you ain't never gonna prove . . . Those Hollywood big people are behind tall walls, man. Big goddamn walls. You got to go real soft and take 'em down fast or you're in trouble . . . You know?"

"I know," Fahey said. "But what is it that *you* know?"

"Yeah, I hear that Sterne was movin' some coke around. Movie people and music people. Some with big names, I heard that, too."

"And nobody went after him?"

"You sound stoked now." Cullis relaxed into a chuckle. "You think you just walk into some bigtime studio and ask 'em to hand over. . . . You need a bench warrant and a truck of facts to get one, and then you got to get by studio security without them yellin' upstairs before you're outta the car."

"But he was in it? Sterne?"

"S'what they say. The boy, not his old man. Never heard any talk about the father."

"That doesn't mean anything."

"I wouldn't try that fishpond if I was you, Fahey. They make you into no-find-ems."

"No-find-ems?"

"Little bones. Real little. You're messin' with big weight there."

"That why nobody talks about the son's game?"

"See, you got to talk to the State Bureau of Investigations, don'tcha. Anything left out of those reports, that's their lookout."

Fahey knuckled his chin, feeling the bristle there. A longer than usual inning in bed that morning with the wife, and he hadn't found time to shave.

"What was he? Small time, middle size—"

"You wanna know for sure?"

Fahey nodded.

"Better you call the undertaker then, 'cause I don't know. And nobody ever bought stuff from him is going to tell you no how, no way."

"You never found anything here or anywhere?"

"Photos and the letter, that's the whole haul."

Fahey got all the way up from the couch. He straightened his red blazer, buttoned it, then gazed sorrowfully at his shoes, dusty from his walk down the road. He wiped them off on the back of his yellow pants, leaving dark smears. Cullis grimaced. Then Fahey stretched his arms, saying, "Know what?"

"What?"

"Your shit's so high it's historical."

"Look here, Fahey, I said to you what you asked. You got no reason to get on me!"

"Wouldn't try, Lieutenant. Wouldn't even think of it."

Fed up, Fahey left. Closing the door, Cullis tested the knob, then smoothed down the edges of the tape holding the sheriff's seal in place.

Lloyd Pritter waved a cheery goodbye to the receptionist at Oldes & Farnham. He had just finished a three hour session with two partners in one of the best litigation departments in Los Angeles.

A courtesy visit, and one for figuring out the next courtroom tactics. Julio Sterne, out of his own pocket, had made available the services of his personal lawyers. Pritter had spent part of the morning ticking off the options available to the defense—when Burke became fool enough to put Romaine Brook on the stand. One by one they closed them off while reviewing Pritter's tactics for her cross-examination.

Shoving his way into an elevator, jammed with other people, he stood there, moist with excitement. When the trial was over, he would be sending in his resignation as Assistant Attorney General. The next time he waved to the receptionist it would be as a senior member of Oldes & Farnham's litigation staff. Nice. A hard promise. All they told him was to get the job done.

Good money for the first time in his life. He had borrowed from his bank to make the down payment on a condo in Santa Monica, a two story affair three blocks off the beach.

He'd been thinking a good deal about power lately: the legal punching the state could throw at will, that kind of power. But the obvious skills and sharp minds of the elitists at firms like Oldes & Farnham were even more impressive.

Burke was going to have to put his client on the witness stand. What else could he do? They had agreed on that point only an hour ago in one of the conference rooms. Hungry at the prospect, Pritter almost rubbed his hands together at the thought of roughing her up, forcing her back and back some more until the jury would have to convict her.

Burke was no Wheeler, not even a wheezing sick Wheeler who had said he might want to recall Audrey Sterne to the stand. But for what? A ruse, that was for what. No worry there, thought Pritter, agreeing once more with the Oldes & Farnham attorneys.

Leaving the elevator, he stepped clumsily on a woman's foot, but he was so afloat in his future that he failed to hear her pained cry. Only one woman, a young one, occupied the cross-hairs of his thinking at the moment.

The walk to the visitor's room to see Tommy Burke is the best walk of the day. And the walk back is the loneliest most awful one in the world. Like lining up for the gas chamber. But we're close now and he told me, "Chin up" and all that rot. He held my hand twice, smiling at me.

He brought a letter from my agent, who is really the sweetest and dearest man. One of the not too many. A magazine is making me an offer for a serial—to tell all—when the trial is over. I might do it, too. God knows I need the money.

I'm depressed. My period's coming on. But I can't wait to get on that stand. It's the illusion you create, making them believe you, and I can act circles around the Barrymores if that's what it takes to stay out of prison. Or worse, which would actually be better.

I should have won the Oscar for Tonight or Never. *I got screwed, but it's the last time that'll ever happen. One thing about Prince Marc Sterne—he gave me a post-graduate course in the fine art of sticking it to people.*

Have to go over that part about the photos again. Rehearse it a few more times.

Later that night, hunched over a console, a television director spoke softly into a head mike. He sat on a low stool inside a small cubicle overlooking the ballroom of the Beverly Wilshire Hotel.

"Four, three, two . . . We're on!" he intoned, and chopped his flattened hand at the cameraman.

He leaned back and dragged on a cigarette. Nothing more he could do now, though he wasn't worried. Those were all pros down there, the best in town, and that made them the best in the world.

Blue and white spotlights swept the audience of over a thousand luminaries seated at tables for twelve across the ballroom. The gala reached its high point. The dinner had been endless—seven courses—and the taping of the show, for a delayed network broadcast, had run late.

The director had listened and occasionally laughed as Red Buttons warmed up the crowd with a fresh bag of jokes.

The cameras aimed at the stage and caught the orchestra playing a few bars of music as Julio Sterne bowed to loud, loyal applause.

Long enough applause for Buttons to stand aside and clap faintly. Out of the corner of his smiling mouth, Buttons whispered: "All yours, you cheap prick." They'd been disputing a contract for six months. A stand-off.

Stubbing out his cigarette, bored, the director made a fast calculation. Probably a billion dollars of talent down there in the audience; about a hundred million of it in current deals; maybe another three million in cosmetic surgery on all those public faces to keep them camera-worthy and beautiful and bankable.

About the right formula, he supposed.

George Burns, the great comedian, had escorted Fritzi to the event when Rhodes had told her how impossible it was for him to sit at the same table with the Sternes. Nor could he even attend a function where Julio Sterne was serving as chairman. He'd been adamant. "You gone soft?" he had reproved her when she asked him to come.

Fritzi knew she was sitting at the head table only because Masquers had offered to cater the event at cost. But the hotel insisted on serving so Masquers had bowed out. Instead she had donated the wine. The second best stock in the Masquers cellars, a mix of California and French vintages, and she had leaned on Masquers' wine merchants to reimburse her for half the cost.

Julio Sterne's speech closed with a short, almost predictable ending: "And I'm so very pleased to say we have raised another two million dollars for our charities this year ... That does not include, ladies and gentlemen, all the private donations of the members of our industry, or especially the time given by our outstanding actors and actresses to countless causes.... Fair to say, and I think you'll agree, that no other industry in America does so much..."

Taking her cue, Audrey stood and hugged her husband when he returned to the table. They were bathed instantly in a flood of white light while the cameras whirred away.

"Just perfect," said Audrey with her diamond spray smile.

"Short enough?" he asked.

"I think too short."

"Hate these damn speeches." He wiped his forehead with a red square of silk.

"You're the right guy for it," said George Burns, overhearing.

Fritzi blessed Julio Sterne with a smile of her own.

The orchestra struck up a new medley, Andy Williams singing "Moon River." Audrey pulled Julio off to the dance floor. They twirled around in the crowd, fielding compliments, a rash joke or two, and a flip remark from Red Buttons's agent.

Julio unpasted himself from Audrey as they found more room, and told her: "You did most of this. Proud of you..."

"Your name, your fame."

"Nothing without organization."

"It did get a little heavy there at the end, I guess."

"I could tell. You haven't been yourself for the past few days."

Audrey smiled flagrantly. "I didn't know it showed."

"Showed?" he grunted. "You've been pacing the night away. For two, three nights anyway."

The orchestra played "Stardust." They danced off to the edge of the crowd.

"Julio?"

"Umm-hh."

"I need a real rest."

"Good idea. Check into the hospital for a few days," he suggested. "Get some sleep. I'll have the office take care—"

"No. I mean get away. Maybe to Main Chance or go over and see the boys in England."

"Not now."

"Why not? I'm really bushed."

She drew him closer. He resisted.

"Slow down. You deserve it," Julio told her.

"I expect to. This last week really got to me. I need to get away before I split in half."

"When the trial is over, we'll both get away. Hong Kong perhaps. I've business there to look after. Or Hawaii, how's that? Possibly Cap Ferrat?"

"By myself, Julio. I've had it with the ef-fing trial." Audrey's face stiffened. Her mouth parted, but her teeth were tight enough to be slightly off center.

"Oh, you have? That's almost interesting . . . It was only my son—"

"Darling, I know! I know it all by now. By heart, I know it. By the news. By you. I'll collapse, damn it, if I hear any more."

They stopped dancing. Sterne's hand moved up to her shoulder. He dug his fingers in as Fritzi Jagoda twirled by in the arms of Barry Diller, the head of Twentieth-Century.

"You're hurting me."

"You'd be better off learning your place," Julio warned her.

"Stop it. You're making a fool out of—"

"You want to get away, do you? With Ferenc, I suppose. A little tryst for two. Maybe Budapest—"

"Julio! How dare—"

"You think I'm blind. He tells me everything I want to know anyway."

"He doesn't! He never would."

A cruel and knowing smile—the smile that was the brace of an empire, a smile that would harden arteries—twisted Julio Sterne's mouth.

"No, you're right, he doesn't," Sterne said. "And frankly I don't care as long as it stays in the house."

"People are watching us." Audrey's hand flew nervously to her neck.

"Let them. They've been watching us all night."

She glowered.

"Possibly, Julio, you should remember a thing or two about Ferenc."

"Such as?"

"Such as the night when the police were there. And you weren't home again. And Ferenc had to lie that you were upstairs. Fainted, and that you couldn't come down for a . . . a statement or whatever."

"So they wouldn't find out about your bed jumping. That's what you mean. That's why you lied. So the police wouldn't get suspicious about you and that Hungarian cocksman."

"That's not true, dammit."

"Who in hell do you think pays that slick Hunkie anyway?"

The tops of Audrey's breasts swelled over her low cut Dior as she breathed heavily. She was wearing a gold sequined gown, and with the blond upsweep of her hair she seemed like a bejeweled mannequin escaped from Cartier's window for the night.

"Julio, I'm leaving before you really create a scene." She spun away to dodge her way through the tables, her bare shoulders rigid with anger.

Julio saw some of the bystanders staring at him. The music seemed louder, too loud. He needed air. Get away, at least from this cloying mob. Standing there like some lost waiter, he felt like a fool and the feeling upset him.

Outside he called for his car and driver. She could find her own way home. After all, she knew how to find her way into the pants of the hired help. But then he knew he'd had something to do with that arrangement.

Hell with it, he thought. He'd send the driver back for her. It would look better. How was she going to leave town until the trial was over? They were going to recall her, they said. Better her than me. Slumped in the back seat, Julio still smoldered. Ingrates. The whole lot of them. Suck his blood dry if he wasn't careful.

He thought about Marc, whom he supposed he never really understood. Plenty of men he knew said the same thing about their sons. Maybe it was every son's duty to understand his father rather than the other way around.

Marc never had. He was born when Julio was already forty-five and that was more than a quarter century ago.

Too long a leap in age differences. The boy had never liked work, only wanting to play around, screw actresses, dog it at the beach, drive expensive cars. Marc had liked the glamour of studio life, but he had no interest in the banks, the ranches, the food companies or the chemical works—all that Julio Sterne had worked so hard to amass.

Drugs. Marc and his friends were the useless floss of the drug generation. Julio had spent a small fortune on clinics and therapy for the boy. For a while the therapy had worked, before Marc went crazy on the stuff again. The Brook girl had been a good ally. She wasn't a user, Julio knew, because he had checked on her.

Then she dumped Marc. So he said. He moped, acted withdrawn, pulled fast ones, was irritable as hell for weeks. As irritable as Audrey had become recently.

The girl, she had killed Marc. One way or the other, she had sent him into a spiral of depression. Sent him swimming back into that sea of drugs again.

Feeling sorry for himself, Julio Sterne hit the seat with his fist.

Nearing the Santa Monica hills he began to recall the night, really the day, when he had learned of Marc's death. He'd been in Seattle at a board meeting of a chemical company in which he owned a one-third interest. He would've been there in Malibu that night had his private jet not been grounded with a hydraulic problem. The pilot wouldn't fly—which was why he was still the pilot—and Julio had stayed one more night at his hotel, calling Audrey to tell her he'd be back very early in the morning.

At five the next morning, he had walked right into a brilliant sunrise and a nightmare at the same time. He was senseless with shock for hours. He had brooded. Wept then raged. And then he had begun his questioning of Audrey and Kardas.

Why were they away when Marc was there?

What was Marc doing there anyway?

Had he called to say he was coming?

Where were they?

Out in the boat?

Why was the girl in the house?

And other questions, before he would even agree to meet

with the team of sheriff's detectives. The living room where Marc had died was shut and roped off; coffee cups and sandwich dregs were everywhere; stale cigarette smoke had spoiled the air.

Audrey, then Ferenc, had explained what they'd already told the sheriff the night before. That all three of them, including Julio, were out on the boat. Wouldn't that look better, sound so much better? Julio Sterne's new wife, relatively new anyway, didn't go larking off on a boat ride with the hired help—one man—when her husband was away. Surely he could see the wisdom of going along with that story.

A day later, Julio had shut the pilot up. That was easy, only money. A couple of thousand and a trip to Mexico for a long vacation.

Julio had played along, deciding it was probably the smarter choice at the time. A stupid thing to do, an untidy cover up, but he'd been broken hearted. Whatever he did would never bring his son back, and he hadn't wanted any loose gossip flying around about Audrey and Kardas. The Malibu sheriff had swallowed the story—that he was upstairs that night, in shock, and no statement would make sense until he could gather together the smashed glass of his tragedy.

Audrey. She had her virtues and faults, and he had thirty years on her. She still surprised him with her sexual demands. Wasn't it better if she had a willing servant rather than some Beverly Hills stud of a blabbermouth? Rescued the beautiful bitch from a broken marriage with Lord What's-his-name, and what did he get from her in return?

If she had stayed home, where she belonged when he was away, there would've been no funeral. Marc would be alive. All of them—the girl and Audrey and the Hunkie—had caused Marc's death.

Ferenc Kardas was another roll of dice. He knew a lie was loose. A fairly small one but loose nonetheless. Was that an advantage for Kardas? If so, how much of one?

Julio Sterne flipped a switch on the armrest. A glass panel lowered behind the driver.

"Any good bars open at this hour?" he asked.

"Take you to Masquers, sir."

"Not there."

"There's the Chart House up the way. Or let's see, yes, La Scala or Moonshadows over on Pacific Coast Highway."

"Moonshadows then."

Up went the window. Down went his thoughts. He would have a drink by himself and he didn't really give a pink piss if he looked out of place in his evening clothes. He wanted to think, and be alone, with no Kardas or Audrey around, now or later, to remind him of deeper suspicions.

What if Audrey and Kardas were up to something much more deadly? Had they taken the opportunity while he was away to put Marc out of his drug misery? Tricked the girl into coming to the house so the murder could be blamed on her?

Julio supposed he had at least ten years left, if he was lucky and took care of himself.

He had one younger sister in Dallas. And a net worth that his accountants said was closer to a hundred million than the fifty or so he was usually credited with. But no other real heirs now except Audrey.

Had he made the greatest mistake of his life, throwing Audrey and Kardas together? He no longer cared about sex, but knew she still needed it at her age. He had fixed that up discreetly, like he fixed up so many other things.

Was she outsmarting him for his money? Had she some sort of a black deal with Kardas?

In his present frame of mind Julio Sterne wouldn't put it past her. She was acting so strangely, up half the night. He could hear her in the hall sometimes, doing the sleepless walk of the damned and the guilty.

Chapter Thirteen

Fahey rapped on the door.

He had waited until dark the next day before coming back to the apartment. Wouldn't do to appear too obvious, and it was the right hour for what he wanted. Cullis would be off duty, safely out of the way.

The door parted and Fahey sniffed fish and garlic cooking, strong enough to park his convertible on. Mrs. Noor poked her head around the edge of the door. She yawned, and in the faded light Fahey saw dull flashes of gold on her teeth.

"Sorry if I'm troubling you." And he put a wicked smile on the words.

She peered closely.

"I'm Fahey. Remember? I was here yesterday with *my* lieutenant. Cullis, you know."

"Ya-ess."

"Are you Iranian? Great country."

"Lebanon. Why you ask?"

"Ah, yes of course, Lebanese. Gorgeous women, the best. Should've known right off."

"E-what you want, Mr. Fah-hay?"

"Left something upstairs yesterday. Forgot all about it until an hour ago. Came right over."

"Why you don't call first?"

"I should have, Mrs. Noor. I was out in my car and didn't have your number handy."

She seemed to juggle the idea for a whole minute. Fahey wanted to slam her door before the fish odor passed him out cold.

"I have dinner now," she said.

"You'll be a good woman, won't you, and let me borrow your keys?"

"Cullis have key."

"I know. He'll be here later. I thought I'd just run up to the apartment and wait."

"He come?"

"Within the hour, for sure."

"Why he come too?"

Fahey though fast, hard. "We're going to look around once more. You see, Mrs. Noor, we're trying to get out of your way . . . turn the apartment back, get your rents up again. Pull down sheriff's paper . . ." He made a paper ripping motion with his hands just below her hawk nose.

"Es-ss so?"

"Is very much so, Mrs. Noor. Your dinner, better not let it burn. Smells delicious."

She nodded. "I get you key. You stay here."

Fahey waited. He heard a drawer shut, then a shuffle of feet before Mrs. Noor was back dangling her ring of keys. With one bitten fingernail she tapped on the key to Sterne's apartment. It had a lilac dot painted on the upper part.

"You never lose the-ese."

"I'll just be upstairs."

"Cullis. He get my apartment back for me?"

"He's fantastico, Mrs. Noor. An iron man." Fahey flexed his arm. "Black magic, you know."

Her mouth showed more gold this time.

Upstairs Fahey switched on the lights. The fish smell had temporarily flooded his nostrils, so the mildewy odor of the apartment he knew was there, wasn't this time.

Ten minutes went somewhere.

Fahey had tipped the floor lamps upside down and shaken them. Nothing there, and the same with the sectional couch. He had pulled it out from the wall and patted it down. Flipping the sections over, he examined their bottoms, and found more of nothing. Nor could he find anything behind the chrome-framed art posters. He picked up a phone from one of the side tables and saw the line was no longer plugged into the wall-jack.

Then he checked the shag carpet for torn seams. A floor safe? A small trap door? Again, nothing. He hadn't expected to find drugs. But he might learn where they'd been hidden away.

It looked like a fight had taken place. Fahey had things littered everywhere, and he began to replace them.

He shoved the last couch section against the wall when he saw his note pad on the floor. How had he forgotten that? Blessing his luck as he stooped to pick it up, he saw one of the wall outlets slightly askew, its metal plate angled and loose in the baseboard. He counted three other sockets.

Pulling at the loose one, he found it stuck but still movable. He peered closer. The screwheads were fake, and he pulled again but the plate wouldn't come out. Taking Mrs. Noor's keys from his pocket, he tried jimmying one of them behind the plate.

Not enough leverage. He leaned back. The kitchen, he thought, would have something better. Then he remembered the knife in the side table drawer. A moment later he squatted near the wall-plate, and slowly levered it away.

A bent metal track began to appear. He pried harder until a shallow metal drawer finally showed far enough out so he could yank it, and the drawer slid fully into view.

What he saw made him smile. In the back of the drawer a clear plastic bag was fastened at the top with a wire twist. A tag on it read: Ferenc Kardas. A smaller bag underneath it was marked: A. Noor.

Fahey opened the smaller one, wet his finger and sunk it into the crystallized powder. White as a fresh snowdrift, and he tasted it, and then again. Re-wiring the bag, he put it back, and shoved the wall-plate flush against the wall.

Bingo.

A second plate came out more easily. The bag in this drawer was three times heavier. No name tag—Marc Sterne's, he guessed. Private stock, a fortune there at street value. Once more, he pushed the plate home.

Christ and Mary! he thought. A whole bank there, enough to fund the regiment for years.

Sweating, doing most of the work with his good arm, Fahey was about to stand up. His brain whirred around like the spots on a slot machine, and seemed to go even faster as he stood up to hear his name called out.

Mrs. Noor came down the three steps to the living room,

a look of hand-tooled suspicion on her face. She stopped on the lowest step, resting a hand on the iron banister.

"Where Cullis?"

"Should be here. Any time now. Have to dock his pay, won't we?"

"What you doing?"

"Oh, me?" Fahey laughed nervously. "Well I—you see, ah, the phone. Was going to call Cullis. Trying to plug the phone in..."

"Es dees-connected."

"So I found out." Fahey wiped his brow. "Hot as your old good granny in here, isn't it? Let's kick a window out. Cullis won't mind."

Coughing loudly to cover the sound, he let the knife drop on the shag carpet as he came out from behind the couch.

"You find what you want?" she asked.

"Right here on the couch, Mrs. Noor. Dumb of me, wasn't it? Pressure of the job."

"You stay here or go now?"

"Be going soon. Have to call old Cullis and bang his head around for him, won't we?" said Fahey, advancing on her now. "You know, Mrs. Noor, I'm new on this Brook case. The girl, you know, you ever meet her?"

"I see her many times. I tell police."

"You ever talk with her? Have tea? Pass the time?"

Noor nodded.

"What's she like? Friendly? Happy?"

"Actress. Strange peoples. She dress ver-ah nice."

"Any trouble between her and Marc Sterne?"

"He es-sa dead. How you need more trouble than that?"

"Parties here? People coming here all the time, I suppose? That sort of thing?"

Fahey was right on her, two feet away, noticing a glitter of amber beads against her neck. He detected the aroma of fish again.

"Young people," she said. "They have party, but not so much."

"Hard worker, Marc Sterne?"

"Nice good man. Very polite. Always pay he-esa rent on time."

Pay you with *what*, Fahey wanted to ask. But that might

tip her off, and he couldn't see how she fit in anyway, not really. Hustling some action on the side, that was her style. He was certain of one thing, though. She obviously had no idea where Marc Sterne kept his treasure chest, or those bags of hot sugar would have been long gone by now.

"I'll be going," he said. He handed her keys back. "Can't thank you enough."

"I go with you."

She locked the door again, clucking strange words to herself that Fahey didn't grasp. No fish cookers in the regiment, he thought. Red meat only. She had small feet besides, pig trotters that could never keep up with the assault troops. Not quite the right shape to qualify as a camp follower.

"What I say if Cullis come here?"

"Tell him he's to quick march the square in full battle gear. Till dawn."

"I—es-what?"

"That I've been here and gone," he said, giving her his most pious smile.

Fahey was impatient to leave. He had trouble reading this dark and suspicious Levanter. Was it too late to call Rhodes? Burke? Now that he thought of it, he had no idea where Tommy Burke even lived.

Alesia Noor dozed through her favorite comedy show. Her dinner of carp in garlic paste, sweet yams and chickpeas rumbled in her soft belly, bringing her awake.

Cullis hadn't come by. Unless somehow she had missed him, which she doubted. She didn't care for this new man, Fah-hay, who talked so fast, and smiled so often, she couldn't understand him most of the time. He reminded her of a quick-tongued trader in the Beirut *souk*, before it was bombed into a mountain of rubble.

She kept thinking of the man Fah-hay. Why had he appeared so surprised when she found him behind the couch? He had dropped something on the carpet; she was sure she had seen a bright flash falling from his hand. From the arm that wasn't stiff as a stick.

The idea of going into the apartment by herself bothered her. That seal on the door. She had enough trouble with the eight thousand dollars of her money gone, probably lost forever, the amount paid to Marc Sterne before the girl killed him.

A belch was followed by a lusty sigh. Tomorrow she would have to call Ferenc Kardas.

Chapter Fourteen

Full of energy, Fahey contemplated a party, one of those rip-roaring celebrations he and Rhodes used to have in times gone by. Burning with excitement at his good fortune, he saw headlines and possibly added retainers from his insurance clients when the word got around that he'd found what the sheriff's detectives had missed like so many blind mice.

He'd tried to call Burke, only to find the lawyer still spending his hours with Romaine at the detention center. Flogging her with his attentions, no doubt. The matter of getting the cocaine-find into evidence at the trial was beyond him. Worried him, even.

So he'd taken off for Rhodes's house. He'd wrap the whole thing up for Burke, and hand deliver this, his gift, later on.

"Stroke of luck," Fahey was saying, pacing around but looking down. "I'll admit the luck but I hate to." He admired the shine on a pair of paratrooper boots he'd recently bought at a surplus store. "Jesus, Cliff, break the whole trial open, won't it. Eh?"

"Not so fast. How much you figure is there?"

"Bags. Make a beach with it."

"Half a million? More?"

"Maybe." Fahey shrugged. "Depends on whether it's been cut or not."

"Kardas had his name on a sack of it? And what's the lady's name again?"

"Noor. Alesia Noor. A Levanter, drinks fish oil."

"They're in on it?"

"Name tags are on the bags. Like neon lights. The Brook girl was telling us the truth."

"You put all the bags back, Alonzo?"

Fahey shot back a look hot enough to remove paint. "That's not so damn funny."

"I was asking if you put it back the way you found it."

"The hell you were."

"Don't start anything, okay. A simple question, that's all it was."

"Nothing so simple about the way you said it, boyo." Fahey's voice and facial expression went from sarcasm to hurt this time.

"Sorry."

Rhodes's mind was turning. He had been swimming when Fahey, agitated as a firefly, found him in the pool. But he was glad, very glad that Fahey had come this time.

"While you dry off, I'll see if I can raise Burke, tell him what I found," Fahey was offering.

"No, no, don't do that."

"Why not? He'll want to know."

"Later, maybe. But not now."

Rhodes left to change, leaving Fahey to fume and fuss until he returned a few minutes later.

"Burke is the lawyer here. He's got to know what I know," Fahey told him, still pacing and still upset.

"Fine, Alonzo. Maybe we can also keep Burke from screwing up. Think about that for a moment."

Fahey looked into Rhodes's unblinking eyes, and they seemed cold, almost empty. The crescent scar on Rhodes's brow seemed to go whiter.

"Trying to help Burke a little. I know he's a rookie," Rhodes explained. "He'll need help, all he can get."

"By holding out on information?"

"Which may not be admissible as evidence and probably isn't."

"So why not tell him?"

"Why not loosen your screws a little so we can sort this out," said Rhodes, covering his intentions.

"I don't like this at all." Fahey darkened.

"Let's just see what develops first, Alonzo."

Fahey turned his back. He put his hands on his hips and breathed audibly. "You could be talking about my ticket here," he said as he swung around.

"I doubt it."

"If Burke finds out I knew about Sterne's stash, that I didn't tell him, he can hang me on a nail."

"I don't think he'll make a fuss."

"What makes you so sure?"

"Just a hunch."

"A hunch, is it? On my license? On my living you want to try hunches?"

"How's he going to know you found that stuff?" Rhodes asked, then added, "don't tell him yet . . . I'll tell you when, and how, and that'll be best for Burke and for you."

Slowly into Fahey's otherwise very alert senses, a light grew larger. A light with a yellow cast of caution.

"What're you up to, Cliff?"

"Nothing. Just trying to make sure we don't start the trial again with another free-for-all."

Rhodes cinched his belt and then, sockless, slipped his feet into a pair of brown moccasins.

"Don't like it, I tell you that for nothing."

"Look, finding a pile of drugs doesn't do much to hurt the prosecution or help the defense. And I don't want another ruckus."

"Hell, it might help the girl."

"Not if I disallow it as evidence," said Rhodes, greatly relieved the more he thought about it.

"I shouldn't have told you. You went and wrecked a helluva good day for me."

Rhodes gave Fahey a deep look, one that could mean anything. "And I like to think I know what I'm doing in a courtroom."

He had finished dressing now. He ran one hand through his blondish hair, smoothing it down. He hung the towel he'd been using on a hook, strapped on his wristwatch, and said to Fahey:

"Let's go up to the house."

"I've got to get going." Fahey spoke sullenly.

"I need an hour with you. It's important." Rhodes had been thinking of something while he dressed.

Fahey hesitated, then said: "I'll need to make a call or two first."

"Sure."

Rhodes had come out of the bathroom carrying a green polo shirt. As he stretched to slip the shirt over his head, a dozen or so weals showed where the shrapnel had sliced into his chest and shoulders. Raised and thin scars, curled like earthworms after a rain. Fahey wondered if the scars still hurt when rubbed or touched. He almost reached out to trace one with his finger and find out.

Up in the red library Fahey made his phone calls and then was handed a yellow legal pad. Rhodes leaned against one wall, talking slowly, giving him a dozen questions for Burke to consider using when Romaine Brook went on the witness stand.

Fahey protested at first, asking why couldn't they be typed out? He fairly howled when Rhodes gave him still other queries, depending how the first ones were answered, if at all, by Romaine. As he jotted away, cursing, Fahey thought he could see where Rhodes was heading. If she answered the first set of questions one way, Burke should keep right on going; if another way, use the second line of inquiry.

Fahey scanned his writing during a pause. "I think you lost your sonar, Cliff."

"Not really. As a judge I could ask any of those questions myself. And I probably would, if Burke doesn't."

"Why don't you then, instead of breaking my bleeding hand."

"Because I'm not the defense counsel. And I don't care to look like one."

"Well, you are." Fahey looked down at the yellow pad. "You sure as hell're doing Burke's work for him, aren't you?"

"Judges help beginners all the time. Courtesy of the trade."

Some ten minutes later, Rhodes finished. Fahey shook a cramp from his fingers, then repeated all the questions, complaining now that he wanted stenographer's pay.

"You wish you were her lawyer, don't you?" he asked.

"Nope. Frankly, I wouldn't touch it with gloves on."

"Yes you would."

"You're exactly wrong, pal."

"You think she's innocent?"

"I wasn't there."

"Cut that crap, Cliff. I was asking what you think."

"And I told you."

"I'd say Pritter has got her by the shorties . . . She admits she was there. A threatening letter. And the money he owed her—"

"What money?"

Fahey recounted what Romaine had said the day they'd met at the detention center. Money that Marc Sterne had borrowed—maybe for drugs, Romaine had said—and the other money for her share of a screenplay idea sold to Parthenon Studios.

"Much?" Rhodes asked.

"Thirty or forty thousand. Have to look at my notes . . . You know you're asking me to take a big chance by shutting Burke off."

"You trust me, Alonzo?"

"I always have."

"Trust me some more." But Rhodes quickly looked away.

The money thing was a new factor. Thinking about it, Rhodes tapped the wall with his knuckles in a slow rappata-rap-tat rhythm. A money motive was a doubtful reason for killing Marc Sterne. Would Pritter know about the money? Probably not or he would've used it by now, and so it might never come up.

Rhodes had put himself right out there in the no-passing zone, and now he was going to have to stay there. He had gone over the line of judicial ethics. He supposed that Fahey probably sensed it already. He was trusting their friendship to hold firm, at least for a time, until he worked out the rest of Romaine's defense.

"You're doing something up there in your head, aren't you?" he heard Fahey ask.

"Who isn't?"

"On the kid? About this trial?"

"She's not a kid. She's twenty-two."

"A kid," Fahey insisted. "What're you really up to?" He pestered Rhodes with a piercing look.

"An open story for the jury, the press, everyone. And on that lovely prayer I think I'll have a drink. Want one?" Rhodes moved toward the bar.

He took two tumblers off the shelf. That's enough, he told himself, lay off or you'll start tripping the switches so early all the lights will go out. Smarten up.

"You know Burke might wonder where I got all these cute questions," said Fahey as he took his drink.

"I was about to get to that."

"So what do I say to him?"

"That inspiration suddenly wet your pants for you."

"He may not be in your league, but he's no dummy either."

"Tell 'em you were talking an idea over with one of your lawyer friends."

"Whoever had one for a friend." Fahey smirked.

"Funny, fuh-nee, Fahey. That what they call you now, the funny man?"

"Well, boyo, I'm not funning you. So what do I say?"

"Just tell Burke to look them over or he might be missing a bet."

"Really."

Rhodes only shrugged, taking a long sip to hush a jumping nerve in the back of his neck.

"Don't cost me my license, Cliff."

"You're already insured, pal."

"How?"

"Because if you ever told anyone about this little chat we're having, you could cost me a seat on the Supreme Court."

"Burke would love to know what I found in that apartment."

"So, you and me, Alonzo, we're even, aren't we?"

"I guess we are at that."

After another drink Fahey left. Rhodes hoped the questions Fahey had written down were the same ones Burke would think up by himself anyway. But he couldn't take that chance. Burke had never tried a case on his own, and he'd be standing up there like some farmboy taking his first

Latin lesson. It wasn't that Lloyd Pritter was so frighteningly clever, but he'd been around for a long time; had enough experience to dice up a Burke for cat litter.

So Rhodes would help defend her. He wasn't going to face the rest of his life knowing he had failed his own daughter when she was spread-eagled against the firing wall. He had never thought that the case against her, largely circumstantial, was all that strong anyway. Enough to convict her, under California law, of first-degree murder, if the jury went against her. But Rhodes knew how easily juries could swing their views.

Trick shots, a surprise party, a few bent mirrors to confuse everyone, and some way to handle Burke by remote control without the young lawyer suspecting anything.

His daughter, he was hearing her. For days he had been hearing her in his jumpy mind, and recalling how she sat there so mutely in the courtroom for all these weeks. Unable to talk, unable to tell the jury her story. Silent as a mummy. She had a new ear to talk to now.

He would need Alonzo Fahey again, as he had needed him so often before. The Fahey who was one of the great dreamers on earth. So fierce in his ways, of such deep passion, Fahey had once bought a mountaintop in Oklahoma for some new religion he was starting up to save the Commanches—white vestal robes, tribal women only. In the heat of summer he could imagine the sound of fresh snow falling in Hawaii; hear the song-chant of mermaids in the Caspian Sea as they passed caviar to the czar and to Fahey himself.

That Fahey, the one who lusted for adventure.

The one-man road company; the mask on, the mask off, who knew? Rhodes knew he would need him to help bring off the plan rapidly coming alive in his thoughts. But right now it was time for another visit with old José Cuervo so the guilt wouldn't keep dragging on him like a ball and chain.

At Malibu Pointe Ferenc Kardas sat in the butler's pantry, writing up a list of liquor and grocery supplies for the house. On a few items he increased the size of the order. Those would never arrive. But the full bill would still be settled at month's end, and then Ferenc would pocket the difference in cash when he dropped by the grocer's for a friendly chat.

The phone rang.

"Sterne residence," Ferenc answered.

For two endless minutes he listened as Alesia Noor told of Alonzo Fahey's visit the night before. As she gasped excitedly for more breath, he asked, "Have you been up there to see for yourself?"

"Es-sa forbidden. I tell you all that many time."

"Go up and look," Kardas urged.

"No, no. You go up."

"It might be there. He had it somewhere." Kardas fingered his lip.

"I not going up."

"I can come on Saturday. Call me back if they come again. And you stay with them next time. Watch them."

Hanging up, he cursed. The Noor woman was a scourge, but useful for the time being. Somehow he needed to find Marc Sterne's supplier or a new source of top grade Colombian. He meant to keep his gold-coined business alive before someone else moved in on him.

Kardas's thoughts leaped elsewhere. How, he wondered, could anything so valuable be left behind a couch? That's where Alesia Noor had said she saw some new policeman fumbling around. Ferenc had been to the apartment many times and could think of any number of safer places.

Every day in the papers he had followed the trial. Never once was there any mention of the police finding drugs at Marc's apartment. Another idea, one that alarmed him, causing his eyes to darken: the police might've found it already, saying nothing, and stolen the drugs for themselves. It was known to happen. He had to get up there, soon, and check it out for himself.

One floor up, Audrey coated the backs of her legs with more tanning oil. She lay on a chaise on the deck outside her bedroom. The sun was high, the lapis-blue sky clear of any clouds. Below, she could hear ocean slurping lazily against the huge black rocks on this side of the house.

Naked, she flipped over, trying to relax. Julio was giving her the freeze treatment lately. He was worried, she guessed, that a few things might still come out at the trial. Embarrassing moments, or worse, and so he was keeping his distance.

He knew about Ferenc, or thought he did. He didn't seem to care much either, and that wound to Audrey's pride made her seethe. She wondered if Julio kept a mistress somewhere. Older rich men were known for it—one last look in their fogged-up vanity mirrors.

Married for over two years, it was an event to lower the oceans when he asked to sleep with her. Even on those spare occasions, no matter what she tried on him, it started boringly and ended disastrously. What did he expect of her?

Marriage fatigue. Already.

Often witty and sometimes generous, he had usually been good to her, and to her boys when they came over from London on their visits. Tolerant, more or less, of her foibles and not too much of a bastard, so it was worth it to keep trying.

It was a day for taking inventory of men, past and present, in her life. She thought of Lord Robert Hubbard-Hewes, ex-husband and arrogant charmer, who had shown her the world of the theater long before she knew of Romaine's talents. Hubbard-Hewes had swept her off her feet, dazzled her with his brilliant mind, and his circle of fascinating friends in England and on the Continent.

She had needed someone like him in those bleak days after giving birth to Romaine, believing Cliff Rhodes was dead. She had never told Robert about the child she had in California, or about Rhodes. A woman's secret. One that, if revealed, would ruin her chances for marrying anyone with the background and standing of a Hubbard-Hewes. Audrey's gynecologist in London had known she'd given birth before, but he would never betray her confidence.

Audrey had nearly told Robert at the time of their godawful divorce. Told him out of spite, anger, downright malice after she'd been forced to admit to a trumped-up situation of adultery—that never happened—to get her divorce.

She still smoldered, thinking about it. In her entire life she had never known anyone who could manage so many sexual affairs at one time as her ex-husband. He tramped after every actress, married or unmarried, that appeared in the many plays he produced. She had suffered so many humiliations that she had thought she was headed for a nervous breakdown. She ended up hating a man she had loved. To save herself and her young sons from any more anguish, she had taken the fall in the divorce. Ironically, she had almost lost the boys in that so-called bargain, and found out what it was like to go up against England's first families. They stood firm, they had rallied around Robert Hubbard-Hewes as one of their own, and Audrey became a near outcast. People she had thought were her friends suddenly slammed their doors, wouldn't answer her calls, would not even accept a simple invitation to lunch.

They could say what they wanted to about the decline of the British Empire—it had never declined an iota when it came to the peers of the realm shutting their ranks on an outsider. They could burn you alive with one freezing look.

Julio had tagged after her when the divorce was over. She could understand why. He was a first pew player in business circles on the Coast. But socially he wasn't quite seated above the salt shaker in many places. He could go wherever money could go, but that didn't mean everywhere by a long shot. There were clubs and homes and get-togethers put on by the Southern California bluebloods that got along quite well without the Julio Sternes of Hollywood fame and fortune. Or anybody else from Hollywood for that matter.

Audrey could give Julio what he so avidly sought. Acceptability anywhere. Her family had been prominent in California society for years. Her mother a McConnico, an heiress to two silver fortunes; her father a leading physician. They were known, liked, accepted anywhere.

She was Mrs. Julio Sterne now, but to a lot of people who mattered she was Audrey McConnico Sterne.

And then Cliff Rhodes drifted into her mind.

Somehow Audrey knew she had to get her hands on those papers at Las Infantas. Close down for good any path of discovery by an outsider, no matter how remote the chance.

One romp in bed—no, a good many romps—with Cliff Rhodes and then God sent a Romaine Brook to this world. The bewitching stranger—the criminal, Audrey thought—and her own flesh and blood. How can you live with the knowledge that your own child is a killer? Linking us all up again, these many years later. I never would have told Cliff about her if he hadn't ended up as the judge, thought Audrey. Maybe, I shouldn't have told him anyway.

God, if Julio ever even guessed.

Cliff Rhodes had come pretty far, farther than she ever supposed he would. Is he as smart, as good as they said he was? Making money defending crooks?

Hardly more than a cowboy when she had first found him at a sorority dance. Rough-edged, tall and awkward, almost shy, and hung like a horse that could go all night . . . whenever they could sneak a night together.

What if Rhodes betrayed her? Their secret?

The sun beat a sheen onto her oiled skin. But Audrey shivered as if an ice cube had just rolled down her spine. No matter how hard she tensed her muscles, she couldn't stop the shivering.

Resting one of his booted feet on top of his paper-piled desk, Tommy Burke slumped back in his chair. He was scanning the questions Fahey had taken down from Rhodes. Reddish curls fell toward his eyes, and he brushed them aside before putting the questions down on one heap of files. Fahey saw the curls swing right back across Burke's forehead.

"Got 'em from a lawyer you said?" Tommy asked. "Anyone I know?"

"An out-of-town guy. We were talking about the trial, and he threw out some ideas."

"Pretty good stuff there. Cute."

"He's got a good reputation."

"Does he have a name to go with it?"

"Oh, no," said Fahey. "He's an old amigo of mine. He wouldn't want to sound like he's horning in . . . Can you use them?"

"Maybe. I'll have to see," Burke said casually.

"They sounded pretty good to me, too," Fahey said. "S'why I thought you might like to see them."

"I'll see. I'm not putting Romaine on the stand next anyway. Something else came up and it's worth a shot, I think. I'll show you."

Fahey came around the desk. Burke opened a folder full of the Malibu sheriff's confidential reports written up the night of Marc Sterne's death. Fahey had perused the folder before. One set of reports dealt with the statements made that night by Ferenc Kardas and Audrey Sterne. Another report dated the same day carried Julio Sterne's statement.

"But the transcript reads differently," Tommy Burke told Fahey as they thumbed the pages. "You weren't around at the opening, but Mrs. Sterne testified that her husband went upstairs that night. All broken up. Crushed and all..."

"So what?"

"So the sheriff took Julio Sterne's statement the next day. But look here, Alonzo. See, it's dated the day before, same as the other ones. See? I never noticed it before."

Burke pointed at the date space in the upper right-hand corner. All three reports showed the same date.

"A clerical error, maybe."

"And maybe not. I want to pin it down tight... And another thing. I'd like to hear more about those noises out on the water that night. Boat noises or whatever. You see the way I figure it—"

"What were Wheeler's tactics?" Fahey broke in.

"He didn't say. I always wondered if he was going to go after Julio Sterne."

"Raye didn't exactly bury you alive with his plans, did he?"

"I was his research department. That's all, Alonzo."

Tommy explained his theory. He wanted to go after the Malibu sheriff, who had appeared as a witness for the state at the start of the trial. But as he talked, a new cloud of doubt arose: how had Fahey come up with those clever questions? Whoever thought those up had to be very familiar with the trial.

Across the desk a green-shaded lamp painted a sickly glow on Fahey's face. The yellow edge of green. The light showed deep creases over Fahey's nose, moving in unison with his restless eyes.

Tommy wondered why Fahey, usually so easy-going, was so nervous today.

About what?

But now he had to call Pritter. Tell him he wanted the

state's third witness recalled—the one from the Malibu sheriff's station. A little more grilling on a few open points. The thought of making the call both excited and frightened him.

Frightened him because he wanted so terribly to win. To do something big, really immense, big for Romaine and big for his career.

He no longer cared whether she ever paid him a bent tin can for all his hard work. All those headaches, the late and grueling hours. He only wanted her freed. He wanted her around him, her honeyed laughter, that soft touch, and those doe-brown eyes filling him with waves of pleasure.

Would they titter at him? The press and the onlookers, would they laugh at his awkwardness? His high voice? He'd rather die before he made a fool of himself in front of her. Dialing the Attorney General's office, he knew he'd have to pull it off somehow. Melt down Pritter's iron-sided case.

And for Tommy Burke, that meant taking another look at a few people in Malibu Pointe.

Tomorrow it all begins again. Tommy will never pull it off by himself. He's not tough enough. I'll have to do it by myself. Just that toad Pritter and me, chasing each other around with our words. Tommy said he hopes he won't have to put me on the stand. He's nuts. I'm the best thing he's got, and I'm the only thing I've got.

I'm going up on that stand. They're going to see my performance of the century. Rehearsals are over.

PART II

Chapter Fifteen

Two weeks had passed, the oddest two weeks of his life, Rhodes thought as he climbed up to the bench. The bailiff called for order. The spectators stood and stirred, coughs sounded, and Rhodes saw a few people nodding hello and shaking hands. The jurors sat alertly, very stiff-jawed. The press rows turned this way and that way to see if any notables were present.

Rhodes looked squarely at his *daughter*. She wore green today, a prim apple-green dress with a circular neckline trimmed in white. He wished he could take her out to lunch, tell everyone out there she belonged to him.

"Call your first witness, please," Rhodes said to Burke. And do a good job of it, he thought.

"May I approach the bench?" Tommy asked.

"Certainly."

He came stiff-legged, as though on stilts, his thick-soled boots scuffing the floor. With his mouth half open, he seemed to smile, and his head bobbed loosely.

Christ Jesus, thought Rhodes dourly.

"Your Honor, I've been trying to get an earlier witness back on the stand. The sheriff's deputy from Malibu, the one who opened for the def—"

Rhodes nodded. "What's the problem?"

"He's away for another day or so."

"So?"

"I want to lead off with him."

"The state's witness? What for?"

"A couple of small items to clear up, that's all."

"Can't you clear them up when he gets back?"

"It will be more confusing, I think, for the jury, and anyway—"

"What do you have in mind, counselor?"

"A delay. Just a day or so until the deputy—"

But Rhodes was already on the second shake of his head. "We've had all the recess we're going to have for now."

"But, I've got—"

"We're on our way again, Mr. Burke. Today. Anything we find confusing we can straighten the jury out on later."

Burke's eyes pleaded. "Just another day—"

"Listen, if we put that jury out one more time, you and I will both get thrown out of here."

Burke blinked. His mouth shifted into an odd shape, and he dragged himself back to the table where Romaine sat, her face uplifted and serene and eager.

"The defense calls Miss Dee Dee Lessig," Tommy said. The pale petal of his face went to beet red as he forced his voice down from a contralto to a quivering tenor.

Some journalists in the front glanced at him. Burke turned redder. Heads swiveled to watch a woman, twentyish, with pony-tailed hair, come up the aisle.

When he had her sworn in, Tommy began to identify her.

"Yes, I was Marc Sterne's secretary for about six months," said Miss Lessig.

"And before that?"

"I worked in the costume department at Parthenon Studios."

"For how long?"

"Over a year."

"And how did you get selected to become Marc Sterne's secretary?"

"I heard there was an opening and asked for an interview."

"And you got the job?"

"Yes, I did." Dee Dee Lessig beamed.

"Ever go out with Marc? Have a date? Dinner?"

A chair scraped loudly. Pritter was up. "Hold it! Now, your Honor"—he was trying to keep his eyes on Burke, Miss Lessig and Rhodes—"I can't see how this is relevant to even one issue in the defense's—"

"Okay." Rhodes held up his hand. He turned to Burke, asking, "Where're we going here?"

"I'm trying to establish the trail of events on the night Marc Sterne died."

"Can you get to it a little more directly?"

Burke lifted his hands, a gesture of resignation. "I'll try." He wheeled around awkwardly, facing his witness again. "You knew him pretty well, Miss Lessig?"

"Quite well, yes."

"Did you ever take messages for Marc Sterne? Messages, for example, from his stepmother? Or from his father?"

"Often from his father, or his father's secretary."

"And from Mrs. Sterne?"

"Sometimes, yes."

"How many times does sometimes mean? Once a week? A month? How often?"

Dee Dee Lessig's brow furrowed. Burke let her think on it as he pivoted around to catch a quick glimpse of Pritter and Pritter's two human sidearms watching silently. Tommy was nervous. He only had himself . . . and then, back about six rows, he saw Fahey waving, and wearing some kind of a fire-engine red jacket.

"Once a month, or maybe twice a month," said Miss Lessig in a voice that spun Burke around.

"When Marc wasn't there in his office, you always took his calls?"

"Just about."

"Did you keep a record? Incoming and outgoing logs of callers? Or their messages?"

"That was studio practice . . . all executive secretaries did."

"And you did too?"

"I just said so—"

"Not exactly, Miss Lessig, but you've answered us now."

Tommy had circled back to his table, and then returned to a spot before the witness. "Is this an executive telephone log from Parthenon?" He handed her a light gray sheet of paper.

"Sure is," said Dee Dee Lessig, looking up. "It's mine. One I kept for Marc Sterne."

"And the one you kept on the day he died?"

"Ye-yes."

"The sixth call down from the top? What's that one say?" His voice slipping on him again, he balled his hands, embarrassed.

"From Mrs. Sterne?"

"Yes. What time? And what's the message?"

"2:14 in the afternoon. 'Would he please come for dinner that night at 7:30. Dress informal.'" Dee Dee Lessig peered at her writing more closely before she added: "'And to thank Marc for doing it on such short notice.'"

"Good . . . that's what I thought it said. And you gave the message to Marc sometime later?"

"Always."

"But that specific message. Do you remember giving that one to him?"

"I think so."

"Specifically, Miss Lessig."

"Yes. I could hardly help remembering after I heard the news the next day."

"I can imagine," said Tommy. "So you told Marc his stepmother wanted him for dinner at the house out at Malibu Pointe?"

"That's my memory of it."

"Did he call her back?"

"I don't know."

"You didn't place a call to Mrs. Sterne for him?"

"I don't believe so."

"You're not sure."

A pause.

"Yes, I'm sure I did not," said Dee Dee Lessig.

"And I'm sure I want to thank you for your time here today, Miss Lessig." Burke smiled a shy smile but one wrapped in appreciation. He stepped back, looked over his shoulder, and said to Pritter: "Your witness."

Romaine watched Tommy shuffle back to his chair. He is the living Tin Man from *The Wizard of Oz*, she thought. Her facial expression was completely empty, forced empty, from her training and natural capacity to act a role.

I know more about that call than Dee Dee Lessig ever could. Or anyone else.

Romaine hardly noticed Tommy when he sat down. Her attention was glued to the woman on the stand and then to Pritter's wide back that bunched in a thick roll under his arms.

"Miss Lessig," Pritter began, moving even closer, "you continue to work at Parthenon Studios, do you?"

"I'm still there, yes."

"They treat you well there?"

"Wonderfully."

"And Marc Sterne, how did he treat you?"

"Oh, fine. He was a good boss. Very bright, humorous."

"How about Mr. Sterne, Marc's father?"

"Well, I don't know, I guess so."

"Can you amplify, Miss Lessig?"

"I didn't see him that often. He was on . . . up on the other floor so I rarely saw him."

"You knew Mrs. Sterne?"

"I never met her."

"A few minutes ago you told us you had."

"I only meant I knew her on the telephone. By her voice."

"You never saw her?"

"Not at the studio."

"Anywhere else?"

"Her picture in the newspaper. She was in the papers quite a lot."

"But you never heard her voice, talking with her face to face?"

"No."

"How can you say it was her, then, who called the day you said she did?"

Romaine felt a tremor under her kneecap.

"She called before," Dee Dee Lessig answered. "She always said who she was and I got to know her voice."

"After, let's see, six months as Marc Sterne's secretary

...And you testified that Mrs. Sterne might've called a dozen times. Is that right?"

"About, yes. I'd have to look at the logs to be sure."

"How can you be so sure it was Mrs. Sterne calling?"

"Because of her voice."

"But how," Pritter hardened on the young woman, "when you couldn't see her talking in plain view? And never had before."

"I don't know. She has a, well—"

"Yes?"

"Her voice is distinctive, sort of."

"Sort of?"

"I mean it's different. It's sort of aristocratic. British almost."

"Sort of. Almost. You're not really sure, are you?"

"I'm sure."

But Dee Dee Lessig was confused. Why were they making such a big thing over a phone message? She became uncomfortable for the first time that morning. Pritter, wide as an ox, was blocking her view of half the courtroom. She looked up at Rhodes, whose face she found attractive, but he was busy studying the jury.

"Did you know the defendant?" Pritter started again, pointing at Romaine. "Ever meet her?"

"A few times. We all knew her by her film."

"In person?"

"Yes."

"You knew, or didn't you, that she was seeing Marc Sterne?"

"Everyone knew that."

"Did you take her messages for Marc Sterne?"

"Sometimes."

"Was there any message from Miss Brook to Marc Stern on the day he was murdered?"

Tommy Burke's feet hit the floor hard as he stood up. "No, your Honor, the prosecutor can't frame a question that way—"

Rhodes swung his gaze to the clerk. "Strike that last question," he said, and then instructed the jury: "Disregard the term murder. The State is here to prove a murder took place...No questions will be allowed that presume an act of homicide as a foregone conclusion." To Pritter, he spoke sharply: "You can rephrase, if you want to. But you'd better do it correctly or sit down."

Pritter shrugged. He went to work again. "Did you hear from Miss Brook, there, on the same day you say Mrs. Sterne called?"

"I don't remember any calls from Romaine Brook that day."

"Did Marc Sterne ever talk to you about Miss Brook? His relationship with her?"

"Not really."

"Never?"

"Hardly ever. Sometimes I ordered flowers, or a limousine for a special night. Things like that."

"And so you knew they were close, or more than close?"

Dee Dee sighed. She had a sudden urge to go to the bathroom, and was too embarrassed to ask in front of the looming Pritter and all these strange people. She pressed her thighs together.

"I assumed they were close," Dee Dee said in a pained voice. "Everybody knew, I guess. They were in the newspapers—"

"So you assumed?"

"Yes!" she said crossly.

"Just as you assumed it was Mrs. Sterne herself on the phone that day?" said Pritter, stepping toward the jury, trying to make his point. "No further questions," he added hastily in a bellow that rolled across the courtroom.

He sat down. He hadn't expected Dee Dee Lessig this morning. Pritter was aware that she was on a possible witness list made by Raye Wheeler at the pre-trial conferences. No matter, she had done no damage. But for the first time he began to estimate where Burke was headed, and it didn't smell right to his keen nose.

At all costs he was supposed to keep Julio and Audrey Sterne either out of the trial or as far from it as possible. That hint had almost been hand delivered to him from his newfound friends at Oldes & Farnham.

Was Burke trying to lay groundwork to retrieve the Sternes? The thought nagged Pritter. So did another one, seemingly unrelated, of why the defense counsel wanted another go-round with the Malibu sheriff's deputy. Burke had mentioned on the phone that an item or two didn't seem to tally.

What items, Pritter had pressed.

Small ones, Burke had replied at the time.

"Next witness," said Rhodes.

Tommy Burke sent an urgent look to Romaine. "Look," he whispered, "we'll stall. Just follow me carefully . . . That guy'll be back tonight, and we'll get him tomorrow. You hear me?"

"Of course, Tommy."

"I'm so nervous I can hardly swallow."

"You're great, Tommy. The most fabulous, really."

He flushed in pleasure.

Romaine stood up. So lithe, proud and resolute, as if she had just alighted from some throne, ready now to grant any favor, even to her captors.

In the witness chair she cast her eyes toward the jury, also sweeping the press rows. A reporter from the Associated Press penciled a quick note to himself: "The look of the Vestal Virgin in a ring of golden ice."

Romaine took her oath, and under Burke's guidance was identifying herself for the record.

Her belly fluttered as she spotted Pritter again. Did he know? Not possibly, she thought. But all the same he'd come very close. Smoothing her green dress, making sure it covered her knees, she arranged her face into the innocence of a child.

"Will you tell us, Romaine, how you first met Marc Sterne? And when that was?"

She began, slowly at first, to convey how shocked she was that Marc Sterne was no longer alive. How wonderfully warm he'd been to her. Helping her. Offering the little attentions any woman adores. Building up her confidence, making her feel like the person she had not yet become—a real movie star.

Romaine took an hour, coaxed here and gentled there by Tommy Burke. He loathed hearing her. All of the previously censored moments of her love affair with Marc Sterne came at him like so much scratched film.

Rhodes listened intently. His daughter was speaking, the first time he had ever heard his flesh and blood talk. He watched her mouth, the movement of her jaw. Her eyelids would drop. Her hands changed position, up and up higher as if she were gospeling from a pulpit.

She didn't speak like Audrey.

She spoke—he finally put his finger on it—like someone trying to brave out a deep crying pain. Only a few feet away, she was walking right into his soul. Her voice was tinged with sadness, with loss and hurt, and he wanted to hold her hand, hold all of her till she was breathless.

Romaine went on, her voice sonorous, talking in the way angels were supposed to sing.

The courtroom stilled. The press stopped jotting on pads and the jury leaned forward. They had come for this—to hear, at long last, her side of the story. Everyone sensed a glow in her face that wasn't so much beautiful as it was handsome and clean, so very clean, and her lean body so erect and unafraid.

This was no murderess. But a vision instead, the one of millions of women, past and present, who had been wronged, trodden upon, pushed out of the way. Then falsely accused by their tormentors.

Burke let her talk on in her compelling way. She had become a part of him, his private stage dream.

The wall clock pointed to 12:30 before the clerk was able to flag Rhodes's attention. He nodded, let her go on, hoping she would never stop. She was becoming his every other heartbeat—one for her, one for himself.

He was learning her life. Enthralled, taken by her and amazed at her. Of one thing Rhodes was certain: she knew who the real audience was, and she rarely unlocked her eyes from the jury.

Five minutes later he recessed for an hour and a half to audible groans from the front rows.

Fahey sat across from Tommy Burke in a booth inside a small restaurant three blocks away from the courthouse. "Like she read it from a script," he was saying as he wiped a bubble of beer from his mouth.

"She's really something."

"And so she may be," Fahey said, "for some of us."

Burke was impervious, though. "God, Alonzo, I've never been through anything like it."

"You're not through it yet, old cock."

"I know!" Tommy said excitedly. "But she's got 'em, Alonzo. She's got 'em standing in the aisles."

"Well, there's Pritter yet to go. He might stand her right on her head."

"Maybe he won't even try. Juries get upset if you start to bark at people too hard."

"Then maybe you ought to get him mad, suck him in. Get him to go right for her beaver pelt"—Burke warned him with a look sharp enough to shave with—"well, her scalp anyway," said Fahey in a fast switch.

"That's kind of you, Alonzo. Really very polite."

"The truth, Thomas. Comes a moment in these trials, especially the murder ones, when the psychology shifts . . . Go for the underdog, they do. It happens. From pity. They see themselves up there, and they think of all the times they had cause to smash the guts out of someone."

"She didn't smash anyone. I'd swear—"

"Easy, Thomas. Don't throw your lunch at me. I'm just saying."

Burke tried more of his salad before he pushed it away. He was too upset to eat, and he was almost too upset to think clearly.

"Roll back, Tommy. Slow down. I'll go yank that deputy sheriff by his short hairs, if it comes to that."

"Would you?"

But Tommy refused the coin. "Alonzo, whyever did you quit trial investigations? I know you're good at it. Everyone does."

Fahey hadn't expected the question. He waited, wondering what to say. "I dunno. All the fun went out of it when Rhodsey-boy sold out to those pols. I tried for a while. One day I had to quit when I started puking on my pillow. You see, it all got so serious and all the fun flew out of it." His voice sounded far away and hollow, even to himself.

Tommy pondered the words, unsure if he understood them. It sounded as if something had been stolen from Alonzo Fahey. Something he would never find again no matter how hard he hunted for it.

"Satan's honor," Fahey promised. He gulped the last of his beer. "Stuff is awful," he said, wincing. "Ought to stick to the real clover juice."

"I've got to get back. Are you coming?"

"As far as the door. Got something on my book this afternoon that won't stand waiting."

"Care to flip for the lunch check?"

"Always, old son. You think because you're a big time mouthpiece now, we suspend the rules?"

Fahey reached into his pocket, feeling around. "Call it," he said, flipping a gold Kruger in the air.

"Heads."

Fahey caught his special coin with the tiny notch on the rim of the head's side. He felt the notch, knew that Tommy had won, and deftly reversed the coin with a flick of his fingertip.

"Tails," he reported, showing it to Burke. "You'll do better this afternoon." He slid the Kruger across the table. "Here you are, pay with this."

At the door, Fahey clapped Burke encouragingly on the back. "Hit 'em with those cloppers you wear. Right in center crotch. And let that songbird of yours keep humming away . . . And, by the way, are you doing anything about those other questions I gave—"

"I'm thinking on them. We'll see."

"Use them. The Pope's own treasury there. You'll see," Fahey said. "Now go at 'em. Grow your tree to the sky, Tommy, and you and I, we'll sit up there on the highest limb and laugh at all the poor people, knowing they're us."

Fahey quickly moved up the street. He liked Tommy, liked him a lot, but the courtroom wasn't for him today. For days now he had wanted to see the gypsy, needing her again in his life. She'd been too busy when he had the time for her, and then it was the other way around.

Today they would have all afternoon together. Time and more time for one of her spectacular séances.

Mostly, though, he wanted to get away from that trial and from Tommy Burke. His conscience had been edgy all morning. He had looked at Rhodes, then over to Burke, and knew something was way out of place. And he, Fahey, who always gave his best to clients, was keeping something back, something Burke should know.

The gypsy would counsel him.

Rhodes slid into his black robe again. He'd come to the court that morning taut and tense over his own decision to slip the aces for Romaine. He was still tense. Macklin Price helped him on with the robe, she did it anyway to make certain it hung correctly.

"Two calls," she reminded him.

"Too bad."

"What'll I say when they call again."

"That I'm busy, in case they've forgotten how to read up there."

"I won't say that. Not to the governor's office—"

"The hell with 'em . . . call Fritzi, would you? Ask if she wants to come for early dinner tonight."

"Sure." Macklin smoothed his hair.

"We'll wrap up today around 3:30. Get any paperwork together I need to sign or look over . . . How're we coming on those forms for my confirmation?"

"Everything's done except the financial part."

"Nosy, aren't they?"

He owned some good real estate, a half-interest in several oil and gas leases in Canada, and a hefty list of corporate bonds. In good shape, very good. But it still irritated him that he had to show his finances to outsiders.

Opening the door, he went through it headlong, almost bumping into Romaine as the bailiff led her to the witness chair. She looked at him appraisingly, then deeply, and he thought he saw an amused look flicker across her face.

Tommy looked up at the clock. Rhodes is punctual, he reminded himself, yet he needed a judge with patience. He stood before Romaine again, pausing briefly while the court reporter fed a new tape into her transcription machine.

"Let's go on," he said to Romaine. "When we recessed, you were talking about how you got along with Mr. and Mrs. Sterne, I believe." He glanced at the court reporter, asking: "Would you read the last few sentences from this morning's session?"

The reporter droned them.

"Now," said Tommy, "let's proceed from there. You were saying that Marc's father and stepmother welcomed you. Were warm and friendly at first."

"Yes, wonderful really."

"Did they ever talk to you about the film *Tonight or Never* you made for their studio?"

"All the time, for a while. It made them a lot of money, I think."

"You were nominated for an Oscar, weren't you?"

"Yes." Her voice lowered slightly.

"Then what? What came about in your relationship with the Sternes?"

"They cooled off. Became sort of aloof, if you know what I mean. I didn't know why at first."

"Did they ever say?"

"Mrs. Sterne dropped hints two or three times."

Rhodes leaned forward.

"What did she say or hint?" asked Tommy.

"Various things. That Marc and I shouldn't be so serious about each other. That we had lots of time. Once she said 'Hollywood marriages are like a wet match in a strong wind' or something like that."

"Anything else?"

"Oh, well, yes. I told her I was adopted one day when we went shopping. She said, 'That was too bad, wasn't it?'"

"Didn't seem to think too much of that idea?"

"She mentioned it a couple of times later to Marc. He told me—"

Pritter bounced to his feet. "Hearsay," he roared.

Rhodes agreed and had Romaine's comment struck.

"All right," Burke went on. He moved to his right, using Pritter's trick, and blocked the prosecutor's view of the witness. "Can you tell us about your relationship with Mr. Sterne? Did that cool off as well?"

"After I turned down an offer he made me, things went sort of downhill between us."

"What offer?"

"He made a terrible suggestion. That if I would stop seeing Marc, he would arrange a two-picture contract for me with another studio."

"Wanted to buy you off?"

"In so many words, that's what it sounded like. Isn't that terrible?"

Tommy Burke let that one sink in. Out of the corner of his eye he saw the heads of several journalists lower as pens went down to pads.

"What did you reply to Mr. Sterne?"

"That I was shocked that a man like him would think so little of me. Of us. His own son . . . We were in lo-love, you know . . ."

Romaine's head turned away from the jury for the first time. Her shoulders sagged, and then she buried her face in both hands. A muffled sob seeped out.

Tommy waited. So did Rhodes, who watched Pritter fume.

When Romaine recovered, Tommy asked her quietly: "You all right?"

"I'm sorry. I just hate to think of how they used me."

"We understand . . . So you refused Mr. Sterne's offer?"

"I had to. Anyone would, wouldn't they?"

"Perhaps not everybody would," Burke observed quietly. "So that was the end of it? Did he make the offer again?"

"No. And Marc and I decided afterward that we'd see less of his parents."

"You never saw them again? His parents?"

"Not as much. Things were strained, and I didn't want Marc on their list because of me."

"List?"

"Their shit list, oh sorry."

A few guffaws erupted. Romaine looked up at Rhodes as if to ask forgiveness for her gaffe. He smiled at her.

"Did either Mr. or Mrs. Sterne ever indicate to you, in any way, that they thought you were after their money? Anything like that?"

Romaine's eyes went glassy. "They say, those people there"—she pointed straight at Pritter—"that I killed Marc. Why would I kill someone whose money I wanted?"

"Yes, why would you?" agreed Tommy. "But did either Mr. or Mrs. Sterne ever accuse you of going after Marc for the family money?"

"She did," replied Romaine, barely audible.

"Louder, please!" Pritter complained. "Your Honor, I can't see the witness when she answers."

Rhodes asked Tommy to stand somewhere else, and for Romaine to repeat her answer.

"Mrs. Sterne took me aside one day and said they were very wise to me. They'd looked into my background. That I might be a good actress and all that, but I wasn't going to marry her stepson, not ever... Nor would I ever get a drop of their money."

"She said that?"

Romaine nodded. "Yes, when she invited me for tea at the Polo Lounge, and let me have it right between the eyes. I was flabbergasted."

Tommy glanced at the courtroom clock. He couldn't figure a reason to ask for a recess, but he didn't want to keep going either. The germ of an attack, forming in his mind for the past several days, was taking shape. He thought he saw a way to go after the Sternes. But he needed the deputy sheriff on the stand again before he really could begin to take a swipe at them. Even then, it was still a long shot.

Romaine saved him.

Tommy hadn't sent her another question, yet she had expertly used the moment, as he had looked up at the clock, to make her face become intensely alive. As if some new thing of crushing importance were suddenly recalled...

"Is it all right to finish?" she asked. "Can I say more?"

"Oh, well, yes, of course," said Tommy, embarrassed, hearing snickers again. His hands fumbled nervously in his pockets.

"About Mrs. Sterne?" Romaine asked.

"Yes, please go on."

"She was angry with me for other reasons."

Burke waited with no idea of what was coming, letting her have her way.

"Yes. Other things too. I think that's what made her so mad at me," Romaine said.

"Other things?"

Romaine brought her breathing under strict control, the trick of a trained actress. Forcing a blush to her cheeks, she looked down at her toes as if caught out in some humiliating secret.

"What other things?" Tommy urged her.

"I don't think I should say," she said looking up, blushing deeper, beautifully too under her flaxen hair.

Romaine allowed a stage-loaded moment to pass. She'd had the scent of Audrey Sterne and Ferenc Kardas for some time. Seen their quick glimpses, those knowing looks, and then the stay away looks they gave each other at times. Little things. The ones a woman always notices about another woman when a good looking man is around, paying attention to only one of them.

"Mrs. Sterne, well, you know—"

"Yes," urged Burke.

"She had a thing going on with the houseman, and one time I stumbled in on them," said Romaine, rushing out the accusation.

"A what thing? Please be precise."

"An affair, I suppose you could say," Romaine said chastely.

Pritter roared something that was lost in the rising murmurs racing across the courtroom. Burke jumped with elation. No one saw him or observed Rhodes who was agog. A stream of reporters headed for the aisles.

Two tumultuous minutes elapsed as Rhodes threatened to clear the courtroom. Banging the gavel, he knew instantly that his daughter, sitting wide eyed below him, had opened a floodgate. Was Burke clever enough to catch his chance?

He summoned both attorneys to the bench. Pritter was livid, pounding his fist against the meat of his other hand. Tommy Burke could hardly open his mouth. He leaned against the bench, agape—in all their meetings never once had Romaine spoken about this miracle of information.

"Okay," Rhodes said. "We're gonna hear her out."

"You can't!" Pritter insisted.

"I can't?" said Rhodes.

"It's absolutely unsupportable."

"Let's find out."

A loose straw blown about in an ill wind. Rhodes would grab at it, at anything. If the testimony was off the mark, he could always strike it later.

Pritter's chest heaved. He pivoted quickly and his coat flared around his hips like a matador's cape. Sitting down, his arm swept over the table, and ended up knocking half the wind out of one of his assistants.

No one had seen the smirk buried behind Romaine's placid expression. Perfect, she thought. Played it just like a throw-away line of dialogue, one that snaps back fast as a whip.

Burke again stood to the side of the witness stand, waiting for quiet in the courtroom.

"I knew I shouldn't have said it," Romaine whispered to Tommy, who was not yet woken to her change of tone.

"You did and you should."

He asked her to resume.

And with the half-truth that can ruin lives, she spoke quietly, almost prayer-like. But they heard her all the way down the room, clear to the very last rows.

"I'd gone to the pool house in Malibu one morning. I'd left a bag there. Some beach clothes I wanted. I was going to meet Marc later on and take off for a beach we liked."

"Marc wasn't there?"

"No, I was going to meet him later."

"Then?"

"I let myself in the back gate. I knew where the key was hidden by the little birdhouse . . . It was early and I didn't want to bother anyone."

"Yes."

"And, well, I went into the pool house and they were there."

"Who? Exactly?"

"Ferenc. The houseman. He testified here. Remember?"

Tommy nodded.

"They were on one of the chaises. The red and white striped one by the bar."

"What time was it? Do you remember?"

"Sevenish. I had an acting class at eight, and I had to hurry to get back for it."

"Seven in the morning?" asked Tommy, nailing the point.

"About then, yes."

"And what did you see?"

"They were lying there on the chaise. He wore nothing, and she . . . I think she had her bottoms on."

"Bottoms?"

"Panties or something. Maybe it was a bikini bottom... I took off, I just closed the door and ran."

"To where?"

"My car."

"That's all you saw?"

Careful now, Romaine commanded herself—look slightly shocked, not too much, just enough. Open the mouth, dilate the eyes.

"Mostly all."

"What else?"

"She was going down on... oh, you know." Romaine forced her lungs and blushed deeper.

"We'd like it in your words," Tommy said.

"Playing with him. With her mouth." Romaine closed her eyes, and her breasts rose under a deep breath.

"Fellatio, you mean. Do you know that word?"

"Fellatio is what she was doing."

Two of the women jurors looked at each other, and put the backs of their hands up to their mouths. Mirror images. More reporters romped out. Someone in the back of the room clapped hands until a court bailiff found the offender and marched her out.

It was 3:21.

Rhodes, a thousand watts flashing in his head, called a recess until the next morning. A besieged daughter in front of him, and a flow of memories about her mother needling him from behind. He felt like he was in clamps, semi-paralyzed: lurid photos of his daughter in evidence; her mother having an affair with a butler?

He had expected that Audrey might have to testify again. Nothing unusual about that, but not like this, under a storm that could rain on her for years to come. Make her a gossip target all over Los Angeles. He'd have to cancel dinner with Fritzi tonight. She would howl but it couldn't be helped.

Fahey loved his spiritual banquets with her. He was savoring the magical insights of his gypsy. Adoring her, his other wife he called her, and his truest conscience.

She hushed him.

His head lay deep in her lap, and her flowing yellow caftan surrounded him. On each hand she wore two rings set with lavender stones. Thin gold circles jangled on her wrists as Fahey gently turned one of her breasts. She was talking to him, warning him again of life's obstacles, and to be even more wary of its joys.

Twice he'd already pleaded with her to perform a smaller séance. But today, she said, the stars were in very poor alignment and might bring harm to them both.

"What of the young one, the girl?" he inquired.

"I've never seen her. She's only a vague image."

"Christ, she's all over the airwaves."

"But not mine. She is hardly a shape."

"I saw her, Gypsy, I did. In the cell house. Swear to you she's got one of those strange lights about her."

"Then she'll come to no good."

"Hang her you mean?"

"Who would know?"

"You would. I need you to tell me."

"Another time, perhaps."

She wouldn't play their game today. She avoided his queries, wondering if Fahey, her humorist, intended her for bed today. She might even put another herb poultice on his bad elbow. He always liked that, and then he would stay longer, and that would yield a chance to persuade him into the new partnership she had in mind. A few nights earlier a drcam-like vision had suggested the whereabouts of some stolen art Fahey had been stalking for nearly two years. One of his rare failures. She would gladly share her secret if he would split the bonus he would receive from the insurance company. Ten thousand, at least. She knew the figure because he'd told her in a fit of frustration one day.

Fahey stirred. From his pocket he drew out the Turkish medal, his good luck charm the gypsy had given him for his saint's day a year ago. He saved it for occasions that could only occur once, the last time being Raye Wheeler's funeral.

"How do I shine this up? Vinegar? Beeswax?"

"Leave it with me," she offered.

"Can't, my blessed one. What would I put under my pillow?"

"Ancient dreams."

She pried the medal from his hand. With one strong lift

of her thighs she sat him up, telling him she was tired. That he must go now. To come back later in the week, Sunday would be best.

But he wanted to stay. He looped his good arm around her, saying he wanted to start composing her history this very day. Where would they begin? In bed? The best place to talk, always. Get the biology down pat, and the rest of it would skip right into place.

And by the way, he could find no history of the Turkish army in any important battle during the past century. What sort of gift had she given him anyway?

Herself, she would tell him later.

For now, though, he asked for more tutoring. He wanted to know who wrote the first love song. And why did love always strike without warning? So unfriendly, wasn't it? He divulged his latest theory, that to get along with the women he adored—"you most of all, Gypsy"—it was better to have a few deeply nourished faults . . . else, how could the women forgive you and start you over?

Gypsy love, tell me, why do women recall everything as if it were written on the stones of Moses . . . whether you praised them or didn't, for their jewels; how their hair looked on a certain night; the dress they wore. Or if you should've made love to them and somehow forgot to. It was like taking a test, except school never let out, not even for one fucking day.

Women were such circular creatures with those lovely faces and intense emotions and their hearts so miserable half the time. Those rounded breasts and that other lambent mouth up their thighs. That inner, silent mouth, so deadly silent, but filled with so much knowledge, that took in your private chemicals and gave back life. Was that really fair? Would men behave with all that guile, Gypsy, if they'd been given those magic chalices between their legs? What was he missing, what cryptic code evaded him?

With his head on the gypsy's lap again, his hand under her caftan stroking her nest, Fahey's eyes shone brighter though with a certain peace to them. Gazing down at his damp face, she widened her knees for him.

"You know what I see?" she asked.

"But I never know."

"Behind his back your God holds trouble for you."

"You think?" Fahey sat up abruptly.

"I know. You must find yourself a different life and soon."

"Life? Life is a high dive. A quick fuck is what it is, Gypsy. You get a few grand moments out of her, then a hot towel and a fast goodbye out the door... and Jesus, look what she charges you even if you don't want her."

"Am I that life, Alonzo?"

"Never, my great one. It's you who keeps me safe from the others. I wish every day with you had a hundred hours."

"And no stones of Moses?"

Fahey laughed and his gypsy laughed with him as he lifted the caftan off her great hulk. She warned him then, before they began, of the girl at the trial. A girl who the gypsy could not see, but did not like at all.

"That young one," said the gypsy, "who seems to beguile you so much."

She knew her Fahey, and then she knew his caressing hands.

Returning home early that evening, Audrey found a message written by Kardas on the front hall table.

—Please call Mr. Pritter at 136–2400 or 399–1921.

Slipping the note into her purse, she walked across the marble floor to a study, where she could find a drink to soften her worries. She wanted a bath, the longest one ever. She had heard a news break raising her hackles on her car radio as she came down the Pacific Coast Highway from an afternoon hair appointment.

Walking into the study, she saw Julio jerk suddenly at the mention of her name. He was watching the 5:30 news blurting out of the television.

Tommy Burke stood by the flat black window of Raye Wheeler's office. He could hear nothing of the life ten stories below. Crowds milled around, neon lights blazed, smells would be rising from the stands of the taco and burrito vendors, hawkers of every hijacked wristwatch, radio, appliance in the city announcing their wares. Streetgirls in their finery of pink and purple satin awaiting their clients in the doorways.

It was Broadway, the same in Los Angeles as New York, the same as every Broadway of every city that harbors those ghettos of the night. Tommy stared down at the one below just as he had now for six months.

His swollen knees ached. He'd been on his feet for too many hours, so he sat down in the swivel chair behind the desk Wheeler had used for nearly fifty years. After the trial adjourned, he had given Romaine a light lashing for holding back on him.

What would Raye do?

The question puzzled Tommy.

Chapter Sixteen

The door chimes sounded. She was here again. Macklin Price had called her, and then run a little interference so no one in the Sterne household knew who was really calling.

Consuelo sauntered off as Audrey entered the library. She came in walking a little stiffly, her green eyes flashing.

"Getting to be a real rendezvous, your house."

"Can't think of any place better. Safer I mean," Rhodes said.

"I heard all that nice news from your courtroom," she said. "On the car radio. For the second time today."

"You couldn't have heard very much."

"Enough."

"Like a drink?" He stood a few feet away.

"No, thanks. I've got to be home by six."

"Mind if I have one?"

"Of course not. Have ten, dammit... What're you having anyway?"

"A double dammit is what I was thinking of," he said, trying to ease the strain.

"All right, I'll have one too. Anything. On the rocks."

It was the Sabbath day for some, but not for them. Audrey sat down as he poured two at the bar. He wanted her. Her and Romaine together, but in very different ways; wanting them as much as he wanted to see the next dawn.

"I can make this quick," he said, handing over her drink.

"Not quick enough. That little wretch! Lying about me like that right in front of all those people."

Still standing, he said nothing.

"Well?"

"I don't know of her as a liar," he said.

"You don't know her then."

"You got that right. Not about what she said yesterday, anyway. That's why I asked you to meet me... I'm in this too, remember."

"So what is it, Cliff?"

Rhodes gave a quick rundown of Romaine's testimony, and the obvious meaning it held for Audrey.

"You really believe that nonsense? You couldn't, Cliff, it's idiotic."

"It isn't important what I believe, Audrey. It's in the air now. The press, everyone listened... and how they listened," he emphasized so she would know he was serious.

"I'll kill that kid, by God I will. I'm going to—"

"Slow down—"

"I'm damned if I'll let her smear me!"

"They'll probably call you back on the stand. Give you a chance to refute her testimony... Probably pull Kardas back, too. You'll have to come."

Audrey glared over the rim of the tumbler. "Who'll call me back? You?"

"Pritter."

"Pritter wouldn't dare!"

There it is, he thought, said so vehemently. The prosecutor was in their pocket. And all this over that damn syringe filled with drugs, the syringe with no fingerprints on it.

"Would you dare," he asked, "leave your reputation all over the street that way?"

"Why should I say anything at all? I've nothing to hide."

"You sure?"

"You can bet the ranch I am." Audrey crossed her legs. One foot seesawed in the air, up and down.

"Maybe I can help, Audrey."

"How?"

"By controlling what can be said, and what can't... at least for the record," he added.

"I'm not doing it. I'm not going back there again."

"You refuse and you'll be in contempt of court, and the trial is all but over"—forcing her now—"and all Burke has to do is open the door wider."

"What do you mean?"

"That you and Kardas had something going. And possibly the two of you had your own reasons for getting rid of Marc Sterne."

"That's the most rotten thing anyone ever said. You are some bastard to say—"

"Lots of money. Your husband's an elderly fellow and a handsome Hungarian comes on the scene—"

"Stop it!" Audrey's hands went up to her neck, down, up once more.

"I want you to see how it can go," Rhodes pointed out.

"Please stop it."

"You've got to understand how—"

"Into that sewer? I don't have to look down there, thank you."

"No, that's right, you don't. But any lawyer with half a brain can make a jury look there."

"And she'd go free. Wouldn't she? Is that what you're saying?"

"All they need is reasonable doubt."

"You'd love it, too. That's what you'd love, isn't it?"

"I've never been convinced Romaine is guilty."

"Oh, my God! How I wish I'd never met you."

"But you did. And we've got a tricky one on our hands... I'm trying to help, Audrey. Really, I am."

"Oh, God, Julio will go crazy."

"It's your word against Romaine's. Remember that."

But Audrey missed his words. A stark image toiled at her thoughts. She saw Julio smiling contemptuously as she sagged against the back of the couch. "You know what?" she said.

"Tell me."

"You know why we're on earth? It's a grandstand to watch everyone go crash. Your dreams, everything."

"We'll get through it. I'll help—"

"You'll get through it, you mean. Wait till your number gets pulled out of the hat."

"You've had a good life. Look up, and out, while you're at it."

"Bullshit."

"I'll go to bat if I can, Audrey. But I'd like to know one thing."

"And what's that?"

"Was there anything between you and Kardas?"

"Are you crazy?"

Rhodes appraised her. "Okay," he said as he stood. "I'll walk you out to your car."

"She's a liar, Cliff. Believe me. You have no idea how hard it is to think that about your own child. No idea at all," Audrey said, thinking again of Marc's sprawled body, her emerald bracelet, and once more guessing at Julio's boiling wrath if she and Kardas ever became public gossip. "It's so damned unfair. I'm really sorry, Cliff. Sorry I called you a bastard. I'm just so undone. God—"

He led her out to the driveway and watched her leave, musing how a woman in mow-down anger was a worthy sight once every few years or so. Could put the Fourth of July to shame. No entry fee for watching them either, if you didn't count the cost to your eardrums.

What Rhodes couldn't muse about was that either Audrey or Romaine was lying. Which one? He heard the misery of choice calling to him again, demanding a fast answer.

She won't even give me a straight answer on the photos, Tommy complained to himself. She evades, says she can't remember. How could she not? Fingers all over her, things stuck inside her, a dog on her.

Pritter will get his opening eventually, and one way or

the other mop the floor with her. Even if no one could see the photos, he'll somehow manage to describe them.

Tommy failed to hear the night line until the second ring. He picked it up. "Wheeler offices."

"Burke's, you mean."

"Alonzo? That you?"

"S'right. All organs accounted for."

"What's the news?"

"Your boyo is in town. I checked. He also got the word from Pritter's office."

"Monday?"

"Up to you."

"That's when we want him."

"What about your girl?"

"I'll ask the judge to delay Romaine."

"See you later."

"Oh, Alonzo, ah, do you have a number where I can reach Judge Rhodes?"

Fahey rattled it off.

"This is terrific, Alonzo. Thanks for everything."

"Take care, lad. Go home, it's Saturday. All good Irishers and Jews are supposed to be home."

Tommy let out a whoop that filled the room. For a moment he rehearsed what he would say, then quickly made the call.

Apologizing to Rhodes for bothering him at home, he quickly explained that the Malibu deputy sheriff was back from his vacation. Could they put him on first thing Monday? "The sheriff's force is busy," Tommy said, "and I don't know when we can get him again."

Rhodes agreed.

Tommy thanked him, hung up again and forgot all about what day it was.

A small point. But if the sheriff's office had made an error on their write-ups of Marc Sterne's death, then they could've made other ones. Tantalize the jury with the idea of other mistakes, ones that he would somehow invent if he had to. A syringe, for example. And a letter written by Romaine that could be read at least two ways.

Chapter Seventeen

"You can't remember?" Tommy Burke asked the deputy sheriff from Malibu.

"Does it make any difference?"

"I think it does. Would you like a moment to think it over?"

"I don't have to."

"Then you must remember who it was."

"It was Mrs. Sterne."

"You're sure?"

"Yes, I am now."

"But you weren't so sure a moment ago?"

"I had to think. It was several months ago."

"That's right, it was," said Tommy. "Easy to make a mistake of that kind . . . You're saying that when you came into the house, the Sternes's home in Malibu, Mrs. Sterne and Ferenc Kardas were there and Mrs. Sterne showed you where Marc's body was?"

"No. Ferenc Kardas did. He discovered the body first."

"You're certain?"

"That's the way it was told to me."

"And then she said Mr. Sterne was upstairs. Too devastated to talk to anyone?"

"Words to that effect," the deputy agreed.

"And that all three of them—Mr. and Mrs. Sterne and Ferenc Kardas—had just come in from a boat outing?"

"That's right. It's all in the investigation report."

"Now, deputy, you testified at the beginning of the trial that several neighbors heard a sound on the water. An engine perhaps . . . engine noises carry over water very well, don't they . . . perhaps that was the Sternes's boat coming in?"

"We assume that."

"Assume?"

"There's no other explanation."

"Some things never get explained, do they?" Tommy said.

He backed away from the deputy. Slowly because his wobbly knees were still swollen to the size of cantaloupes and shooting pain up his legs. He picked up copies of the two investigation reports, the first exhibits marked and entered for the record by Pritter at the opening of the trial when this deputy had appeared as one of the state's leadoff witnesses.

Tommy showed them to the deputy, asking: "You recognize these?"

"I do."

"You wrote them?"

"And signed them."

"You're a trained criminologist, right? You hold a degree in criminology, correct?"

"That's right."

"Can you tell me why the dates on those reports are identical?"

The deputy frowned again at the reports in his hand. "I—the one here—the other, I think, that's the one for Mr. Sterne—they shouldn't be—" He stopped, flustered.

"They're both dated the same day," Tommy said. "You dated and signed them, right? That's your signature. One report describes the statements of Audrey Sterne and then of Ferenc Kardas. The other, for Julio Sterne, is dated the same day. How could that be when Julio Sterne was too undone over his son's death to make a statement then?"

"A mistake, I guess. Probably a typo."

"A mistake?"

"Yes."

"Well, that's two mistakes, isn't it?"

The deputy reddened. He looked away from Tommy and away from the jury. Pritter straightened in his chair.

"Isn't it?" Tommy repeated.

"Minor ones."

"How about the syringe, deputy? The one you found by

Marc Sterne's body. The one the forensic lab says was used to inject a fatal dose of drugs in Marc Sterne. Was there a mistake there?"

"What do you mean?"

"You handled it, didn't you? Picked up the syringe and put it in a plastic bag. Could you have made a mistake and wiped away any fingerprints when you did?"

"No." The deputy wagged his head. "I picked the syringe up by the needle. I used forceps."

"You couldn't have made a mistake?"

"Not on that, I couldn't."

"You remember it so clearly?"

"I sure do."

"Only a few minutes ago, you couldn't remember whether it was Audrey Sterne or Ferenc Kardas who first told you that Julio Sterne was upstairs, indisposed."

"But then I did remember."

"About the dates of your reports, too?"

"A typo, I said."

"We all make mistakes all the time, don't we?"

"Sometimes, yes."

"And you, just possibly"—Tommy hesitated—"just possibly might've made one when you picked up the syringe."

"But I didn't."

"You say that, deputy. But anyone in a time of turmoil can do something, and afterward not remember doing it, can't they? I can and you can and we all can, right? Sometimes we don't even know we've made a mistake until later."

"I handled the evidence correctly. By the book. I told you," the deputy retorted vehemently. His fists balled up on his knees.

"You assume the noise on the water was the Sternes's boat? An assumption unproved. You didn't immediately recall whether it was Audrey Sterne or Kardas who told you Julio Sterne was upstairs . . . You think, and you assume, the identical date on Julio Sterne's statement was due to typographical error, though you took his statement down the following day . . ."

Tommy paused again.

". . . Yet you're certain as the sun rises about the syringe. That's what you want us to believe?"

"Absolutely," answered the deputy.

Burke shook his head. He turned to the jury with a whimsical expression, shook his head again, and said: "I wish we could all be so absolutely sure."

"You seem to be, Mr. Burke."

"Not really. This is the first case I ever tried and I have to say I'm confused . . . Let's go over your statement of a few minutes ago. You said—and please correct me if I'm wrong—that Mrs. Sterne called the Malibu sheriff's station soon after Marc Sterne's body was found. Right after that she apparently called the gate and told the guard you'd be coming through. The guard said, when finding out from Mrs. Sterne that Marc was dead, that Romaine Brook had been there earlier and then she left. She arrived at Malibu Pointe after Marc had already come through the gate . . . Later, Mrs. Sterne told you about Miss Brook, and you checked it out with the same guard. Is that correct? Do you want to change any of that statement?"

"No," said the deputy. "That's what I told the court the first time I was here. And so did the gate guard as I remember."

"I just wanted to be sure, deputy." Tommy Burke looked at Pritter. "Your witness."

"No questions at this time," Pritter announced. He didn't think Burke had done any real damage. But he didn't care to open any new avenues for him to explore.

Rhodes had closely followed the exchange between Burke and the deputy. Yet his eyes rarely strayed from Romaine's demure and cheerful face.

His cat sense got the better of him. Someone here was bullshitting. The record wouldn't be clear, and Rhodes thought of the governor's assistant, all those calls, the heat Burke would never know about. Burke was failing to close up the box now, when he had the chance. As the deputy waited to be excused, Rhodes mulled before asking: "Deputy? On Mr. Sterne?"

"Yes?" The deputy craned his neck, looking over toward the bench.

"Did you or anyone else from the Malibu station look in on Julio Sterne the night of Marc Sterne's death?"

"We respected Mrs. Sterne's wishes. We left him alone."

"You're not sure where he was?"

"Upstairs. His bedroom, I guess."

"You guess? Wouldn't you have verified his presence, his condition, one way or another?"

"It was a pretty rough time for everyone, your Honor, and we had our hands full."

"I'm sure. But all the same, wouldn't it be the correct procedure to fix the identity and whereabouts of everyone at the scene?"

"Usually, yes."

"Usually or always."

"Always."

"But not that time?"

"I guess we were so busy that . . . pretty hectic time and all . . . I, well, we—" the deputy stumbled again.

"So you didn't look in on Mr. Sterne?"

"I think not."

"Was that another oversight?"

"In hindsight, yes."

"You don't know for certain that Mr. Sterne was upstairs or someplace else?"

"We took Mrs. Sterne's word for where he was."

"Well, supposing he wasn't?"

The question hung there. Pritter did a slow die in his chair. He wanted to raise an objection to the line of questioning, but he knew Rhodes would hardly rule against himself. He was stuck. His mouth tasted coppery. The one thing he'd been instructed to do—take all steps necessary to keep Julio Sterne out of the trial—was slipping away from his control.

"Can you answer me?" Rhodes requested of the deputy.

"We took his statement the next day and that's where he said he was. Up in his bedroom, in shock."

"That's what your report says?"

"Yes. Mine and the one taken down by the state investigators."

"Why was the state called in so soon? The very next day, weren't they?"

"The Attorney General's office insisted on taking over. Sending their own men in."

"How many men?"

"Four or five."

"Which?"

"Five."

"Quite a few, isn't it? Is it usual for the state to take over on this sort of an investigation?"

"No, not in my experience."

"And they were present when you questioned Julio Sterne the next day?"

"They were, yes, five of them."

"Who did the questioning?"

"They did."

"But you signed the report as if you'd conducted the questioning. Is that right, deputy?"

The deputy nodded.

"Please answer aloud."

"Yes, sir, I did."

"Why didn't they do the write-up?"

Agitated, Pritter shifted in his chair. Murmuring something to one of his assistants, he sent him out of the courtroom. Several of the jurors watched the man scurry off.

"They told me to do it," said the deputy.

"For you to do their work?"

"This was an unusual situation, your Honor, and we cooperated."

"Other than an alleged case of homicide, how was it so unusual?"

"I guess—well, it was them—the Sternes, you know."

"Know what?"

"They're so prominent and all and, well, I think you know what I mean."

"Big enough to get you elbowed out of the way. Make you write reports the way they wanted them written?"

"I guess so."

"You have any more guesses, deputy? Did you make a guess that Mrs. Sterne was factually correct when she told you her husband was upstairs?"

"I took her word."

"Because she is Mrs. Sterne?" asked Rhodes, cutting deep for the deputy's nervous bones.

"I didn't think of it that way."

"Never crossed your mind? Not once?"

"Yes, I suppose it did, later on."

"Did you mind the state coming in and peeling you off the case?"

"We didn't like it much."

"But you went along?"

"We had to."

"Why?"

"It wasn't my decision."

"Whose was it?"

"The sheriff's."

"And how did he explain that situation to you?" Rhodes asked as he saw Pritter conferring with his other assistant.

"The sheriff said we were out of it. 'By direct request from the governor's office,'" the deputy said, putting it as delicately as he could.

"The governor's office?"

"That's what we were told."

"Do you have any idea why?"

The deputy was confused. Confused and somewhat frightened, as he had been warned to keep his mouth shut about all the griping at the Malibu station when the state had horned in.

"I think your work could've been a lot sharper," Rhodes said to him.

Letting it sink in. A giveaway to Burke, a swipe at Pritter, and a point he was sure the jury would put in their pocket. As he was sure his ears would soon ring from more yells out of the governor's office. But at least he'd gotten it all out in the open—that political finagling was going on behind the scenes.

"Any more questions?" Rhodes asked.

Pritter said no. Tommy shook his head.

Rhodes told the deputy to step down. Halfway down the aisle he picked up a gaggle of reporters who followed him out. Rhodes called Burke and Pritter to the bench.

"What now?" He searched Burke's face. "Are you going to continue with Miss Brook?"

"No. We've got to hear from Mr. Sterne."

"You agree?" Rhodes said to Pritter.

"Not for an instant. Why does it make any difference where Julio Sterne was?"

"It might mean everything," offered Tommy. "I've got plenty of reason to believe Marc Sterne was on the outs with his father . . . Romaine Brook has told me plenty."

"What're you suggesting?" snapped Pritter.

"Maybe Julio Sterne was involved," Tommy said.

"Did away with his own son?"

"I don't know. Do you?"

Pritter's normally florid face paled. "That's the stupidest thing I ever heard of."

"Aren't we here to find out?" Rhodes said.

Pritter snorted.

"How much more have you got with your client?" Rhodes asked Burke.

"A long way," said Tommy. "But I want to tie this down—the whereabouts of Mr. Sterne—before I go on with her. We have to."

"Am I going to have to subpoena him?" Rhodes said to Pritter. That word again, *subpoena*, he thought.

"Look, the man's been crushed by all this," Pritter replied. "How can you drag him through it again?"

"You've been dragging my client through it for months now . . . We can knock Sterne off in an hour," Tommy retorted. "Maybe less."

"Knock him off, you say." Pritter's shoulders rose. "You mean the way Brook knocked his son off?"

"Okay, that's enough," Rhodes said to Pritter. "Let's get Mr. Sterne out of the way . . . subpoena or not?"

"Won't be necessary. I'll talk to him," Pritter said in disgust.

"Tomorrow?"

"I'll have to see." Pritter looked off, far away, up at the clock, through the walls, across the city, watching his future, his desk at Oldes & Farnham riding off to another planet.

"We'll have to recess . . . I'm requesting that you," Rhodes said to Pritter, "get him here as quickly as you can. Tell him that comes straight from me. And we'll try to inconvenience him as little as possible."

As Pritter sensed his future catapulting into oblivion, Tommy Burke's world seemed like the light at the end of the pier. Almost floating back to where Romaine sat, he could hardly wait to tell her what was up.

What would Julio Sterne be like? Tommy wondered.

Rhodes had swung the gate open. Tripping the deputy on the way, showing the court how the state had pounced on Romaine. The judge, he thought, had paid out the telling questions. Nice sharp belly cutters.

Tommy would have sent him a thank you note if that weren't so improper. His knees stopped hurting.

That evening Rhodes sat with Fritzi on her veranda. They dipped chips in guacamole and drank margaritas in the cool air fanning across the hills. Loosening his tie, Rhodes put his feet up on the railing.

"I love this hour of the day," Fritzi observed.

"The best."

"Are you staying? Say yes."

"Can't. I want to look at some of the trial transcript tonight."

"Do it here. I can be back by ten, maybe earlier."

"The script won't get to my house until eight or so. I need time to go over it."

"Why not have them send it here?"

Rhodes shook his head. "We've walked that track before. That's the way mouths start rumors—"

"Plenty of people know about us, Cliff."

"Let's not add the court system to your fan club."

"That damn trial owns you, doesn't it? I hardly see you anymore."

"It'll be over soon."

"Will we be all over, too, Cliff?" asked Fritzi, her face somber.

"Don't ever say that. This is a big, big trial. And I've got to be damn careful with it."

"Because you got raked so hard over the last one?"

"That's as good a reason as any."

A stillness settled.

"You're really hard in the head," Fritzi said eventually. "Sometimes I'd give a lot to fall *out* of love with you. Just be friends, the sort of friends who only *say* they care."

"That's not my idea of a friend, lover-girl."

"Mine either. That's exactly what I mean." She sighed, looking beyond the veranda rail to a sky painted in coral and lilac. All that remained of the sun were those fabulous colors she would love to have woven into fabric for an evening gown.

"You know what?" she said.

"Sometimes."

"Here's one you don't know."

"That makes twenty don't-knows for today."

"I went to my doctor today."

Rhodes was watching a plane descend on an imaginary line in the far distance. At the word "doctor," his attention fastened again on Fritzi.

"Checkup time," she continued. "Told me I'd better get on with having children before I'm forty. My biological clock is galloping."

"They actually charge you for that advice?"

"No, that's gratis."

"They persuade you to have a kid and then bill you for screaming it into the world."

"You're so smart."

"I'm a lawyer, kiddo. Doctors and lawyers all use the same method to pickpocket their clients."

He tried to find the plane again, but it had dropped out of sight. He sipped at his margarita, betting a hundred-to-one with himself what was coming next.

"And do you know," Fritzi was saying over his thoughts, "he's right. I don't even have an heir."

"You've got a whole gorgeous head of it."

"Oh, are you ever one and the same today with Bob Hope." Fritzi smiled halfheartedly. "You can do better, much better."

"You don't have an *air*. That's what I like about you. Not a lot of bullshitty veneer and posturing—"

"Oh, God!"

"That's who you'll need if you want an heir."

"Is that so?"

"That's so. Unless you're in line for one of those immaculate conceptions."

"Be pretty hard to prove how immaculate it is in my case."

"I'll vouch for you."

"Would you? You're not around enough to really know."

"You'll get all of me pretty soon... I'm putting in my resignation soon. And what do you think about a few days in Mexico? Fishing? Cabo St. Lucas?"

"How about a month?"

"Really?"

"I was only teasing. I couldn't get away for a month. Would you think of an adoption..."

"And marriage?"

"It'd sure look better, wouldn't it?"

"Much."

"Would you?"

"You could always go to one of those artificial insemination banks."

Fritzi tossed her heavy dark hair. The lower curls blended perfectly with the black velvet collar of her bottle-green suit, an Austrian get-up, a dirndl, that for some odd reason made her seem smaller. Rhodes thought he could see a flush growing under the pearls around her throat.

"Oh, I don't think I'd have to pay for it," she said, slightly annoyed. She looked at her watch.

"I know you wouldn't... And how in hell're we on to this subject anyway?"

"A child," she said. "It'd be nice to have one, I've been thinking."

"Wouldn't it, yes."

"I'd be willing to adopt one if—"

"If we paired up legally," he finished for her.

"Correcto."

"What the hell kind of marriage can we have if I'm up in Sacramento most of the time?"

"We could manage. Vicarious thrills. And we can send each other singing telegrams every Wednesday."

"We manage all right now, don't we?"

"So-so."

"I wasn't talking about the sex part."

"Neither was I, Cliff."

"Marry and adopt a kid?"

Fritzi nodded with the pure vigor of a woman who knows her mind exactly.

"I'll be in Sacramento. How can I help raise a child? Won't work, Fritzi, and you—"

"We can make work whatever we want to make work. Here I am damn near proposing to you again and you just look for excuses. Thanks a whole bunch."

"I'll—let's talk about it later."

"Sure. Later. Like your going to a psychiatrist, it's always later."

"They're quite different things."

"For you, Cliff... I'm not so sure for me."

Rhodes's feet hit the patio, making a sharp sound that served as an exclamation point to his feelings. He was worried. He had trouble, trouble he chose to bear alone. He didn't care for any more of it, even though he knew she was perfectly right to ask all the questions in the world about their future.

"Think on it," Fritzi said in a voice tremoring with complaint. She got up to leave.

"I have, sweetheart—"

"Future tense."

"Christ, I come up here to have a drink with you, get a feel of your sweet ass, and you want to settle the next twenty years on your way out the door."

Fritzi smiled. "Cold steak in the 'fridge if you want it," she said brightly.

"Thanks."

"Think on it," she reminded him.

She was gone then, abruptly gone. He could hear her heels tap, tap, tap on the hardwood floors in the hallway.

Habit.

He knew a lot about her thinking habits, and then supposed she knew even more about his. Women always did. They had some very unfair advantages in sonar technique.

They hadn't kissed each other goodbye. That bothered him, strangely enough. He couldn't remember the last time, if ever, when they hadn't at least hugged goodbye. He supposed, too, that he deserved it with what he'd been giving her lately. Fritzi had just told him off, but so nicely it had taken him a minute or so to realize it.

Adoption?

He needed an heir, too. An heir other than Uncle Sam, he of the voracious appetite who lived in Washington by the Potomac. Thoughts of Romaine danced on his escalating mood: a lot he would like to do for her. He had the money, barrels of it, enough barrels anyway.

As it stood, some of his money would go into a trust, and the rest become an outright gift to the law school. He'd have to alter that formula soon. Romaine Brook was his heir. Not his legal and present one, but that could be fixed up with an hour of dictation. Who would witness it, though? Who could even type it up without finding out what he could never afford to tell anyone? He would have to write it in his own hand when the time came.

If he got her home, sound and safe as the sun.

A robe of deepening twilight wrapped itself around the sky. It had come fast tonight. The air cooled and Rhodes shivered. There must be some rule somewhere about adopting a child of your own blood, who had already been adopted once. A reverse spin of the family tree?

Fritzi would never understand. Adopt Romaine Brook? Ridiculous, let alone the explanations that would have to be made everywhere. No, Fritzi would want a little bundle in blue or pink booties. Diapers, nannies, a cradle...

Thinking about it, he felt as if someone had lobbed a hefty rock onto his head. Making him reel, almost the way Audrey got to him. He needed to get her out of his life, head, and heart. Two months ago he had a happy and mainly sound habit going with Fritzi, one that was three years young, uptick, and with a promising future.

Until the sight of Audrey again had made him come down with a first-degree case of brain confusion. The error had compounded when she let him in, after twenty-two years of silence, on the news about Romaine.

He ought to send himself out to whoever it was that gave out kicks in the ass. To wake up. Yet he wanted these women in his life. He loved them, or wanted to love them, and was trying hard to love Fritzi the way she deserved to be loved.

Rhodes walked off the veranda. He went by the living room to look for some matches and found a packet resting in a crystal ashtray on the lowered leaf of a breakfront desk. Lighting a cigar, he looked down through a pillow of smoke at the miniature Correggio on its brass stand.

A rare and beautifully executed oil of a woman and man locked in embrace on either side of a decaying wall; the man offering flowers, the woman only herself. Fritzi had loved the painting, spotting it one rainy afternoon in a gallery on Bahnhofstrasse in Zurich when they had been there for an address he was giving to a group of international trial lawyers.

He gave it for her Christmas, her birthday and her next birthday. It cost him nearly as much as his own house. But then he didn't often make gifts unless the cost really dug a hole in his bank account. Otherwise, it wasn't a gift but only a token and tokens were for subways.

Down the hallway he stopped again. He saw another gift, a much smaller one. The two love birds in their gilded cage. They were preening and fluttering their little wings, chirping, delighted with their small and fearless world.

He felt pretty high himself, and not from the margarita either. He didn't know why. Excitement seemed to sting his veins. He felt so alive, as if he were not the referee any longer but right down there in the trenches slugging it out with Pritter. Hands down, he knew he could take Pritter out with just a few hard moves and quick steps.

Dance-mastering him.

Burke had set the deputy up, and it took hardly half a punch to mow him down. They were a team, he and Burke. Burke just didn't know it yet.

Out the door now, locking it, one matter still bothered him. Why had Audrey called and left a message for Marc Sterne to come for dinner in Malibu? That's how Marc Sterne's secretary had testified. He'd come, too, obviously, but no one was there to dine with him.

Except Romaine had come there later on. What large hole did that little ball of mystery drop into?

None he could see, nor any he really wanted to see.

Chapter Eighteen

Julio Sterne had been at Parthenon Studios, when first learning of Romaine Brook's damning words in the courtroom. A reporter had called the studio's public relations department to verify whether Julio had offered to secure a picture deal for Romaine if she stopped seeing his son. The call had been forwarded to Julio's office. After thinking it over before getting on the line, he had decided the best course was to agree. Why deny it?

He had told the reporter: "Yes, I had liked her acting and offered her a deal; no, not at some other studio but with Parthenon. She's confused. And definitely not a deal if she would call off her romance with Marc, but just good business. She *was* a great actress."

Julio knew the press. He'd given them no fresh story, and he thought his statement was reasonably fair. Tit for tat. Romaine had told an outright lie. He had simply answered her with a lesser one.

The trial touched him in another way as well. Two other ways, he thought, sitting across from Audrey on their glassed-in deck. That afternoon Pritter had given him the unfriendly news that he must testify in Rhodes's courtroom. Audrey was expected to go back on the stand to answer a few questions herself.

Julio had taken the message from Pritter with utter calm. Just another problem was how he saw it. But then he dealt with problems all day long. Business problems, people problems, tax problems, even political problems. He looked at all of them in the same way. Neatly and so coldly it froze most of the problems stiff. Stiff enough so they stayed locked in his man-made ice until he was ready to melt them down to size.

Audrey, he started to convince himself, was becoming more trouble than she was really worth. A beautiful bore, but one he no longer needed in his life. He didn't relish the idea of going to court. Still, it offered nice possibilities for setting her up and then getting rid of her. And he knew she was watching him now.

She broke up his thoughts: "You're not listening to me, are you, Julio?"

"Most certainly I am."

"Well, I'm asking what you're going to do."

"Just what I have to do. Go to that goddamn court and speak."

"And say what, darling?"

"The truth, what else?"

"That you weren't here that night? You'd tell them that?"

"If they ask, I will."

"You wouldn't."

"You think not? Don't be a fool, Audrey. You don't think I'd perjure myself, do you?"

Julio had been calm and remote for as long as he was ever calm and remote. She had expected him to be in a flying rage. But he talked so smoothly she knew he was calculating trouble somewhere in that nimble head. He wanted something. Only when the glow of his cigarette faintly lit the shallow planes of his face could she see him.

"What if they find out? Then what about me?" she asked, her voice quavering.

"I don't think they'll ask me about you."

"They'll know I was on the boat alone with—"

"Ferenc. Yes, I would bet someone will rapidly reach that notion."

"Do you care?"

As Julio inhaled, the night seemed to stop and listen, then send in more of its dark.

Neither of them heard or saw Kardas, who stood inside the sliding door behind the blinds. Something was up. Kardas could sense it, even more so when he heard his name. But he had difficulty hearing the rest. He suspected it was something to do with the trial, and the accounts of it in the paper that morning. A hint that he was romantically linked with Audrey. Sterne had said nothing to him so far.

Julio snubbed out his cigarette. "I don't know if I care or not," he finally said. "I tried to cover for you as any husband should and now it's come out . . . as it sometimes does. Even the girl knew about you, I gather."

"She's a liar."

"Is she?"

"You know she is."

"As a matter of fact I do, Audrey. But she's not lying about you and lover boy Kardas."

"Julio, if you thought that, you'd have fired him out of here long ago."

"That's where you're one down and all the way out."

"You would too," Audrey insisted.

"I hired him and I pay him."

"So?"

"Why the hell do you women think you're the only ones who really understand how a marriage works?"

"Do we? We probably do at that."

"Yes. And you're wrong," said Julio slowly. "I know men who are quite aware that women, even their wives, fool around."

"Why don't they divorce them?"

"Over a little outside screwing? Are you serious? Divorce is too expensive for the league I'm talking about . . . Sometimes the wives get to know too much. Cheaper to keep them and let them have their intrigues. If they keep their heads about it . . ."

"That's nice. What a really great way to live."

"A lot of wives don't mind. Not after they think it over when they're forty or fifty, and realize how much sweat they sweated to get where they are . . . Give it all up? For what?"

Audrey listened carefully, catching the cynicism. Julio was telling her something that had never before crossed her mind. Her temper rumbled from somewhere deep near her toes.

"Are you saying," Audrey said, "what I think you're saying?"

"I had an idea you'd like Ferenc. Nice looking chap. Good manners."

"Thanks very much!"

"You seemed to like him well enough."

"And you didn't care at all."

"Audrey, turn on your lights, for God's sake. I'm a good thirty years older than you are. I can't keep up with you, and we've both known that from the beginning. Someday that'll happen to you and you'll see what I mean. I know you need that part of your life . . . that's plain enough."

"So you got Ferenc for me."

"Let's say I let it happen."

"And you did the choosing for me?"

"Better that way. Right here where, more or less, I could keep an eye on the situation. And a lot saner than having you pick out one of my men friends. Or going off with some Hollywood jocker."

Audrey was shaken, shaken and flabbergasted. Her own husband. Not only did he know what she'd been playing at with Ferenc, but he had, by God, set the affair up. She was utterly humiliated, and now her temper sailed up a notch.

"You're so callous, Julio. You're the worst cynic I ever met, saw, or ever heard of."

"Kept me out of trouble, those qualities. So don't think you're hurting my feelings."

"Hardly."

"Well, don't worry too much—they may leave you alone. Why do they care if you're having a bouncing balls contest with Kardas. I figured that out the day I got back from Seattle to find my son dead . . . and I knew that what you and Kardas had was so very alive. The police might easily find out. They're not all that stupid, and they'd add two and two together and finally get to you, Audrey."

"I never thought about that side of it at all," Audrey said. But she had thought about it quite seriously ever since Cliff Rhodes had rinsed her out in the same theory.

"That's what I do all the time, keep thinking," said Julio.

"And what do I do?"

"Keep looking beautiful. You are you know . . . you're good at a lot of things. Tennis, golf, running a house, charities. In bed. Here's some advice, cheap... let me do the hard thinking for us both."

They sat in silence for several long minutes. Audrey supposed she was lucky Julio wasn't giving her the hot steam of the enraged and jealous husband. He'd actually been terribly civilized, even nice. But then he had known for a long time, and hadn't really bluffed her at all on the night of the charity ball when she'd denied everything.

She felt idiotic, he'd fooled her so easily. "Julio, that girl is dangerous," Audrey said quietly. "She's telling so many lies it scares me to death."

Julio knew it but wanted her side of it in case he'd missed anything. "What lies are those?"

"I never met her for tea at the Polo Lounge."

"I thought you might've. It sounds like you."

"Well, I didn't."

"Any other ones."

"Lies?"

"Yes, that's what we were talking about, I thought."

"She never saw Ferenc and me doing anything."

"Fucking?"

"Must you, Julio."

"That fellow Pritter gave me a rundown on Romaine's testimony." He laughed quickly. "She caught you down by the pool. My God, I'd think there was enough room in a house this size—"

"Stop this, Julio. I mean it. You're trying to flatten me, aren't you?"

"No, that's Ferenc's job."

"I'm hating you right now."

"I can feel it. I did a damn fool thing when I covered up for you with the police. I suppose I was covering for myself at the same time... Now it'll be in the open and they'll play it to hell and back."

"How are you planning to explain yourself?"

"I'll think of something."

"Such as?"

"Such as there may be more than one explanation for how Marc died."

There. He'd said it. He could almost see the words as they slapped Audrey's features. He could barely see her face in the dim light, but he knew her eyes, usually green as spring leaves, would be dark with anger.

"You thought... my God, Julio, how could you think I had anything to do with Marc's death?"

His good ear was the right one, and Julio turned his head slightly. Audrey knew something important was coming.

"You're ten-tenths hot-blooded, I found that out. Anything can happen."

"I can't believe you'd even think... oh please, Julio."

"What I believe isn't so important. I wasn't here. You were. And so was Kardas—"

"And Romaine Brook!"

"Yes, her too. But at a different time, though close enough apparently so the sheriff could've drawn one of two conclusions. Either the girl did it or you and Kardas did it. But then to cover your hot-pantsy ass you got me involved by lying to the sheriff. So then they could reach for a third possibility—that I did it."

"Julio, you have—"

"Let me finish," said Julio. "That's why I acted so fast once you caught me up in your lie... That's why I got the governor's people, the state people, involved. So I could keep my hands on things. I wasn't going to have anyone think I killed my son. So when I had to protect myself, then you and Kardas got a free ride on me."

"I never dreamed anyone could think up anything this ludicrous. The way you're doing."

"You bet they can. I've often wondered, Audrey, whether you were actually clever enough to tell them I was here when I wasn't so you would force me to cover for you."

Nervously Audrey's hands rose to her neck. Her face, hidden by the starless dark, was white as a snowflake.

"I'm not that clever. But I suppose I see what you mean."

"Well, maybe you are that clever."

"But I'm not. I know that side of myself. I couldn't kill a flea and you know it."

"I think you didn't," said Julio. "But I don't *know*. Those are two different things—"

"You must believe me."

"Oh, I want to all right. I believe you because I saw the Brook girl do it. Slowly, for a year, she got into Marc's brain and blood and made him crazy. Cock happy. That's what she did, made him cock happy. She put him back on drugs when she tramped on his heart..."

"You're right, Julio, that's exactly what she did," said Audrey, relieved that he admitted what she'd known for a very long time.

"She's a very strange young woman. One of those who kiss you with their fangs. I've known a few others like her. Knock you over with charm and you fall right on their knife."

"Calling her foxy would be—"

"You're all foxy. Everyone who's got one of those jade boxes between their legs is a fox. Women don't get really polite and safe until they're at least seventy."

Audrey smelled more tendrils of trouble rising. She'd already told Rhodes there was nothing at all between Ferenc and herself. If she admitted the truth in front of him at court, what then?

"Let me remind you," Julio said, "of how close a thing it was for you. When I came home that morning from Seattle, I drove in through the low road by the golf course only because it's shorter and I was tired... If I'd come the other way through the front gates the guards would have known I probably wasn't here that night. Your story would've been shot to hell, Audrey. That's how lucky you were."

"You've only told me a dozen times, Julio," she said irritably.

"Yes, I have. So perhaps you'll let me do the thinking around here until this trial is over."

"I couldn't agree more and—"

They both turned their heads at the sound of a sneeze.

Ferenc Kardas appeared, rubbing his nose. "Is there anything I can bring you before I retire?"

"Alone?" asked Julio.

"Julio," warned Audrey.

"Pardon," said Kardas.

"Never mind," Julio said. "I'm going up myself. Need my sleep, don't I? Get in training for the lawyers." He dismissed Kardas with a casual flip of fingers.

Audrey hugged herself. She'd left her sweater inside. A

breeze had stirred and goose flesh dimpled her arms. Julio had gone, but he left enough of himself behind for her to really think about and very hard this time.

What would he do if he ever learned that Romaine Brook really belonged to her? Worry pleated her forehead, and then it knuckled her backbone. Worries about Romaine, who chewed ceaselessly at her conscience. To have a daughter—or anyone—act the way Romaine did. The girl was a pathological liar, a user, a thief. Was Romaine crazy? Why was she the end result of what had been the love of Audrey's life? And why, oh why, did she kill Marc Sterne? How can anyone take a life like that?

And then there was Kardas. What a fool I was to get involved with him, Audrey thought. But Julio was right, damn him, I was starving....

But Romaine. God help me, what if she didn't kill Marc? How am I to bear that? We were in an absolute panic that night, and there was no time to figure anything out.

And why any story when that bastard of a Julio knew about us anyway?

Audrey knew she wasn't as quick off the mark as Julio; still, she supposed she could've been more agile, gush with enthusiasm, rush over and hug Julio. Tell him what a wonderful darling he was for giving her her very own lover, whenever she wanted, and so discreetly. Mock him so thoroughly, he would never forget he was as fallible as anyone else.

Upstairs Ferenc Kardas shaved as he always did before bed, his dark beard needing two passes every day with an electric razor. He hadn't heard much of anything downstairs, but enough to know it was serious.

Time to pull out, he told himself. The buzz of the razor kept rhythm with the feeling in his gut. A feeling that sent sure signals of dangerous weather to come.

The Noor woman. He'd have to get over there soon. He had delayed long enough. Pick up the coke, if they could find it, close out his bank accounts, and then a ticket on the next plane out.

Nassau. He liked the name, and the weather was supposed to be terrific, and he'd heard there were usually fabulous women hanging around for someone to blow them to a good time. He would need to find a woman, maybe two, preferably rich now that Audrey Sterne had spoiled him.

He switched off the razor, but the buzzing hidden in his belly went right on.

In bed he thought of the Gabors. They were Hungarians married to rich men and would know people in Nassau. Perhaps he could approach them. Hungarians were sentimentalists, looked after each other...

A soft rap on the door startled him and he leaped off his bed.

"Me," said Audrey when she opened the door. She saw the thin line of ebony hair descending from his navel. "Put a robe on, get decent."

Ferenc's chest tightened. "Are you stupid to come here with your husband home?"

"We have to talk, Ferenc. Now, while there's still time."

Kardas saw the look on her face. He could pack his possessions in an hour, but would rather stay on for a few more days. He'd listen.

"You're going to have to back me up on something," Audrey told him. "It's for your own good."

Switching on a light, Julio poured a glass of water from a carafe on his bedside table. As he drank, he debated whether to take a sleeping pill. Wouldn't do, he decided, to be groggy tomorrow. He'd try going to sleep again.

It's the appearance thing, he thought.

A man who couldn't keep a leash on his own wife—how could he be expected to manage five enterprises? Several times the directors of various boards that he chaired had dropped edgy cues his way. He was in his seventies, and shouldn't he be stepping aside to make room for the younger men? "Times have changed, Julio," they would tell him. "Why not enjoy what you've got?"

He had bailed Audrey out of her miseries in London, partly to show them all that he was still strong enough to attract and satisfy a much younger woman.

This was the second time now that he'd bailed her out, and it would be the last. The first time, in London, he had agreed to be named as correspondent in a divorce over adultery. Audrey got her divorce and he got her, though he'd never laid a hand on her. Not in that way. He had wanted Audrey as he had wanted few other people in his life. So he had agreed to be a patsy only because her London lawyers had said it was the surest way to get Hubbard-Hewes to agree to a quick divorce. It should have been the other way around. He knew all about Hubbard-Hewes, a good showman, and one of the most notorious cocksmen he'd ever heard of—in a class with Errol Flynn or one of those players. Now that Julio thought about it, he remembered that he and Audrey hadn't slept together for at least a week after their wedding.

He hadn't bargained on all her bedroom urges, though. But he could take care of that at home, out of sight of the world, throwing a Kardas her way.

That plan had backfired. But how far?

If he were to be sniggered at in public, he would have to show that his husbandly trust was misplaced, sneered at, and spat upon.

Audrey had no idea what oceans he'd moved to protect her when Marc died. Calling the governor, where he had influence—the real push—asking for some help. Which was immediately provided by sending him Pritter, who they claimed was their best man in Southern California.

Yet Pritter had failed to keep him out of the trial, and that item would not be forgotten on Julio's agenda. Because now he would have to make a public spectacle of his wife—as that little piece of witchcraft, Romaine Brook, had done so blithely. Hold himself up to public gossip as well. Even scorn. Bad for one's appearance, a man in his position.

Julio tossed again, on his side.

Audrey, he knew, put a high premium on money, on her personal security. What woman didn't? And what man, for that matter? But Julio was quite sure she would never involve herself in the murder of his son. She was too keen, reasonably loyal, and didn't have the instinct of a killer.

Get Marc out of the way so she stood to have all his millions? Not likely.

But Kardas, he was a different fish. Cunning, even sly, and someone trained in a foreign army.

Julio knew what the investigator's reports said: Kardas

had preceded them up to the house by several minutes, while Audrey and he straightened up the boat.

And there were lights on, lights that hadn't been on when they had left the dock earlier. *They* said. Kardas had spent several minutes up there, alone, to do anything he pleased.

To Marc, when Marc was drugged?

Two hours later, sleep finally tapped on Julio's eyelids.

Chapter Nineteen

"I've given you my answer, young man," said Julio Sterne to a very impressed Tommy Burke.

"But if you weren't at your home that night, where were you?"

"Seattle."

"But the sheriff's reports have you in Malibu Pointe. At home."

"Somebody got mixed up then. Probably me."

Surprise washed over Rhodes. Seattle? The courtroom stirred. Four jurors hunched over the rail of the jurors' box.

"Would you explain that for us?" Tommy asked.

"I can't. Not very simply anyway."

"Try, Mr. Sterne. We have to know."

"I arrived home very early in the morning. It was still dark. I knew something was wrong the minute I went through the front door. There were those ribbons across the entry to the living room. Coffee cups, cigarette smell, chalk dust on the floor. All those things."

"And then what?"

"My wife told me my son was dead," said Julio. His eyes bore in on Romaine sitting ten yards away.

"The first you knew of it?"

"Yes."

"But then why did Mrs. Sterne say you were upstairs all the time?"

"Ask her."

Audrey lied to us, Rhodes thought. How many times? A small gnawing doubt started in the center of his stomach.

"Yes, I will ask her," Tommy said. "But you know you gave that same impression when you made a statement. The one to the sheriff and the state investigators."

"I was sick about it, under strain. Confused too."

"Confused?"

"Yes, confused and broken up about it. I don't know if you've ever lost a son. When you lose one it breaks you down and tears you apart. Like a truck hit me . . ."

"I'm sure it must have been awful, Mr. Sterne. I'm sorry. Everyone is—"

"Not so sorry if you have to call me down here to talk about it forever."

"We have to know what happened," Tommy said. Sorrow tugged at his face, but he pressed on. "Mr. Sterne, could you prove, if you had to, that you were in Seattle that night?"

"I'm no liar, young fellow."

"I'm not implying you are, sir. But we have to square everything up, you see, and this is vital to Miss Brook's interests."

"Why? She killed him. Don't you know that by now?"

"You can't say that. Not here, you can't. Your Honor"—Tommy Burke glanced up at Rhodes—"please have that stricken from the record. In no way is Mr. Sterne competent to—"

"Agreed," said Rhodes. He informed the court reporter and told the jury to disregard the statement, and why they should.

Pritter dug at his ear with one fat finger. For over an hour he'd gotten nothing more than frosty stares from Julio Sterne.

Tommy went on. "Mr. Sterne, would you be willing to amend your statement to the sheriff and the state investigators as to your whereabouts that night?"

Sterne agreed.

Tommy itched his pink chin. "Mr. Sterne, how is it the gate guards at Malibu Pointe never mentioned seeing you that morning? I don't believe they listed you as coming through the gate."

"They never saw me."

"Never saw you?"

"That's right. I came in by the lower road. The one that goes by the golf course."

"Why did you do that?"

"It's closer to the Santa Monica airport by nearly a mile. That's why. I use it frequently."

"So the guards never saw you."

"No, the guards aren't there to keep track of me or the other residents."

"Just to protect your privacy?"

"That's correct."

"How many residents are there at Malibu Pointe?"

"Twenty-one."

"And you, or your property, occupies the tip of the Pointe?"

"Yes."

"How big is your home there, Mr. Sterne?"

"About 14,000 square feet. Six bedrooms, two ocean decks, eight rooms on the first floor. About that big."

"That's pretty big... Would you say it's big enough so that four or five people could be in different parts of your home, and none of them would necessarily know that *all* the others are there?"

"I don't understand the question."

Burke repeated it.

"I suppose so, yes," replied Sterne. "But I don't think that's—"

Burke interrupted. "We're more interested in what you actually know, and not so much about what you *think*, Mr. Sterne."

"Don't you be flippant with me, young man."

"I'll try not to... But someone else could've been there in the house that night. Someone else besides your son and Romaine Brook?"

"Who?"

"It doesn't matter who. Anyone at all. And they could even have come there by way of the golf course road, yes?"

"Not easily. You need one of those electronic clickers to open the gate on that road. Only residents have them."

"I see," said Tommy. "Well, someone could come in by water then?"

"Probably would've been heard, if they had. I'm sure of it."

"Possibly. But what about some other resident of Malibu Pointe. Supposing one of them entered your home?"

"Without being invited? That's hardly likely."

"But it's possible, isn't it? And in a home your size, others already there might not even know it."

Sterne didn't have to think long about where Burke was headed. "Especially, I suppose, if you're referring to my wife or Ferenc Kardas."

"Precisely. Or anyone else. But let's say them... Supposing, Mr. Sterne, that someone lured your son and Romaine Brook to your—"

"I won't listen to this!" Sterne cut Tommy short. "Those're nothing more than cheap insinuations—"

"Maybe so, Mr. Sterne, maybe so. But they are not *cheap* possibilities... you already admitted that others could be in the house at the same time and not be discovered. That goes for Mrs. Sterne and your houseman, who both know the house so well, wouldn't it?"

"So would the architect who designed it."

"Of course. But just so we agree that others may have been present that night. That's all I want to point out."

Sterne pulled a face, saying nothing.

Tommy Burke quizzed him for a time about his son. How did they get on? Was he aware of Marc's drug habit? Marc had even spent time in a rehabilitation program, hadn't he? Did he know that Marc might have been dealing drugs?

"That's an absolute untruth," stormed Julio Sterne. "By God, I'll have you for slander if you keep on this way."

"All right," said Tommy. "I'll take it back, but there may be testimony later that he was a dealer."

"By her. She's a cute liar. So don't you believe it." Julio Sterne half rose out of his chair. His lean and serious face surveyed the room, the press and the jury to whom he said: "My son had a drug problem. But he was a good boy, a fine boy. I spoiled him. He had too much, too soon. But I'm a well-to-do man, and my son never had to sell drugs. Don't you believe it and another thing—"

But Rhodes stopped him. Calming Sterne down was no easy task. The man was a power, used to being heard whenever he wanted to be heard.

"Have you got anything more?" Rhodes asked Burke when the air settled again.

"I'm through, your Honor."

No, you're not, dammit, Rhodes was thinking. But he could let it ride for the moment. He would see what turf Pritter would smooth down first.

Pritter approached the stand. He started a friendly smile at Julio Sterne, but as suddenly it disappeared. "Romaine Brook testified to this court," he began, "that you personally offered to get her a contract for several films if she would stop seeing your son."

"That's as wrong as it can be. A damn lie," said Sterne, changing his story from the one given to the reporter who had called the studio.

"A damn lie?" Pritter repeated for the jury.

"That's what I said."

"She imagined it somehow?"

"Don't ask me. I never offered her anything of the kind."

"But you didn't like the idea of her seeing your son?"

"No. I did not. Especially when I found out what she was like."

"What is she like?"

"She's a master at using people. Ten sides of deceit and trickery to you, young lady," he accused, looking straight at Romaine, whose mouth opened slightly. She tugged at Tommy's sleeve and one soft sob carried across the first rows.

"She's a good actress, you'd say?" Pritter went on.

"First-rate. I'll give her that. She lives in a world of make-believe. A sociopath, I'd say."

"Sir!" Tommy gangled to his feet. "Your Honor, no! Wait a minute. The witness can't say that. He's not competent to make a psychological profile of my client."

"Sustained," ordered Rhodes. "Strike that . . . Mr. Sterne, you'll have to—"

"Can't I have my own opinion?" asked Sterne.

"Not unless you're qualified as an expert first."

Pritter had made his point, though. He hardly heard Rhodes

finish his ruling. "All right," he went on. "Let me ask you this, Mr. Sterne. You are currently chairman of how many companies?"

"Five."

"How large are they? Together?"

"About 10,000 employees."

"And in sales?"

"About 2 billion."

"How many executives work for you?"

"Several hundred."

"And you personally select them?"

"Many of them, yes. The top ones."

"So you do know something about reaching judgments on people. On managers. Their habits and capacities, ability to operate, how they make decisions, how skilled they are with people?"

"I think I do."

"You do it often? Assess people?"

"I have to, or I couldn't run the businesses."

Pritter smiled. "That's all, Mr. Sterne. Thank you very much for your time," he said trying to ingratiate himself as he thought again of Oldes & Farnham and the new condo he'd bought on the strength of their offer, which was really Sterne's gift. He went back to his seat, believing he had shown Julio in a favorable light.

Tommy Burke took one more turn. "We know you're a very busy and very successful businessman, Mr. Sterne. A really great reputation for it, I guess... But you're not a trained psychologist, are you?"

"I read up on it."

"You do?"

"Yes, I do."

"But you don't hold a degree?"

"I don't have to. I never had time for college, young man. My degrees I keep at the bank, where I've received all sorts of degrees. Green ones."

Laughter erupted across the room.

"But you're not competent, are you, to make a professional diagnosis of my client?"

"Why not? I hired her, or my studio did. Made her famous."

"Yes, but that doesn't entitle you, does it, to have an expert's opinion as to her personality makeup? Traits?"

"For me, it does."

"But another psychologist, a trained expert, one with years of study and practice, might not accept your opinion?"

"And yet they might."

"But not as a professional?"

"Not that way, no."

"Thank you."

About to leave the stand as Tommy Burke returned to his seat, Sterne looked imposing, able to issue orders to anyone there. And leaving no doubt with anyone those orders would be carried out with precision.

Alley rules, Rhodes was thinking.

This was ring time, and you had to belt away whenever an opening came. Circle and hit and hit again until the jury, who were the only judges who counted here, began to score their cards. Your way.

Was Burke saving it for Audrey? That might be too late, the last round.

"Mr. Sterne, one moment please," Rhodes said.

Both Burke and Pritter came up fast with their heads.

"What is it?" Sterne asked.

"If you'd take your seat again for a moment."

"Aren't we done here? I'm quite busy."

"I'm sure you are. But we wouldn't want to call you back if we can avoid it."

Sterne inspected Rhodes with care. A shrewd look, the one of the jeweler searching a stone for its more obvious flaws. He saw the crescent scar over Rhodes's eyebrow, and noticed that neither eyebrow moved over his eyes.

Julio Sterne sat down. Never before in all his seventy-odd years had he set foot in a courtroom. He found it a nuisance.

Anger rattled Rhodes's feelings. Had Audrey lied to him about everything? No question of it now; she had assuredly lied to the deputy sheriff about her husband's whereabouts on the night of Marc's death. What else?

Was there a conspiracy to get Romaine, hang her on a limb and let her swing?

Audrey or Romaine? A woman he'd loved mightily or

the one he wanted to know and love? The surest way of getting Romaine out of trouble was to start some for Audrey. Whatever choice he made, it would count as a betrayal.

Rhodes forced himself to speak: "Mr. Sterne, one of the things we must do here is compile a straight record. Testimony is taken, pulled apart, and put together again so we can all see everything as clearly as possible. Time goes by, we forget. Errors of memory are made sometimes. We have to try, try again for the truth..."

He hesitated. Go on, he told himself. That's your daughter—look at her, she is you. She smiles at you, needs you.

"I want you, Mr. Sterne, to answer a question of a most personal nature. Someone needs to ask it so that everyone has their say. Are you with me?" Now Rhodes's eyebrows did move up.

"I believe I am. What is it?"

The front row reporters poised over their pads, two of them whispering something to each other. Romaine looked blankly at Rhodes, who saw Pritter rolling up a paper in his hands.

"Two days ago," Rhodes said, "some testimony took place here by the defendant. And in part of it she revealed—"

"About my wife? I've already heard about it."

"Would you care to have it read to you?"

"I would not."

"Then I'll ask you. Are you aware, or ever been aware, of some, well, romantic attachment between your wife and Ferenc Kardas?"

Julio Sterne's pause was lengthy. He looked at Burke, over to the jury, then threw a broken bottle glance at Pritter. He was no longer bored.

"Why not ask them?" he replied coldly.

"I'm asking you, Mr. Sterne," said Rhodes, wondering if the floating pause was a tactical slur against a straying wife. Had the jury gotten that nuance?

"Those are matters a man doesn't always know about."

"Agreed. But the question is, *did you*? Were you aware?"

"I'm aware that Miss Brook, there, says anything that runs through her mind."

"Please stick to the question."

Another silence.

"I can't say," said Sterne.

"Can't or won't?"

"Anything is possible between men and women. Are you asking me to call my wife unfaithful?"

Rhodes heaved a deep breath. An image of Audrey making love to Kardas emerged in his brain, engraving itself forever. He tried to erase it, but the fog of jealousy had taken up full time residence. Was Sterne lying, trying now to cover for Audrey's earlier lie? Was that it? Were they trying to hang Romaine in some family conspiracy?

"Not at all, Mr. Sterne," Rhodes went on. "I have no wish to embarrass you. It's possible the allegation may have a bearing on this trial. You are one person who might shed light on it."

"What bearing?" asked Julio. But he already knew and guessed it was bound to come up again.

"The question. Please answer. Directly."

"I never saw anything," said Sterne.

"Never?"

"No."

"If you didn't see anything, were you at any time aware of anything between them?"

"They're young. Younger than me. Perhaps they had some attraction for one another. Who would know better than they?"

"No one. But you, you yourself, never harbored any suspicion?"

"Let me put it this way," said Julio Sterne bluntly. "I never saw anything, and don't you try to say I have. Suggest that I'm a voyeur or one of those deviants."

"That's your answer."

"It is."

"Thank you very much. And for your time."

When Sterne stepped down, Rhodes adjourned for the day after Pritter said he had nothing more to ask. His thoughts lay in broken coils. He needed time to think, to find Fahey and meet with him before Burke started in on Audrey.

The jury gathered in one of the back corridors, ready for their trip back to the hotel. A few talked of Sterne's testimony. The bailiff gave them a warning glance. By the time they'd taken their seats in the van headed back for the Biltmore, they started gabbing again.

They were thinking, talking and thinking some more.

A new bailiff raised his voice. He reminded the jurors sharply that there was to be no more talk of the trial. "Against the judge's instructions," he scolded. "And you know it."

One leggy juror, the brunette with the horn-rimmed glasses, was thinking that everything really fun was against some rule or other. She liked Julio Sterne. Suave and obviously powerful. What kind of a bitch would cheat on a man like him?

She saw nothing wrong as she worked her way up the aisle to sit next to the new bailiff. He was there, cute and available, studdy-looking. She was sick and tired of this trial. Whoever had done away with Marc Sterne would be the last thing she intended to think about tonight.

Chapter Twenty

A voice inside Audrey coached her to say what she was incapable of saying. She tried to shout it down, but the shout wouldn't carry. Not uphill, not sideways, not anywhere.

Sitting there, she looked as unlikely as an Arctic rose in her pink linen suit, white blouse, and a lilac paisley scarf caught by a circular gold pin under her throat. Beautifully nervous, her face struggled for calm against her moist eyes and modest smile. She looked exposed, yet indignant at having to explain herself.

Fleetingly she looked at the jury. Was that a wink from the tall brunette with the horn-rims?

Rhodes shifted his eyes away, so vast and sudden were

the echoes of her again. Real ones, imagined ones, every kind, and especially the latest one. As a liar.

And where in God's name was Fahey, he wondered.

Tommy Burke reminded Audrey she was still under oath. He read to her from her earlier testimony when the trial had first opened; then of Romaine's testimony; and finally Julio's evasive remarks of the day before.

"Some of these matters," finished Tommy, "are unclear to us. So if you'll help, we can try to straighten them out."

"I'll be glad to."

"Good," said Tommy, thinking he'd rarely seen anyone so ravishing.

He moved away, getting her in fuller view. Standing by the jury, one hand on the rail, he eased the weight on his tired knees.

"Several weeks ago, Mrs. Sterne, you stated that Mr. Sterne was upstairs when the Malibu sheriff arrived . . . That was after you called the sheriff, and after the body of Marc Sterne was found."

"I thought so at the time."

"Can you tell us why you thought so?"

"The whole ordeal was so wretched. A big blur."

"But your statement, that wasn't so blurred."

"I was."

"What made you believe your husband was upstairs?"

"The lights were on."

"And they weren't on when you left on the boat with Ferenc Kardas?"

"The dock lights were, but not the upstairs lights in the house."

"So you believed Mr. Sterne had come home and was upstairs?"

"Yes."

"You didn't think your husband might've come home while you were out on the boat, and discovered the body?"

"It's a very big house. I thought—well, I wasn't exactly—I don't know. But no one expected Marc to be there that night."

"Well, your husband said to this courtroom that he spent the night in Seattle."

"It turns out he did."

"While you went off boating with Mr. Kardas?"

"That's where I was—"

"—During the time," Tommy kept going, "when your stepson Marc was supposedly being put to death by Romaine Brook."

"She was there."

"We all know she was. But why did you say your husband was there when he was actually in Seattle?"

"I was in terrible shock. My wits weren't about me."

"Must've been terrible," Tommy said sympathetically.

"It was, believe me."

"But you admit you made a serious mistake thinking your husband was at home?"

"I erred, yes."

"And didn't retract the statement later? With the sheriff or the state investigators?"

Audrey looked at Rhodes beseechingly. He barely nodded, as if she were a stranger passing on some deserted stretch of beach.

"Mrs. Sterne?" said Tommy.

"I didn't retract it, no. I guess I thought my husband straightened it out . . . when he met with them the next day."

"But he didn't, did he?"

"I suppose not."

"Did you think that was right?"

"I didn't think about it at all. We were all so upset. A nightmare."

"Mrs. Sterne, have you ever seen this?" Burke waved a piece of paper. "It's one of the sheriff's reports."

"Should I have? I don't think I have."

Burke read an excerpt.

"It leaves one," he said, "with the distinct impression that three people were on your boat that night, doesn't it? The third one being your husband?"

"Well, he wasn't. That's obvious to anyone."

"Not so obvious from this report, though." He waved it again.

"I didn't write it either."

"One wonders who did. And who's covering for whom, Mrs. Sterne? You signed it."

"I would've signed anything, I was so undone."

Right there Tommy could've put her to the stake, but his aim was merely to cast doubt about the true events of that night. He wanted to be cautious about this woman, who might capture the jury's sympathy. So he trudged elsewhere.

To the other places of her life within the Sterne family. Marc's relationship with his father? So-so? Good, devoted, enviable? Bad?

The usual, she replied—arguments at times, even fights, but a strong bond had existed between them. An only son, a successor.

And narcotics?

Yes, Marc had dueled with his demon. So many young people did nowadays.

"And now, Mrs. Sterne," Tommy said, "Marc's secretary testified here a few days ago. She told us you left her with a message for Marc to come to your home for dinner that night. He came but you had gone out on the boat."

"I never left any message that day. Otherwise, if dinner was planned, I would've been there."

"The secretary said you spoke to her."

"I did not!" Audrey cried.

"Who then?"

"I haven't the foggiest."

Romaine settled back in her chair. Behind her dreamy mask she kept studying the woman she never knew was her own mother. Sitting only ten yards apart, they were separated by the distance to the sun and back.

"Was it some practical joke? Calling him out there for dinner?"

"Not by me," Audrey said.

"But you'd called other times. The secretary said she knew your voice."

"I know when I call and when I don't."

"On that day. Seven months ago, you remember?"

"I wouldn't forget asking Marc for dinner. Not that night or any other."

"Are we to believe the secretary is in error, Mrs. Sterne? She logged your call."

"Not mine. I made no such call."

"You're sure?"

"Of course, I am."

"Just as you were sure your husband was upstairs that night?"

"Anyone, when you're under stress, can make mistakes."

"They often do, yes," Tommy agreed. "And we seem to have had a lot of them in the past several days."

Burke aimed his remarks squarely at the jury. Leaving them now, he passed Pritter's table as he came closer to the witness stand. Pritter stared straight ahead, not at Burke or Audrey or even Rhodes. But at the wall clock silently ticking away, a tangible reminder of how the hours and minutes cut away at the state's case. And himself with it.

"Mrs. Sterne," Tommy said respectfully. "The night you came in on the boat to the dock. You told us when you first testified that after the boat was tied up, you stayed behind to clean up."

"That's right. Some dishes and things."

"What things?"

"Glasses. Spoons and forks. I can't remember exactly."

"Glasses? Had you been drinking?"

"A cocktail or two."

"By yourself?"

A trap, and Audrey knew it. "Yes, by myself."

"Mr. Kardas, he had no alcohol?"

"Not that I saw."

"Would you have seen him if he did?"

"Most certainly."

"He was steering your boat?"

"Yes. Sometimes I did, though. I like handling the boat."

"While drinking?"

"Possibly."

"Do you often drink with your help?"

"I resent that."

"Do you?"

"Yes, I do. And no, I don't get overly friendly with the servants."

"Not even that night?"

"That was different. The boat's only forty-eight feet long. So you're close together sometimes."

"How close."

"Close enough," Audrey replied resentfully.

"He went up to the house ahead of you?"

"Yes."

Burke referred to some notes from his pocket. "By about ten minutes or so. That's how you testified."

"About."

"Did he go up to see what those upstairs lights were all about?"

"I asked him to . . . Those weren't on when we left, as I said."

"You weren't sure, perhaps, who was up there?"

"No."

"Kardas was gone ten minutes?"

"Approximately, I guess."

"That's a long time. He discovered Marc's body, and he didn't come back to tell you?"

"I don't know why. He told me he was shocked when he found Marc."

"Too shocked, I suppose, to run upstairs if you both thought Mr. Sterne was there. Grief stricken, powerless to act or talk. That's what you said in these reports . . . that your husband was there, and you knew the condition he was in."

Audrey seemed flustered. The tips of her fingers alighted on the pin on her scarf, and she twisted it back and forth.

"I don't know."

"Could it have been, Mrs. Sterne, that you knew all along Mr. Sterne wouldn't be home that night. That Marc would come at your invitation . . . and you and Ferenc Kardas meant harm to Marc?"

The courtroom simmered. Murmurs climbed up into spoken words. Rhodes rapped for order. Pritter scrambled up, bellowing an objection.

Rhodes heard him out, then allowed Burke to proceed with his question. He saw a freeze gathering in Audrey's eyes. Her chin shoved out, and her face assumed the texture of marble.

"And while Kardas was up there something happened," Burke nearly shouted at Audrey.

"Any you seem to forget and forget that Romaine Brook was there first . . . That's been proven!" said Audrey, her voice rising feverishly.

"But what's not proven is that she contributed to Marc's

death. There was opportunity for at least one or two others to kill him, wasn't there?" returned Tommy. "And why did you lie about where your husband was?"

"That's stupid. Marc had everything in this world to live for," said Audrey, evading the point.

"One would surely think so. But the fact is, and it is a fact, Mrs. Sterne, that none of us really know what happened. Just a bunch of accusations, isn't it?"

"You forget another thing," said Audrey with a triumphant gleam. "We . . . I never knew Marc was even there."

"So you say. His secretary says differently. She is misleading us?"

"A nice way to put it, I'd say."

Tommy turned again to the jury. He met them with an honest, open expression. "Well, we have a good jury here. The best, and they've heard quite a lot already. They can decide," he said before wheeling around again, nearly stumbling, to face Audrey.

"Mrs. Sterne, are you now, or have you ever been, intimately involved with Ferenc Kardas?"

"The houseman!" she cried out.

"Your houseman, yes."

"That's insulting. You're trying to throw dirt around." She looked up at Rhodes for the second time.

There she was, mother in front of their daughter, getting scalped. She'd lied to him, perhaps. Rhodes loved her, always had, a love ordained a thousand years ago. Now, though, the blue flame of her that warmed his heart flickered out. Inside, he had become two men, torn, all in a matter of days. He looked briefly at Romaine who seemed steady enough at the moment. Mother against daughter, and it began to remind him of a grim Greek tragedy.

"You'll have to answer," he told Audrey quietly.

"Why? He's offending me."

Because, Rhodes told her, a statement under oath had been made. Other circumstances now coming to light made a reply necessary. Someone, he said, was playing with the truth or had forgotten it.

"You mean things she said?" Audrey glared again at Romaine, who was suddenly pale as the first winter snow.

"Yes, Mrs. Sterne, by *our* defendant," Tommy confirmed.

"She's a blind liar then!"

Romaine shrugged. Rhodes thought he saw tears glistening below her eyes. She wiped them once, and the jury saw her.

"But did you have an affair with Kardas? That's my question," Burke reminded Audrey.

"You're just being ugly and horrid."

"We're not all blessed with your beauty, that's true, Mrs. Sterne . . . For now we need a horridly straight answer."

"Never is your answer."

"Never?"

"I just said it."

Her hands were at the gold pin once more, worrying it around. The women, more than the men, in the jury began to notice her movements.

"And so," Tommy said, "we're all to believe that Marc's secretary and now Romaine Brook are both not telling the truth. But you and the deputy sheriff and your husband never make a misstep. Never get anything wrong. And never, in your case, looked at another man, or took up with one?"

Rhodes wanted to stop it but he couldn't. He was surprised Burke could swing so hard.

"I said I hadn't!" snapped Audrey.

"But you were divorced, weren't you?"

"I was."

"In England, and on grounds of adultery."

Audrey gasped, then groaned softly.

"You've been a real help," Tommy said. "Thank you, Mrs. Sterne."

Pritter glided her through a few steps. He let her go after a few attempts to show her as a woman who had it all: many more years ahead of her; marriage to one of the most prominent men in the west; a golden life. Why would she risk everything, her reputation, on a servant? Pritter asked the courtroom.

Why would she hide the existence of my daughter from me? Rhodes thought later in his chambers. But he failed to answer his question. There was a call to take from Sacramento. Not the aide, Macklin Price was telling him, this time it was the governor.

Chapter Twenty-One

It was raining again.

Rhodes swept his sleeves as the door opened, and he glimpsed the willowy shadow of Wanda Fahey, then saw all of her as she dried him off with a quick hug.

Tall as Fahey, slim and dark haired and with high cheekbones, she'd been a model when younger. Before Fahey had written on her, given her a life of despair, she'd been a lively woman of deep religious feeling. Not overly pious but a real kneeler, twice each week at her parish.

Rhodes talked with her for a few minutes. Where had he been? Damn the time, how was she? Sacramento? Wanda told him he was a waste, that he should marry and never mind what they said about it. Admiring him then, the way a suffering woman admires a trip around the world, one only for and by herself.

"Wears my clothes, he does, like some fag," Wanda said without rancor. "Never know what to make of him anymore."

She has become Fahey, he thought, a clone if that were conceivable. Even talked the same way. "Your clothes?"

"My silk scarfs. Uses them for belts. Ascots too."

"We'll have to take him shopping."

"He's in his hole over the garage," she said. "Doing arts, he says. Trying on my bra, more likely."

"I'll find him."

"Tea? I'll make some for us."

"Wonderful, Wanda."

"Come for dinner soon? We could go out for a change," she said dejectedly." "Say you will."

"Yes and yes. Has he been around lately?"

"I gave him your messages." Wanda sighed. "He's having those moods again or something." She tapped her head. "Won't even give me a good morning most days."

"Maybe I can gas him up."

"Would you?"

"I'll try."

"He's such a runt at times. Takes mothering, Cliff. Grown like him and he still needs it."

"But what a runt, eh?"

"Ummhh . . . Well, you know the way," said Wanda, thumbing the air.

Up the half-flight of stairs, Rhodes turned left, went through a crawlway, and knocked on a Dutch door. Entering, he saw Fahey sprawled in a leather chair beside a desk made from a long plywood plank. Art books were scattered everywhere, some open, and others lay about in small stacks.

"Judges are forsaken," Fahey offered, twirling an ivory tipped walking stick. "Going to the opera soon. Getting my duds cleaned up."

"Didn't think we had opera in Los Angeles."

"They're mounting a new company soon. Specializing in Balkan works. The city needs a fleck of culture . . . Take that chair that I spent my life making."

The chair was a wooden stool. One leg was shorter and the stool wobbled. Rhodes sat anyway.

"Have a cure? A what-ails-you?"

"Wanda's putting tea on."

"Is she now? Next thing we know she'll have us on those nature grains she eats. Sickening stuff, makes holes in your bones."

"You ought to take her out, buy her a steak."

"Won't eat one. Loves the cows too much. She's gone Buddhist on me."

"Make her an offer."

"Ahh! Then she wants the dress, and the hairdo. Be Tiffany diamonds next."

"Nice woman, Alonzo, you're lucky."

Fahey looked away. He rolled the walking stick across the plywood, and it stopped at the wall. He tightened the collar of the brocade robe he wore; silk, a dark Chinese maroon, threadbare at the elbows, and the back crocheted with dragons.

"How's my lad Burke circusing?"

"All right, far as it goes."

"And his glowworm? The enchantress?"

"Romaine Brook?"

Fahey yessed with his head. He dropped his hands and at the same time a curl of black hair fell across his brow.

"She's holding up, I guess," Rhodes told him. "I came to see you about her."

"Not out for your stroll then?"

"Not on this night anyway."

"Let's talk about the lady Sterne. A real looker, is she?"

"Pretty nice, Alonzo."

"Here she's been, all this time, having it off with the butler in the belfry . . . Got that tidbit from that he-man Burke late this very day."

Rhodes tried not to wince. "That's not a certainty by any means."

"The rich ones, you have to chain 'em up. Get ideas, go guilty over the poor. Have to fuck their way across their moats, try the muscles of the peasants for a change."

"Alonzo . . ."

"They all do it, mind you. Had a few myself. Think their cunt's the Grail. Have to wiggle it now and then with the lower ranks."

"What's aching you anyway?"

"On the wagon and it's breaking my soul apart. Blood went yellow overnight. Piss it out four times a day. So weak now I have to stay home and listen to Wanda pray."

Rhodes laughed. "You? On the wagon?"

"The gypsy went and hung me on the peg. Going to whip me into shape, ready me up for the opera season."

"What gypsy?" Rhodes had a faint, disturbing recollection but wasn't sure.

"A woman I know, a real thrasher, Cliff. Solves the sins, does it all, sees a great century ahead of us. Ought to have her on one of your juries. Clean things up in no time, she would."

"I'll have to meet her one day," Rhodes said, unsure if Fahey's imagination was about to burst its pipes again.

The door swung wide as Wanda came in with the tea. She slid a tray onto Fahey's plank, then poured from a silver-bellied pot, dented on one side. She handed Rhodes a white mug and another to Alonzo, whose hair she combed twice with her fingers.

"Thank you, mermaid," said Fahey to his wife, leaning forward to wrap a hand around her thigh, pulling her against his chest. "Isn't she the whole bolt of satin? I tell you the best, a gift of the Khahil . . . Look at her, will you? Get a castle for her on the Saudi slave market."

Wanda whirled away, laughing, her lithe body arching like a dancer's as she closed the door.

Rhodes burned his mouth on the steaming tea. The wet night thrummed at the window behind Fahey.

"It's time to find Cullis, is that his name?" Rhodes said. "Get him and take him back to the apartment. Show him what you found. But keep the cocaine there, and if there's any trouble on that one, call me immediately."

"Why now?" Fahey asked warily.

"The trial is swinging everywhere. I want all the possible evidence out in the open."

"Maybe it's not connected. You told me that once, as I think you'll easily remember."

"What if it is?"

"Let it go, Christ—"

"That's the jury's choice. Always."

Fahey pondered again, then said: "Not for me. I'm out of it. Got a smell to it dirty as the German High Command."

"You did everything asked of you. I thank you, I really do."

Fahey glowered. "First time I ever held out on a client, even a non-paying client."

"You can tell him now. Or soon."

"You're over the ledge, aren't you? Way over the mark . . . why're you doing all this?"

"Everything in this trial is finally out on the laundry line. I want it *all* out there."

"For her?" asked Fahey, not knowing which *her*.

"For me," Rhodes evaded. "A problem either way if she's convicted and it goes up on appeal." A weak excuse but all he could offer as a reason, and he'd already used it once before.

They crisscrossed excuses on how Fahey could ask for an opportunity to go back to Marc Sterne's. Rhodes made a suggestion. Fahey had a better one. More talk, endless, talk enough for a U.N. treaty.

"Send me Tommy-boy. I'll tell the louter where it is. Christ, he's a tall one, isn't he?"

"That's too fishy," Rhodes reasoned.

"Got a stink to it like—"

"Do it for me, Alonzo . . . You're really doing it for your client," said Rhodes, ready to grasp at anything workable.

"Ah, but the client is still in the dark . . . The glowworm. Listen, Cliff, the gypsy told me about her."

"I don't care about your damn gyp—"

"She's real, real as the night, has stars for eyes," Fahey informed him. "Don't you slur on her."

"Sorry. But you have to listen to me now."

Rhodes explained what was going on in court. Suspicions were loose. Ferenc Kardas would be on the stand the next day, and this was the time to get everything out in the open.

"I've got myself some work. A fat old mogul up in San Francisco has hired good Fahey to find art his wife walked out with. Pair of Monets . . . Can't trust the bitches, can you?"

"Can you?"

"Will I?"

"Yes, will you?" Rhodes was pleading.

"Have more tea. Cheer up. This'll take a moment, and I've still my license to think about, boyo."

Though Fahey, the gourmand of the unseen, had said neither yes nor no to Rhodes's appeal. "There are other rules need looking at," he'd said on the way out, hobbling along on his walking stick, feigning a gimp leg to go with his gimp arm.

Holding Rhodes back at the door, onto his women thing again, Fahey spelled out an ultra-sheer theory for marveling at—very close now, he expounded, no more than a short fathom away to explaining women for all of posterity. Getting the true range now that the gypsy was putting him wise.

"Fantastic, she is, Cliff, and with elegant sentiments. Still wears one of those garter belts."

And did this long sought revelation qualify for a copyright? Or at least a patent? "A man, any man, reaches his highest level of sanctity, of earthly heaven, when he learns women were sent here to keep us out of God's busy way . . . That's why they have all those round and gorgeous tree ornaments on them. To distract us from real sin. That's for honest. Don't you see, Cliff, the women are given to us as presents. Treat them like God and they're ours forever. They are Him, aren't they? Have His eggs inside them too, and that's why."

Aren't they?

Yes, Rhodes patiently agreed. He could do no less, actually, knowing that three of them were front and center in his life at the moment.

Outside, all the other rains came down harder. Even the Bentley looked drowned, but no more drowned than Rhodes was feeling.

He was putting the fix in, something he'd never done before. Fahey might end up owning him forever. Fiercely wrong what he was doing, but he had no other ground on which to fight openly for Romaine. Slinking around behind the scenes, asking his best pal to pull a stunt on the jury . . . and about juries Rhodes knew plenty. How they turned their feelings one way this day and the other way the next. A slow and hidden thing like the rotation of the earth. There was no sensing them hour by hour. So you saved up till the end, then hit them with the haymaker that usually put their lights out.

He'd done it to juries before. Many times. But never cheating them and never as judge.

Chapter Twenty-Two

A replay.

Once again the jury was led deep into a bewildering jungle. Kardas had come back and foiled most of Tommy Burke's questions that morning. Denying everything, his answers laced with hostility, though always speaking in nicely accented English.

They remembered Ferenc Kardas. His well knit soldierly stance was hard to ignore; an ex-Hungarian army captain, of honor, he explained again, and never a communist. A gentleman and now a gentleman's gentleman, hired by Julio Sterne.

Pritter stood in front of him, all two hundred and forty pounds shielding Kardas from any harm. Heads in the press rows weaved back and forth trying for a better view.

"You're certain, now," Pritter asked, "that there was never anything between you and Mrs. Sterne?"

"How could there be? As I said to Mr. Burke, him there, I am only the houseman."

"She never encouraged you?"

"Encour—" Kardas halted, baffled.

"Made you think she was interested in you?"

"She is a very correct lady, Mrs. Sterne. Always very proper and good to work for."

"You never touched her?"

"By sometimes I did that—when I serve the dinner or drinks. I brush her—" Kardas made a tentative, quick motion with one hand.

"In no other way?"

"But you embarrass me, sir."

A few more questions as Pritter refuted Romaine's earlier claims of a love affair. Rhodes digested it all minutely. Neither Burke nor Pritter knew anything about the cocaine in Marc Sterne's apartment. Only Fahey and he knew, and Julio Sterne had denied his son ever dealt in drugs. A user perhaps but not a pusher. Rhodes decided to gamble. He had been watching Romaine closely for days, and he began to worry he was too obvious.

"Mr. Kardas, before you leave us, just a little more on one or two things," Rhodes said.

Kardas swung around in his seat. His face showed surprise, then composed itself into an even look, very straight and very sure.

"Please, sir," he said formally.

"You knew Marc Sterne quite well? Saw him frequently?"

"Quite well, sir."

"Remind me if you will. For how long?"

"Almost two years before he died."

"Did you ever go anywhere with him? Go out to a ballgame? A bar, for example? Anyplace at all?"

"I saw him at the house. We joke sometimes. Tell men stories. Those things."

"Nothing else?"

"No, sir. Nothing else."

The lie. Perjury. Rhodes wanted it on record so that he might come back to Kardas's denial later. How much later he could only wonder. It depended on Fahey. And was Kardas also perjuring himself about an affair with Audrey?

"You never had any business dealings with him, good or bad?" Rhodes inquired.

"Naturally not, sir. I am not in the movies."

"Thank you very much."

Rhodes smiled benevolently. He wished he could get Romaine alone for a few hours and ask, and keep asking, till he had a feel of what was really going on here. He was angry. Lies and more lies seemed to be the invisible graffiti written on his courtroom walls.

Had Audrey, then Kardas lied about an affair? Did it make any difference? It hurt, but Audrey didn't belong to him anymore if she ever really had anyway. Romaine belonged, though. Kardas had lied only a moment ago. Julio Sterne may have lied about his knowledge of his son's drug dealings. Both Audrey and Kardas had persuaded the Malibu sheriff that Julio Sterne was home that night when he was actually in Seattle.

Were they all covering up something deeper? Or just those other sins they didn't want the world to know about, the ones now coming out. And Audrey's affair, if indeed there had been one, had no real relevance to the trial.

Or did it?

Rhodes didn't know. He was only sure he was going to tip the weight if he could in favor of Romaine. He wondered why they were gunning for her so hard when the evidence against her was so circumstantial at best. A dry cottony taste filled his throat.

Macklin Price interrupted his fruit salad lunch with the news that Pritter was on the phone. He took the call to hear there was another request for a return to Marc Sterne's apartment. Burke's leg man wanted another look.

"Uncalled for," said Pritter in a bark that would startle a Doberman. "They've had their turn. The Hollywood sheriff's station isn't a courier service."

Rhodes settled it swiftly.

As the court went into afternoon session, Fahey, miles away in the Hollywood hills, tramped up the steps by Cullis's side. The lieutenant took them two at a time. Fahey lagged back, breathing, admiring the man's quick march.

"My ass is heavy with work today," Cullis complained. "Where'd you go?" He looked around for Fahey. "This got to come and go in half an hour. No more, you hear?"

Fahey tapped on a step with his walking stick. "Slow it, will you? Bad traction today. Can't get the right foot grip on the world."

"You got a broken ass, too, if we don't hurry."

"Mind your manners, Cullis. I'm an invalid this month."

"In the head, too."

"You don't sound so good today. Been kissing your frog again?"

"Whats'at!" Cullis swung around, putting a hand against

Fahey, who jerked back as if a red-hot coal just landed on him.

"You're getting a bad habit with that hand, Cully-boy. Looks like your loving hand to me, and I'd hate for it to go home crippled."

"Watch your mouth, mister."

"The hand."

"I oughta throw you down the stairs."

"I wouldn't. You geniuses have enough trouble as it is."

"I got no trouble."

"No? What about all those fancy reports you filed with the state? Sound to me like they were written on confetti."

"That's Malibu's worry."

"But this is your hand." Fahey peered down at the splayed fingers on his chest. "You making a pass at me, lover?"

Cullis mumbled as they went into the apartment, still rife with the spoiled meat smell of the decayed plants. He flipped on the lights. The place still made Fahey think of a bordello, the only business he knew he could never improve upon.

"What'cha looking for now? More of them photos?" Cullis asked.

"Something I remembered or didn't remember . . . It clicked later on in my head after we were here the last time."

"Like what?"

"Something the girl told her lawyer and me one day in her dungeon. Christ! Never go near one of those lady's schools for the chosen . . . Steal your whiskey, the sodders."

"Let's get moving."

"Sure, lover. Help me with this couch."

They yanked the long white couch away from the dull lavender wall. On the shag rug the steel table knife used on Fahey's more secretive visit gleamed its presence. He picked it up, hefting it lightly in his palm.

"Where'd that come from?" said Cullis.

"Search me."

"I just might."

Cullis eyed the knife suspiciously. Stepping back, he opened the drawer in the sidetable. Only a spoon lay there, but he remembered a similar knife from his previous visit with Fahey.

"There was one here, remember?"

"Sure do, boyo."

"Don't call me boy."

"Sho-nuff massa."

"Get on with what you want." Cullis glared at him.

Fahey put his walking stick down. Then he followed it and on his knees began to inspect the wall-plates again. The fake ones and the real ones. He swayed on his knees a few times, humming a Dublin lyric learned from his days when crawling the lesser pubs there.

"What're you lookin' for?"

"A way to save your world, Cullis. Now stand the fuck away."

Fahey pried one plate loose, the middle right one. It came right out easily to reveal the bags again. One for Alesia Noor, the other dangling a tag with Kardas's name. He smiled into his ruffled yellow shirt.

"Lemme see. What's that?" Cullis was almost on Fahey's shoulder.

"Guess. First ten don't count, handsome."

"Give it here."

"Uh-uh."

Fahey opened one bag. He dipped a finger in and then tasted the dust. Looking up he said: "That's not Aunt Fanny's ice cream . . . Hand me the spoon and we'll take a ride together, Cullis. Have you flying over Baghdad in no time at all."

"Gimme that, you hear!"

Cullis took the offered bag, sniffed into its opening, then tasted a tiny amount. "Shit-sake! I'm damned, Fahey. How'd you know—"

"I knew you jumbo brains were blinded by those precious photos."

"There more there?"

Fahey moved over, worked on the next plate, and retrieved the larger bag. This one he gave directly to an astonished Cullis.

"Marc Sterne's by the weight of it," Fahey said.

"You're gonna tell me how you knew about this?"

"Tell me first how you Einsteins missed it. You've been sitting on this place for months."

"I gotta call the station." A harried frown creased Cullis's leathery face.

"Not from here, you won't. The line's been canceled."

"Mrs. Noor's place."

"So she can hear you. Her name's on one of those happy-bags. Tip her off, will you? Do another Einstein for us?" goaded Fahey.

Cullis thought it over, deciding Fahey had the better argument. "Okay, I'll talk from the car."

"Not so fast. *We'll* talk from the car . . . Let's put the merchandise back."

"You crazy?"

"You want to run off with the evidence for a murder trial? Possible evidence?" Fahey was enjoying himself. His grin spread in all four directions.

"I'm not leaving it with you."

"So we'll put it back. We can repair to your car, boyo. Make calls up to highest authority and listen to how they'll fuck up again."

In Cullis's sedan the call was put through to the senior officer at the Hollywood sheriff's station. Fahey sat back, his game arm resting on the muzzle of a shotgun locked in a brace by the dashboard.

Chatter rose over a faint hum of static. Cullis explained everything. Fahey whistled another ditty, then asked for the mike.

"Whoever this is, here is the Fahey talking. For the defense . . . I know how to raise the temperature of the water you're in if you tamper with this evidence . . . Stay on the wireless here and patch this call in to Judge Rhodes's chambers . . . We'll wait for you. Savvy?"

After giving Fahey an earful, a truce was reached, and they waited. Waited more as Fahey whistled to a stone-faced Cullis who shoved Fahey's arm off the shotgun.

Macklin Price had taken the call from the Hollywood sheriff's station. Sixty fast steps later, she panted a brief message to Rhodes. He recessed the court for twenty minutes with no explanation to anyone.

In chambers, immersed in the three-way cross-talk, Rhodes's heart leaped. He wanted to kiss Fahey. Two live witnesses, including a law officer, vouched for the presence of the cocaine stash.

"Sheriff," he said, "leave it there. We'll have to see if it's evidence in this trial or not. I don't want it touched."

The senior sheriff's officer in Hollywood started on a tirade, began to bitch, and almost yelled.

Rhodes broke him off. "You want a restraining order, you got one . . . And you listen. The news'll be out in no time once your station hears of it. That means newspapers, that means the attorneys will know, and that means it'll be brought up in my court. Maybe it shouldn't be, get it? You want that sort of trouble on your backs?"

No.

Rhodes replaced the phone. The mosaic was nearly complete, he was thinking, as Macklin appeared once more. "Time to go," she told him.

He floated there. The sudden image of Romaine filled the corridor as he walked back to her. Fahey, he remembered, must say nothing.

"We'll put a guard up there. Twenty-four hours," Cullis said when he told Fahey to get out of the sedan.

"That's the best idea today. You can tip off that old sexpot Noor and maybe she'll tell Kardas for you."

"Shit!"

"You already have, lieutenant. Don't do it again, not in those nice gabardines you got on." Fahey peeled himself out of the car. "Have a swell evening," he said, giving Cullis a drum majorette's twirl with his walking stick.

At Malibu Pointe.

Audrey sat before her dressing table mirror finishing the seventieth stroke. Her hair shone like a dewy daffodil. Putting the brush down, she placed her hands over her bare breasts. Not bad for forty-two, she thought. They swelled under her slight squeeze, stayed round, the pink nipples erecting.

A cat with her fur up now and Audrey thought: ef-him! Rhodes had betrayed her. Had allowed her to be scorched in public when he had promised to help her.

She'd had it out with Julio again that morning. Hardly

listening to her, he had calmly read his paper, munched his grapefruit, and kept right on reading the financial section. Audrey had ranted, blistering Rhodes in a near rage. He wasn't a judge, he was an enemy, letting them flay her alive in that damn courtroom.

Julio had better do something. "Put down that idiotic newspaper and listen to me . . . He's not fit to walk a dog, let alone go to the Supreme Court. A disgrace! You'd better let the governor know before it's too late."

Julio had only folded the paper, stared and blinked slowly across the table as if she were a child talking out of turn. He had flicked lint off his sleeve, then walked away without uttering a single word.

Looking in the mirror again, Audrey sipped from her first late afternoon scotch. Outside the sky began to darken, but she hardly noticed. Inside she felt the slight burning sensation of the liquor, and her vaulting burn of anger and despair against Rhodes. He would never believe one thing she'd told him about Romaine. The thought galled Audrey. She knew she would be a target for a lot of very unfunny gossip soon. The thought depressed her so much she failed to hear the phone.

"They here again. This afternoon. Two of them," Ferenc heard from an excited Alesia Noor.

"How long?"

"Long time."

"Were you with them?"

"No. They not let me go up. You better come . . . You say you come here four days ago."

"I'll come tomorrow. In the afternoon."

"You better. That tall one, hee-sa the trouble."

Ferenc had no idea who she meant. "I'll have to go now. Someone's coming."

Ferenc sensed an end to his luxurious world of Malibu Pointe. He thought hard. He could empty nearly all his bank accounts in the morning.

Was the cocaine still there? Hidden someplace? He didn't know, but it was certainly worth one look. Noor saw something, she said, the last time the police were poking around there.

He blew a kiss up to the ceiling, somewhere toward Audrey's room. Goodbye, they might get you, but not me...

Chapter Twenty-Three

Alesia Noor watched raptly as Ferenc Kardas spilled the contents of the largest sack into two glass bowls, dividing the white crystals evenly. They sat in her kitchen on either side of a small table covered with a red checkered oilcloth.

She had taken him up to Marc Sterne's apartment an hour earlier, showing him where Fahey had stood behind the couch the night when he'd come back alone. Kardas found the knife still laying on the shag carpet behind the couch, and then he saw the scratches the knife had made on the baseboard. One socket-plate was slightly ajar.

The rest was easy. Fahey and Cullis in their haste had left an easy map to follow; one that led to more treasure than Alesia Noor ever imagined would shine into her widening eyes.

"You have no scale here?" Ferenc asked.

"Not any good one."

"I do my best then."

She nodded but said nothing. The pour of the crystals, white as clouds, drugged her senses. She was embalmed with joy at the money, white money, piling up by the inch.

Kardas asked her to come around the table. In both bowls he smoothed off the grains with a metal spatula.

Kneeling down, he examined his work with an approving grunt. Knowing she would insist on an equal cut, he had favored her bowl with slightly more than his own. He knew she would notice. A few grams' difference was worth hundreds of dollars; thousands if the cocaine was pure, which Kardas doubted.

As Alesia Noor kneeled beside him, he leaned away. She smelled of odors strange to him. Nauseous ones, and he tried not to breathe through his nose.

"Is okay," she said after examining the bowls minutely.

"You are certain?"

She nodded approvingly.

Only a ritual, he knew, but a necessary one. Alesia Noor smiled at him, her gold teeth showing a dull gleam. She might holler, so it was better to go ahead, divide the win, wasting time but gaining her trust.

Close enough now. She seemed distracted, happy with her share. That was just before she became a dead weight in his arms and then hit the floor. A short hard clip slightly underneath the point of her slack jaw drove a quick shock up into her brain. Her eyes rolled back on the trip to his waiting arms.

Dragging her out of the kitchen, he propped her in a chair facing the television set. Her breath came evenly. To make sure, he loosened a few buttons at the top of her dress, knowing it wouldn't help her, but the gesture still made him feel better after hitting her that solidly.

He finished his burglary in the kitchen, taking only a moment to pour both bags into a larger one, which he knotted.

On the way out, checking the woman again, he set the lock, closed the door, and sauntered off. Miami was on his route sheet only two hours from now; Eastern Airlines held two reservations for him under different names.

From the trunk of his rented car he yanked out a pigskin valise, small enough to carry on the plane. Releasing the brass catches, he pulled out a partly empty five pound tin of highly aromatic Jamaican Blue Mountain coffee.

Scooping the coffee beans over the glassine sacks, he sealed the tin with blue plastic tape. He hid it under some clothing in the valise.

Kardas hated to leave. California had been the most stupifying path of promises he'd ever known. Golden girls, sun swept beaches, gilded dreams, the heaven of every mother-lucking hustler with half a brain.

He threw the car into gear. Nassau by way of Miami lay less than a day away. He'd already added up his score—and all that honey was right in the back of the car. So easy, he thought, rounding the corner. The American dream had come true.

Chapter Twenty-Four

There was hardly any more sound in the courtroom than a hummingbird makes; everyone in limbo, watching her. For her truth or for dodging of it. Her face, was it on a straight line, or would it shift around? And her voice, falter, or stay full of her heart?

Romaine wore a crisp white organdy dress. A modest coral necklace graced her throat that sometimes moved as she uttered small gasps of disbelief. Her tawny hair swept across the full width of her shoulders when she shook her head. Then other looks, full of sudden surprise, or soft and endearing. She could do them all, even the more intense ones of anger and shock. She was on her stage, every actor ever born.

Tommy Burke paused next to their table, holding a glass of water. His mouth and his teeth felt like a hair dryer had worked them over all morning.

A flash of memory then, of the night before, when Fahey had called, telling him not to use those questions—the questions sent by whom? Tommy wondered.

He looked over the ranks of impatient faces, anxious for him to get going again. Showtime. They all had their free tickets, and they wanted more. More of Romaine's hide or more about her romance with Marc Sterne, he wasn't sure. Action, that's what they'd come for. He hated Marc Sterne, loathed him. That coroner's report was sure to be on today's menu of trouble.

Only a short hour ago, he had raised nervous giggles from the faces staring at him, tying his nerves in knots. Trying to re-stage events on the night of Marc Sterne's death, Tommy had stripped his jacket off, unbuttoned his shirt, and bared his knobby ribcage.

But it had been for her.

They had performed a small playlet together, with Tommy lying on an old camp cot as a prop. A crude model of the couch where Marc was lying the night he emptied one last cocaine cocktail into his arm.

Around his own arm Tommy had wound a length of surgical hose, tightening it until a vein swelled blue with blood.

He pricked his vein with a hypodermic syringe bought only a few days before in a drug store. Blood had flooded the syringe, and he had asked Romaine to put her thumb on the plunger.

And push it down, so everyone in the jury could see.

Just exactly as he had rehearsed her to push it down, she had, so that everyone in front could see the blood rushing back into his arm. He came off the cot then, a little shaky but smiling.

Lunging at Romaine, she had fended him off, his shirttails flying. They were close, close as a mother's hug. In the flurry of their arms, Tommy had slithered an edge of his shirt over the syringe still sticking out of his arm; then, close as they were, he wiped the plunger's top very quickly.

He had worked on that trick for over a week now. Had he gotten away with it? Had the jury seen him do it?

"Was it like that? That sort of a rush at you?" Tommy had asked her. He turned so the jury could see him, the syringe still in his arm, filling again with blood pumping out from the vein.

"Something like that, yes," Romaine agreed.

"Would you say he was hopped up?"

"Yes. Speeding his brains . . . Oh! poor Marc, he'd just lost himself all over again."

Everyone's eyes had been riveted to the red flow flooding the syringe.

"He was going for you? Meant to harm you?"

"I was petrified. His eyes were devil black. That's what I remember most of all."

"Harm you again?"

"It was so fast. He wouldn't, though, not really . . . I mean that's what I hoped. He was so hurt, way down. Beautiful Marc, but still . . . oh, I don't know."

When their act was over, Burke had come before Rhodes and raised his eyes up to the bench. "Would you have someone remove this syringe," he asked. "Just so they don't touch the plunger top. I want someone else to remove it. The last person to touch the top was Romaine Burke." And he had looked at the jury again.

Rhodes had eyed the blood-filled syringe, wondering how Burke could spare it.

"A doctor perhaps . . . Wait—" he had said, glancing over at the jury. "Aren't one of you ladies a nurse?"

The brunette with the horn-rims raised her hand. Rhodes asked her to come forward. Tommy pulled a clean handkerchief along with a thin white box from one pocket. Untying the surgical tubing from Tommy's arm, the nurse had carefully removed the syringe, dabbed Tommy's arm, then placed the hypodermic in the white box. They were no more than ten feet from the jury when she handed Tommy back his handkerchief.

"Your Honor," Tommy had said, holding out the box, "this will be our only exhibit for the defense. I ask that it be marked for evidence and sent immediately to the police department's forensic lab so they can check it for fingerprints. Romaine Brook's prints especially. No one has touched the plunger top since she did . . . You all saw that, didn't you?" He had ridden his eyes across every juror.

Rhodes had ordered a bailiff over, giving him a very precise set of instructions. His respect for Burke was mounting, and he had shown it with a deep look at the younger man.

But that had all happened over an hour ago.

Tommy put his water glass down, and turned to see Romaine floating a baffled look his way—what was taking so long? He would skirt around the issue of those photos and see how Pritter clawed her on that one.

"I want to know only one more thing, Romaine," he said to her, up by the witness stand.

"Yes," she said eagerly.

"This morning you and I re-enacted, as best we could, how you described the events of your last night with Marc Sterne."

"Yes . . . So sad and everything."

"You remember how you pressed your thumb on the plunger, running my blood back in."

"But I didn't touch the syringe that night."

"This morning you did."

"I know."

"So your fingerprints should be on it, shouldn't they?"

"I guess so, I—"

Unless in our little scuffle they somehow got wiped away," said Tommy, leaving the thought hanging.

Pritter's jowls puffed out and in. He jostled an assistant with one elbow, saying something.

"I don't know," Romaine said. "I couldn't say, Tommy, for sure. You were all over me . . ."

Knowing laughs from the front rows.

"Now tell the jury, in your words—did you kill Marc Sterne?"

Something magical came again. Her face lit up and seemed a size bigger as her lips parted slightly. A vacant daydreamy look appeared for only a fleeting moment. Going pale, as if suddenly blessed to see what went on at the fiery core of earth, Romaine's eyes shone with stark amazement.

"We, all of us, are in God's hands, and I know that," she offered. "Some people, whoever they are, forget how I loved Marc Sterne. He did everything for me, don't you know . . . Oh, please, don't you know," she said, gift-wrapping her sentiments for the jury again.

She misted up before loaning out wet sobs to the hushed onlookers, spellbinding them for that instant of time. No one there could remember her coming apart so visibly. Not even once, in all those months of observing her so closely.

Tommy crouched. Her words. He already knew them and had known they were coming, but they still ripped at him.

Blood had rushed from his vein earlier, and now, it seemed, a scythe slashed across his sunken ribcage.

"Your witness," he said to Pritter.

Pritter began easily. He took Romaine back to the beginning, back to the coroner's report, back to the traces of drugs found in Marc Sterne's body. "Acute poisoning from cocaine, heroin and Meperdine," intoned Pritter, adding, "Do you know those drugs?"

"Not very well."

"How well?"

"I've heard of them. Everyone has, I suppose."

"Meperdine? You know what that is?"

"Like Demerol, isn't it? A painkiller?"

"Yes it is," agreed Pritter, surprised but pleased that she knew. He handed her a page he'd been holding. "Recognize this?"

"The letter, isn't it, the one I wrote Marc?"

"You tell us."

"A copy, yes, of my letter."

"Your handwriting?"

"Mine, yes it certainly is."

"Care to read that letter out loud so we can all hear how you threatened Marc Sterne?"

Burke moaned. He labored to his feet, sounding an objection—the jury had already seen the letter. No purpose was served by spilling it out to the press. A few reporters shot unfriendly looks at him.

"Sustained," said Rhodes to Pritter. "I'll let you go at it another way."

"How would you characterize the letter?" Pritter asked Romaine.

"Sort of angry, which I was."

"Angry? How about threatening?"

"No."

"No?" Pritter wagged his head. "You explicitly said in it that you were going to talk to his parents. Tell the newspapers certain things. Expose him as a criminal."

"I was upset, Mr. Pritter. Really boiling."

"Upset? The letter sounded to some of us as if you wrote it with sulfuric acid."

"I shouldn't have been so mad. I was wrong . . ." Pritter,

trying to stop Romaine right there, failed. ". . .he owed me money I needed, and I believe Marc took my share to finance his drugs. The ones he used on himself and the others that he was dealing."

Rhodes breathed a prayer of thanks. She'd gotten the issue of drugs back into the record.

"Perhaps, Miss Brook, you'll favor us with answers to the questions asked," Pritter said.

"Oh, excuse me. I thought that's what you wanted to know."

"Not precisely. And how can you say that Marc Sterne sold drugs. Did you buy from him?"

"No, never. I don't take drugs, Mr. Pritter."

"Never?"

"Oh, no."

"You saw him negotiate drug sales?"

"Many times."

"Where?"

"Parties and places."

"What parties?"

She told him of strings of parties she had attended with Marc. Often he would leave her by herself when he drifted out to his car for his stash.

"Could you name names?"

"I wouldn't. That would be terrible."

"So we can't verify your statement that Marc sold drugs?"

"Not by me. I'm not saying who those buyers were. Anyway, it was done in privacy."

"Why didn't you report it to the authorities?"

Romaine gave the jury a look of astonishment. "I wouldn't ever do that to Marc. I loved him."

"When you don't report violations of the narcotics laws, Miss Brook, it's the same as if you conspired in the sale yourself."

"But I loved Marc. How could I . . . Besides, Mr. Pritter, you'd have to report on half the people in Hollywood."

Rhodes joined in the laughter flooding the room.

Plugging on, Pritter asked: "You said he owed you money. From the sale of drugs?"

"Please don't accuse me of that anymore. I never sold drugs in my life."

"Or used them either?"

"No, of course not!"

"I'm trying to find out why Marc Sterne owed you money. He was a wealthy young man."

"Yes, but money to him was like water to me. He really spent."

"If he did, why wouldn't he ask his father? Why borrow from you?"

"He didn't exactly borrow . . . We did a treatment of a screenplay together. A story I dreamed up. We wrote it up in thirty-two pages and Parthenon Studios bought the rights to it. He kept my share."

"Which was how much?"

Romaine told him.

"Wouldn't the usual thing be for Parthenon, when they bought story rights, to pay each author separately?"

"I think so. But Marc went funny on me. He submitted the story under his own name."

"Not yours?"

"No, you see that's why I sent the letter. I was hopping mad, I tell you, because I was the one who created the story . . . And really I needed money then."

"Can you prove you were legitimately a co-author?"

"I know the story by heart."

"Which doesn't make you a co-author."

"But I was."

Pritter scratched his round chin, thinking. His mouth pursed in the shape of a horseshoe.

"You trusted Marc Sterne? A man you say was a drug dealer and a thief. Who took your money. Money you say was yours but we have only your word for it. The same, isn't it, for those people who supposedly bought drugs from Marc? No names, just your word?"

"It's all I have," replied Romaine, sheepishly. "And my word wouldn't be worth much if I started telling on people."

"But you have!"

"On who?"

"On Marc Sterne. Just now."

"That's not the same," said Romaine defensively. "Marc's gone."

"How about Mrs. Sterne? And Ferenc Kardas? Didn't

you tell us slanderous things about them? They're not gone. Maybe they wish they were now that you've lied about them, trying to kick innocent reputations apart."

"I didn't lie. I saw them."

"They deny it."

Pritter wheeled on her. He'd been facing the rows of reporters, but now he loomed so close Romaine could part his hair with a fingernail. Oily black hair, she thought, and slick as eelskin.

"That's the third time now where you've said something we can't verify as truth. The money. The drugs. Mrs. Sterne's alleged behavior. Except in her case, she claims that you're lying blatantly."

"God will punish her one day. He'll have to . . ."

"You're getting very hard to believe, Miss Brook. Even Mr. Sterne denies he ever offered you a picture deal with any studio—his studio or anyone else's—so that's the fourth example of your lies to us."

"I never thought—yes, you're right, that's what they say. But I'm not lying to anyone. You just say I am."

"You want us to think everyone else is lying to us except you. Four liars to one truth teller."

"I'll admit, Mr. Pritter, it may seem strange—"

"Strange!" Pritter fired back at her. "That's not so strange for you. You're not in the same world as the rest of us! Everyone's a cheat and a deceiver but Romaine Brook. The put-upon actress!"

"I'm proud to be an actress."

"So you are. Now act the part of truth for a change."

They went on, Pritter snarling, fencing, cornering her. Painting Romaine as a female Lucifer, the Eve of all Eves, he swayed the jury at times. Their heads often nodded in agreement.

Burke became nervous, and started to sweat. He watched for an hour as Pritter hounded her, setting one burning match after the other to her claims of innocence. Pounding like a hammer, then pounding away even harder.

What would the lab report show? wondered Rhodes. Would her fingerprints show up?

Pritter lowered his gunsights. "You've seen these?" He

held out a packet of 3 × 5 color prints. Those notorious photos came into the imagined view of everyone there.

"I've seen them, yes."

"Do you know where they were taken?"

"In Palm Springs. I was there with Marc. And the other hands in the pictures, I think I know who they belong to."

"And who would they be?"

"A Mexican couple."

"Their names?"

"I don't know."

"You don't know again. You don't know the names of people who you let roam your body?"

"That's not very nice of you, Mr. Pritter," said Romaine quietly. "You shouldn't ever say that to anyone."

Pritter stepped back from the witness stand. She'd caught him off guard with her slight rebuke. "Miss Brook," he said, "these photos've been withheld from the public and the press. Do you know why?"

"They're awful. Pornographic, I suppose."

"And therefore they might unjustly influence people. Is that right? Or cause undue harm to your reputation, the way you've been causing it to others."

"I think they would harm anyone, Mr. Pritter."

"Yes, I would imagine so," Pritter said, softly for a change. He held the fan of photos out at arm's length, studying them, knowing he was mortifying Romaine. "How are you dressed in these photos?"

"You can see."

Tommy Burke sputtered an objection. Any way you looked at it, he complained, Pritter was defying an earlier ruling that the photos would be restricted to the jury, the court, and the attorneys.

Rhodes overruled, a small ploy.

"What were you wearing?" Pritter repeated.

"I was quite bare."

"You certainly were." He shuffled the stack of pictures, showing Romaine another one. Pritter's jowls went pink, and then he mocked her in a conspiratorial tone: "You were—sort of wearing something here, weren't you? What do you call that?" He pointed at a spot on one photo.

"A dildo."

"Where is it exactly in this picture—"

"Okay," Rhodes said to Pritter. "That's enough. You made your point and the jury's seen the photos."

Pritter protested. "I want to find out the circumstances under which the photos were taken. And I—"

"Then ask the defendant," Rhodes said.

"I am," Pritter replied.

Rhodes gave him a look, and Pritter shrugged. He sidestepped a few paces until he faced Romaine again.

"Miss Brook," he said, "those of us who've seen these photos are aware that other people were present when the pictures were taken . . . Hands other than your own show up. In one picture a large dog— Were you posing here or what?"

"I would never do that." Her head shook. Golden hair swirled back and forth across her shoulders.

"But you did!"

"Not knowingly."

Then Romaine, in sonorous tones, told the entire courtroom how she and Marc had gone to Palm Springs for a long weekend. While there the first day, swimming, he'd made her a cool drink at the outside bar. A short time later, she was on the wildest journey she could ever imagine.

"I was drugged-out," she told the jury. "I don't think I really woke up for a day or two."

"What sort of a drink did he make you?" asked Pritter.

"A spritzer. A white wine spritzer."

"You drink alcohol often?"

"Rarely."

"That day you did."

"I asked for some iced tea. But it was all gone by then. So he made me a spritzer."

"And you say you were drugged."

"I was."

"And yet you said earlier, Miss Brook, that you don't take narcotics. Remember?"

"Not by habit."

"You didn't say by habit, you said—"

"Mr. Pritter, I don't take them by choice," Romaine retorted, "and I don't sell them either . . . Please stop badgering me that way. I'm asking you—"

"You don't take drugs. You don't drink alcohol."

She shook her head again.

"Perhaps you just engage in orgies," Pritter rapped at Romaine, not waiting for an answer.

"I dizzied out. Everything became yellow and red and—oh! I don't know. Freakish."

"And we're to believe Marc Sterne drugged you?"

"Who else could have?"

"Didn't you say there was some Mexican couple there with you?"

"I did, yes. The doctor and his wife."

"A doctor?"

"A Mexican doctor from Tijuana, or one of those border towns. A friend of Marc's."

"And you don't know their names?"

"Arturo and Maria something-or-other."

"That's all?"

Romaine nodded, then said very solemnly, "I think Marc was trying to make it easy on me. That's why he drugged me."

"Make what easy—" and Pritter tried to stop his question, but Romaine grabbed her chance. "The abortion." She hurried. "We'd gone there because I needed an abortion and—"

"I'm not asking you that," Pritter scolded her.

"Oh." Romaine patted her mouth as if to apologize.

Once again Rhodes spoke. "You go on ahead," he told Romaine.

Pritter stabbed him with his eyes. "That's not my question, your Honor."

"It is now. You began it. You told the court earlier you wanted us to learn the circumstances of the pictures. Get to it please."

Pritter sighed deeply. "You were having an abortion in Palm Springs? To be performed, I suppose, by some unnamed Mexican doctor?"

"Yes, you know about it then?" Romaine asked innocently.

"No, Miss Brook, I don't know about it," Pritter said wearily. "And neither does anyone else."

"Well, Marc, he wanted to relax me, I guess. I was very upset and he was being so nice and caring."

"He cared so much he drugged you?"

"He knew I was terribly upset."

Tommy Burke was staggered with curiosity. He was also furious. Romaine had never really explained the photos nor had she ever uttered so much as a comma about any abortion.

"Are you saying," Pritter was asking, "that Marc Sterne drugged you prior to an abortion procedure? Drugged you when there was a doctor, supposedly, present?"

"Marc liked to do things his way . . . You can ask anyone who knew him."

Pritter already had. She was right.

"And this abortion. Your fetus, of course. Was he the father?"

"Yes, naturally, Mr. Pritter . . . Ohhh-hh, you're being terrible. You're implying it was someone besides Marc."

Pritter didn't know how to break the front he was sure Romaine was putting up. She was either too coy or she gushed in pained surprise whenever he closed in on her. She was acting very cleverly—his lawyer's sixth sense could tell. But how could he prove it?

"Miss Brook, have you ever posed nude for what some call 'men's' magazines. *Playboy* or *Penthouse*? One of those?"

"Anyone who knows me knows I wouldn't."

"Uh-huh. Just in Palm Springs?"

"When I was asleep with drugs."

"Having an abortion?"

"Yes."

"Why didn't you go to a clinic? A hospital?"

"Marc wanted it done very privately. So did I."

"Why?"

"People talk."

"Doctors?"

"Their nurses or secretaries or someone. They can, Mr. Pritter . . . and they have."

"What were you afraid of?"

"Mr. Sterne. Marc was afraid his father would raise holy cane, even kick him out of the studio."

"About an abortion?"

"Oh, no, not that. Supposing I'd decided to have the baby. That would've made it a Sterne heir. Marc told me his father would wring his neck. And then mine. Mr. Sterne is so powerful. He might've had me blackballed in every Hollywood studio . . . That's why I agreed to the abortion. And now I wish I hadn't."

Pritter swore under his breath. It was all too plausible, and she was too cunning. Spinning one web after another, and all of them so intricate he couldn't unwind them. He had to shake her somehow. Quake her was more like it, he thought.

"Why would Marc Sterne—the father of your unborn child—the man you loved, and who presumably loved you, take those pictures?"

"Maybe he didn't take them, Mr. Pritter."

"Who then? The Mexican doctor and his wife?"

"Possibly."

"Why?"

"I don't know. What if they had some scheme?"

"Such as?"

"Blackmail . . . I don't know."

"The pictures were found in Marc Sterne's apartment. If he didn't take them, how would he have them?"

"Maybe he bought them to protect me. I don't know. Possibly your state investigators could find out."

The courtroom burst into titters. Pritter flushed. "We have no names to go by, Miss Brook. No place to start."

"You started easily enough with me . . . And look what you've done to my life."

The wall clock showed 11:40. Some of the reporters covering the trial for the European news services had already left to telex their stories home.

Rhodes recessed. An abortion? He had nearly become a grandfather before he knew he even was a father.

A technician slid a set of print images into a small tray on the side of a square gray machine. Under a pale green light the images magnified. Side by side she saw these latest prints line up next to those of Romaine Brook's, taken when she had been booked for homicide.

Less than two minutes had passed since the first prints

were retrieved from the two million sets stored by the Los Angeles Police Department.

Adjusting a knob, the technician looked down at a backlit screen. Romaine's prints stood out in sharp relief, magnified a dozen times. With a tiny chrome pointer the technician traced the loops, whorls and arches on the thumbprint lifted from the chrome plunger top of the syringe sent over from Rhodes's court; next, she did the same to other prints left on the syringe's finger grips.

She compared, looked again.

Swiveling in her chair, she stood up and went over to a bench to peer into an electronic microscope. Once more she saw the red and white fibers also found on the plunger top.

Only twenty minutes had passed since the bailiff brought the syringe to the forensic lab, telling the Latent Prints Section of L.A.P.D. of an urgent request for a speedy identification. Pretty simple, she thought, sitting down and rolling a form into a typewriter.

ROMAINE BROOK, she typed on the second line, then remembered how much she enjoyed seeing *Tonight or Never*. One film actress down the pipe, the technician thought. How could people screw up like that, when they had it all?

By 1:30 the jurors were in their seats again. Three of them had skipped lunch, using the time to make calls to their families, who hadn't seen them for over five months.

Romaine was still on the witness stand. She tried a weak smile on the jurors, getting small reward for the effort. As she smoothed the pleats of her white organdy dress, she wet the inside of her mouth when Pritter approached.

A little more, she told herself, *be the character you have to be or he'll grind you into red hash. Be Joan of Arc or anyone who ever went through an inquisition. Smile more. Show him you're not frightened.*

For the next half-hour Pritter hacked away at her with more questions. He was out to break her down, rip out the weak seams of her story.

Romaine stuck to her beliefs. Occasionally her slim hand would touch the coral beads of her necklace and Rhodes was reminded of Audrey's nervous habit.

By mid-afternoon, Pritter was nearly through. He stood

near the jury, his wide face in a rumpus of contempt. His vest was partly unbuttoned over his deep belly that seemed to grow when he rammed his hands deep into his pockets. Rocking on his feet, he was distracted as a bailiff handed a paper to Tommy Burke.

"Miss Brook," Pritter started in, "you remember well the night you last saw Marc Sterne? The night he died in your presence?"

"He was still alive when I left."

"Was he really?"

"Yes."

"You knew he was in trouble? Injected with a fatal drug dosage?"

"I knew he'd taken them . . . I didn't know what drugs exactly. Or if they'd be fatal."

"You knew earlier. You knew about Meperdine, you said."

"I knew what they said Marc died from. But I know very little about actual drugs."

"How did you know?"

"Reading, in the newspapers. And Mr. Wheeler showed me the coroner's report once."

Pritter rocked again. "Why didn't you seek help for him? Call a doctor? Do something. Wasn't this man dying before your eyes the man you supposedly loved?"

"But I didn't know." Romaine gulped visibly. "I was so frightened when he went after me. Sort of crazed and everything. I didn't know he would OD."

"OD?"

"Overdose."

"You know that term?"

"Doesn't everyone? You hear it a lot."

"So you let him die on you. Your love, your lover?"

"I said I didn't know he would die. I'm not a doctor. I couldn't tell."

"You wouldn't take even the simplest precautions to save a life? Come now, Miss Brook."

"But I was so scared when he tried to seize me. Later was when I worried."

"Worried?"

"Well, you see, if I called a doctor or the paramedics and

Marc was all right, there could've been a lot of publicity. I don't think the Sternes would've ever forgiven me."

Tommy Burke approved. His pleased look caught up with her.

"For saving their son?" asked Pritter.

"But I didn't know," she repeated innocently. "How can you always know? It's been slapping at me for months... Now you're doing it all over again."

"When you made a statement to the Malibu sheriff, and again to the state investigators, you said," Pritter read from a sheet: "'I came to the Malibu house when Marc called me that day. Inviting me out to have dinner there.' Like to see this?" Pritter offered her the report.

"I remember that. Thank you anyway."

The other call. Does he really know? Suspect? Romaine felt her breath shorten.

Pritter dropped the report in front of an assistant. "But there was no dinner planned at the Sterne house that night," he said.

"I didn't find that out till I arrived."

"But you were willing to have dinner with him anyway?"

"Of course."

"With Marc Sterne, whom you hadn't seen for a while. Who had drugged you in Palm Springs? Perhaps had those photos taken of you. Had even stolen your interest, you say, in some film story rights."

"Yes."

"That's implausible."

"But it happened."

"After what? How long had you split up by then? A month?"

"We hadn't split up. We'd been apart for six weeks."

"Why so long, Miss Brook?"

"I was recovering from the abortion. I had classes to attend. And for two weeks of that time he was filming up in Oregon. On location."

"Did you ever talk? By phone?"

"Once a week perhaps."

"Hardly very often, was it? For two young lovers?"

"I don't know. Enough for us anyway."

"That's why you agreed to go for dinner with him in Malibu? For a patch-up?"

"We weren't patching up. We were in love. I was going to give up my acting career. Make a home for us. I could do it for Marc, give him a destiny."

"A destiny in love?"

"Yes, Mr. Pritter. And another thing was that Marc said he'd pay me the money he owed me."

"Oh, he did?"

"I really needed it, too. I was late on my tuition. The rent was overdue. Had a pile of other bills."

"He could've sent you a check."

Romaine folded her hands. Sparkles shone in her eyes.

"I went for the biggest reason of my life," she said.

"Tell us."

"We'd decided, Marc and I, to tell his parents of our decision to marry... We couldn't stand being apart any longer."

Tommy Burke thought his head was coming loose. Never had Romaine mentioned any marriage. Ever. And Pritter looked like someone had knocked his molars out. A hush blanketed the courtroom. Rhodes sat back. Rows of elated faces whispered to each other, trying to absorb this newest change to their expectations.

"How touching," said Pritter. "Isn't it too bad Marc isn't here to tell us what he thought about marrying you?"

"You've no idea what that would have meant to me. Plea—oh! please—I'm sorry." Romaine's voice became the sobs of a lost child.

A moment later Rhodes asked if she wanted a recess. Wiping the tears away, Romaine shook her head.

Eleven times Pritter had refused to believe her. Eleven. He shook his head like some punch-drunk fighter. His eyes roved the courtroom—the reporters, the spectators, Burke, up to Rhodes, over to the jury. His arms raised, then flopped to his egg shaped sides.

In a rising blast he raked Romaine: "Here I've been twenty-one years in courthouses. Never yet have I seen the likes of you. You're an actress. For my buck you're the greatest actress alive. No, not an actress, Miss Brook, you're a symphony of deceit. Of tricks and moods and a voice that can call birds in from the mountains . . . You've evaded everything, haven't you?

"You won't name the names of persons Marc Sterne allegedly sold drugs to . . . He owed you money, you say, for a film idea but the studio has no record of your co-authorship . . . Mrs. Sterne is, according to you, an adulteress, and of course she hotly denies it.

"Mr. Sterne says he never offered you some picture deal you imagined. Then there's some mysterious Mexican doctor who performed an abortion . . ."

Pritter stopped, looked around again.

". . . And photos, but no one knows who took them. Nor do we know if Marc was father to your aborted child."

Romaine closed her eyes, but left her moist lips slightly parted.

"Then you say," Pritter went on, "Marc Sterne drugged you before the photos were taken. But Marc's no longer here to confirm or deny anything. You tell us he invited you for dinner at the family residence. You were going to tell his parents that you were to marry . . . And at the end, you want us to share your convictions that he was alive when you left the Sterne home.

"Your word, Miss Brook, against everyone else's. Or your allegations that we can't check. The roads to those facts are all so much lost dust. Isn't that so?"

Pritter hesitated again, waiting for her.

"But why is that my fault?" she asked.

"No, we can all see you're faultless. You've had months to figure out how to get away with a capital crime. By lying, and lying, and lying more"—Pritter pounded a rail until it actually wiggled—"and you expect to get away with it, don't you?"

"But Mr. Pritter, it's you who's doing all this to me," Romaine cried out.

He ignored her. Patches of sweat had begun to appear under his arms. A thin gleam entered his eyes.

"Maybe you'll tell us something else," Pritter pounced again. "Have you ever had medical treatment for gynecological disorders?"

"The abortion."

"Yes. Do you know what a D & C is?"

"I do."

"Have you ever had a D & C other than at the time of your alleged abortion, the one done by the Mexican doctor who lives God-knows-where?"

"No."

"Then, Miss Brook, so that we might ascertain whether you might've had an abortion, would you submit to an examination by a competent doctor?"

Tommy Burke hadn't expected this looper. He shook his head, praying that Romaine would see him.

"What doctor?" she asked.

"Why, yours."

"I don't have one."

"You don't have one? A woman your age?"

"I don't believe in them. Besides, I'm very healthy."

"A healthy enough liar, I'd agree," said Pritter, seeing Tommy's face contort as he fumbled out of his chair. "All right, counselor, I'll save you the trouble . . . statement withdrawn," Pritter said to him, and again to Rhodes.

Sighing, he continued: "Then by a doctor appointed by the court, Miss Brook. How would that be?"

Romaine was perplexed. "I'm sorry—you know I wouldn't let just any doctor examine me!"

"We'll get the best in the city. I'll even ask the state of California to pay the bill."

"No, thank you."

"Why not?"

"It's against my religion."

"Oh?"

"I'm a Christian Scientist and we don't believe in it."

"I see. Where do you practice this religion of yours?"

"In private. My readings. I do them before I meditate."

"Meditate on how you're going to beat—" Pritter halted. He knew Burke would collapse to his feet again if he continued that line. "Never mind," he added.

"So that's thirteen times," Pritter went on, "we can't get to your side of things. An unlucky number." He whewed aloud, then looked up at Rhodes, saying: "We've got a defendant, the last person to see Marc Sterne alive, therefore a witness, who refuses to cooperate. In a trial about murder, your Honor. Yes, murder . . . Will the court rule, kindly, and by seeing the logjam here, that the defendant must undergo a medical examination?"

"On what grounds?" Rhodes replied.

"To get at the truth. Those are the best grounds I can think of."

"I'll take it under advisement."

Pritter argued harder.

"I'll make a ruling after I check the law. But I can tell you this: the defendant is not required to do or say anything that might tend to incriminate her. The state brought the case and the state's now asking the questions, and it's up to the state to disprove any answers it doesn't like . . . That's well held law," Rhodes finished. He wasn't worried, though. He already knew it was medically impossible to tell whether a woman had ever gone through an abortion.

"She's evading," Pritter protested.

"Which is her right, if she really is."

"Can we bring in a minister to find out if she knows anything about the tenets of Christian Science?"

Rhodes knew his answer before Pritter was halfway through the question. "I'd have to check that point, too."

Like someone ready to spit, Pritter stood with his lips and chin twisting. He turned away from the bench. "Thirteen lashes," he said to the jury. "Thirteen lies flailing the unsuspecting heart of Justice." Whirling, he faced Burke. "Take her. She's worse than trying to nail a cloud to the wall."

4:14.

Rhodes called time-out for the day.

Back in chambers, Rhodes's own beating heart fought with his muddy conscience.

No time to spare now. He had to do the wrong thing in exactly the right way. She'd been good. A credit, superb when she had to face the pressure. Yet Pritter had scored on her: high, low, higher again. A pro in what was mostly a man's game, he had slammed away with everything he could muster. And Rhodes knew that the prosecutor had piled up points with the jury. Making Romaine seem a cunning liar, a teller of tall tales.

You can never outguess a jury, Rhodes thought. Fool you every time. You never knew because they never knew. Theirs was the only power that counted, that wonderful power to decide what was fair—and the hell with the law if they thought it was wrong or didn't apply.

Photos, abortions, a marriage?

What if Marc Sterne, tired of life, burned out and drugged up, had busted apart his own life? Lovelorn? That might make Romaine a liar.

Was she? No!

Rhodes's earlier theory was shot all to hell. The questions he'd given Fahey for Burke were designed to show the jury another possibility. Questions that might support the notion that Marc Sterne was a despondent lover. A spoiled boy with the world in his wine cup, but a boy who couldn't have the girl he wanted. He took his own life. In a fit of clever vengeance he wiped the syringe clean of prints, implicating her at the same time.

He had defended more bizarre cases many times. A crime of passion Pritter had called it at the opening of the trial. But if so, then of whose passion?

He trifled with a darker idea. How much more *didn't* he know? He had won when he won as a top trial lawyer because he dogged the facts until they couldn't run from him any more. Dogged them until he owned them. But he didn't have all the facts on this one. What revelation might come next from Romaine?

He leaned back, sweating, then lit a cigar, shrouding his desk in blue smoke, thinking of Audrey. How livid she must be, and that thought led him over more barbed wire.

Tease fate again. His own, his daughter's, Audrey's? Go through with it as planned or almost planned? A gamble he must win this time. Were Audrey ever to confess—tell anyone she was the mother and he the father—the lights in Rhodes's world would go out for good. That was now his greatest risk. If Romaine walked free, would Audrey someday reveal the truth out of anger?

Rhodes wanted that jury badly. The fix was already halfway in place. Plenty of judges had been fixed before, but Rhodes wondered if any judge had ever fixed a jury . . . without their knowing it.

That was one fact he would never know.

Chapter Twenty-Five

"Now if you'll please follow me," Tommy Burke suggested to the jury. "Remember the sheriff's reports? Perhaps they were accurate for once when telling us Marc Sterne had his shirt open when they found him. Like mine was yesterday, when Romaine and I were trying to re-enact the scene. Marc lunged at her. The syringe was still in his arm . . . the needle buried. Just as this one was with me yesterday"—he held the syringe up, waving it back and forth—"and then in the scuffle, with Romaine trying to defend herself, the syringe gets caught somehow in our clothes, and the prints get obliterated when our clothes wipe against the syringe.

"Marc's prints?" Tommy pointed out. "Were they his, only his? Listen to this."

He read from the lab technician's report, explaining briefly what loops, arches and whorls meant. "Those are the tiny lines and squiggles on the pads of our fingers."

Romaine's fingerprints had shown up on the chrome grips of the syringe they had used the day before to show what happened that night in Malibu. "Her forefinger and middle finger"—he held his up so the jury could see how her prints had impressed on the wings of the grips—"you see, like that. But then we scuffled a little, the way she had to that night with Marc Sterne, and my shirt wiped away part of her thumbprint from the plunger top. What was left was just the edge of her print. You remember, don't you, how she had her whole thumb down on the top when she squirted the blood back into my arm . . . And here's what else the lab came up with."

He read more, then looked up.

"Yesterday I wore a red and white striped shirt. I have it over there." He went over to his table, picked up his shirt and dangled it in front of the jury. "The same one. And in the lab report here, the part I just read you, they found red and white cotton fibers on the plunger top . . . So you see, my shirt, when we scuffled, rubbed part of her thumbprint off. Just like that night with Marc . . . But, you see, it could've been Marc's print and only his print that was erased."

He had the jury thinking. Very hard, and in deep confusion.

"The state says, Mr. Pritter over there, he says those were Romaine's prints on the first syringe. You see?"

Tommy knew they didn't.

"But why couldn't someone else's prints have been wiped away? Like Marc's? Or Ferenc Kardas, who found the body? Possibly, and I don't know, even Mrs. Sterne's . . . Do you? Does anyone really know?"

As Tommy moved away from the jury, Rhodes asked him to come up to the bench. Pritter as well. They discussed if either side had any more witnesses.

Tommy shook his head.

Pritter said he still wanted a medical examination of Romaine. Or at least she should be tested on her knowledge of Christian Science. "It's all too pat," he protested again.

Rhodes refused him. His court wasn't about to get tangled up in anyone's religious beliefs. Pritter knew better, didn't he?

"I plan to take a crack at this new syringe," Pritter said. He looked at the small white box Tommy Burke was holding.

"Of course," said Rhodes. "After you do, can you keep right on with your closing arguments?"

"I certainly can," he said.

"No more witnesses then?" asked Rhodes of both, needing to know their plans so he could begin to put his own in motion.

Standing below the bench, facing Romaine, Pritter started on her again. His deep voice bounced off the farthest walls. He was right where he wanted to be, center ring, where he could scorn Romaine and Tommy, and be most visible to the press.

"They're quite a pair, aren't they?" asked Lloyd Pritter of the whole courtroom. "Don't see many like them. They just sit there and dig a hole we can all fall into. They're not interested in bruising justice . . . They want to massacre it. Let me show you."

He exhorted the jury. He singled out first how the charade they had witnessed yesterday was an insult to everyone's good sense. Burke had shown them a second syringe, claiming that in a scuffle some of Romaine's prints were smudged away.

But not all of them were, were they? On the fingergrips some of her prints were clearly identified. The lab report emphasized that fact.

Yet on the syringe found next to Marc Sterne's body, *all* the prints were missing. Where had they gone to? Who stole them?

"Romaine Brook, that's who," said Pritter, crashing his words against the ceiling.

There was no other logical explanation. She had been there. The Malibu Pointe gate guards logged her in and logged her out. She admits she was there.

Who else could've done it? She had tried to stamp out her trail. The motive? Passionate jealous rage. Marc Sterne wanted nothing more to do with her.

Romaine Brook is a sociopath. Someone who knows the difference between right and wrong, but doesn't care. A sociopath can put you under a spell, charm and mesmerize you, make you feel as though you're on some high and great throne.

"All the while," Pritter went on, "you're being puppeted. They don't pull wool over your eyes. They use silk. The silk of deceit and trickery."

Pritter crossed the floor to the jury as he spoke. "Do the right thing," he told them, a bishop reminding his small flock of their sacred duty. "You're fighting for yourselves here, for what you believe in. That the society you live in won't stand for wanton murder. This young woman is laughing at you. At all of us . . ."

* * *

Fritzi Jagoda had never seen a courtroom argument during all of her mostly happy life. Not the real article anyway. She had only watched television shows or movies where actors performed courtroom scenes.

The only scene occupying her mind was of swaying palms, sugary white beaches, and miles of blue warm water. And thrown into the bag of her imagination, a hidden grotto for the kind of loving that begins in the Urals, gets fueled up again in Venice, and then lands right in the lap of her ecstasy.

She was ready.

In her office, lacquered the exact shade of red as Cliff Rhodes's library, Fritzi met with her top staff: Ginty Jellicoe, the chef, the maitre d', four senior captains, and the head bartender.

"I'm taking a breather," she told them. "Next week or the week after. On short notice."

"Off to where?" Ginty asked.

"Meh-he-co, señor. For a week. Maybe more."

"Not by yourself?"

"Nope. I'm shanghaiing d'judge."

She opened a pair of half-moon reading glasses, resting them on the tip of her nose. One by one she told them what she expected while she was gone, ticking items off her list with a gold Tiffany pen held in very anxious fingers. A hundred people would attend a private reception for the British Ambassador in the terrace room during her absence. But it had better go off smoothly, she reminded them.

When the staff departed, Fritzi tried to remember where she'd last parked her fishing gear: the Abercrombie & Fitch poplin outfits, her Topsiders, those straw hats.

Rhodes was a devoted fisherman, when he had the time. She knew how to fish, too. She meant to fish him, this time for good, and right to a judge—the marrying kind.

That damn war, she thought. It had taken a piece of him, but not the best part. A stalwart, and as bright and solid as any man she'd ever come across. Even with his brooding insecurities, he could be wonderful in bed when the urge struck him, or when he wasn't shy about his privates. Even better than other men she'd been involved with before meeting him.

Rhodes could be tenderized. Fritzi knew it. She was convinced she knew how to make him the happiest man who ever laughed. He'd been such a stranger of late, offering excuse after excuse as to why he couldn't be with her.

The answer was simple for Fritzi. She would suffocate him under the warmest blanket ever woven.

Love.

Audrey was trying to locate Kardas, missing for two days. She had dialed two Hungarian restaurants he frequented on his days off. No luck, they hadn't seen him lately. She had no idea where to call next.

Visiting his room that morning, she saw his clothes still hanging in the closet, two military hairbrushes on the bathroom sink, some shaving gear, his toothbrush, and several other signs of lived-in space.

Where in hell had he gone to? she wondered. Should she try the police? That idea entered her lovely head and expired after the briefest possible life. She had enough problems with them already.

By afternoon, Tommy Burke finally got his turn to sum up before the jury. For two ceaseless hours Pritter had ranted and raged, pleading for common sense.

Burke confined his remarks to a smaller target. "The state's whole case is circumstantial," he was saying to the jury. "Romaine Brook was there that night and everyone knows it. But supposing one night I was in your neighborhood," he spoke directly to the brunette with the horn-rims, "and I was at your door, lost, trying to get directions. So I push the bell and your next door neighbor sees me the same way the gate guard saw Romaine Brook come into and leave Malibu Pointe. There's no answer when I push your bell because you're not at home. And certainly no answer comes from the burglar who is upstairs, busy robbing you.

"I go away. You come home to find you've been robbed . . . I was there, yes. No one knows exactly who robbed you. But I was seen on the premises. Am I the suspect? The robber? I took nothing. And Romaine didn't take Marc's life either."

Tommy stopped. He felt as if he were on fire, he was so nervous. Limping across the room for more water, he knew he was an odd sight—tall and lanky, joints so loose they seemed like jelly. But somehow he felt surer of himself, stronger. After gulping down the water, he smiled at Romaine and his Adam's apple rose a full inch.

He still wished Raye Wheeler were here.

"You've heard her," he said as he turned to face the jury. "Has Romaine Brook given you any reason to doubt her? Any at all? Yes, she was there while Marc Sterne hopped himself up. And because no fingerprints were found on the syringe, they want you to think she murdered him with narcotics.

"We've been all through it now. The state's case doesn't hang together, anymore than I was the one who robbed your house," he said again to the brunette.

Tommy was nearly through. He'd itemized every one of Pritter's points earlier, and done what he could to demolish them.

"Ladies, gentlemen," he said, "the Romaine Brook you're looking at is an intelligent woman. An acclaimed actress, a very warm and loving person . . . Does anyone here really think she'd go through the Malibu Pointe gates, sign in and out, in an attempt to kill the man she planned to spend her life with? That's the only question you need to ask yourselves."

Tommy Burke sat down, spent. He was utterly drained of any more fight.

Unfair or not, Pritter had the last inning all to himself. He had two swings at his closing arguments; the defense only one. Quick on the rebuttal, he reminded the jury: "If you find her not guilty, then what you're saying to all of us is that the real suspects are Ferenc Kardas or possibly Mrs. Stern . . . Can you do that? Can you say that's who killed Marc? Because he was killed dead, dead as you can ever be."

Killed dead by himself? Rhodes still wondered. He rapped for a recess.

Five months and sixteen days. The longest trial he'd ever been involved with was almost over now. Looking at Romaine, he thought: You, young lady, are a problem, but you are mine, and you're going to walk free.

In his chambers Rhodes mulled over an iced tea, doctored

with his pal José. He had not broken the law since he ran opium loaves down to Bangkok for the tribe he'd lived with in Laos for nearly a year. He sold their harvest because the war had chopped off their trade routes. They needed what the opium would buy so they could survive.

Now he had to harvest Romaine, could hardly wait to know her, spoil her, begin some sort of life with her. How, he didn't know. How would he ever tell her he was her true father? That was easy enough, for he knew he could never tell her. Yet, if he couldn't tell her, then what was the point of all this. He wanted her in his life. But if he told her then she might slip up one day, say something, and start questions rolling that would shatter their lives.

Rhodes was thinking brutally hard now. He had cashed in Audrey, then turned around and put everything on the line for Romaine. He was willing to risk himself but needed to be very sure of the outcome. Too much was at stake this time.

What he had learned in the past weeks was what he should've known all along. He would never really be a referee of the law. He was the nimble hustler; someone who knew where she was weak and could seduce her by showing others how to turn their backs on her. That was easy, too, and yet it wasn't something you ever left to blind chance.

He broke out of that thought by forcing a new one into his head. Soon he must give instructions to the jury. Points of law. What testimony they should consider, what they could safely disregard.

Above all, he'd teach them the catechism of *reasonable doubt*. That handy tool of the law giving everyone a peg to hang their vote on and feel they had just gotten the inside word from God.

He would engrave it on the jury so deftly that for the rest of their lives they would never see black and white again in the same ways as before. Put new shades of paint on their consciences so they could go home with justice soaking in their hearts forever.

Pritter would holler to the heavens.

Rhodes could hear the braying already. But it was time

to load up and sprint for the wire. This race was nearly over. All he had to arrange now was one everlasting train wreck. And then he could let the whole thing swallow his conscience for eternity.

Chapter Twenty-Six

"What do you mean!" Tommy Burke exploded into the phone.

"Ease it down, boyo. You're stinging my ear. Bad for the opera."

"You found what?"

"Bags of little white emeralds... One for little Marco that he'll never get to sniff. Two more, and one of those for that old skirtchaser Kardas."

"When?"

Fahey told him.

"God, Alonzo. Oh, my God! The jury's out, they're deliberating right now... Why didn't you tell me?"

"Listen, if Cullis hadn't been there, I'd have lammed off with the stuff myself. Finance the opera. I was sorely tempted."

"What a stupid shithead you are."

"Tut-tut. Easy..."

"Easy? It could have meant everything."

"Not too late, is it? Tell old Cliff-boy what's up. He's very imaginative sometimes. Not in the Fahey's league, but he can rise to surprising heights, if you blow the right bugle."

"How can I go to him? Now? Oh, God!"

"Lace up those stormtrooper's kickers you wear and be off. Be sure to tell him Fahey wants a medal."

"Oh, shuddup, Alonzo. Let me think . . ."

"Time is wanting, lad."

"Why the—oh, hell!—why'd you sit on this? Why did the sheriff? Cullis, he's one of theirs?"

"Yes. And it's the sheriff who does sit on it. Know all about it, they do."

"For how long?"

"A few days. Let's see—"

"If Romaine gets convicted—"

"She might if you don't saddle your goofy ass up and move fast. I've got errands for God today. Bye."

Tommy punched the numbers three times before getting them right. He asked to be put through to Judge Rhodes. Minutes later, Rhodes sent a message by bailiff to the jury. They were to suspend their deliberations this moment, pending a new ruling.

At his downtown athletic club, Lloyd Pritter was summoned to the phone. Waddling out of a steam bath, two towels draped around his fleshy girth, he took the phone and listened. Then he crashed it back on the hook. The earpiece broke in half.

An hour later, Rhodes heard them out in his chambers. "Call it my mistake, Lloyd," he was saying. "But I wasn't sure that finding the cocaine meant as much as it now seems to."

"It doesn't mean anything," Pritter returned.

"The heck it doesn't," Tommy said. "You accused my client of lying when she told us that Sterne was a dealer."

"Narcotics aren't in this trial," Pritter replied hotly. "He's not on trial. She is."

"On, no!" Tommy said. "Narcotics are all over the trial. That's what killed him, for God's sake."

"You can't open it up now," Pritter said to Rhodes. "The jury's reaching a verdict—"

"No, they're not, Lloyd. I suspended—"

"You what!" Pritter heaved himself off the couch. "How can you do that? They'll be confused as hell."

"We may have to reopen," Rhodes suggested.

"But then—you see what you're doing? You're tainting the record," Pritter said.

"What's better, Lloyd, a tainted record or an incomplete one?"

"Please you gotta, Judge," Tommy urged. "Romaine's whole life is on the line here."

"That's why we're meeting. I think it's got to come in, don't you, Lloyd? Really?"

Rubbing the back of his neck, Pritter swelled up like a balloon about to burst. "There's no precedent for this sort of nonsense and—"

"Sure there is," Rhodes said. He opened a book, finding a place he'd marked a week earlier. "I looked it up after Burke called me. The Sassounian trial before Judge Nelson," he read. "They reopened the trial twice. A murder trial, Lloyd."

"Look, Mr. Pritter," said Tommy. "If the jury goes against us, we have to appeal. For that reason alone. It'll all have to come out at that time. You'll lose."

"Lose? Hardly. The Appeals Court might not even consider it," Pritter said.

"They'd almost have to, Lloyd," Rhodes offered.

"Appeal then, and we'll find out."

"Maybe an appeal will be necessary," Rhodes said. "But we'll complete the record at this level first."

"Why open it up?" asked Pritter. "Even if Marc was a dealer, *and I'm not agreeing he was*, how does that change anything?"

Rhodes looked at Burke, who looked at Pritter.

"Because," Tommy said, "Ferenc Kardas has his name on one of the bags they found. He's a suspect now."

And Audrey, too? Rhodes thought.

Pritter knew he was boxed. He also knew they were right. His case seemed to float away out the window, soon to be seen dive-bombing on the offices of Oldes & Farnham.

"Tell you what," Pritter said to Tommy. "Let this thing go and we'll reduce the charges. We could go for involuntary manslaughter . . ."

"No chance. Not on your life," he stated. "Judge?"

Rhodes picked up the phone. Ringing the chief bailiff, he issued a new set of orders.

"Tonight," he said, the phone still poised in midair, "we're going to settle it tonight." He made sure Burke and Pritter understood they were to come along. "You tell the sheriff, Lloyd. And Burke, you better have your man there, too."

"If I can find him," Tommy said.

"You'd better."

Chapter Twenty-Seven

A pagan moon lay on her back and kissed a soft glow into all the faces Fahey could see. A breeze pulsed through the trees and the sway of the trees made him think of an Apache dance. He would've given anything for an African drum to tap out some sinister beats, and wiggle the spine of this night.

He arrived shortly after Cullis, who had come with two of his superiors by the look of them. Together, they watched the bewildered jurors file in the door, with Burke, Pritter, then Rhodes following. Barely able to contain his excitement, Fahey begged for a comet to blaze across the sky, a dazzling signal directly from the gypsy. He would name it after her.

By the door Alesia Noor lurked in and out of the shadows. She raised up on tiptoes to see better.

Fahey sported his walking stick. Edging around the room, he chatted idly with the nurse with the horn-rims. Learing of her profession, Fahey complained of a bad back. "From alcohol abstinence. Most likely you could aid me," he suggested. "Front and back. After dinner. Know just the place for us. Caviar the size of jumping beans."

She sniggered pleasantly. There was something about

Fahey. Something that made her want to decipher the deeper messages in his electric blue eyes.

Rhodes quieted the room, telling the jurors why they were there. They would certainly recall how the defendant's credibility had been challenged on the stand. Many statements couldn't be proven one way or the other. Yet the state insisted Romaine Burke was lying. Here was possible evidence that she was telling the truth to the court.

"You can decide," he said. "You know where you are." With wondering minds the jury looked around at the lavender walls. "The sheriff here will show us what they found recently... I was told about it, several days ago, but I wasn't sure the evidence fit in with this trial. I didn't want you, who're the real judges here, to be prejudiced. But then I changed my mind."

"But why?" asked one juror.

"As I said, the defendant's truthfulness is at stake. That's an issue the state put right out in front of you. The state asked the defendant for proof she wasn't lying to us... Perhaps we have it. You'll have to consider everything."

This was the first time in months the jurors had seen a home. They were eager to see why they'd been called out, and to feel their way around in a world they had nearly forgotten.

Fahey stayed in the back, less than a foot away from the brunette. Just over his breath he conveyed how this night was so right for a moon bath. Had she ever partaken? He knew of a place in the Hollywood hills.

Cullis and one of the other sheriffs wrestled the couch away from the wall. They shoved the sections to one side so everyone could easily view the baseboard.

Kneeling with a screwdriver in his hand, Cullis pried out the wall-plates. The jurors, all but one, strained forward. Cullis's two superiors, a few feet behind him, watched intently as first one metal drawer, then the other, were pulled out.

"It's gone," Cullis said, straightening up. "Was here but it traveled somewhere."

Fahey roared with laughter.

One of the sheriffs threw him a stony glance. He stepped forward, moving through the jurors, who parted to make way. "You know something we aren't privy to?" he asked Fahey.

"Lot of things, Admiral. And I think a comet will be on us soon."

"You were here, weren't you, with Lieutenant Cullis?"

"I most surely was. Both times."

"Where're those bags?"

"Beats me. You boys come back and get them, did you? Probably out on the street by now."

"Listen, Fahey, you're on a real quick wick—"

"I'll take care of this, sheriff," said Rhodes, coming through the circle of jurors. He backed the officer away, then asked Fahey, "You know anything?"

"Just that it was here. Cullis saw it, too."

"That's it?"

"All of it I know about. Went off like a bluebird in the night."

Rhodes inhaled a careful breath. His ace in the hole was stuck somewhere up his sleeve, and he'd wagered plenty on this one. Turning to Cullis, he asked: "What about it, lieutenant? You have any guesses?"

"No, sir."

"Okay then, tell the jury in detail what you found here with Mr. Fahey."

Cullis went through the whole finding. Of how he was there twice with Fahey by request of the defense. What they'd seen on the most recent visit, and how they left it. "All on a confidential report down at the station," he ended.

"But where're the jewels?" Fahey piped up. "Those down there at the station, too? You sell it already? Got the new haberdashery business all set up?"

Cullis stiffened.

The jurors wore mixed expressions. Pritter leaned back against the iron railing near the steps down to the living room, enjoying the despair on Tommy Burke's face.

Fahey searched the room for Alesia Noor. She looked as baffled as everyone else, standing near Pritter, plucking nervously at her ivory hair combs.

Fahey hadn't seen Cullis barge through the jurors, but he immediately sensed the brunette melting away from him.

"You sure got yourself a fat mouth, don't you?"

"You should hear my lungs, Cullis. Really, you should. Going to sing the lead soon in Madame Butterfly . . . Might even offer you a discount ticket, old sod . . ."

"Goin' to sing you something, too. You're coming down to the station, Fahey."

"Next month maybe . . . Listen," Fahey lowered his voice, "you'd better get onto the Noor woman. She might know. Her name was tagged to one of the bags."

"I will." Cullis motioned to Alesia Noor, calling her over.

Rhodes, standing near the jurors, threw a glance at Tommy Burke, who looked away.

"You been in this apartment since I was here last?" Cullis asked Alesia Noor.

"Never."

"Where'd you get that bruise on your chin?"

"Cleaning up, mopping. I slip."

"Anyone been here?"

"You. That man." She pointed at Fahey.

"No one else?"

"You tell me apartment is sealed up. Your orders. No one come here," she said. "Him, he come."

"I know about Fahey. He was here with me."

Fahey warned her fatally with his eyes. He tried a smile made only for your first meeting with God.

"But he come the other time. When you not show up."

"When was that?" Cullis asked Fahey.

Rhodes stopped inhaling for a time. He had to when his chest started squeezing so hard. The jurors moved closer to Cullis, as if taking sides.

Fahey explained how he had come back to pick up his notebook after he visited the apartment for the first time with Cullis. Only for a few minutes. It was late, and Cullis had already gone off duty.

"Needed my notes, had to advise Tommy Burke," Fahey told everyone. He'd already been deserted, even by the brunette who joined the others.

"Why did you let him in?" Cullis asked Alesia Noor. "You were told not to allow anyone to—"

"But he with you," she protested.

"With me? No, I'm a sheriff—"

"But he show me the metal . . . heesa badge."

Cullis looked at Fahey. "What badge?"

"Nothing," Fahey said. "A gift from the wife, as I remember."

"You impersonating a law officer?"

Alesia Noor moved forward. Still furious that Kardas had taken her share of the cocaine, she was ready to take a swipe at anyone. Fahey was her best chance to stay clear of Cullis, though they couldn't do much now that the bags were missing.

"He show me. He have it in his wallet."

Cullis and the two sheriffs spent the next three minutes leaning all over Fahey, finally forcing him to display the honorary sheriff's badge, embossed and engraved with a bogus number by his jeweler friend.

"A technicality," said Fahey, who glanced at Rhodes, adding, "Isn't that right, Judge?"

"Not exactly," Rhodes answered. "But the main thing is that you and Cullis found the drugs here a few days ago."

"We did," Cullis agreed. "But Fahey shouldn'ta come back here without an escort. That's a violation."

Alesia Noor sidled around to Cullis. "That man no good"—again she pointed at Fahey—"he come and stay here long time. I find him there by that wall. He dropping something. He say you come later. But you never come."

Cullis's mind blazed. Dropped something? The table knife that was behind the couch when they both had returned the second time?

"You told her I would be here?" he asked Fahey.

"Was trying to reach you—"

"Crap. You're coming with me, Fahey. We're going to have a talk."

Before Fahey could protest, get his quick brain and quicker mouth in action, Rhodes stopped him.

"We'll sort this out later," he said. Turning to the sheriff, he asked, "You're going to make up a report on this?"

"It's a must," he replied.

"You have another report? From when Lieutenant Cullis and Mr. Fahey found the drugs?" Rhodes asked.

The sheriff nodded.

"Please have copies of both in my court tomorrow by nine o'clock."

"Including one on Fahey for breaking and entering?" asked the captain.

"No. We won't need that."

"Now wait a minute here, everyone," Fahey shot back. "You're getting this wrong." A deep flush crept up his ruddy face. He rapped on Cullis's shoulder with the walking stick. "I think Noor knows more than she's giving us . . . she says she saw me there. She could've come back and looked and found everything."

"But why didn't you tell us what you found that first time?" Cullis asked. "We're gonna spend some time near the floor on that one. At the station, Fahey."

Outside, Rhodes walked up the sloping street of the cul-de-sac. The jurors were herded into their van by the bailiff. Fahey caught up with him.

"What're you going to do?" Fahey asked.

"Finish up this trial."

"About your friend Fahey, I meant."

"I'll talk to the sheriff."

"You got me into this. Get me out."

"Later."

"Now, Cliff, right now. What if they charge me, pull my license? Christ, man!"

"Let's worry on it later. Now lower your voice, dammit, and move away."

"Son of a bitch!" Fahey cursed, hitting the pavement with his stick. The sharp sound echoed like a pistol shot. "You're all the son of a bitch there ever was, ever."

Rhodes walked ahead. His shoulders pulled forward as he made the climb to the next street. The moon had dropped, blackening the night. He thought he heard Cullis calling Fahey back. Fahey was among the wounded now. But so was Romaine, and she was all he cared about for now. The trial was costing too much in human pay. Audrey. Now Fahey. And himself?

Trudging up the road to where he'd parked the Bentley, Rhodes worked his brain as fast as it would go. He had come here to sell the jury on one idea: If they believed Romaine about Marc Sterne's drug escapades, shouldn't they believe the rest of her story?

Chapter Twenty-Eight

A new day now. The foreman was polling the jurors for the fourth time. They'd spent the morning in the courtroom, listening to another round of closing arguments, after the visit to Marc Sterne's apartment the night before.

Pritter: "Without evidence there's no crime. If there were narcotics there, they may've belonged to anyone. Someone, perhaps, who broke in to get them back . . . And whether there was cocaine there or not doesn't change one thing . . . the defendant, ladies and gentlemen, is lying to us."

Burke reminding them: "The sheriff's people saw the bags. Here it is on the reports they sent us this morning. Look here! Lieutenant Cullis specifically said the bags were tagged with the names of Marc Sterne, Ferenc Kardas, and Alesia Noor. That's dealing, isn't it? Hasn't Romaine Brook been telling you the truth all along?"

Rhodes once again went over the rule of reasonable doubt—that it didn't mean beyond any shadow of a doubt at all, but was merely a plain test of common sense. *Was it reasonable* in their minds and hearts that a murder would take place this way? That's all, and nothing more. Dropping it on them again, like a bag of cement from ten stories up.

The foreman polled again. She knew how the vote would go this time. She sent out a message—they'd be ready with their verdict soon.

Nearly over now. Months of their lives spent in this courthouse with Romaine Brook, the dead Raye Wheeler, Pritter and Burke and Rhodes. And as many nights at the Biltmore Hotel where none of them would ever visit again by choice. Living and sleeping there like ill-chosen refugees. Bickering, arguing strenuously at times, lonely, laughing, bedding together. Two of the women had learned their way through five of the male jurors and three of the bailiffs; affairs that would soon become lost to memory.

They would face another world soon—their families, neighbors, the humdrum of everyday life—and go back to jobs they hoped still existed for them. And they would probably never see each other again. Things might come out that were better forgotten, denied. Just as some of the witnesses they had seen and heard had denied and denied again.

People. They were all the same.

The foreman finished marking the ballot, then she penned a long sentence at the bottom. They were ready, they all exchanged looks across the table. Chairs scraped, the sound of metal against wood, and they filed out once more.

In the courtroom the foreman glanced at the clock: 5:20. She handed the folded ballot to a bailiff, who gave it up to Rhodes. He read it as if he were seeing his own life exposed, then passed the paper down to the court clerk.

Who stood inspecting the press and hundreds of faces behind the press.

". . . find the defendant not guilty," was all anyone seemed to hear in the tumultuous shouts.

Joy suddenly crowded Rhodes's throat. But he was exhausted and somehow it seemed to him that he'd been standing in one exact spot for the last century. His eyes went to his daughter as she hugged Tommy Burke, tears streaming down her face; tears wet and heavy yet seeming as golden as her hair.

Burke whipped a long arm out to fend off some reporters pushing in, clamoring until the commotion bowed to total chaos. Other reporters, their questions set on rapid-fire, peppered away at the jury.

People thronged around Romaine, Rhodes saw, and he supposed that's how it must be at a splashy film opening. He stopped for only a moment, watching a circle of bailiffs hem in Romaine and Tommy. The human ring moved, creating a gap in the throng of well-wishers and shouters.

I freed her, he thought, and now she's in a human cage that may prove worse than the one with iron bars.

In the corridor, lights were set up for two portable video cameras. Pritter stood before an interviewer from the local NBC station, his eyes as friendly as two bullet holes.

"... And what did you think of your opponent?"

"Which one? If you mean Burke, I can't really say," Pritter told the interviewer. "He has a pretty good mouth game, if you listen closely."

"What's your feeling about the trial?"

"We lost. She got away with it. That happens, unfortunately."

"How about the jury?"

"You ought to ask them."

"Did you feel Judge Rhodes handled the trial well?"

Pritter bristled. "I think he flunked the course. He was a pretty swift lawyer before he came to the court... He did some odd things here. So odd that I'd have to call it a screw-up. I'll be entering a complaint soon."

"About what?"

"Wait and see. Now I've got to go." Pritter pushed off.

"One more question, please." The interviewer moved along with Pritter, furiously waving the cameraman back so the shot would still show them in frame.

"Will the state open an investigation against Mrs. Sterne? Or Kardas?"

Pritter stopped, but he merely shook his head. "No comment."

It was over, but then they were all aware that it would never be over. Lives had been torn apart. Mending them was the same as trying to hide your other life in a thimble. Nothing ever fit.

In a small room screened off by two bailiffs standing outside the door, Romaine sat across from Tommy Burke. They raged with glee and Tommy could hardly quiet her exuberance. He didn't really try. She was so alive and eager and close to him.

They waited.

Outside reporters were still waiting to open up with a fresh barrage. Bashful around any spotlight, Tommy didn't cherish the idea of mixing with them. Besides, he'd fought with all his heart for this moment, and he didn't plan to share it with anyone else.

"You do all the talking, Tommy. You got me away from this hell."

He grinned crookedly. "It's you they'll be after."

"You do it," she insisted.

"You're the news," he demurred.

"So are you."

"Yeah, maybe, but small stuff."

"Oh, Tommy! Isn't it glorious . . . and I owe you everything. Everything! That reminds me. I can't pay your bill for a while. But I'll do it soon as I get work again."

"There're the expenses. A few thousand. But there's no bill for me."

"Oh, yes."

"Nope. I did something I never thought I could"—though a flicker of doubt swept his face—"and you made that possible. I'll get all sorts of cases after this."

"I'm paying, I'm sorry. You'll have to let me."

"We'll talk about it another time."

"You just remember, Tommy. Add it all up."

"Sure." He was more interested in something else. "Can you have dinner with me tonight? My mother's? Or we'll find some quiet spot."

"I couldn't."

"You have to eat. Something to celebrate on after all the prison food."

She went dour. "I can't, Tommy. My agent, Max Shapin, is picking me up. He's out there somewhere . . . And I have to be alone for a while."

"Tomorrow then. Take the day off, and we'll go somewhere. Up to the mountains."

Her hair danced around her shoulders. "No, Tommy. I'm sorry. You've been the biggest saint, but I'm putting all this shit behind me. Everything and everyone."

"Me?"

"Everyone."

Elation was instantly swallowed up by misery. "I thought maybe we could be friends. We could have a laugh with Fahey. He can be fun."

"I don't like him. He's a destroyer."

"He's quite funny actually."

"You're so naive, Tommy. So sweet but terribly naive."

"Yes, maybe. But let's do something. We can go up to San Francisco next week."

"You don't get it, do you?"

"About what?" he said.

"Let's go meet the press, Tommy," she said, standing up. "I've got places to go."

"Without me."

"You'll be okay. But stay away from me." An insolent smile rocketed up to laughter, carrying from one wall to the other. "I'm free," she cried. "Seven months, Tommy, that's how long I've been behind that fucking iron gate. We beat them!"

"I know."

"You could never know. My mind, Tommy, it's all blued out. I have to—"

"I want to help."

"You did, so marvelously too."

"Then more."

"I need someone different, Tommy."

"I could be—could try to be—"

"What you never would be, not for me."

"Try me, Romaine."

"I have."

"Romaine?"

"Yes."

"The press is going to ask a lot of things."

"I suppose they will. But who cares. We won, Tommy."

"There're some things you testified to that you never told me about. Marrying Marc and the abortion, to name two."

"So?"

"Why didn't you let me know?"

"Oh, Tommy, there are some things you can't tell anyone. Not ever."

"But you did. You told the whole courtroom."

"I had to see how things were going first."

"You didn't trust me. Is that it, Romaine?"

She looked down at her feet. Then her head came up with a face full of rapture. "Tommy, trusting other people too much has cost me everything I ever had."

"You told the truth, didn't you?"

"No one'll ever catch me lying, Tommy. The truth is bigger than all of life with me."

Tommy stood with her by the door. He wondered if his knees would ever stop swelling. Or his heart. Nothing seemed to fit right for him either, or for those hopes he had nursed for so many weeks now.

He would've given anything. Anything at all.

Chapter Twenty-Nine

Rhodes packed his gear for Mexico. Fritzi was bursting to go. He was ready himself, and ready to ask her a giant favor but unsure how she would react.

Over his morning coffee he read that Pritter had filed a strong protest to the court. So what? A jury had freed Romaine. They couldn't go after her again.

He tried to convince himself.

According to the articles the man Kardas, wanted for more questioning, was missing. The Sternes apparently didn't know his whereabouts.

And Rhodes had not been able to find Romaine. He had asked Macklin Price to keep on trying while he was fishing in Mexico. Macklin had clucked at him, asking why. There were reports, he told her, on the news that some woman's magazine was approaching Romaine for her story. He hoped to dissuade her, the episode was closed. His excuse to Macklin for chasing after Romaine was another lame one, but it would have to do.

But the episode wasn't closed. Not for him, not for Audrey, and, if he had anything to do about it, not for their daughter.

Rhodes was writing a letter at his desk when he heard the phone ring. Moments later, Consuelo came in as he sealed the envelope and addressed it.

"The Señora," she said. She was cheerful, for he was home and she could fuss over him.

"Which Señora? Will you mail this for me?" He handed her the letter.

Consuelo told him which Señora. He squinted for a few seconds.

"How're you, Audrey?" he said into the phone.

"How the hell do you think I am?"

He said nothing.

"Are you there?"

"Right here. It's over. You'll be all right."

"Says you! The sheriff out here is asking questions . . ." and she burned his ear with how her life was in torment again. And Kardas had disappeared, making matters worse.

"I'd guess they'll go after him," Rhodes said.

"And me."

"Any good lawyer can handle your end."

"I hate lawyers."

"Sorry."

"And what *I'm* damn sorry about, and you should be ashamed of, is what you let them do to me in your rotten court," Audrey said.

"I wouldn't have stopped that, Audrey, even if I could, which incidentally I couldn't."

She sighed deeply, too bitter for tears. "Thanks millions. And now she's off scot-free."

"Thank goodness."

"A disaster. You mark my words, Cliff Rhodes. You let her go and—"

"I'm a little busy right now, Audrey."

"That's too bad . . . I've something to tell you, though I don't know why I should."

"Shoot." He changed the phone to his other ear.

"I'm not taking any more chances, Cliff."

"On what?"

"I want those adoption papers back, or whatever you call them . . . And I'm going to get them."

"That's a mistake, Audrey."

"No, it isn't. What if other people find out?"

"Leave it alone, Audrey. And why tell me anyway?"

"Because I don't know if you're planning to tell your darling Romaine who her parents—"

"I haven't decided anything yet."

"I know you and—"

"No, you don't. And here's some free lawyerly advice. Stay out of it, or you're likely to find hornets all over—"

"I'll worry about me."

"Suit yourself. But I'm warning you, Audrey, those papers could turn out to be a blowtorch for everyone—"

Audrey hung up on him.

By ten the next day Rhodes was packing his car with luggage, his mood bright and his worries easing. Having a good healthy attack of happiness, as he thought of it, when he heard tires flying the gravel off his driveway.

Fahey got out of his Buick convertible, walked up to the garage. Unshaven, his black beret tilted over bloodshot eyes, he stopped a few feet away. "Off somewhere?" he asked.

Rhodes told him.

"I'm not invited?"

"Not on this one. Fritzi wants to get away. Hardly seen her for a month." Rhodes could smell early fumes on Fahey's breath.

"But you saw some of me, didn't you? On the run, aren't you, when my ass is on the cooker?"

Rhodes put down a fishing rod case. "Take the guestroom upstairs. Sleep it off. When I get back we can—"

"You got me into this, old cock, now help me . . . you know what those chummers will do? Suspend my license, that's what. Even got a hearing set up."

"I'll try to figure something out, Alonzo."

"Do it one better than that."

"Meaning?"

Suddenly Fahey darkened even more under the black stubble on his face. "Tell them what came down. What really happened. Don't ask me to fall down for you."

"I can't. You know that."

"Then, boyo, I will. This is friend Fahey you're calling upon to cover your—"

"Alonzo, I've got to go."

Fahey stepped closer. "Cullis is frying me. They're gonna pull on me, Cliff. Know how that feels?"

"I think so."

"Do you, now? And supposing they find out *all* Fahey knows? You'll not be getting the Good Housekeeping award."

"Don't force me to deny it, Alonzo. I'd have to."

"What a sweet one you are. You used to be a fighter. Now—"

"I said I'll try to think of something."

"That's not good enough, laddie-boy."

"For now, it'll have to be."

Rhodes bent over to load more luggage. When he looked up again, he met Fahey's glowering face, those luminous eyes like dangerous stars about to explode.

"A black one, you are. Black as a bloody coal digger's ass."

"Keep your nerve. We'll get by it. I'm sorry, but Fritzi's waiting for me."

Rhodes brushed past him. How could he ever tell Fahey the whole story? About Romaine? Or Audrey? Of why he'd done what he had to do for himself? That he had been caught on the swaying high-wire of protecting the law or protecting his daughter.

As he backed the car out, Fahey rapped hard on the side window, shouting something. Thready spittle dangled from his mouth and his forehead shone with wet. Another fist crashed against the window.

Rhodes was tempted to get out and take a swing at him. Or swing an arm around him, hold him, take him inside, shower him down and sleep him sober.

But he kept on backing down the driveway as Fahey kicked gravel at the car in rage. Turning into the road, Rhodes was swept by uneasy feelings, and he thanked fate that Fahey and Audrey were not acquainted with each other.

They could sink everything, and not even know they were doing it until it was too late.

Gladly, he would have gone to bat for Fahey. In the sweep of the trial Fahey's sin was a trivial nothing. A quiet call to the police commissioner would probably have put the matter to rest.

But now in the Hollywood Division they were hopping mad at Fahey showing them up. His laughing fast mouth had ignited their anger.

Rhodes couldn't lift a finger. The press, for the second trial in a row, were already slashing at him for turning a murder trial into a narcotics chase. This time they happened to be right, only they didn't know why.

If Alonzo Fahey ever talked, really talked, and was believed, then Rhodes knew he would be scouting up one more attorney.

For himself.

Chapter Thirty

A feast of blue.

Every shade of it colored the waters they fished off Cabo San Lucas, a sleepy resort at the tip of Baja California. By their fourth day, blazed by sun and sprayed by salt water and wind, they were brown-red and peeling.

Sunup to twilight they fished from a boat whose skipper and mate were old friends of Rhodes. Fishing hard and fishing well, they had taken and released twelve good marlin with heavy shoulders and strong hips and fast tail-feet, who knew all about the sea and how to dance and walk on it long before the Bible scribes made the Jesus stories.

On the fifth morning Fritzi begged off. She had strained a shoulder, and said her arms had as much strength as two wet noodles.

Sunburned, stiff and sore, they had walked down an almost deserted beach. Two miles from the hotel, they found a natural pool in front of a lagoon, and swam in its limpid waters. Later, in the shade of jutting sea rocks, Rhodes spread out a terrycloth beach blanket. Then he spread Fritzi after slipping off her bottoms. For all the midday they loved, swam again, naked and brave, no cares except the care for each other.

She still thought about it even now, holding him close on the patio by the hotel pool. Around them other couples moved to the slow music or sat at tables and drank, listening to two guitarists strum their ballads along with a pianist.

Fritzi glided along in a mellow haze. She pressed her tilted cheek against the silk of Rhodes's soft white polo shirt.

"I've been thinking," she said, when the beat of the music trailed off. "I don't ever want to quit this place."

"Open up a Masquers—South?"

"I meant just stay crazy here for a while, like you made me so crazy this afternoon."

"Lucky we didn't get arrested," Rhodes said.

"I wouldn't mind."

He twirled her about. "You would after a few nights in a Mexican slammer." Flecks of light shone in her raven hair.

"Would they bed us together?"

"Big enough bribe, sure. But let's *not* find out."

"Any old time," Fritzi hummed.

"There's the other thing." Holding her closer, his arm pressing hard against her lower back. "We could do it, Fritzi, if you really want to." He'd never said it before, not to anyone, and the words tumbled out slowly.

"What's that, Cliff?"

"Marry."

She stopped, dead still.

"Marry?" she said. "You mean—"

Fritzi didn't finish. Her eyes swam into his, and she gripped him around the neck with both arms. Her weight hung on him until he felt his neck give out.

"Cliff, darling Cliff, I'll make you love it. You'll see . . ."

"I'm seeing right now. But I'm about to black out."

He kissed her as she stood up straight, easing her weight away. A long kiss and they were deaf to the music floating on the night.

"When?" Fritzi asked as they returned to their table. "Oh, Cliff!"

"A month or so. After they confirm me." He held her hands.

"Are you going to have any trouble? The newspapers and all?"

Rhodes shrugged. "Shouldn't think so. Why?"

"I don't know. The publicity . . . Oh, never mind," Fritzi said, almost raving to herself. "They're getting the best in the world . . . A supreme for the Supreme." She suddenly went serious. "My God, there's so much to work out, isn't there?"

"I'll say."

"We'll have the best life together. We'll be the talk, Cliff, you wait and see."

He grinned. "I don't have to. We're the talk right here in case you want to look over your shoulder."

"I love you. Forever, I love you," said Fritzi, waving cheerfully at two couples sharing a nearby table.

They drank and danced for hours, lost in their own cocoon. Near eleven, arms entwined, they walked in the moonpath up to their bungalow. Fritzi joked exuberantly, silly little jokes that meant nothing to anyone else.

Pouring himself a José Cuervo, Rhodes sat on the edge of the bed, feasting on Fritzi's deep breasts, rounded belly, the smooth flanks and wide hips and thighs as she slipped into a cotton shift. A born breeder, he thought. She came over, took his drink, sipped from it and smiled.

"Sit down for a jiffy," he said.

"How about lie down?"

"Coming up. But I have to ask you something first. A favor."

"Anything. Name it." Fritzi sat.

He asked if Romaine could stay with her for a week or two until things settled down and some sort of a life could be planned for the girl. Get her out of the public eye, away from the glare.

Though he was not obligated in any real sense, he had found out she was the blood daughter of someone he knew very well. A random coincidence. He had become aware of the situation halfway through the trial.

"The parents, her real parents, want to see that she's helped"—how weak, he thought quickly—"and I said I'd see what I could do." Knowing he was being evasive, Rhodes played directly to Fritzi's generous nature.

"They can't help or won't help?"

"Can't admit they're the parents, no."

"Well, well—"

"I'd put her up myself," said Rhodes, "but that wouldn't go over at all."

Fritzi gave him a look. "I agree . . . Sure, she can stay for a while. Be a little strange, I'll say that."

"Strange? How?"

"Taking in a murderess. Imagine?"

"But she's not. She was let go."

"That won't make any difference to some people," Fritzi offered.

"A jury's a jury," he said, though he knew she was right.

"I guess so . . . Anyway, doesn't she have friends she can stay with?" asked Fritzi, having second thoughts.

"Probably does, sweetheart. But maybe she needs time to adjust. She's been a prisoner for months, you know."

"Who're the parents anyway?"

"I'm sworn on that, darling. I'm sorry, but I can't tell you."

"Not even me?"

"No one. I can't."

"Important people? With names?"

"Sort of, yes."

"I'll be damned." Fritzi sighed wistfully, though she was alive with curiosity.

"They couldn't have been more astonished. Or helpless, as it turned out."

"Do I know them?"

"I'm pretty sure you do and that's all I can say."

"How strange. The whole trial. I hope she doesn't expect to entertain or anything. At my house, I mean."

"I'm sure she doesn't. And I don't know if she'd even stay or not. A gesture, that's all."

"Your friend, whoever it is, must be some friend."

They talked on, with Fritzi inquiring whose house they would live in after they married? How big a wedding? Wasn't everything so wonderful? In her joy she laughed that laugh that was like no other. There was nothing false about it, nothing contrived. It was simply a symphony of sound that started somewhere deep inside Fritzi, then gathered its full melody on the way up and out. He could always tell when it was coming. The low purr, followed by a long roll, finally a deep and warm embrace of music that made Rhodes think of Ella Fitzgerald's singing. But it wasn't, it was something better. He loved hearing her.

She made love to him again, the length of him, and even where he was shy. She told him she would gladly have made love in the middle of the dance floor if he had wanted her there. Maybe not, but then maybe yes, too. So excited she couldn't sleep. She thought earnestly about their life together and what a drag Sacramento would be. By comparison, Romaine Brook would be a lark.

She thought.

Past midnight, a thousand miles to the north, a light still burned in another bungalow. Romaine sat with her legs curled up in a chair across from Max Shapin, her agent. Some said he was the best agent in the film business.

They played backgammon and Romaine was beating him four games to two. Very soon he would score her for five.

Max's wife, Julia, had left early that morning for Los Angeles where she taught speech and breathing and dialogue technique to actors. On Thursdays she spent the day at Hollywood Children's Hospital, where she struggled with the speech defects of retarded kids; five, six, seven years of age.

They were good friends, the Shapins and Romaine, and it was Julia who had first spotted Romaine one night at a small theater in Santa Monica. At her urging Max had caught the next performance. Two days later he had signed on as her agent.

The Shapins had picked her up after the trial was over, and Romaine spent the night at their Beverly Hills home. The next day the three of them drove down to La Costa, a resort on the northern rim of San Diego.

La Costa was a great favorite with some of the film colony: a very nice playground with a spa, a dozen tennis courts, a championship golf course—a place where loud money came to quiet down temporarily.

With real privacy.

Which is why Max had chosen it. He was known there, a regular. And the onlookers, if they heard Romaine Brook was in residence, wouldn't get in the way. A brief word with the manager had taken care of that nuisance.

Romaine rolled her dice. Double fives. In glee she said: "Snakes and bad breaks. I'm off the board, Maxey."

He grimaced. "You're a guest here, kid. You got to ease up on me."

"You're letting me win, Max. I can tell."

"Never threw a game in my life."

"And you never throw anything so far you can't reach it, right? You told me that once."

"S'right. Shapin's first commandment."

Max began to pencil up the score. Before he could finish, Romaine's hand shot out and she ripped the scoresheet off the pad.

"We'll finish tomorrow, okay?"

"Tomorrow is never. Don't forget that one either," Max said.

"How could I? You tell me every week."

"So's you don't forget."

A teddy bear, thought Romaine. Right down to the tight curly hair, the paunch, the heavy sloping shoulders; a bear who made wisecracks through four thousand dollar teeth. Teeth that chewed money out of the studios so Shapin clients ate and lived the best in town. Except for her.

"Quit moping," he said, tossing the pencil aside.

"You weren't even looking at me."

"My peepers are here." Max touched his nose. "You like a drink, a beddy-bye drink?"

"No thanks."

"Smart girl. But I need one to switch off my engine." He ambled over to a small tiled bar in one corner of the room.

"What am I going to do, Max? No one wants me anymore."

"Cool it, kid. There's nothing else you can do."

"I'm really flat, Max, and I owe everyone in the world."

"You can't get it," Max said over the splash of water from a tap. "Studios, they're like anyone else. Sensitive. But they got a lot to protect. Don't take chances with their audiences and why should they? You're too hot."

"Hot the wrong way."

"The wrong way is right," Max agreed. He came back, talking. "But you're the best. Never you forget that, beautiful. I know. I handle some of the biggest."

"I've got to get work, Max. I have to."

"But you can't, not here. Not now. Next year, we'll see."

"Next year is the next century. Either you find me some work or I'll take up *Cosmopolitan*'s offer."

"Stay out of the mags. Like I told you, that only heats things up again. *Cosmopolitan* we forget. Yesterday we already forgot it."

"But it's fifty thousand, Max."

"Not for ten times that would I let you."

Romaine's shoulders slumped. She fiddled with the backgammon board, making a loose design with the ivory discs. Where were her friends? Who were her friends? Frustrated, she swept her hand across the board, sending the discs flying across the table.

Max barely noticed. "Like I said, and like Julia says . . . go to London. You can study at the Royal Drama. I got friends there in the business. Get you some parts, I'm sure, on the London stage. You work hard, knock 'em flat, like you can do"—Max snapped his fingers—"and whammo, you're back in Hollywood and them with their checkbooks open."

"London's rainy, isn't it?"

"Who cares? You start again, but there and not here."

"I already started once, Max. I had it all going for me. Everything."

Max skipped a palm off the side of his head. "The moment you're born, you start. It's who finishes that counts."

Romaine stood up yawning. No more advice tonight, not even from her darling Max.

"I'm tired."

"Sleep it good. Tomorrow I gotta get back to the office. Like some tennis in the morning?"

"Sure, if you'd like. What time?"

"Whenever we wake up. Eight, maybe."

But Romaine didn't sleep at all. She lay for an hour in murky depression, the rails of her young life twisting off into a shapeless future. The trial wasn't over yet, not for her; she might even be on the unwritten blacklist. The studios had one, even if they denied it. And the Sternes could make sure she went to the top of it.

She thought of Max's advice about London. She didn't know anyone there. It would be wet and lonely, and she would have to make new contacts in a theatrical world strange to her. Though Max would help her, he'd said so. She remembered how Audrey Sterne had once discussed her first marriage—to a Lord Hubbard-Hewes, a famous producer there. Maybe...

But Max turned and turned again in her anxious head. Grizzly Max, so affectionate, so kind. He knew her ego, her sensitivities and how to protect them. Occasionally he would even grab a friendly feel of her breasts, always with a small joke to distract her.

Any man right now, Romaine thought.

She slipped out of bed, padded down the dimly lit hallway and opened his door. She could barely make out the hump of him under the sheets, but heard his snoring.

"Whaz-whoz'at?"

Her hands were on him, fondling, and her leg was draped across his thick middle.

"Me, Max, just me for you," she said in a low voice.

"You crazy? Julia'll kill us."

"She won't, Max, because you'll never tell her, will you?"

"Stop it, kid...oh, Jehu, sto—"

"It's been ever so long for me, Max. I can feel how strong you are. Hard, Max, really hard. Shall I stop? Just tell me, Max."

He groaned from somewhere in his soul.

About the only way Max could have stopped would have been with a straitjacket wrapped around him. They rolled and tossed, and afterward, chuffing for breath, Max clamped one hand on her smooth bottom, the other over his heart. He lay there fallen and full of doomed ecstasy.

No tennis the next morning; only room service with steak, eggs, a pot of coffee and two champagne mimosas for Max, who was strangely quiet. He had called his office. "Be here another day," he told them. "Coming down with a cold or something." Later he'd figure out something more original to tell Julia.

Max wrote Romaine a check for five thousand dollars that afternoon.

"Shopping money, that's all," he said to her, figuring that he'd reap it back dozens of times. His hunches about talent rarely failed. Romaine, she was spectacular—in bed, too, he thought as his eyes rolled—and she was yet to truly find her range and depth as an actress. Another Garbo, maybe, Max thought, signing the check.

He always trusted his instincts. The kid had the right fire in her to become a top actress. She would just have to cool her heels till he could get her packaged right and back in front of the cameras.

Chapter Thirty-One

Audrey listened closely.

She was trying to fathom her chances with Sister Marius. The first time they'd met seemed ages ago, though it wasn't much more than a year, when Audrey had sought help in finding her daughter. She had begged then and paid then—with hefty monthly donations to Las Infantas.

And there had been the call from Sister Marius a few weeks before, telling Audrey that a subpoena might be issued for precisely what she was now after. The call that had started an avalanche. *That call*. Audrey, afraid she might scream at Sister Marius, wisely decided not to bring it up now.

Best to be patient, but then she'd been so patient for the

last half-hour. Cut the butter up, pay off, and be gone. But only please, please, please let me have those God-forgotten papers.

So she listened.

". . . quite a problem for everyone it seems," Sister Marius was saying with upturned palms.

Audrey forced a smile out of cold storage. "*Quite* is a very wide word, wouldn't you say?"

"Forgive me, Mrs. Sterne, but no, I don't think so."

"But why? Why this problem? It's so simple."

"Not necessarily. Please remember a detective was here to make inquiries."

"What was his name again, Sister?"

"Fahey. Quite a charming man. Or rascal, I should say," said Sister Marius pleasantly. She remembered the flowers he had brought her.

"But you told me you didn't tell him anything."

"That's absolutely correct, I didn't. He only knows Romaine was adopted from here. Nothing more."

"You're sure?"

"Quite."

That word again. *Quite* this and *quite* that, said so pertly and with such finality.

"I suppose," Audrey said, "you know why I'm here again."

"But you surely understand that we're a religious order. We have our obligations and those papers are part of our records." Said so nicely and with a beatific smile.

"And my record as well, Sister Marius."

"Yes, when you put it that way. And your daughter's."

Sizing each other up, they traded the quizzical look of two strangers who sensed an opportunity, but were not sure whose turn it was to bargain.

"We were very sorry about your son, Mrs. Sterne," said Sister Marius a moment later.

"Stepson."

"Stepson, yes. May God rest his soul."

"Well, I'd like some rest for my soul right now."

Audrey reached into her Hermes handbag, drawing out a cashier's check. She placed it on the desk blotter in front of Sister Marius. "I'm prepared to rest that much of my soul on Las Infantas in return for the file. We can even destroy it together if you like."

Sister Marius's eyes widened. She'd never seen a gift this size: twenty-five thousand dollars, sent straight from her Savior. A sum that would solve her worries for many months to come. Unpaid bills galore were stacked in the drawer right beside her very excited knees.

She handed the check back to Audrey. "I'm afraid you misunderstand us," she said, nearly weeping inside. "We could never accept your generosity this way."

"But I want to be generous, and I'd like you to be generous with me."

"The material aspects of this world are of little concern—"

"Sister Marius, let's not kid each other," Audrey broke in. "This place'll be condemned if you don't do something. I'd like to help . . . But I want some help, too. What do you care about those papers? They're twenty-two years old for goodness sakes . . . They've done far more damage than good."

"And the young woman?"

"My daughter. Naturally I want to protect her. She's been through a hell of . . . excuse me, an extremely tough time . . ." Audrey placed the check on the blotter again before continuing: "My husband doesn't know anything about this—that I'm the mother. I'm in a terrible bind. That was his only son, and we've been through . . ." Audrey stopped, afraid she might say *hell* again.

"You needn't go on, Mrs. Sterne. I had a pretty fair idea why you wanted to come here today."

As if in search of guidance from above, Sister Marius steepled her hands, glancing again at the cream-colored check on the blotter. The devil's work or God's? Temptation teased at her for the third time.

"The check is a gift," Audrey said. "Think of it as the start of more gifts."

"A gift with strings."

"Yes. Strings around my neck if you wish, Sister."

"I wasn't suggesting—"

"But I am."

Again silence. Suddenly Sister Marius swooped out of

her chair. Her blue habit flew about and lifted up around her high laced shoes. Audrey was reminded of a greater heron rising in sudden fright as the nun disappeared from her office.

Waiting, Audrey was no longer so sure of herself. Would Sister Marius call someone for advice? Take a community vote?

Curtains thin as a negligee fluttered by the open window; laundered a thousand times, Audrey supposed. Ceiling paint threatened to come down in a gentle snowfall. The floor carpeting, once a shade of plum, had faded to a sickly brown.

A bell rang, and again, out in the hall.

The brass door latch clicked a few minutes later. Another swirl of blue cloth as Sister Marius came back in, and Audrey blinked as a smile lit up her face.

Sitting down, Sister Marius clasped a file to the starched bib hiding her bosom. Then she placed it on the center of the blotter, untying a mothy ribbon that bound the file covers together. She pushed the opened pages, yellowed with age, toward Audrey.

"I'm due at the noon Angelus soon. Read this if you wish. I'll be gone a while."

Audrey thumbed the brittle pages. A drop in the bucket of history. Less than a drop, she thought, and all because she had let a man enter her body at the wrong time. The wrong monthly time and the wrong any other time.

All the brutal grief that comes from the crazed flight of what you go through when you're in love. Or when you think you are, or hope you are. She wondered what Cliff Rhodes would say, or think, if he were here now and could see his name on the form fixed to the second page.

She didn't care. Yes, she did. He would have to do some of the sweating for once. Somehow he'd gotten Romaine off. Or perhaps he hadn't, but he had been there all the same. And he had definitely been there when Romaine lied about seeing her with Ferenc at the pool house one morning. That was possible, faintly possible, and Audrey resented Rhodes for not stopping Romaine flat in her tracks from talking so openly.

The ashes of the trial seemed to cover Audrey like chimney soot. Snide jokes were traveling around about her affair with Kardas. And the worst of it now was that the Malibu sheriff wanted Kardas for more questioning about Marc Sterne's death. Audrey, too, had been interrogated again, quite politely but with enough innuendo to let her know she was under suspicion.

She was stained. She could tell by the way some people looked at her. By their cool greetings. By what they *didn't* say to her.

She read on, turning the pages. There was a sub-section about the adoptive parents. Chatham Brook, the father, a theatrical musician, though without the devilish talents of his adoptive daughter, Audrey would wager.

Glancing at her gold watch, Audrey noticed ten minutes had passed. She shut the file. Her eyes strayed to the desk top to see the check was missing.

An unspoken signal, a deal sealed with an invisible handshake?

Audrey smiled and slowly bent the file, then squashed it into her handbag. It wouldn't close. She tried again, then gave up and headed for the door.

She looked both ways down the corridor. Nothing there, only silent walls that knew little of laughter; walls that never sheltered a lover's embrace, of that she was certain. Walking quietly, hugging her open handbag under her arm, she reached the wide front door, inched it open, and tried not to run for her car.

At noon it was still dark in the deeper crevices of Fahey's spirits. He avoided lunch and instead was testing a low-calorie whiskey he'd recently seen advertised on a billboard.

Fahey smacked his lips twice, then wiped them on a napkin. He sat in a booth across from Tommy Burke in the small Mexican restaurant where they had drinks after the first day they spent working together.

"We better get out of here if you have to talk this way," Tommy told him. He put his coffee down, trembling slightly.

"Who can hear us? Hi! ho! and fuck 'em anyway."

"Anyone can. Lower your voice, will you?"

"This voice," said Fahey, "has only begun to shout. Telling you right now, Tommy boy, *never* fucking *never* trust your friends... Kiss only your enemies."

"I'm leaving if you don't shut up." Tommy leaned forward. "And I have to tell you, Alonzo, I can't help you either."

"Someone has to. That filthy bugger Rhodes doesn't know us anymore."

"He can't help you eith—"

"Drawing a line in the dust for him, Tommy. Do it with fighting sticks. Pearl tipped. You'll be my second."

"Alonzo, you were wrong. Maybe they'll only suspend your license. Sixty days or something."

Fahey glowered. His black eyebrows fell and spliced together over his nose. He whistled a few dry-lipped notes at Burke. "Who are you people? Fair-weather farters, the lot of you."

"You'd better be careful, Alonzo. You can't prove anything on Rhodes. That's a serious charge you're making."

"He danced me about. Told me—"

"Even if he did, so what? You can't prove it."

"The wife was there. Christ, she never lies . . . and never marry that sort of woman, I tell you. Ruins everything when they're too honest."

"Still won't make any difference... God, why didn't you tell me about those narcotics when you first—"

"Told me to save it. Rhodes did," Fahey pleaded. "And those were his questions I gave you. He gave them to me."

"You told me they came from a lawyer friend of yours."

"He is a lawyer. He *was* my friend."

"I can't believe it," Tommy said. But then he did.

Tommy's forearm, lying idly on the table, was suddenly seized in such a crushing grip that his eyes watered. "Believe me," Fahey growled so intensely a passing waiter stopped to watch him.

"I'm just astonished... and you're breaking my arm." Fahey's fingers relaxed. "Why? Why would he do it?" Tommy asked.

"Fair trial and that sort of toilet talk. I think he wanted to try the damn thing himself."

"From the bench. Don't be silly—"

"He's a cute one, Thomas. Could kick a hole in a Rembrandt and you'd never even notice."

"What you're saying, Alonzo, I just can't buy it."

"We can talk to the papers. Fuel things up a touch. They're already on to him."

"You're nuts, all the way."

"Listen, hey, of course. How do you think I survive all the treachery around me?" Fahey, almost in form again, smiled gallantly.

"Alonzo." Burke leaned forward again, desperate for some quieter talk. "I think you're great. But I can't represent you. If all this comes out, you'll wish you were a manure pile. And that's how I'll look, too, if they think I was involved. And I wasn't. They'll fry us both."

"But he was—Rhodes was," Fahey reminded. "He jitterbugged on us. On me anyway."

"Thanks all the same, but I don't think I'll tangle with him. Even if you *could* prove it."

Across the coarsely woven tablecloth they looked dejectedly at each other: Burke glum and Fahey grinding his teeth in disgust.

Tommy was grieved. He wanted to do anything for Fahey, who had been so helpful. But Fahey was shattering his illusions now. All those long hours practicing, trying to conquer his fear of facing Pritter. He hadn't, by himself, saved Romaine, the way he wanted so much to believe. Wasn't good enough to do it by himself, and the reality was swallowed slowly, hurting as it went down.

Rhodes had pulled all the switches that really counted. Tommy could see the full possibility of it now. Then again, he had no proof because Fahey had none either.

But why? There was no answer. He was swept by an urge to tell Fahey how Romaine had behaved after her acquittal. Such elation. Then, out of nowhere, she had become so iron minded. Didn't want to see any of them again, ever. Actually had called Fahey a destroyer.

Tommy Burke would never repeat her insult to Fahey. He loved Fahey, loved the loose swinging gate of Fahey's many ways that knew no season, and were so full of golden fun.

"Alonzo, let's go."

"Not till I finish pissing on your shoe."

"Take a walk with me." Tommy started to slide out of the booth.

"A walk? Know the gypsy, Tom-mo? She'll walk us to Bulgaria. Has her own camel, I think. We'll go see her. Drinks and fucks on me."

Tommy stood up, a frown galloping across his thin face. "I can't drink like you can, thank God."

A distant look passed across Fahey. He bit his lip and his eyes shimmered up to a brilliant blue. "Maybe a church," he murmured. "If you find me here tomorrow, get me to a tall holy church. Nearest one."

"A church?"

"Right. Time for a small talk with the big Crusader."

"That's tremendous, Alonzo. But I'm taking off."

Fahey waved at him sullenly.

"Alonzo, I can't help you," Tommy repeated. "It's not that I don't want to."

"Panty-ass lawyer, aren't you? Can't expect more."

"Alonzo, please, for your own sake. Let's leave."

Fahey looked straight ahead, unhearing and unseeing as Tommy shoved his hands in his pockets and moved off. Halfway out of the restaurant he turned to see if Fahey had changed his mind.

All he saw was Fahey's back slanting out of the booth. An errant hand was groping for the bouncing front of a giggling Mexican waitress. He would give anything to be another Fahey. Be that good looking, that crazy and sentimental, a man who put his name on every day he lived.

Tinged with friendly envy, Tommy Burke wheeled around once more. His thoughts skipped to Romaine. Where was she anyhow, would he ever see her again? He wondered how it would feel to touch her, just once, the way Fahey played with the waitress.

A strange feeling caught at him, cold as a gust of winter wind, and it wouldn't leave him even after he reached the eighty-degree heat of the streets.

The most exciting time of his life, over now. He had won a big trial, but something had hollowed out the victory. He honestly doubted whether he had really won anything. Slaps on the back, a sizzle of fame, a bunch of television interviews—that's all he had really won.

But all those he'd lived with for so many months were nothing but fading shadows now. Names and faces he would probably never see again.

If only he could be like them, he thought, with all their style and verve. Romaine he would give his life for. And then Rhodes, who was probably the best trial man the West had seen for years. How could Fahey ever imagine Judge Rhodes stooping to such tricks?

Tommy crossed the street in a daze. He had nowhere to go, and he didn't even know how to get there.

PART III

Chapter Thirty-Two

"She's on the phone. Got her finally at her landlady's," Macklin Price told Rhodes.

He was sorting out papers at his desk, and Macklin detected an excited gleam in his eye. Rhodes's thoughts collided. Some were like the alarming ones of a boy calling a girl for a first date. The hand-on-the-knee thoughts of a sixteen year old.

When Macklin left, he picked up the phone.

They talked for a solid ten minutes. How she was getting along? Was the press bothering her? He had resigned the court; a small and flat joke, telling her, "She'd been too much for him." Would she come to his house for a chat?

When he hung up, Rhodes sat with his elbows on the desk, his head anchored to his hands. Fritzi had said she wouldn't mind for a couple of weeks. That would at least be a beginning.

The next day at four o'clock, they saw each other again for perhaps the hundred-and-fifteenth time. Still strangers, they acted somewhat uneasily.

They sat on the terrace of Rhodes's home while he talked about the hurdles faced by the accused, who had been freed but still suffered from the wagging tongues of skeptics. Rhodes wanted to imply that he could help if she would let him.

"They call it," he said, "the criminally innocent syndrome. Big words. Sort of like having social flu for a time."

"I know," said Romaine, hinting a smile but with eyes glum as tar. "They asked me to leave my acting classes. Said it's too distracting for the others."

"Give it time."

"Who has time? I feel like a leper."

"You've got your whole life."

"I'm an actress. If I don't keep going, I'll lose it."

"No, you won't. But you may have to rest it. Do something else and come back to your acting later."

"When they've forgotten? When ten new actresses have passed me by?"

"A risk you'll have to take."

"I can't. I'm good. Everyone knows it."

"I'm sure they do. I'm not much of a movie goer but I'm told you were great."

"Thanks." Now Romaine really smiled. "I can even be better."

"You'll get your chance. Just be patient a while."

"Fuck it." Romaine bristled. "I want to live now."

Rhodes was jolted slightly but he understood her youth-filled worries and let it pass.

She reached over to pour herself another cup of tea. As she stretched, he could see her legs perfectly defined by skintight dungarees. Audrey's legs. How much of her was himself? He consciously divided Romaine in two; so much belonging to her mother, so much to him. But that was stupid, and when he became aware of exactly what he was doing, he stopped.

"Why're you so interested in me? Isn't that a problem for you?" Romaine asked.

"A problem?"

"You being the judge and everything."

"I resigned from the court. Besides, judges have a certain

latitude in their cases . . . I have to tell you something. My interest is more than the usual here."

"Like how?"

He steadied himself. "I know your parents, Romaine. They live in this city, and I think they'd like to know that you're all right."

"My parents? That's a laugher, Judge. My parents are dead and more dead. My mother is anyway, and my father might as well be. He hit the road years ago. Goodbye and good riddance."

"I meant your real parents," he said, tensing for her reply.

"Real? What's real about them?" Romaine stopped and thought again. "You must know, then, I was adopted."

Rhodes nodded. "They'd like to help you. Your real parents, I mean, and maybe they can."

"Who are they?"

"They're not in a position to come forward right now."

"That's certainly courageous of them. Are they real live heroes?"

"It's a complicated situation."

"Are they rich?"

"Enough to help, I'd say."

"Where were they when the bombs dropped on me?" Romaine smoothed her hair back, and the fall of the sun's light gave it the color of freshly cut hay. "No. I don't need them at all. They never needed me, did they?" She sounded so faraway to Rhodes.

"Maybe more than it seems to you."

"Are they in the industry?"

"Films? I couldn't say."

"Or won't?"

"Not now I won't."

"I don't want them around . . . I loved my mother. She was a singer who took an early curtain call. My father was a pig. I hated him! Parents are baggage that I don't really need."

Rhodes lit a cigar, watching Romaine grimace at the sight, then got up and leaned against the stone balustrade a few feet away. Not going to be easy, he could see that, and he hid his disappointment behind a fan of smoke.

We all need someone to help us, he said to her, somebody

to look out for us. So have some trust—and he thought of Fahey, then Audrey—and give your own wave a chance to grow. Easier to ride it that way, and for the wave to carry you. You've been through a bad time but he'd seen worse. People might help, but not if she kicked at the offered hand, walked away. Her acting career, where had it led her? A hard game at best. You get used, thrown aside, the phone stops ringing one day. Build your own life, so you can control it better—not completely, just better.

Rhodes mentioned Fritzi. Who she was, her ranks of friends, how much everyone liked her. Romaine could stay there for a while. A lovely house, a place to ease off and work out the next steps.

"Why her?" asked Romaine. "She owes me nothing."

"She's close to me. We're getting married soon."

"All because you know my parents? She'll help me because of that?"

"She's willing to do a favor, let's say. About the most favor-doing woman I ever met. You'll like her, believe me."

"I sort of know who she is. I went to Masquers once or twice . . . I like St. Germain the best."

"What do you say then? I'll see you as much as I can, and in a few weeks, who knows, you might be on that wave."

"I need a job. Acting. I've got some money but not enough with all my bills—"

"That, too. Make a list. We'll see what can be done."

"Mind if I ask you a question, Judge?"

"Go right ahead."

"Have you got a *thing* for me? Are you into some sort of weird thing because you think I'm flat on my ass? Want a young girlfriend?" Romaine's throaty voice suddenly rose.

So steeped in trying to establish some sort of a beginning with her, he'd never thought about her side of it.

"It's on the level, all of it. But you'll have to see for yourself," Rhodes tried to assure her.

She had seen him as many times as he'd seen her over the months. Nice looking, she thought, deeply tanned, trim and hard, and with good shoulders and arms. She had even known him in fantasy, in the dark loneliness of her cell, needing a man. There were times—the more vicious ones at the trial—when he had seemed to help her and Tommy Burke, especially at the end. He was well off, that much was easy to see, and probably well connected too. She could handle him—what man couldn't be handled if you came right down to it?

"Please don't think I don't appreciate this," Romaine said after a moment. "You're very nice."

"So are you."

"Tell me who my parents are."

"Someday maybe I can."

"That's not a good way for us to start trusting each other."

"That's how it has to be," he said around an easy smile. "At least for now."

"Are you pretty tough?"

"Never."

"You always smoke cigars?"

"Two a day. Sometimes three. Bother you?"

"I don't think anything you do would bother me, Judge."

"Are you doing anything special tonight?" he asked, avoiding her eyes. "Care to have dinner here?"

"I think I'd like that very much."

"Wonderful. Afterward I'll see if we can get you introduced to Fritzi."

"Is there any chance I could stay here?"

"No chance. Sorry." Rhodes pulled on his cigar again. "That might start a real fracas."

"I see . . . I guess it would. Can I call you something besides Judge? I don't like to think about being in court and—"

"Sure, you can. Call me Cliff."

"You're pretty smooth, aren't you?" Romaine's voice had the texture of silk.

"I'm about to smooth my way into a five-thirty drink. Want some more tea? Anything else?"

Romaine got up and stretched. With her arms raised over her head, the pink pullover she wore became carpet-tight over her breasts. Though shifting her gaze away, she had an unerring instinct of where he was looking. Exactly where she intended him to, and it pleased her.

"I rarely drink, Cliff. This time maybe I will. A little one."

"Don't start on my account."

"You're really very nice. You're different than other men, aren't you?"

"Not a bit."

"I think you are."

She drank like a small bird, as if lapping from a dew-misted flower. Chatting, they came to a necessary understanding—to never discuss the trial again. Every so often she would slide in an inquiry about his past life. He knew the game and kept strictly to the rules of letting her find her own way with him. The ice, if not all the way broken, was at least getting chipped away.

After dinner he called Fritzi. Romaine stayed in his living room, listening to the jazz of Dizzy Gillespie, one of his favorites, and someone she'd never heard before.

A beginning, Rhodes thought. Small enough but what could he expect? Bound to be somewhat on guard, wary, and there were many more days to come. Days for listing in a book of private dreams, days for remembering always.

Knocking back a brandy, he thought about the time when he had been nearly the same age as Romaine. He'd gone to war and come out a changed man, but he staggered through it somehow. And like her, he'd been desperate to know if life held any promise whatsoever. He understood her dread of what was to come. Or wasn't to come—an even worse feeling.

In the living room he found Romaine asleep on a chintz-covered couch. Her blond-lashed eyes in repose; her honeyed hair winged across one rosy cheek; her lips moved, barely, to the rise and fall of her breasts that were as beautifully shaped as Audrey's, though smaller.

Rhodes wanted to carry her upstairs to the guest room. He felt a slight sexual burn for her, and then a mild sense of shame.

Candlelight flickered and Audrey strained to see what was going on at Julio's end of the dinner table. Surrounded by two executives and their wives from the Seattle chemical company, he was laughing at something she couldn't hear.

The dinner bored her. Seated next to her were the head of studio production at Parthenon and a film distributor from

Rome. No wives. She tuned out and in to their trade talk, smiling and nodding, trying to seem attentive.

But she was still recoiling from Julio's blunt warning before the dinner guests arrived. "Better find yourself a lawyer," he had advised her. "If you know where Kardas is, that might make it easier for everyone. You most notably."

Not more, not less either. She made a new effort to dial in the Italian, who waved his hands as if he were rehearsing an orchestra. His breath was laced with an aroma of garlic that hadn't come from her table.

Audrey was nauseated. Whether from the garlic or the incessant talk of films, she wasn't sure. Most likely, she guessed, it was from fear.

She sensed Julio was also putting distance between them as fast as he could. At bullet speed it seemed, and pressuring her, she suspected, with the sheriffs who came nosing around every few days. She was beginning to actively dislike her husband.

Picking up on the conversation again, Audrey turned to the Parthenon production chief saying:

"Do you think Julio is getting senile?"

"Why?" he asked, startled.

"Because," Audrey said earnestly, "he's talking of firing you soon. Wouldn't that be absurd"—then she looked at the Italian—"as his idea for cutting you out of the distribution rights for Italy."

"You can't be serious," the Italian said, jerking his head toward Julio.

"There's a mistake. You probably misunderstood," the production chief added, alarm sagging his face.

Audrey smiled. "Perhaps. Have it your own way . . . He always does, doesn't he?"

The two men stared absently across the table at each other. Audrey finally caught Julio's eye. She waved affectionately.

Chapter Thirty-Three

Rhodes refused to see the press. Calls had come in on three occasions since his return from Mexico; politely, he told them no go. The trial was over, a verdict given. The state attorney general's office could complain all they liked, but he had resigned, and that was it.

They went after him anyway. Echoing the cry of Pritter, one local paper printed an editorial headed: THE WRONG MAN.

"...Rhodes may have done nothing illegal," it stated. "But his actions at the end of the trial clearly influenced the jury to return a verdict of not guilty. In the end it was the deceased Marc Sterne who went on trial for the yet unproven charge of dope trafficking... A blind spot remains in this long and often ugly trial that cost the taxpayers well over a million dollars... Yet Rhodes is now in line for an appointment to the highest court in our state. In our view he has disqualified himself. We deserve better..."

It was the third hatchet sailing by his head that week.

Cleaning up his affairs at the courthouse, he was forced to stop at one point. To satisfy a committee of senior judges he answered their questions with a memo of his own.

No two trials are the same, he wrote, and this one was hounded by publicity, enmeshed with politics, and forced into limbo when Raye Wheeler passed away. And the specter of narcotics lent some credence to other motives as well as other persons in the still unsolved death of Marc Sterne.

Was it someone else? he asked in the memo. If so, then let the police decide, not the court. Or was Marc Sterne's death by his own hand? Some jurors, when polled, thought so after Burke's demonstration with the second syringe.

Set aside for the time being was a far more interesting task: finishing the draft of new criminal justice statutes for the governor. He wanted to put the finishing touches on that work before going up to Sacramento.

There was his own estate, and his will and last testament to go over. He would change that, too. Over the past several days he'd thought pretty hard about how to do it.

How would Audrey react? He thought he didn't give a damn. But then in the next instant he found that he really did care and very much.

He paused, pen in hand, doodling on a piece of scrap paper. Romaine had been at Fritzi's for several days. Getting along well together, it seemed, yet he knew he must soon come up with a better solution.

For the past four nights he dined with her while Fritzi was at Masquers. Delirious fun, as they explored some of the lesser known haunts in the beach towns south of the city. Places where they were not likely to be noticed. A ruse for both of them. Romaine had worn dark wigs and blue-tinted eyeglasses. Using a makeup trick, she even changed the shape of her face by inserting small dental sponges around her upper gums. Romaine had merely seemed like any young woman out on a dinner date.

Her humor had improved. He could see, and with pride, why men found her attractive. She owned a natural charm and often gave the impression that she could do anything, and would, and only for you. Bright, too. More than once she surprised him with her satirical comments on politics or religion or an especially devastating one on the theatrical world.

Sometimes she made the same mistake he had at her age—of thinking she knew more than she really did. About the theater and film business she seemed almost scholarly.

A few times she had tried to impress him with people she had met and known, and places traveled. Somehow he doubted she could have crowded all of those people and places into her young life.

Never once had he tried to trip her up. She was too

precious a find. He was building bridges to her, sturdy ones, and he couldn't chance a wound to her confidence.

She was an actress, he told himself, and they had their own prisms: not how life actually happened, but of how it should be, was always meant to be.

Like Fahey would see it.

At Masquers, Fahey, in a gray suit, black shirt, and matching black tie, worked harder on Fritzi. They sat in her office, Fahey downtrodden one moment and fighting mad the next.

"I'm sure he'll help," said Fritzi, who was finishing a fruit salad at her desk.

"Don't go deaf on me, love. Crank his ear, will you?"

"I already have once."

"Again then. Near the well known pillow."

"He says he can't now, Alonzo. It's not an opportune time or something."

"Opportune. Christ! Opportune, did he say?"

"Something like that. What can I do?"

"Cut the bastard off. Turn him out on the streets."

"You know we're getting married?"

"He called to tell me. My heartiest to you, that's one reason I came. You're getting a dog."

"Alonzo . . ." Fritzi gave him a baleful look.

"All right, then, a blind, ungrateful dog. Needs a whip, he does."

"Alonzo, I don't know what the heck is really between you two, but he loves you. You know he does."

"Love!" Fahey's chin shot out. "Listen, that was my friend. *Was*. I am what I give, and I always gave him everything of me."

"Cliff told me you hung up when he called you about us. That's a no-nice, Alonzo."

"Forgive me, love, but Fahey's got trouble. Clients giving me the brush-off. Gypsy's giving me a bad time—"

"I'll talk to him again."

"Do, love. Till he sees the lighted path." Fahey brightened at a fresh thought. "Found a church for you, Fritzi. Just the place for the marry-up. Great stained glass all painted up with high minded virgins and the Magi... Run you by it someday."

With a light knock at the door, Ginty Jellicoe stepped in. "Health inspectors, Fritzi," he said. "They wanna talk about the kitchen. We need new stoves. Somethin' like that."

"Oh, no they don't," she said. "Those stoves are only, what... three or four years—"

Fahey came to his feet. "Let me. I know the type. Have them in for a jar and we'll thrash it all out in the bar."

"Stay right where you are, Alonzo," said Fritzi, and then to Ginty: "I'll be right along."

The door closed.

"Pay them off," Fahey advised her. "Get some brandy, lower quality stuff. Works every time."

Fritzi stood, laughing at him. "You stay right here. I'll send in some lunch." Nearing the door, she turned to face him. "Alonzo."

"Yes?"

"How would you like to give me away? At my wedding."

Fahey's face became a celebration. "You mean it?"

"Sure do."

"You're a hug. The whole win, you are... Carriages, get that Budweiser team with those white chargers. I'll drive—"

"And I'll be right back. Have your lunch. We'll figure something out," she added hopefully.

"Right as a diamond rain, Fritzi. And kick those Healthers to hell out of here. Tell them we're planning a ducal wedding, a misery of dry tears, tell 'em so, and then—"

She skipped through the door. Fahey was left alone, newly enthused yet mired in his worry. She is the best, he thought. God, why hadn't he landed her a thousand months ago? Free drink, set the place to rights, poison every last sonofabitch lawyer in town.

He would have his lunch, and then lend counsel to Fritzi on the more fatiguing aspects of marriage.

Romaine read through a screenplay that Max Shapin had loaned her. Finding the pace slow, almost sleepy, she flipped the script over to a coffee table.

Rhodes was fun, she thought. Disarming even, and there

were flighty moments when she imagined him as a genuine lover. Why not? Only twenty-two years apart in age, and she'd seen others of her generation go with older men. Make the moo-eyes, hang on every word and jaded joke. Cars. The clothes . . .

He had staked her to some lovely clothes. Wouldn't go with her to Giorgio's and Nieman-Marcus, but gave her permission to charge four thousand dollars of frills. A few of the boxes were delivered a short while ago, others had arrived the day before.

She had shown the ones from Nieman's to Fritzi, who gushed over them until Romaine told her who footed the bill. Fritzi's jovial face instantly soured into a look that would roll up a sidewalk. She had tried to conceal it, but Romaine's alert eyes didn't miss a trick.

Gathering up the boxes, Romaine decided to go back to her bedroom to try on her latest gifts. She passed by Fritzi's room. On a sudden whim she stopped, rested the boxes against a wall and went in.

She sat down at the mirror-topped dressing table, whiffing one bottle, then two others. Fritzi was a three-perfume woman.

A nice enough woman and popular by the count of silver-framed photographs scattered about the living room: film personalities, diplomats, business tycoons, five astronauts. Pretty enough with her smile and rosy skin and blue-black hair, but haunchy and with the legs of a country girl. Romaine couldn't grasp what Rhodes saw in her.

They'd talked, giggled, run the gamut of chatty gossip together on Romaine's first days there. Gossip from Masquers, mostly harmless. Items one would never hear in a detention cell. Always though—Romaine had noticed—Fritzi steered clear of the trial, or what jail was like and how she was treated there.

Admiring herself in the mirror, Romaine posed herself in different moods and faces, liking the one of the ingénue best of all. Her hand wandered idly to a small leather-bound address book lying on one corner of the table.

She mimicked Fritzi's mouth, how it curled up in laughter. She tried Fritzi's voice, aloud, by lowering her own natural pitch. Tried again. Better this time. Again, for several minutes, putting a shade more inflection on the vowels.

Romaine leafed through the address book. Who would know Fritzi's voice, but not intimately? A hairdresser? She put one end of an eyebrow pencil in her mouth, then dialed the Borendo Salon.

"H'lo," came the answer.

"Hi. Fritzi Jagoda here." Romaine moved the pencil to one side of her mouth.

"Yes?"

"I have to cancel . . . oops, sorry, I'm eating an apple," said Romaine, slurring, trying Fritzi's laugh.

"You wish to cancel on Thursday?"

"Borendo, is that you?"

"Of course."

"Cancel me, would you? I'll be away," said Romaine, shifting the pencil again.

"Shall I re-book you?"

"Monday. What do you have open?"

"10:30, all right? I'll mark it in."

"And a manicure."

"We have you down."

"Bye, thanks so much, Borendo."

Romaine dialed again, this time to a tree service. Would they send someone to cut the oleander hedges in front of the house? Take them down two feet or so? Thanks awfully.

Smiling into the mirror again, Romaine thought how easy it was to act. Reasonable looks, photogenic bones, the voice of a choir, and an active imagination. Either you were born with the desires to move people's emotions, or you could never understand.

Where was he taking her tonight? Donte's? Some jazz place in Hollywood, he had said. She would make herself look older, sag her boobs somehow. Thirtyish at least, ugh!

If they were so in love, why didn't they sleep together?

Getting up from the dressing table, it crossed her mind how much Rhodes amused her, could probably open the palace doors, so why waste it? He could protect her too. Besides, she needed him more than Fritzi Jagoda ever would.

Her hand reached out to a peg at the side of the mirror that held twists of glittering gold chains. From one of them swung an enameled gold pendant, a lion with small ruby eyes. Fritzi had worn it one afternoon over a light gray sweater, the lion lost somewhere in those dairy-like breasts.

Untangling the chain from the others, Romaine twirled it around in her fingers.

On her way out of the bedroom Romaine overhauled a plan she'd been fussing with: edge Fritzi over, drive her nuts. She would be worth studying closely enough so she could make Fritzi's reactions her own anytime she chose.

Be every woman you have to be, and a few more while you're at it. Fritzi might be good for a chuckle, but everyone had things to learn. Castles crumble. Romaine's certainly had, so you build another. Isn't that what Cliff had told her?

At the back of the house the garbage disposal hiccuped, grinding up the chain and gold lion, and with it a friendship that might have gone somewhere.

The air was wintry in Julio Sterne's office at Parthenon Studios. At a round table in the far corner sat Julio, the two Oldes & Farham lawyers who had loaned advice on prosecution tactics, and Pritter, fiddling with the lower buttons on his vest.

"Bungled," raged Sterne. "Screwed up investigations. The trial. Me, made to look like I don't know what was going on in my own home." He glared at Pritter with the sort of look one sends a relative who's owed money for too long.

"We did everything to keep you out of it," Pritter said. "Everything we could think of."

"Not enough," Sterne replied.

"Couldn't be helped. Rhodes decided who had to testify—"

"All over that damn Malibu sheriff's report," Sterne interrupted. "Can't even"—his shoulders shook—"God, one of our janitors would do a better job of it."

Pritter clamped his teeth tight. Two errors had been made: Sterne pressuring the governor to bring in the state investigators too early; and Sterne stupidly implying he'd been at home when he was in Seattle the night his son died.

"Has Kardas been tracked down?" Julio Sterne wanted to know.

"We're working on it," Pritter said.

"Drop it."

"What?"

"Drop it, I said."

"I don't understand—" Pritter's eyes bolted to the other two lawyers. Calmly they returned his puzzled gaze.

One of them, the elder, said: "Lloyd, what Mr. Sterne is suggesting is that someone else may be responsible for his son's death."

"And that's just the way we want it handled," said Sterne.

"Why now?" asked Pritter. "We've got the FBI alerted about Kardas. All Points Bulletins were sent to every state police headquarters. Immigration was notified and—"

"You're not to press it," said the second lawyer.

"Mind telling me why?" asked Pritter.

"You'll be too busy with us, Lloyd, for one thing," said the elder lawyer. "Clean this business up, and then come across the street to us. Your new office is two doors down from mine."

He didn't have to say more. Oldes & Farham still wanted him, even after the trial had gone off the rails. Pritter was sufficiently overwhelmed not to ask why. But he knew there was a hitch somewhere.

"Mr. Sterne," said Pritter, his senses ringing, "let me get this straight. You want us to let Kardas get away without any further effort to find and question him?"

"You figure it out," said Julio Sterne. "Be sure you figure it out the right way this time... By the way, can Rhodes give us any more trouble?"

"He resigned," said Pritter. "He's out of it now."

"You're keeping up the pressure with the newspapers?" Sterne pressed him.

"As much as we can. We can't make it too obvious."

"Good." Sterne arose. "No mistakes this time," he reminded Pritter, who remained puzzled. Sterne ushered all three lawyers to the door.

A short and crisp meeting, just the way Julio liked them. Back at his desk he examined the monthly budget runs on films in production. Both films currently being shot were well over their estimated costs; three properties in pre-production were in trouble until the right actors were found;

another film was being readied for release next month and its publicity outlays were higher than a skyscraper.

He'd been hearing howls from his company directors, the same from the banks. Parthenon hadn't sent a film into the winner's circle since *Tonight or Never*, which was still racking up steady money all over Europe.

The irony of it pumped his veins dry. The trial had done that, he thought. A damn good film and the free publicity had fueled the box office take astronomically.

Still, the studio profits slumped. Grumblings were heard: "Sterne's too old. Out of touch. Has his fingers in too many companies."

He figured he saved himself two, possibly three million dollars on Audrey. Bluff her silly, then settle for a sandpile. Ten minutes with three lawyers and he was that much ahead. No, he hadn't lost his touch. If anything, he thought, it was maturing into one with a far more subtle reach.

Audrey would get the message of her life, and so would Cliff Rhodes.

Julio buzzed for his secretary. Time to nudge the governor into action again, and he would stop in Sacramento on the way to San Francisco the day after tomorrow. Rhodes should be easy enough; the newspapers were dogging him nicely. He would show the doubters how Julio Sterne could still draw breath and exhale fire.

In the studio parking lot Pritter conferred with the Oldes & Farham lawyers. He wanted assurances that he had heard Julio Sterne correctly.

He had.

Back in his office an hour later, he called the Malibu sheriff. They were to press the investigation further, adroitly and with finesse this time. If Kardas turned up, they would deal with him separately. Meanwhile the sheriff was to shift his attention to Audrey Sterne and rap hard on her.

"Work the money motive," he told the sheriff. "Keep her guessing but squeeze her."

The situation was now vividly clear to Lloyd Pritter. Julio Sterne was about to pasture his wife. An investigation hanging over her would put ice under her heels.

* * *

In the half-dark at Donte's in North Hollywood, Romaine listened to Rhodes play his trombone. On the small stage by the piano, he leaned into his muted golden horn. His toes pointed slightly at each other, and his head tilted and swung as deep notes of the blues floated across the smoke-hazed room.

They'd come after their dinner at a small Italian restaurant in Burbank. So-so food, a nice Chianti, but a perfect hide-away. Romaine had no idea he would be sitting in with the small jazz quartet appearing at Donte's that week. She hadn't even known he played the trombone, and found herself pleasantly surprised.

Two nice looking men, seeing that she was alone, had dropped by the table. They were probably as old as Rhodes, older perhaps; in the dark she couldn't tell. Offering to buy her drinks, one of them even asked if she'd like to take off for a discotheque.

She had shooed them off, nicely though, assured that her disguise made her look thirtyish. A black mid-length skirt cut full, black boots, a black wig. Her long sleeve blouse was white except for a red velvet ribbon threaded through the cuffs and around the high collar. She had even flattened her breasts with an Ace bandage.

Shadows and clever makeup did the rest. And her bold-ness. Romaine decided to go for it. Why not? It was hers now, and hers always. Small enough payment for what they'd done to her.

She stretched open the cuff of her left sleeve, then lowered her hand. The platinum bracelet slid smoothly down her wrist, feeling cool as a winter window and looking so fab-ulously expensive.

Applause when the set was over, and Rhodes thanked the quartet's leader as the stage emptied for a break. He lingered there, putting the trombone back in its case, then handing it over to a waiter.

"Attracting the barflys. Class always tells, eh?" He smiled at her a few moments later.

"Don't leave me then."

"Need to do the songs once in—"

"You're neat. Really terrific."

He sat down across from her. She clasped his hand with her left one.

"Like some wine?"

"No thanks. I had another glass while you were playing."

"I've worked up a thirst." Rhodes motioned a waiter over.

"Cliff?"

"Yep."

"Would you take me to church on Sunday?"

"We're chancing it as it is, don't you think? Frankly, my nerves are getting hit . . . too many people."

"A small church."

"Only takes one person to see us."

"Fun, isn't it?"

"Be a helluva lot more fun in Bali."

"Are you sorry? About me?"

"Nope."

Romaine breathed audibly. "Are you going to kiss me ever?"

"I have."

"Only on the cheek." She pouted.

"That's where all kisses start."

"And in my case, finish?"

"I'm your—" he stopped, stunned at himself. "I'm twice your age, Romaine, and twice a lot of other things, too."

"Oh, but I don't mind, Cliff." She was about to go on, but the waiter came by.

He set the glass on the table close to Romaine's left hand. Rhodes had been looking at her face as they talked, not at her wrists. Reaching for the glass, he stopped as suddenly as if a viper lay coiled on the table.

The green stones framed by pavé diamonds caught the light from a candle. They dazzled like lasers in the shadowed light.

"That's a knockout," said Rhodes, touching the bracelet with his fingertips.

"Looks real, doesn't it?"

"As the sun." He pulled her hand closer.

"They're only paste; unfortunately."

"Certainly looks like the real article."

"Do I ever wish."

A round dime-sized clasp appeared as Rhodes turned the

bracelet on her wrist. Small markings stared back at him, eighteen empty eyes forming the letter A, then forming a hurt that scraped all the way down to his heart.

"Beautiful," he said. "Paste or not." He knocked the tequila back, unable to speak.

"A charity bazaar. When I saw this I had to have it. Eighty bucks."

Times how many thousand, he thought. There was a sting in his throat, and another one coming up behind his eyes. "A charity bazaar?"

"Oh, one of those they put on all the time." Romaine pulled her hand away. "Saint John's Hospital, I think, a few years ago."

You are tearing me to bits, lovely one of a hundred disguises, and you don't know what you're saying. Or do you? I hope by God you don't. Not after all that's been done to give you your life back—at least some kind of life. Rhodes thought he would get sick. He knocked back the rest of the tequila in one swallow.

"Let's adios," he said, getting up.

"Are you all right?"

"Sure."

"Let's stay," Romaine protested, aware of the quick shift in his manner. "It's not that late."

"The older you get, the faster the light comes . . . C'mon."

On the way out, with Romaine behind him, he picked up his trombone case. He walked too fast for her, not even turning when she wailed at his pace. In the twenty minute ride to Fritzi's he kept to himself, leaving her bewildered and huddled against the door. Twice she tried breaking through his crusty silence, only to meet the higher wall of his unspoken fury at himself.

His thoughts fled to Audrey. Had she been telling the truth all along? Romaine was wearing her Bulgari bracelet. Was he sitting next to a felon?

And then he realized something else. At the trial he had scorched the Malibu sheriff's deputy for shoddy work. They would still be in a burn over it, rolling heads, sounding off that it wasn't their fault. Anxious, too, for a remedy. Kardas? Or Audrey? Unable to think straight, he nearly swiped a parked car as he pushed up the winding road to Fritzi's.

She was home, he could see her car in the open garage. He'd stay with her tonight. To hell with trying to play it so sacredly in front of a daughter who didn't know she was, and might never . . . his precious thief.

"Fritzi's home," he said, turning off the ignition. "Let's have a nightcap with her."

"Are you upset? So quiet and everything?"

"Lot to think about."

"Me?"

"Yes, and how much I'll miss you," he said, trying not to raise any alarm.

"Why? I'm right here."

"I meant when I move up to Sacramento."

"Cliff, I adore you. We could be so great together and . . ."

Her hand grazed his knee. But he was halfway out of the car and barely heard her.

Chapter Thirty-Four

A day together.

At the shallow end of his pool Romaine turned, flipped over and free-styled her way back. Lithe and golden, and he recalled how Audrey had weakened him in other days with her body.

Laying on a chaise longue, he dozed, sometimes awakening when she called to him. He watched her swim, her body almost like another fluid in the shimmering water. Thinking and thinking about her, and in a fuss of confusion. Yet Rhodes was very aware there was nothing confusing about it at all.

Romaine had lied flatly. Instinctively he knew that nothing she could say about it would persuade him differently.

He dozed again and then he quivered down his entire length, at first believing he was dreaming. A cool and liquid stroke moved up and up higher on his thigh. He opened one eye. Romaine was rubbing him. In one hand she held a bottle of suntan oil.

She had slipped off her top, and the rounds of her breasts, pale and firm, wavered as she oiled his skin. He closed his eye but the vision of her nipples, little ruby bullets, stayed with him.

"Didn't want you to burn away," Romaine murmured. Unabashed, she rubbed more. "Kiss me."

"Absolutely not."

He moved her fingers away, but she strained to keep them near to where he began to bulge. He opened both eyes, seeing that she noticed his rise, and how she smiled at him. On his second and more forcible try he bent her wrist slightly, holding it away.

"Let me."

"No," he said.

"For un souzand pesos I show you my see-ster, but I geeve you me," she mimicked.

"Cut it out." But he smiled.

"Fiva hon-dred. Ees better, no?"

Rhodes laughed.

"Sen nossing, señor. You good man, so I fuck you for nossing. Am vair-y clean, señor."

"That's not funny."

"Ah, but I make you laugh, no?"

"Not any more."

"I might surprise you," she said in her real voice.

"Don't talk that way. I don't like it."

"Take me. You'll never again want anyone else."

"Beat it now and get your top back on." He sat up fast, a savage scowl on his face.

Romaine stood next to the chaise. Bright as a flash bulb, the sun shone down on her and he could see the downy fluff on her upper legs. Fahey's summer snow, he thought. For a long moment she was Audrey again, and that was a thought he wanted to assassinate.

"Why don't you want me? You've been so nice. Let me."

"I'm out of season, kiddo. And so are you. Scrammo, right now."

"I know you're not gay," Romaine teased, watching how his eyes passed across her breasts. "Fritzi told me."

"Fritzi would tell you plenty more if she caught you like this."

Romaine leaned over, very close. "If Fritzi were here, she might kiss you like this." The kiss missed his face completely, going lower as intended, much lower.

He brushed her away. She merely smiled again at him.

"You're behaving badly."

"And you're being stubborn . . . Fritzi isn't the one for you. Don't you know that?"

"No, I don't. And thank you, I'll be the judge of that."

"That's what you just resigned, I thought."

"Not in that department," Rhodes said, wondering, and alarmed.

"I could be much better for you."

Standing over him, lusciously perverse, she wiggled her fingers into her skimpy bikini bottoms.

"You do that," Rhodes said, "and I'll slap your ass till it's purple."

"How exciting."

"Get going." Hot and angry, he pointed to the pool house. The muscles on his shoulders bunched up.

Romaine pouted. Before, her face was relaxed, almost softly inquisitive. It changed suddenly, all of its lines and planes and shapes becoming a stone frieze, the face of a statue.

"I could hate you. I really could." Tossing the bottle of oil off into the grass, she sauntered away. "You are a fag. I bet you are," he heard her taunt, and then what sounded like a forced and shrill laugh echoed back at him.

She disappeared into the pool house. Rhodes balled his hands into fists, whether in anger or frustration he couldn't tell. He wanted to love her, fend for her, create some kind of a life together. It was becoming impossible, even childish at times.

Could he tell Fritzi? Tonight they were supposed to go over their wedding plans. She had already informed him that Fahey would be giving her away. "A surprise," she'd said, then landing on him for the way he had failed to help his friend.

He had sprung his own trap on himself, and he could see no way out unless he bared everything. Make trouble that none of them would ever live down.

And now was the time, if ever, because tomorrow he would be meeting with the governor in Sacramento. Rhodes knew he would never spread the story out up there—not with the guv, not to Romaine and probably not to himself either.

Not the real story anyway. He doubted whether he could face it...

But it pounded away at him all the way up to the house, where he went to shower and dress. Had Romaine lied her way through the entire trial? He had been ready, he knew, to hear her out, twist her meanings to his own design, move the west end of hell itself to save her.

Had she killed Marc Sterne?

In the pool house, Romaine unpeeled before a mirror in one of the changing rooms. She studied herself, posing, lifting the fall of her hair over her head.

The face could be better, but the body has all the right sights in the right places. Why doesn't he want me? Is he for real? Knowing my real parents and wanting to help me—is that some sort of a trick? In bed I bet I could find out.

Fahey refused to take another call. Three times Rhodes had tried, and now the hell with trying it anymore. Wanda, aloof and distant on the phone, said Fahey was on a private pilgrimage. Couldn't be disturbed. "Ever," she said in a tone for making icicles.

Saddened, Rhodes called to confirm his reservation to Sacramento.

Chapter Thirty-Five

A dream kissed goodbye after two years of waiting for it to circle and land. His chance at what he hoped to do for the rest of his life exploded like a soap bubble right in front of his nose. Rhodes stared out a window, barely listening as the governor rambled on almost piously.

"... this state's, any state's, Supreme Court must be above this sort of controversy. Cliff, are you hearing me?"

"Not too well, Harry."

"You've got the newspapers on your neck again. The legislature is growling about your appointment... I've got a letter here from a senior judge on the Supreme Court who's bitching. Surely you can see the wisdom—"

"Out on my ass," said Rhodes, swinging around. "Is that it?"

"Not necessarily. Let's let things quiet down for a bit. You can have the next vacancy."

"Which could be ten years away."

"Yes it could," the governor agreed. "But two of those fellows over there practically need crutches. A little patience."

"All over the damn trial, isn't it, Harry? Your boys lost one, and it was one of the most fouled up investigations I ever saw."

"You didn't have to rub their noses in it."

"Harry, they had a kid up there on... on a bum murder rap," said Rhodes with weak conviction.

"Some people don't think so."

"The hell with them."

"Easy for you to say, Cliff. But I have an election coming up and it's no time to upset anyone."

"You seem to forget pretty fast, Harry. Damn fast. I helped you stump this state, and gathered up a lot of dough for your campaign. I don't say I made the difference, but I sure as hell helped."

"And I'll never forget it."

"But you are. Right this minute."

"It's all very regrettable. Very embarrassing for me. But there it is." The governor opened his hands, outward, as if to protect himself from new and heavy burdens.

"Is Sterne in on this?" Rhodes asked. "The two of you set up an ambush?"

"A terrible thing to say," the governor said. He laced his hands together, cracking the knuckles nervously.

"The terrible truth, you mean."

"Don't talk so foolishly—"

"I wonder what people would think, Harry, if they knew how many times I got phoned by this office during the trial."

"What're you suggesting?" The governor blinked.

"That Sterne wanted pressure put on me . . . You know it, Harry, so don't look so goddamn innocent."

"Begging your pardon, Cliff, but all I ever called you about was the court appointment."

"Your ninny of an aide did it for you. How do you think the newspapers would play that one?"

"Well, he shouldn't have."

"Sterne never met with you about the trial?"

"We're old friends. A shocking thing," the governor soothed, "we could hardly avoid talking about it at times."

"I'll just bet."

"Are you saying I used this office to influence you?"

Rhodes could feel the cords tighten in his neck. His lungs heaved. He didn't really believe what he was about to say, but it wouldn't hurt to troll a few doubts before his host.

"Your pal Sterne damn near perjured himself in my court. He wasn't even there on the night he said he was . . . Think about that one, Harry. Think about whether he was covering for his wife, Harry, and then, Harry, you can think about whether she and her boyfriend did away with Sterne's son . . . And they needed a victim to take the gaff and the girl was unlucky enough to be around . . ."

"I'd say that's preposterous."

"But you weren't there and you weren't the jury, were you, Harry?"

"You're reaching for straws."

"You'll never know. Neither will I, but it happens and happens," Rhodes said.

"Perhaps so. But you obviously don't know Audrey Sterne at all. She'd never in a thousand years . . ." The governor's voice trailed off.

Rhodes was tempted to set the governor straight, and watch him fall right off his sanctimonious throne. But instead he said: "The jury knew Audrey. Well enough anyway to reject her story."

"You know, Cliff, there's such a thing as a man being too good at what he does. Gets folks upset sometimes. Maybe you ought to go back to lawyering again. You were the best in California and maybe that's where you still belong."

Rhodes knew he had forced the governor to deny any tampering with the trial. One look at that craggy evasive face told him it was time to leave before a war party started up. Circles of deceit. Top to bottom, everyone was side-stepping. Strange, he thought, how the trial had touched lives not even remotely tied to an act of murder. Everyone on the dodge, himself as well.

He had coached Fahey, hadn't he, on the timing of the cocaine discovery? So he could use the moment to sway the jury. Get them to side with his own beliefs.

He owed Fahey plenty. So did Romaine. The governor seemed to owe no one anything, except for the IOUs held by Julio Sterne.

Rhodes started for the door. The governor made an effort to rise but was stopped with: "Don't bother, Harry. I know the way home."

"Cliff . . ." A flicker of anxiety there under the voice.

Rhodes hesitated. "Harry, we've got one chance left to stay on speaking terms. And that's only if we both say not another damn thing right now."

Outside on the circular driveway, he told the waiting driver that he would make it back to the airport on his own.

Opening his collar, yanking down his tie, he walked into the gritty hot afternoon, other hot steam baking his emotions. He stumbled over a curb, as if the sidewalk were grabbing him by the ankles. Wet patches of shirt clung to his back. He moved along almost aimlessly, barely aware of others on the street.

Two years frittered away. Save the daughter, lose the dream.

Pritter and his bosses pissed off, and Julio Sterne yelling because the memory of his son was left bruised and beaten. Family pride sullied in public, a wife with loose hips, a son who sold the only kind of snow ever shoveled in Los Angeles.

He couldn't get away with it, would somehow have to pay up. His friendship with Fahey on the crash pad, his appointment to the big court blown away. Audrey. He doubted whether she would ever speak to him again.

Romaine, darling Romaine, was getting to be the most expensive kid in history. His history at least.

Had she?

Rhodes pushed open the door to Frank Fats, a saloon that fed nicely, a home for some of the sharpest hucksters in the country. He waded through the guzzlers, two deep at the bar even at this hour. The biggest bar in California, long and oval shaped, built of a mahogany that shined gratefully from the thousand elbows rubbing on it every day.

Four in the afternoon. Rhodes looked around at the rows of faces up and down the bar. Without knowing their names or where they slept, he knew those faces belonged to lobbyists, hangers-on, legislators and whoever else had a deal to cut in Sacramento. Favors. Laws passed. A game for grownups where sooner or later white bribery takes over and then green cash starts to move like a river after rain.

Rhodes ordered a beer. He shook hands with two bartenders he knew from days when he used to come to Sacramento to appeal cases to the court he would never sit on now. Well, fuck the court anyway. He had won a daughter, hadn't he? His new princess?

Now that he had her he didn't know what to do with her. Or with himself.

He drank his beer, feeling cooler, not much but some cooler anyway. Unaccountably he began adding up his life.

Marriage was about to say hello. Step right this way, hold your breath, Rhodes, this won't hurt any more than the usual lobotomy. Out of work, though far from broke, but still far from what he hoped and believed would be the rest of his life's work. How nice. Big invoice, that one. He would rather be broke, do what he wanted to really do—so few had that opportunity.

The girl he had wanted to marry an eternity ago, when he was young and slightly dumber, was already hip by hip with the sonofabitch who had the guv on a leash.

He could always go lawyering again. Always plenty of crooks around to defend. Some of them, he bet to himself, could be found within two feet of where he was draining his beer.

Teach? Cap and gown, and pass down great wisdom to the students. Show them how to beat the law and yourself at the same time. Here's how you blind juries in one very, very difficult lesson.

The best lawyers he knew had poets living in their mouths. Could really spin silk out of air, talk their way in and out of a safe-deposit box. But the better you were, the bigger dollars you earned, the less people ever trusted you. Bigtime lawyers weren't supposed to be honest. No one really expected it of you, which is why most people never wanted a top gun to become a judge. They wanted safe and they wanted someone blessed with modesty, full of pale as the corner minister.

That wasn't entirely right, but he was too numb now to get his thinking off the napkin and into his clearest senses.

He was out of it for good, a sometime player. Rhodes glanced at his wrist. An hour to go before his plane departed, so he headed for a pay phone in the back of the saloon to call Fritzi, tell her the honeymoon could go on for ten or twenty years. He had nothing else to do. If Fahey ever talked hard enough, convincingly, they might even qualify for a free suite at San Quentin. Game for that trip, Fritzi?

In the phone booth he dropped in a handful of coins.

"It's me."

"Are you back?"

"I'm just about to leave for the airport. I'll be there in a couple of hours."

"Come to the house," Fritzi told him in a shaky voice. "Soon as you can—"

"What's the matter?"

"Don't have time," said Fritzi hurriedly. "But she's crazy. A fiend."

She hung up before he could tell her how the governor had so recently canonized him. She'd probably celebrate, he thought, throw a big dinner and send a campaign donation in thanks.

Feeling like he'd shot himself in the gut, Rhodes worked his way through the bar mob, feeling as wounded as he had that night in Laos.

The plane circled Los Angeles for over an hour before landing. By the time he reached Fritzi's, he was tired and hungry and still coming apart inside. But those things were forgotten when he saw the fret she was in. Sizzling.

She could get upset and, at times, touchy, but her storms usually faded as soon as she found something funny to start laughing at again. But now her chin shook when she talked; up and down she paced, eyes swollen, and her arms grabbing at empty air.

He threw his own arms around her as she spoke into his shoulder, looking up occasionally with her filmy eyes, seeing if he was getting it all.

"One thing af-after th-the other. Hexi-hexing me," Fritzi sobbed. "Sc-creamed at me like I was the one who was wrong."

"You have to calm down, darling," he tried to tell her quietly. "I still don't know what you mean."

Fritzi moaned. She gripped his forearms and he felt her strength shoot right up his arms. "Goddamn her, she's really—"

"Okay. C'mon, let's go sit down. You can tell me... Where is she?"

"Drove off in her car to who cares where." Fritzi rubbed

her eyes, and Rhodes passed her his hanky. "I'm sorry," she said, sniffling.

"You don't have to be sorry about anything."

"I just hate to disappoint you."

"About what?"

"You wanted her to stay here. But she's got to go. Tonight!"

They stopped after taking only a few steps toward the terrace. Fritzi clasped his hand, and led him off toward the living room.

"Look." She pointed to the small Correggio on the breakfront-desk.

Rhodes bent down. The two lovers had their faces blotted out with blue ink.

"Does she know where the painting came from?"

"I told her."

"Why, Fritzi?"

She shrugged. "We talked about you a lot. Romaine was curious, I guess... She tried to wreck the painting, and those little lovebirds you gave me are gone—"

Fritzi told him how she had found the cage door open, the birds missing. Romaine said she watered them, and may have forgotten to close the cage. Fritzi had asked her how they'd flown out of the house. Romaine said she was mystified—maybe up the chimney. Then the Correggio was noticed when Fritzi answered the phone because it was skewed slightly on its brass stand.

"Did you see the oleander shrubs along the fence?"

"No."

"It's all knocked down in half, practically. They say—the gardening service—said I called and told them to cut it."

"And you didn't?"

Fritzi shook her head. "I certainly didn't, but they insist it was me. The same as my hairdresser. He called yesterday, wondering why I failed to show up."

He thought about Audrey's bracelet, and then he thought about the phone call Audrey denied making to Marc Sterne. Why would Romaine behave that way? And her seductive attempt at his pool yesterday. Was she mentally slanted?

"She's going tonight, Cliff. I won't have her around here anymore. I don't care who her parents are . . ."

"I don't blame you. She say when she'd be coming back?"

"I didn't hear and I don't care. I gave her hell and she swore at me. Then took off in a snit."

"God, I'm hungry. Are you going to Masquers?"

"Not till this is settled."

"Let's go pack her up then."

"What're you going to do with her? I felt so sorry for that kid. Now I think they ought to put a fence around her."

Rhodes shut his eyes, counting the shots to his heart no one could see and only he could feel. "Yeah. No. Something's wrong, Fritzi. I don't know what, but I'll find out."

"What is she to you anyway? Get rid of her."

"I can't. Not now, I can't."

"Why not for God's sake? You're acting like an idiot."

"Someday"—he exhaled—"not now, but I'll tell you one day."

"Who're her parents? Why do you have to get into it?"

"Long, long story. Some other time."

"You must owe them the damn world, Cliff." Her eyes questioning, she waited for a reply.

He thought before he said: "They owe her something. I've a feeling life scraped Romaine once too often. Set her off. I just don't know. I honestly don't."

"So what're you going to do with her?"

"Put her up at my place, I suppose."

"Jolly. Isn't that the silliest thing I ever heard you say. And what about those damn disguises she wears?"

"Let's pack her up." Rhodes put his hand on Fritzi's shoulder.

"Fine. I can't wait."

"I'll start on it. How about if you do me an omelette or a sandwich?"

She saw how haggard and punched out he looked. "Sure. Let's have a drink first. We can pack her up later."

He needed to be alone for a moment. "You go ahead, I'll make the drinks."

Waiting until Fritzi headed for the kitchen, Rhodes went out to the hallway leading to the bedrooms. He passed by Fritzi's, a linen closet, the door of another bedroom, before going into the one at the end. A gay bright room all colored up with flowery chintzes against powder-blue walls. The furniture was country French, and two side by side windows overlooked a rose garden full of early spring bloom.

Rhodes opened the outer doors of an armoire and slid out the drawers full of panties, bras, some sweaters, silk hosiery and several flesh-colored garter belts he thought had gone out of fashion years ago. He opened another drawer. Cotton shirts. In the lowest drawer he found a jewelry box made of green leather embossed with gilt scrolls.

Inside the box, along with several pairs of earrings, gold bangles, and a signet ring was Audrey's emerald and diamond bracelet. He dropped it into his pocket just as Fritzi poked her head through the doorway.

"I thought you were going to pop the gin," she said, then saw the pained look on his face. "What's bothering you, Cliff?"

"Bad day, I guess. Got more holes in it than a sink strainer."

"How was Sacramento? I forgot to ask."

"Where's Sacramento?" he said glumly.

"What happened?"

"Harry dumped me on my ass."

"Oh, no!"

"Oh, but yes. Rolled me into a doughnut, one he doesn't want to touch."

"You poor thing." She was near him in three quick strides, holding his face between her hands. "Tell me."

He did. In four clipped sentences he painted the portrait of his afternoon with the governor.

"I can't say I'm really sorry. I know you wanted it, but I'm so glad you'll be here. Very glad," Fritzi whispered to him, her eyes filling again.

"I'll get your drink."

"God, I'm sorry I bothered you with all this."

"I'm not, honey. I had to know. Cliff?"

"Yes."

"Do you think she's whacked out?"

"Something's wrong. Has to be."

"Is she safe to be around? I don't like her being at your house. If anyone finds out, it'll look funny. They'll talk and—"

"I can't lose track of her. Not just now anyway."

"Well, when then?"

"Soon as I can get her squared away. I have to, I owe it to someone."

With suspicion edging her voice, Fritzi asked: "Why did you buy her all those clothes?"

"Her father paid for them," he said, feeling like a damn fool.

They left the room. He joined Fritzi in the kitchen where, drinks in hand, they talked as she made ranchero omelettes with ham and chili peppers. As they ate, Fritzi worked him over on the wedding, then about Fahey, and his own plans now that Sacramento was in the past tense.

He nodded to almost everything, or shrugged, sometimes answering her with an exhausted silence. Woman questions, get to the bottom of everything, check out the new compass bearing, all in one fell swoop. He loved her, but he was washed out and needed a century of quiet.

They packed up Romaine in three suitcases, a dress bag and a duffel. The new dresses were folded back into the boxes they found on the closet shelves.

"This is a pain for you," said Fritzi as she zipped the duffel.

"I don't mind."

"Doesn't she have friends who can put her up?"

"I'll find out."

"Don't take her out places anymore, all right?"

"I'll see."

"No. Look at me. I want you to promise me."

He looked at her.

"Promise?"

"How can I? How would you feel if you'd been through what she has?"

"Like I was lucky to be alive. That I might even wiggle myself before the judge who may have saved my neck. And when miraculously he comes to my rescue again, I might really get ideas—"

"That's nutty and you—"

"She is nutty for sure." Fritzi latched the last of the suitcases.

"I'll take this stuff out to the car."

"Why not let her . . . I'm almost sure she can brush her own teeth. Or will you do that too?"

"You're beginning to sound very married."

Fritzi huffed. He gripped two of the suitcases and lugged them out of the bedroom door. She wasn't there when he came back. He made two more trips. On the last one he heard her on the phone. A few minutes later she appeared in the living room, wearing a black chiffon dress and a strand of pearls around her neck.

"I'm going over to the restaurant. Want to come?"

"Thanks, no. I'll wait."

"Don't be ridiculous, Cliff. We've both had a rotten day, and somehow, when you think about it, she caused it. Let's get out of here."

"That's why I'm waiting. I want to be sure we don't have another rotten one."

"Well, I don't want to be here if she comes back tonight. I don't trust myself."

Rhodes went to her. He held and kissed her, but Fritzi was as wooden as some child's toy.

"She's trouble."

"So everyone says. I'll give her a saliva test first thing tomorrow."

Fritzi turned away. "Try one on yourself too. The one for a wilted brain . . . oh, Cliff." And she left.

Rhodes sat and waited. He waited into the breathless night and once, for a twenty minute spell, he blew cigar smoke out on the terrace after pouring himself a force-ten tequila. He had no luck at all trying to understand this day. He had known other bad ones, but he tried to believe those were behind him. A foolish thought, but you could always hope you'd been through your quota of bad ones.

He looked a long way out into the night as he pondered his situation. He thought again of what Romaine had done here, and of how she damaged the Correggio. He supposed it could be repaired, but the very act of spoiling something that rare vaporized his patience.

Abandon Romaine? Not one chance in hell he would. If Romaine was sick, all the more reason to help. Maybe she was high-strung, flighty, full of the fragile emotions of the talented actress she apparently was, and some lunar force was shaking her. He didn't know. He could only try to find out.

His thoughts became the older memory of the mountain cave where, wounded and bleeding, death had kept its watch on what remained of him. The tribesmen had never abandoned him, not when he needed to have them. The Cong had gotten him anyway, but at least those mountain peasants fought and died to save him.

He recalled another of those bad days in the hills. A day when he had done away with four Cong, taking two of them out with his bare hands, another with a rock to the skull, and the last one, and the toughest—a woman—he had strangled with a length of wire. It was the kind of killing you had to do without making any sound. That day, with all the blood on it, was a Christmas day, though he'd forgotten all about it at the time. He had hoped God would, too.

In his pocket Rhodes felt for Audrey's bracelet, and then he tossed it lightly in his hand a few times. Tossed jewels. Was Romaine a tossed jewel?

Fahey, for the tenth time that week, came to mind. A nagging item that had to be squared somehow. As he was starting to pick the lock of that problem, too, he heard the front door open.

"I saw your car," said Romaine. She wore no disguise tonight. Her hair was pulled back, and she had on white slacks, red sandals, and a blue pullover. She looked like one of those ten dollar posters of a California beach girl, blond as a daisy and just as fresh.

"Have a seat."

"What're you drinking?"

"White blood. My own. Want some?"

Romaine grimaced.

"I guess it's time for you to move on," he said. "We packed your gear up. Didn't know when you'd be home to do it for yourself."

"I can't wait to leave."

"That's wonderfully nice and ungrateful of you."

"She told you? About getting mad and everything?"

"I'll say."

"Fritzi has everything mixed up. She's really got the wildest imagination when she's not humming the right way."

"We all do."

"Not like her. She was nasty. God, and how nice I thought she was . . ."

And still is, he thought. "Let's skedaddle. You can stay at my place."

"Really? Can I?"

"Where else? It's almost midnight, you know."

"You don't sound so enthusiastic."

"A long wait, Romaine. Longest one I ever made. Twenty years or more—"

She laughed. "No one waits that long."

He got up. Romaine went to check her room and returned quickly. "I suppose I should leave a note . . . I guess I should. She was really very nice sometimes."

"Call her and tell her."

"I'd never do that. She isn't worth it."

"Right you are. She was only your hostess for almost two weeks."

"You don't have to be sarcastic."

"Sarcastic truth. We're going now before my head cuts out."

Once out the door neither of them looked back: Romaine because she didn't care to; and Rhodes because he didn't have to, knowing the house and grounds by heart.

A day ended that would never forget him, nor would he ever forget the day that had now become night and the very last of the hundreds of times he would ever come there to Fritzi's home.

Chapter Thirty-Six

Audrey read the card for the second time. She had just opened the small box from Cartier, unsealed the tissue paper, and seen the card. Her eyes almost jumped out of their sockets.

Lost and Found,
Cliff

said the handwritten scrawl.

A medley of elation raced through her as she draped the emeralds around her wrist again.

Curious, she called Cartier. She was referred to the service department and told the signature diamonds on the clasp had been missing. The settings were replaced three days earlier. They had sent the bracelet on as requested—urgent service, they told her.

Was anything amiss?

"Not at all, and thanks very much," Audrey said, rather surprised. "Is the bill coming separately?"

Already paid, she was advised.

Audrey debated what to tell Julio. Would he think she made the whole thing up from the start? She tore Rhodes's handwritten card into tiny pieces, tossing them into a wastebasket. Better that way, she thought. She could never explain to Julio why Cliff Rhodes was sending her something from Cartier. Or worse, how he'd ever come across the bracelet.

Audrey's mind turned the point over and over—how *had*

he come across her bracelet? Obviously from Romaine, but how?

Struggling with more curiosity, she decided not to call him after all. Perhaps a letter. But that didn't seem such a good idea either. Yet if he paid for the repair, decency said she ought to do something.

Then again, maybe he owed her that much and more.

Two blocks down from the gypsy's house, Fahey dropped to his knees. Sober and massively serious, he settled into a pew in the unfamiliar haven of a small church.

This is me checking in from Your forgotten planet. I sing of my friend and my friend is Alonzo Fahey . . . We are again under siege down here. Many feet are stepping on me. So for God's sake . . . I mean for Your sake, listen . . .

You still need me.

Sinners are everywhere. It's so much fun, You know. Rhodes, I'm sorry to say, can no longer be counted on; Cullis, whose heart is black as his face, has red teeth getting even redder on my bones; and about Burke, he of the wounded walking, You must also dismiss him as another disloyal.

By the by, the whiskey swear-off doesn't work so well. You could've told me, You know. Besides, what's a soldier without his jug?

I know what You're about to say. The ladies, right? But You who have known me for these thirty-seven years also know it's always been the married ones for me. Much safer. So neglected they are, and spiritually too, of course. Can't have them running around with their straps loose, can we? Or out on the streets? Why have You made them so soft breasted and hardheaded?

At Your signal I shall ignore them all. A very, very clear signal. Nothing halfhearted this time.

I'm off to see the gypsy. Shan't touch her this time. No more, anyway, than a kiss of her mad eyes, I swear to You. She's a true gift You've given me, and it shall not go forgotten.

I'm studying her powers. Uncanny ability there, and I think of her as one of Your closest cousins. Take her over to Las Vegas one day, and tithe You for the usual ten percent.

So I'm off now. See the front lines and how goes the troop morale. Remember that friend Fahey is Your first soldier and he will suffer a mortal blow if his ticket is lifted. It's my Calling, just as You have Yours. Who'll stop the art thieves at the Vatican, those cardinals You and I already know about . . .

Bless You.

Is heaven crowded these days?

Come see us sometime. Do wonders for our spirits. Be delighted to make the announcement for You.

Outside the church Fahey walked at a quick clip and with mountain-hard resolution in his face. He seemed in less of a coma, and his mood began to lighten.

Over his shoulder he glanced back at the church, then up to its belfry. They ought to be ringing the church bells more often, or what was the point of having them at all?

Ring them hard for every golden sinner, he thought. All those gorgeous sounds to wake the living, tell of the dead, open the saloons up and after the saloons the schools for the childies. And what of the biggest bell of all, the one for midnight? So that whoever kept the Book of Hours would know another day had died, and all of us were still here to mourn it.

Who *did* shut the fucking bells off? he wondered. And he cursed at them, whoever they were, because they were against his newest friend, God.

He'd have to look into it. But first the gypsy. He would confess her now that he had so recently sanctified himself.

A week had passed since Romaine moved to his house. Fritzi was still boiling. The only thing to do, and fast, was to get her away somewhere. Some place where they could help her.

Rhodes spent most of the day—one appointment in the late morning, the other in early afternoon—with two psychiatrists. He wanted different opinions. In other years, when lawyering, he had hired these men as expert witnesses.

He described to them everything he could think of about Romaine without mentioning her name. Making casual inquiries, he said, though neither doctor was prepared to say very much unless a professional visit could be arranged.

Impossible, he told them.

With caution the doctor he visited in the morning made a possible prognosis and referred Rhodes to several textbooks. As a favor he also said he'd contact a clinic in France that might help. Rhodes had said his client wanted to take the unnamed person abroad. "Convenience, and a few other reasons besides," he informed the doctor, who smiled irritatingly and asked for more details.

On the way to the medical school late that afternoon, he summoned images of Romaine: in her bikini, reclining, thrusting, laughing, her face and eyes so innocent and then filling with scorn.

He ought to chuck it all, leave her to her own life. But he could not, anymore than he could explain himself to Fritzi. She'd had it with his Good Samaritan act—told him so too, and that he was behaving like an imbecile. He knew he would have to settle it with her soon.

In the medical library he requested the reference texts, and then slid into a chair at a long table, where bleary eyed students moped over books as others of them nodded in sleep. Tense and tight-packed, he studied and absorbed for two hours, losing his way sometimes in the murky vocabulary running through his mind.

Pathological Narcissism. A new one for him.

How it was that certain people can behave acceptably most of the time. Can work, even excel, to fulfill great ambitions. Earn the admiration of others. Who live with a terrific need for praise and are quickly bored when others don't heap it on them. Exploit you without any feelings of guilt. Charm and engage you and play you as if you were a harp. Scruples—those are for others, not for them. Love of self, never apologize, brush off any insult . . . and if one doesn't give in to their basic desires, then one must expect harm.

Rhodes finally shut his last book. An empty feeling swept over him. He stared off into space, thinking of her again. Was she dangerous?

Was she even a pathological narcissist? He didn't know. Like having a broken leg, but of the mind?

Maybe she was cut from the same mold as other actresses he had known. They lived all those make-believe roles when performing, and then were abruptly jerked back to reality, if they could face reality at all. Their personalities in many places at many times. Artists without anchors.

Was she lying? Had Audrey lied? He had all but lied to save Romaine. Most certainly Rhodes knew he had created a deception to influence the jury. He detested liars and in the past had thrown out clients he'd caught fibbing with him.

Romaine needed help. Probably, he thought, the same kind of help an Army head fixer had once offered him. An offer he had rejected out of absurd pride.

She had survived the ravages of Marc Sternc, of being doped and aborted and lewdly photographed. One night recently, she had even numbed him with how her father had forced incest on her when she was only twelve years of age.

Was that all a lie too?

Anyone deserved better. He was more determined than ever to get it for her.

Blinded by the splash of Hollywood, she'd fallen in with the wrong crowd. He blamed Audrey partly. Then he reprieved her, for at least she had found Romaine, tried to brighten up her chances in life. That very same Audrey, he thought, who might tell who I am if she is ever charged with the death of Marc Sterne.

He would help Romaine and then he would have to let go of her. Sooner or later someone was bound to find out about them. He'd taken too many chances already. Get her away, and France sounded just far enough away to be as good an answer as any.

At his own home an hour later, he found Romaine in the pool house, tucked into a chair, writing in her journal as she'd been doing for the past few days.

Sometimes she would sit for long, vacant-eyed spells whenever she wrote; at others, she would wander the yard, or sit solemnly on a white wooden bench under the sprawl of a magnolia tree. One entire day she had kept to her room, meditating, she told him, with Consuelo bringing her meals up.

She was either exuberant, or else put out if he neglected to take her out at night. Miffed even when she couldn't try out some new disguise.

At the pool house, he fixed them both soft drinks. Romaine played with the ice cubes in hers; indifferent, impatient too, as if he were a nuisance for barging in on her.

"I put some money in your account today," he said, leaning against the wet bar.

"How much?"

"Enough to carry you for a while. Several months."

"From *my* parents, I suppose."

"That's right, Romaine."

"I owe everyone in the world. Are you charging me for staying here?"

"Just for the days when you go surly on me."

"Thanks . . . I mean for the money." She suddenly threw him a smile that broke the tension. "I'll pay you back."

"Pay *them* back."

"Can we go somewhere tonight?"

"I'm seeing Fritzi."

"Pooh! What the hell am I supposed to do? And you can tell her something for me."

"You tell her."

"She'd deny it."

"I doubt it."

"She takes things."

"She took you in as a guest. Is that what you mean?"

"No, it isn't what I mean at all."

"Well, then what?"

"Oh, nothing." Romaine pouted.

He would bet half he owned that she was thinking of the bracelet. He intended to wait her out on that one until she told him straight, if she ever dared. He would go on as if he knew nothing about it. Otherwise, he would have to reveal why he sent it back, and she would guess that he knew Audrey Sterne on more than casual terms.

"How'd you like to jump off to Europe with me for a while? A week or so," Rhodes asked her.

"Europe?"

"France, actually."

"Really? Paris?"

"Sure, then down south."

"Oh, God, Cliff!" Romaine catapulted out of her chair. "I'd love it. Oh, yes." She stood right by him, her hand pulling excitedly at his arm, eyes coming eagerly into his, and he thought he'd never seen anyone so alive. "Is she coming, too?"

"Fritzi? No. Just a quick trip and some business to take care of before we get married."

"A girl? An elegant girlfriend you've hidden away for years? Going to tell her goodbye?"

"Not exactly."

"I know. A fling for us. Bathtubs of champagne, violins, a tree of candles in a beautifully black bedroom—"

Rhodes laughed. "You sound like Fahey."

She winced. "You know him? He's crazy."

"Not really," Rhodes said. A mistake, and he knew it the moment he'd opened his mouth. "Have you got a passport?" he diverted.

"What about Fahey?"

"What about him?"

"What's he to you?" Romaine scowled.

Rhodes shrugged. "Known him for years. Lots of people know him."

"He's the sneaky kind. Thinks he's so funny, and all the time he's a snake charmer if I ever saw one."

Right on, thought Rhodes, and he may well have saved your sweet ass in a bargain still clamoring to be paid. "Well, you get your passport, and whatever else you need, and we'll get the airbird on Friday or Saturday."

"Yummy! It's at the apartment. My passport."

"How long is your lease on that apartment anyway?"

"I have to give it up next month. She only takes students."

"Okay, then. I've got things to do up at the house."

"I can go there tonight. Maybe I'll stay there if you're going to see *her* again."

"Stay wherever you like, of course."

"Cliff?"

"Yes?"

He'd been going for the door. He turned around now to see Romaine with both arms stretched out behind her against the counter of the bar. Her long legs were apart, and the place above her legs arched out, inviting him again.

"Why're you doing all this? Europe, the clothes, money?"

"I thought I told you."

"Not really."

"There'll come a time when I'll tell you."

"Futt!"

He smiled. "Glad to see your language is improving."

"You swear sometimes."

"But I don't know any better . . . See you later."

When he left, she went back to her journal. She wrote some lines and then drew a sketch of Rhodes. The drawing, quite good, showed him blowing on a trombone, adrift in a cloud of musical notes.

Ah, Cliff, what's the use—was the tag end of Fritzi's thought as she listened to him over dinner. They were at Chasen's. He had taken her there because it was impossible to be alone with her at Masquers.

She listened, hating it.

Are you so dumb stupid, she wanted to say, that you don't know you are killing me over this silly-ass business with your little actress? Are you trying to get even with me for something? Do you know what you mean to me? What we can have together if you don't wreck it before it really begins.

He stopped talking so he could eat his steak before it got any colder. Rhodes knew she wasn't taking it any better than he expected her to take it.

"But why Europe?" Fritzi asked.

"Because I want to get her out of this town. Off this acting kick, at least for a while."

"She's some actor all right. A bad actor."

"Romaine needs help. And I don't want her all screwed up with more Hollywood fantasies."

"But why you? It's like you're on some romp with that girl."

"The hell of it is I don't think you'd believe me, Fritzi. I hardly believe it myself sometimes."

"Try me."

Rhodes braced himself. He didn't know where to begin because it was all such a great maze; and he had to keep Audrey out of it, though he wasn't sure why. But he began, in a low voice, and told Fritzi the bare essentials—the ribs of a mirage.

A long ago heat rash that began as a college romance and ended, he thought, in the passage of swift hours on his way out to war. A baby. He'd never been told because he'd been among the missing, the time when he was a prisoner and before he escaped—which Fritzi already knew about. The Army thought he might even be dead. And so, in the end, Romaine had been put up for adoption.

Stumbling out the words, Rhodes saw Fritzi go from her usual rose color to fish belly white. As her color changed so did the shape of her face, as utterly amazed as if someone who was stark naked had just come over for a friendly chat.

"I can't believe this," Fritzi said when he finished.

"Neither can I. But there it is."

"You're trying to kid me. You're making it up."

"I wish to hell I was."

Fritzi looked off, then back again. "Aren't you in trouble then? I mean couldn't they do something to you?"

"I am if you ever let on what I should never have told you but had to."

"Oh, my dear God!" Fritzi cried out loudly before she rushed a hand to her mouth. A woman sitting at a nearby table glanced over, full of quick interest.

"You can't say anything. You realize that."

"I wish you hadn't told me, Cliff."

"You asked and have been asking me now for weeks."

"I should never have pried. I'm sorry."

"You had to know sooner or later."

"You had me so worried . . . and now it's worse."

"I know it looked crazy," he said. "Running around with her, especially with all those disguises. But I needed to learn about her. Get to know her somehow."

Still poised on the teeter-totter of disbelief, Fritzi was bothered by all the very real trouble that might chase him down. The newspapers were already riding him hard. The governor had swung the worst punch of all. A real blow to his pride, that one, and so she knew never to mention it again.

"Does she know who you really are?" she asked when he flagged the waiter for coffee.

"I don't know how to tell her."

"And if you did she'd have you right by the neck."

"And a few other places."

"Who's the mother, or shouldn't I ask."

"You can ask, babe, but I'm not saying."

"I suppose you wouldn't. Someone I know, isn't it?"

"Yes, you do. That's one reason I'm held on it."

"Can I ask you something else? Did you get her off? Is that really why Alonzo Fahey is in trouble?"

"Something like that . . . yes, I suppose I helped get Romaine off. I've been getting a lot of people off for the past sixteen years. And she's my daughter and I couldn't help myself. So I did everything possible and now Alonzo is taking it right in his chops. I'm sick over it, but I'm damned if I know what to do about that either."

"What a mess." Fritzi tried a weak smile. "What will you do?"

About his future he didn't know precisely, and said so. At forty-four there was still plenty of road ahead. But his plans had changed so swiftly he hadn't the time yet to draw up a new map. He had received two offers recently to join law firms.

"But you always liked being on your own," Fritzi said.

"I do and that's the way it's going to stay."

And, no, he would not go back into criminal law again. Maybe he would teach. Or hold up one end of the bar at Masquers, how was that? He could always ramble around Europe, thinking it through. But as soon as he said it Fritzi reminded him:

"No, you don't. We've got a date, remember?"

"I damn sure do. But you better think on that one for a while."

"I have."

"Well, think some more, Fritzi, because I honestly don't know what'll happen if the milk gets spilled."

"You mean Alonzo?"

"For one, yes."

"Who else?"

"Romaine's mother."

"Does Alonzo know all this?"

"No, and he never can either."

"You can't leave him hanging, Cliff. He's your great friend."

"Was my great friend is more like it."

"Can't you help him?"

"I don't know how to. I'm swinging in the wind as it is."

Serving their coffee, seeing their bleak expressions, the waiter eased out a joke. They had to laugh politely when the punch line was forgotten.

"How long will you be in Europe?" Fritzi asked a moment later.

"A week, maybe two. A clinic in southern France, in a town called Gorbio, was recommended to me. I don't know how she'll take it. Probably not good, so I'll have to persuade her somehow."

"Well, it's for her own good."

"Maybe I'll check in myself and let 'em change my lightbulbs while they work on hers."

"That isn't exactly a ha-ha."

"What is? I can always say I went crazy and had to hole up for a while."

"Don't, Cliff. Don't say that."

"It's been a helluva strange time. I'm boxed forever. But I want to get behind her and help. I'm going to . . . still it hurts. I can't tell her who I am. That's too risky. And I can't really have her in my life or someone's going to suspect something. I think of it by the hour. And then I think about what you said not so long ago, Fritzi. About having kids. Adopting one. I'd like a family. You. Romaine. But that won't work either. Maybe we should adopt one. We'll have any kind of a family you want, if you want. A promise. But as I said, sweetheart, you'd better think over this marriage again, because I don't know what'll happen if it gets out that I'm her old man."

"Don't ever tell Romaine anything," Fritzi said, reacting to her fears.

"You're overlooking her mother. Someday she might yap and then what?"

"Deny it."

"How? After I've taken Romaine to a clinic and all the rest of it . . . And the more I do, the worse it gets."

"I should never have sent her away."

"Yes, you should've and did. And that's about the hour when I woke up and to no music either."

"Do you think she killed him?"

"I can't think about it."

"You have to, don't you?"

"I don't because I can't . . . They never had anything like an open-and-shut case on her anyway," he told her—and himself, again and again.

"Which is beside the point," Fritzi made herself say.

"You're so very right. But they were up to all sorts of tricks including sloppy work and plenty of political heat on yours truly."

"You never told me that," Fritzi said.

"It happens sometimes. It shouldn't but it does anyway . . . Got me mad as hell, Romaine or no Romaine."

"Can't the mother do something? Take her to France?"

"Not a chance," said Rhodes, swallowing the last of the coffee.

"You want me to come with you? To Europe?"

"I'd love it, but I need time alone with her. I'm going to get as close to Romaine as she'll let me. Try to sell her on what's best for her life, if I can."

"Isn't she going to think that's odd?"

"She thinks I'm odd anyway. She's put the moves on me twice already, and gets all fired up when I rain on her."

"The little bitch. You bring her around me and I'll—"

"Fritzi, she only knows me as a judge. Another guy, older, but not all that much older. She's bound to be confused and don't forget she's got problems."

"That doesn't give her any right to—"

"I know. But nothing is happening so don't get shipwrecked about it."

"Shipwreck her is what I'll do," said Fritzi, bridling.

"Let's drop it and drop our way out of here, too. I'm damn sorry to put you through all this, but I had to tell you."

Rhodes called for the check, signed it, and helped Fritzi out of the booth. On the street Fritzi said she was exhausted and wanted to go straight home. Would he come with her? He kissed her till she struggled for breath, and they were as close as you ever get with clothes on.

"I better not," he said when they broke apart. "I don't

know if she's at my house or not, and I think I'd better find out."

Fritzi held him tight, pressing all of herself against him again, thigh to thigh, belly against belly. She never wanted to let him go, and almost suggested that she go home with him for the night. But if Romaine were there, a bitter flare-up might ensue, and Fritzi wasn't up to that, and knew it would only make things more troublesome for Rhodes.

She drove off. Miles later, up on Mulholland Drive, she pulled over and parked, high above the city. Down below the canyon shadows wavered under the faint light of a cloudy moon. Beyond them a whole sea of lights shimmered, lights enough for ten cities.

Her city, her corner of earth, where she had grown up. Where she knew so many important people whose own lights often blazed like meteors. Blazed and just as often paled and blinked out forever.

She thought of her father, gone for ten years. A wind-walker himself, a wonderful and tender man. One of the old time California bootleggers before he made enough to open Masquers. A man full of life and fun, who had cut his chops as a cardshark on the old trans-Atlantic luxury liners.

A survivor.

He would approve of Cliff Rhodes, another loner, stubborn as a bull bred for the ring. But a really good man who cared, loved deep, though was rarely able to admit it to anyone. Alone now, thought Fritzi, and so am I. Was Cliff a falling meteor? After all his success, were his lights dimming now? Because of that trial? Fritzi detested Romaine, and she couldn't help but wonder about her mother.

Marry him? Not marry him? Would there be trouble? She would stand by him, wouldn't she?

She had never really thought of their relationship as an affair. Other people had affairs, but not them. They had their own private radio station, with only themselves able to hear the signals.

She had rescued Cliff Rhodes from the clutches of a fading actress who was two-timing him. And she had taken to him hard, this brilliant lawyer, a hell raiser who kept no sane hours, trying to fill out his life. She gave him the best of herself. He responded by giving her anything she asked for, and plenty she would never ask for. Anything, that is, except for the whole of himself, which he never believed was there to give anyone.

He had, thank God, avoided marriage all along because he could never see the point of it without having the real point of it—children, a family. They could live any way they wanted to, he had always told her, with strings attached or no strings at all.

Fritzi had waited a long time for the right one, and she knew she loved him the way he would never love her. That's what made it right. As long as she could live with that—give more, not expecting stardust to fall every day—then she sufficiently loved him and could get by on that much. Good as you could expect, and whoever had it even-even anyway? Most people got their love on the installment plan.

Fritzi turned the key, starting the car up. France? Should she go there anyway, surprise him, marry there? She smiled. Thinking about it would make the night pass more easily.

Chapter Thirty-Seven

"Don't you ever listen?" said Rhodes, deeply provoked and showing it.

"This was more fun. Surprised you, didn't I?"

"You've got strange ideas about what's fun."

"Oh, don't be so stuffy, Cliff. I thought you'd laugh at least."

"Hardy-har-har. Good God!"

Turbulent air bounced the Air France 747 and Romaine grabbed the armrests; he caught his drink as it slid across the tray.

"Goblins are slapping us tonight," she said. "Please don't look at me that way." Her mouth went taut.

"What way?"

"Like you're about to bite me." Romaine giggled. "I wish you would though. Softly, by my ear."

"You'd better climb back to your own seat."

"Not until this plane quits jumping around. I might lose my wig. Like it?"

"Very swell, Romaine."

"Well, you never knew until I sat down and started talking. So how could anyone else tell it's me?"

"How'd you ever get through the check-in anyway, looking that way?"

"Easy."

And then it dawned on him. "Are you using someone else's—"

"A friend's. Edy Pachmyer. She's in one of my drama classes."

"And now you're Edy. God, Romaine, do you realize what you're doing?" he asked, a new worry on his agenda.

"Of course I do. But how can we be together if I use my own passport and have to keep looking like myself?"

"It's France we're headed for. Not Beverly Hills."

"That's what I mean."

Leaving Los Angeles in haste, he hadn't taken the time to think everything through. *Tonight or Never* had played throughout Europe, and because of the film's popularity her picture was spread all over the newspapers there during the trial. She would certainly be recognized if she weren't disguised somehow.

"You're probably right," he said a moment later.

"I am right. It's so much better. Think of the fun we'll have fooling everyone," Romaine said. "Anyway, lots of people travel incognito."

"More people don't, chum, and traveling under someone else's passport is illegal."

"I don't even own a passport. And who's to know anyway?"

"One sharp customs official is all it would take."

"Here, let me show you."

Romaine rummaged around in a leather tote bag. As she

bent over, he saw the swing of her heavy reddish hair and the small beauty mark on her chin. He swore he could see faint freckles on her cheeks. But then it might've been a trick of the dim light in the darkened cabin.

She handed him the passport. The inside photo bore a good resemblance to Romaine. At least what he'd seen of her as she swept into the vacant seat next to him, out of nowhere.

Same age. Same address, too. The young face in the photo staring impassively back at him lived in the same apartment house. He handed the passport back.

"Super girl," Romaine said.

"So are you, when you behave."

She leaned over, almost against him, and nuzzled his shoulder. "I'll be so good. All behaved and very upright and say my bed prayers every night."

She rested her hand on his thigh. He tried not to notice, which was the same as trying to ignore that she was a woman. A woman half his age, perfumed, with a slim and youthful neck and her breast pressing against his upper arm. She was that unnoticeable, and he made her straighten up before something in him did. He blushed, glad the cabin was dark.

"Is your ticket in your friend's name?" he asked.

"Hein. Jawohl, Die Samen," Romaine aped. "The Prussian Pachmyers, famous for their beer and the finest of fornicators."

"Stop it, damn it. I only wanted to find out if—"

"I'm at least that bright. I turned in the ticket you gave me."

"Someone'll know then. Good God."

"Umm-hh. Let's go upstairs. There're hardly any people on this flight—"

"No thanks. I'm for some shuteye. And you, you're for your own seat."

"Cliff, I hate traveling alone. I'll stay here. You sleep and I'll count the sheep for you . . . Gosh, Paris! Won't it be fun?"

She unbuckled her seatbelt and hurried up the aisle. A few moments later she was back, leading a flight attendant who carried two pillows. Romaine edged into her seat again, two snifters of cognac in her hands.

"One for me, one for thee," she said brightly, taking the pillows from the blue-smocked attendant. She stuffed one behind Rhodes's head, then held a cognac under his nose. "Sniff. Isn't that how they do it?" She laughed. "Like that old white evil dust." She tasted hers. "Whoo-ee. Yuck, that's awful stuff."

Later, he leaned against the window and tried for sleep again. He'd been halfway there an hour ago when the first voice broke in, warning everyone to buckle up, the air was going to roughen. A nice voice, very French and soft, but a voice for bed and not for waking him at 30,000 feet.

He had already downed two bourbons—Air France didn't include tequila in their liquor kit—and read three newspapers, damn happy to learn he wasn't mentioned in the *Los Angeles Times* for a change. Then the "buckle up" voice sounded, and moments later a woman seated herself next to him. A woman, as far as he could tell in the shallow cabin light, who was dressed in a loose dark skirt, white cowl-neck sweater and black leather boots that crackled when she crossed her legs. Around the slim waist glittered a silver concho-belt.

"H'lo, handsome," she had said, "you look so good to me. I'm from Traveler's Aid. Like a back rub or very possibly a front rub . . . Compliments of Air France-chance."

Briefly Rhodes was speechless. How in hell had she gotten here? They were to fly separately, he on Air France and she on a later TWA flight. He assumed, wrongly, that Romaine would travel on her own passport. His better instincts told him they shouldn't be listed as passengers on the same flight manifest.

Out of the blue, or the night black, she had appeared, stoking him up, jangling his nerves.

As he tried to sleep again, he heard her breathing. Nice and even breathing, nothing to worry about except for the whole outside world.

He hadn't seen any of it; not the diapers or the first shoes, the first walking steps, the spills, the dolls, a bike, a first date for the first dance, an allowance, borrowing the car.

None of those stages of growing up or growing closer or growing apart.

A choice of fate. She had burst into his life and now he was a father. She was filled with all the hopes and wishes, all the makings and flaws of any young woman. Teasing him with her nubile body and guile, and he was sorely tempted at times. As a daughter she was a state of mind; as a woman, very available, flaunting her sexual candy.

Lots of fathers took their daughters on a first swing through Europe. Though this short trip could hardly be called a swing. Not unless you had a new name for a stay at a clinic specializing in . . .

He couldn't finish the thought.

Then he wondered how many fathers took daughters abroad under a false passport. Incognito, in spades. Overnight she would have to become not a daughter but a niece. Those kind of nieces were for sugar daddies.

Sleep evaded him. He took another tilt from the cognac snifter on the way to holding her hand.

The following day Fahey read the letter he had dreaded now for weeks. A notice to appear for a preliminary hearing to answer a complaint filed by the Hollywood division of the sheriff's department.

Cullis was on him.

Fahey scorched his wife's ears with a string of oaths that would make a Naples dock whore blush. Crumbling the letter into a paper ball, he lofted it into a wastebasket several feet away.

"Leave it be," he told Wanda as she went to retrieve it.

"So you won't forget the date, Alonzo."

"I'm not going."

"You have to, don't you?"

"Fuck their filthy minds."

"Please don't, Alonzo . . . Talk like that is blasphemous."

"Christ, you too, now . . . Tell me a better word. A transitive verb with a very creative force to it. What's a more imaginative thing than fucking? Can't even talk about the rumble of the flesh, can we?"

He looked away, roused in anger. They were sitting in his makeshift study over the garage, the same place where

Rhodes had come to open up Pandora's box. On that rainy dark night when Fahey's woes would begin to circle ominously and then crash-land.

"Alonzo," his wife broke into his sunken spirits. "Let's go to Saint Bridget's tomorrow. We'll talk with Father Malley. Maybe he can help."

"Already been to church this year. Spoke right to the big boyo. Haven't heard a word back either."

"You went to see Father Malley?" asked Wanda. "You didn't tell me."

"No, not that old fraud," Fahey griped. "Went to the soldiers' church . . . Didn't even ring the damn bells when I came to pray."

Bells? Wanda had no idea what he meant, and she decided not to ask. His churlish face, those eyes as wary as a cat of the forest, warned her off. She would try another idea, though nothing in the way of her other suggestions had earned even the slightest rise lately.

"I've been thinking, Alonzo." She paused to see if he listened.

No reply.

"Alonzo, I could always go back to work. I know I could. That would make it easier"—Wanda saw those eyes lift—"and I wouldn't mind at all"—and his hand begin to rise "—and when all this blows over, and it will, Alonzo, yes it will"—and the hand thunder down like a drop hammer.

The crash of a toppling table filled the room.

"Are you telling me, woman, you're to money for me now? Can you suppose how that looks to everyone? Especially me."

Wanda flushed. "We have to do something . . . You never ever saved a dime in your whole life. Look where we are now."

"Money!" Fahey shouted. "Money is a disease. Who saves up diseases, for Jesus sake? Green as gangrene, it is. You want to be like everyone else? A serf? Owned by the Pharaohs? Wanda, woman"—he leaned forward as if he were ready to pounce—"all I want is to fucking do what I damn please in this dog-forgotten world. Have you the faintest idea what it costs me to keep us free. Sing, you hear. Sing the song that only I can hear, and that's all I need to save myself for. All this silence in my life is what's killing me. Not money."

Fahey sprang to his feet. He kicked the fallen table out of his way.

"Where're you going?" Wanda asked.

"To burn, that's where. Burn down Rhodes." Fahey smiled suddenly. "Then I'll find that black bastard Cullis and swing him on the bell ropes. Tell that to your priest and tell him to ring the bells, if he knows what's good for him this year."

"Alonzo, please stay. Please—"

But the door slammed on her plea. Wanda trembled in her chair for fear of what Alonzo might do next. She had suffered him for years, his escapades, his women, the drinking. The whims and rages, and the other ways about him that only the Lord and herself understood.

He was heavy pain at times. Yet she craved him, was thrilled and charmed at how he could move her deepest currents. She had no name for those feelings he instilled in her. A long time ago she had stopped wondering how he could make her feel half crazy so much of the time. It was easier to just let it happen. She had learned to suffer from him and for him. But he was outlandish and courageous and wonderful madcapping fun. He asked for so little, though he was as emotionally seized as an infant.

She knew but would sometimes forget; his worst and unspoken fear, the fear Fahey called the tomb-day. A day where no more dreams would visit him: out of music, out of love words and laugh words, and no more imagining of what things were like that could never be seen—and for wondering where Christ had slept with his first woman. Quests, mad ones and usually so sacrilegious.

There would be no more oil paint on the palette of his reckless spirit. His tube squeezed dry, and the one true romantic she had ever known would be all rolled up and used up. And then and there, Wanda worried, the ashes of her own life would heap up until they buried her with him.

Wanda murmured prayers. One for herself and two long ones for her beloved stranger on this earth.

Paristown.

The Ritz.

They four-footed Paris for three days and nights, Rhodes having his best time in years. Romaine was on the fly. She was gay and always smiling under the sun's larger smile, and he was immensely proud of her.

They lunched at the Eiffel, gandered at other well-heeled tourists at Tour d'Argent, saw the rising grace of Notre Dame by twilight, cruised Montmartre and the garish cabarets of Pigalle, scouted for lesser Gallic temples. Everywhere she wanted to go, they went, hurriedly, as if every hour must supply the work of ten.

Strolling the quays of the Seine, they tossed white camellias brought from a flower girl at a nearby stall into the gray swirl, making their secret wishes.

Rhodes spoke of the Parisian poets he had admired as they walked the cobbled streets in the Marais. One afternoon they passed a cinema where *Tonight or Never* was playing. Glancing at him, Romaine saw that he pretended not to notice—neither her look nor her name up on the marquee.

For their last afternoon Rhodes hired a guide to take her places they hadn't visited. He told her of an appointment with a firm of Paris attorneys. One more lie, one more ruse. But then, as he explained again, this was the reason for their trip to France.

Wandering the Left Bank, feeling older, he passed a few hours under the crimson awning of a small bistro. He jotted postcards to Consuelo and Macklin Price. Then thinking and thinking harder, he watched the everyday life of Paris pass before those thoughts. He felt the slow die then, of wanting to be with Romaine for a long time to come. And knew that he could never, for soon she would need herself, alone, and the time to get whole again. How to tell her, persuade her, when she was so gay and exuberant, full of cheer, so fun to be around.

Back at the hotel in mid-afternoon he called the clinic in Gorbio, telling them he would be arriving very soon. Afterward, poised in doubt, he wondered if he was making a grave mistake. That she was as sane and true as the next person.

At loose ends waiting for her return, he went down to the bar on the Rue Cambon side of the Ritz. There he struck up a casual conversation with a Belgian diamond merchant, who was transiting Paris on his way to South Africa.

An hour ticked away. Seeing the bartender smile and give a little wave, Rhodes turned on the stool, and there she was, breathy and so highly alive, her face tingling with a child's excitement. She waved back at the bartender, and hugged Rhodes's arm as he introduced her to the Belgian.

"Oh, Cliff, I saw Versailles and that hall of mirrors . . . I could be Antoinette all over again."

"You are easily more beautiful," said the Belgian, bowing slightly.

"Thanks." She beamed. "Maybe someone'll do a film on her again," Romaine said to Rhodes. "I could do that part."

"You are in films, mam'selle?" asked the Belgian.

"She's trying out," Rhodes said quickly.

"Ah, I see. You are her producer perhaps, eh?"

"I'll say . . . Look, will you excuse us? We've some things to go over."

He led Romaine away to a table, deep enough into the bar so they were almost alone. She ordered afternoon tea, and he called for a Perrier.

"He was nice," Romaine said.

"Men go for you, as I'm sure you've found out."

"You too?"

"Me too, Romaine."

"Then why are you so distant?"

"Am I?"

"You think I'm still a child."

"And I'm an engaged fella."

"So what?"

"So everything. Tell me about Versailles."

"Wonderful how they lived. No bathrooms either, come to think of it. And in all that fabulous luxury. Silly, isn't it?"

"Yep. It's the Ritz for me, or maybe a chateau up in the Champagne district."

Romaine had drifted her eyes over to the Belgian still at the bar.

"What if I ran off on you, and got myself a nice European? Do the old lover's romp," Romaine said as she flashed him a smile.

"I'd say good luck."

Romaine squeezed lemon in her tea. "That's all? Wouldn't you pine away or send out the marines?"

"I'd wave goodbye and lift the glass for you a few times."

"Let's go there. Where they make champagne. We can drown together."

"Another time maybe. What do you feel like for dinner tonight? Make it good—tomorrow we leave, you know."

"Let's stay, Cliff. Paris is . . . God! it's the neatest place ever made. Don't you have more business?"

"All done. Buttoned up. Monte Carlo isn't so slummy either."

"Maxim's."

"What?"

"Tonight. I want to go to Maxim's and have eggs and everything."

"Eggs. At Maxim's?"

"Sturgeon eggs. Those black bee-bees. The kind you pay for by the spoonful."

"Sure," he said. "If we can get in. I'll have to see."

He went to see the concierge to find out what it would take to get a good table on short notice. Rhodes slipped him a wad of francs and asked for a car and driver, though Maxim's was only a few blocks away.

Romaine vamped her face again at the Belgian, who started toward her from the bar. She shook her head, very slowly, so that her message to stay away was tantalizing but clear.

So easy, she thought, as most of them were. All but Cliff Rhodes, her present mystery. No play there at all, and how she had tried—tried the tears, the unpossessive routine, and showing him how happy she was when she wasn't, telegraphing her sex signals and making with hungry eyes. Nothing turned him on. She fretted about it, ever curious about what was in all this for him.

Up in the suite, he showered and dressed in a double-breasted blue suit, a pale blue shirt, and a white tie with small green polka dots. Then, out in the parlor, he called into Romaine's bedroom, telling her he'd be down at the front desk getting francs, and to take her time.

She *was* taking her time. Trying on a black evening dress, she posed two different ways before the closet mirror, then took the dress off. She yanked off the wig that had begun to itch unmercifully.

"Hell with it," she said aloud, and thought, if this is my last night in Paris, then Paris can see the real me. Going over to the sink, she bent over and scrubbed off her makeup.

Off the lobby, Rhodes set in a phone booth talking to Fritzi. At first she sounded grave, then became very uptick as she went over a few wedding details.

The Good Shepherd Church was available next month; Galanos had produced a nifty design for her wedding outfit; wonderful Jimmy Murphy, who owned Jimmy's in Beverly Hills, wanted to throw the reception. What did he think?

"That the two of us fly up to Reno and spend ten minutes with the first preacher findable," Rhodes replied.

"You're a real help."

"A helluva lot simpler."

"Cliff, a lot of friends want to come. The only wedding either of us have ever had," Fritzi complained.

"Let's do Reno and have a party afterward. A month or so later," he urged back.

"We're old news then."

"Perfect."

"Forget it, I'll decide for us both."

"I know you will."

"Where're you going for dinner? Isn't it night there?"

"Maxim's . . . Romaine wants Maxim's."

"That's nice of her. Is she paying?"

"She's been just a bell ringer the whole time."

"A ringer is right."

"And I'll ring you tomorrow or the next day," he said, wanting to hear no more.

"Okay. Bye. Love you. Be very good."

"Love you, too, babe."

He sat for a moment with his hand on the telephone, wondering if he should call Fahey, sew up the wounds somehow? Tomorrow. Call him tomorrow, he decided, as the booth became too warm and his neck began to moisten.

Out in the lobby again, he wondered what was keeping Romaine. Ambling over to the newspaper rack, he scanned the headlines of four foreign papers, pausing to catch a few lines from the *London Times*.

The staccato click of high heels on the marble floor raised his eyes. She looked nothing short of sensational in a silver lamé dress. Good God! he thought as his senses reeled. Romaine was stunning, her blond hair gathered in a topknot with loose tendrils tickling her ears. A matching silver head scarf partly hid the stems of her blue-lensed glasses.

"Well, well, how about you," he said admiringly when he regained himself. "You'll blind the whole town."

"You like?" Romaine pirouetted.

"How do you do that, make yourself look that way?"

"Older you mean?"

"Yes."

"Dab a little warpaint in the right places."

"Where'd you get that rig anyway?"

"The money you put in my bank, for which I thank you again."

Send her back upstairs? Hell with it. All of Paris couldn't feature a more glamorous twenty-two year old. Take a chance, he told himself. Why not parade the glory of her youth and the pride surging inside himself?

She came closer. The slinky dress fit her like a second skin, glittery as she moved her legs. Breasts swelled at their tops, and he thought of two fists fighting their way out of a tight corner.

At Maxim's Rhodes talked Romaine into some champagne after she ordered Beluga caviar. She looked around as the restaurant began to fill up, very aware of quite a few men and at least several women giving her the twice-over.

Rhodes caught sight of a man at the bar that he knew—a lawyer with one of the big New York firms. An aggressive type with a lot of mouth that worked on overtime.

Halfway through the main course, Rhodes looked up to see the lawyer again. Romaine had taken off her blue glasses when reading the menu and now he wished he'd reminded her to put them back on again.

"Hello, Cliff. That's you, isn't it?"

"That's me. Hello yourself, Thurston." Rhodes didn't get up.

"Been in Paris long?"

"Couple of days or so. How about yourself?"

"Came over yesterday on the Concorde. Best thing the frogs ever invented."

"I think they had some help from the British."

"Well, you know what I mean."

"No, I didn't, Thurston, but I think I do now."

"Going to introduce me to your lady friend?" Thurston Garey just stood there, irritating Rhodes.

"You speak Czech?"

"Check?"

"Czechoslovakian. The lady only speaks Czech so it wouldn't do much good to introduce you, Thurston."

Romaine played along. She looked at Thurston Garey, smiled and said: "Praha."

"She's from Prague," Rhodes caught on, the great translator who didn't know one word of the language.

"You look like someone I've seen before," Thurston Garey said to Romaine, who shrugged, looking bewildered.

"She just arrived in town," Rhodes told him.

"Not here maybe, but somewhere . . . Well, enjoy yourself. Maybe we can catch a drink tomorrow. I'm at the Athenee."

Rhodes shook his head. "Sorry. We're off to Monte Carlo in the morning."

"The two of you. Like that, eh?" Garey laughed.

"Yes, Thurston, just like that. And now we'd like to finish our dinner."

"Better that way, I suppose," he said, grinning lewdly. "Can't talk back to you. Or do you speak Czech?

"Only here at Maxim's. Then I lose it somehow."

"I see what you mean. And I see you lost your appointment to the Supreme Court. Too bad." With that Thurston Garey left them alone.

Rhodes began eating again to stop his swelling anger. It nettled him to be intruded upon. Maybe it was because Garey thought he recognized Romaine—from her film, no doubt—if he did at all. Close, nervously close, and the fear of being crowded began to spoil his fun.

"Who's that one?" said Romaine in a half whisper.

"A New York guy. A lawyer there."

"You don't like him. I can tell."

"He's all right. He has a habit of shoving in where he's not wanted."

"Do you think he knows me?"

"Seen you possibly. On the screen maybe."

"I'll wear my other get-up, then," Romaine said innocently. "Sorry if I blew it and embarrassed you."

"You didn't. We just have to watch it. Even here, I guess." He paid her an easy smile. "Traveling with a celebrity, gotta be careful," he joked. But he was worried, thinking about it.

"You're the one he really knew."

"But I'm not the celebrity, bright-eyes. You are."

"Yes, you are. I read about you during the trial. And besides, *she* told me a lot about how big you are as a lawyer."

"I pay Fritzi for all that publicity. She's good at it, but she's liable to say anything."

"Don't treat me like a child, Cliff."

"Believe me, I don't."

"Someday I'm going to the top, too. I know I am."

"If you do the right thing, I'd say it's a certainty."

"People get in your way, don't they? They don't want you to take their mountains away," she said.

"Sometimes, yes."

"Not me they won't. I'm really good, Cliff. All I need is another chance."

"Slow down. You've got a long life ahead of you. Give it a chance to catch up."

"I want it now. Otherwise it'll all pass me by," she said wistfully. "In show biz you have to be there when you're happening."

He wiped his mouth with one of the Maxim's big napkins, thinking how lucky he was to have found her. She was his, she was Audrey's too—but exclusively his for now. He was glad that he had arranged matters so that one day Audrey would have to acknowledge Romaine as her true daughter. He never could, not when he was alive, not without exposing himself to a misery he shuddered to even think about. Romaine would know someday, though. Maybe then she would understand and think nicely of him. God, how he wished he could tell her this minute.

"You finished?" he asked. "Want some coffee?"

"Anything more and I'd split my dress."

"I thought it was a neon sign."

"Don't you like it? I thought you did." Romaine showed an expression of mild hurt.

"Glorious. Half the people in this joint arc rcading you, though."

"I forgot about my glasses. Can we go somewhere fun? A disco? Dance?"

"Anywhere you like. Anywhere at all," he agreed, and watched her mouth widen under the round blue lenses.

In the car she asked him if she was the reason he'd lost out on his bid for the Supreme Court. So unkind of that lawyer from New York to bring it up. "I saw some stuff in the papers before we left California. They think you saved me, don't they?"

"The papers will say anything," Rhodes said. "You have to read them with that in mind."

"You helped me, though. At the end."

"You helped yourself. You told the truth and that's what juries care about most."

"I know you did," said Romaine softly and sensing he didn't care to discuss it more.

They were in no hurry. He only cared about this night with her, and how he would like to remember it for a long time. Lights shone on the streets, the many kinds of light in Paris that painters worked by—the gas-blue light and the Mexican pink, the flame-red one of fire and the green hue of an aquarium. The lights glowed softly as if they were all screened by gauze.

What would happen, he wondered, if he were twenty years younger or even ten, and he wasn't the father. They might be doing anything. Be in bed together, or holding on to each other in the corner of some cafe, where the wine was good and cost only a few francs a glass. On the rooftop of a garret and naming stars for their crazed and craven kisses.

Rhodes had the driver pull over by the stairs built into the steep hill leading up to Sacre Coeur. They'd already walked them once, but by daylight. Now he needed to see the view with her again by the splendor of the Parisian night. Halfway up they rested at a place where the steps sharply steepened.

"I can't make it in this dress, Cliff." Her breath wiping his cheek, she was so close.

"We can stop here."

"These are our stairs, aren't they?"

"Always ours, Romaine."

"I've loved it. I could live here easily."

She turned around slowly under a moon that caught the silvery shimmer of her dress. Above her he could see the great oriental dome of the church and the shaft of the bell tower poking out of the night. Silver was everywhere on her, and the moon painted the church with more of it, so all the glisten filled his eyes.

Romaine felt his hand covering one of hers and part of her wrist. Move it up, she thought. *All the way up my arm and under the strap. Fondle me. I want to faint, so don't be afraid, and don't tighten me up like this. Have me here on the stones, bruise me this once, leave your best marks on me and in me.*

Rhodes pulled his hand away. Whatever it took of time, of anything, he would see to it that she was mended. When she was right, he would be right, and to hell with what the future sent them. He gripped her shoulder and Romaine twirled to face him, pressing close as he would let her.

He loved her.

He told her so under all that silver of the night, and she thrilled. And later he would hold her hips and shoulders as they swayed to music at Regine's. He saw lovers there, the bold and the shy ones. Becoming all of them, he swayed and turned more with her under the ceiling of flashing mirrors and mosaics of glass.

"I'm not going to leave you, Cliff," she said. "Fritzi or not."

"That's different. Very different."

"So am I."

"I know. But we'll see one another often." But just how he didn't know.

"I mean all the time."

"Not all the time, Romaine. But we'll work something out and—"

"Let's go somewhere far and then even farther," she said by his ear. "The Congo. I don't care."

She said something else, too, but the music blared a few loud beats and he lost her voice that he wanted to hear forever. The lights brightened suddenly before the music quickened to a heated pace.

"More champagne?" he asked.

"The whole ocean. I never drank before I met you, but now I love it."

Before dawn crept up on Paris to cast the first light of the new sun, they entered the Ritz lobby. Romaine was not weary, but only as tired as you get from a long stretch of excitement. She hung on Rhodes's arm, tapping her feet in the elevator to music that had stopped for them an hour ago.

She undressed and left a call to awaken her at ten. So tired and yet so raring that sleep never really came. She needed him, in all the ways, and that hunger for him gouged at her for all the short night that remained. She had to snare him away from Fritzi, as foolish as that sounded. It was probably impossible, but Romaine knew she would try anyway. He could make a big difference.

Thinking of her made Romaine stiffen in the dark. Fritzi, who had lifted her bracelet when Romaine had wanted so much to bring it with her. Show it off and give the impression she was the clever young girlfriend of a very smart lawyer.

If Fritzi could walk off with her bracelet, then she could walk off with Cliff Rhodes. A fever for him rose inside her, and she began to imagine again what it would be like to know him sexually. Take him, just as she had taken Max Shapin that night at La Costa.

Feel the weight of Rhodes on her body, smothering her with words of endearment and deep kisses. Feel him grow under her caresses and then grow ever stronger inside her.

Romaine made little motions with her fingertips on her belly. Back and forth, around and around, then down below where he would be, riding her, and she taking all of him.

Minutes passed. Minutes full of longing and fantasy and ecstasy before her explosion came. She gasped into her pillow, then turned and lay in the darkness, wondering if France would always be so beautiful. For her. For them.

Chapter Thirty-Eight

Rhodes leaned over the balcony and gazed down at the winter gardens, then off to the harbor. A navy of yachts bobbed quietly in their berths. Beyond, like some huge blue mouth, he saw the bay spreading out before Monte Carlo to where bluer water touched the sky on a wavering horizon. A wind gusting up from the south dotted the water with whitecaps.

He'd leave soon. They asked if he could try to be there by eight, otherwise the day became so busy it was hard to spend much time with visitors.

He left the balcony and went into the room separating their bedrooms. At a small writing desk, he penned Romaine a note, saying he would be back by late morning. And to order whatever she wanted for the picnic they had planned that afternoon.

Slipping the note under her door, he left the suite and walked down the four flights to the lobby. He asked for the red Fiat he had rented two days before at the airport in Nice.

When the car arrived, Rhodes slipped a Michelin map out of the glove compartment, then listened as the doorman traced the road up to Gorbio with a stubby finger.

Ten minutes later he came around a hairpin turn and nosed the Fiat up through the winding hills guarding Monte Carlo. Rhodes felt depressed, though he knew he'd be worse off if he did nothing at all. He didn't want to give her away, and yet he knew he must.

Passing through villages tucked in valleys or set on the mountainsides, he saw how the small gray stone houses were either washed stark white or painted in pastels. So close together, they seemed to stand on each other's shoulders.

He felt slightly sick. He knew that it wasn't from food—he'd barely eaten for almost a day.

Twenty miles north of Monte Carlo he rolled into the town of Gorbio, circled the tree lined square, and went out the road that was favored by the morning sun. A mile later he saw the sign, hanging on a stone pillar hidden by leafy trees and a stand of stone pines. He almost missed it.

RESERVE, it read. It took a good part of the reserves of his heart now to drive onward. He spun the wheel and backed up.

Up the road, he drove by a dipping meadow full of mimosa and, further on, by a pond with swans gliding across its dark surface. Across the pond he saw a slate-roofed chateau with three smaller outbuildings. He was still uncertain how to break it to her, or how she would take it, or even if she would take it at all. He wanted to look the clinic over at least once, make the money arrangements, meet the doctors, tell them he would deliver Romaine a day late.

Or even two days late, he suddenly decided, bringing the Fiat to a sliding stop. He thought it over again. What was another day or two out of a lifetime? She had behaved beautifully so far. Maybe he was all wrong, and Fritzi was, too; perhaps Romaine was merely suffering from delayed trial stress. From what it was like to be locked in a cell for months. He'd seen it other times, many other times.

So much had been hidden from her. He began to think he was acting stupidly. She didn't need the head fixers, she just needed a good stiff talking to. Wasn't that right?

Rhodes turned the car around. Level with her, he could do that much, act cleanly and straight with her, quit trying to dodge, the way he had dodged the marriage thing with Fritzi for so long.

In Gorbio he stopped at a garage, gassed up the Fiat, and called RESERVE to apologize. "Be coming up a day or two from now," he told them. "A small hitch in my plans . . . thank you."

Romaine found his note, puzzling over why he hadn't taken her along. She dressed and went down to the terrace for orange juice and a croissant, then ordered the picnic lunch. "Yes, they could have it ready anytime, mam'selle, in one of the wicker hampers," the maitre d' promised her.

She liked the smaller hotel where they were staying, the Hermitage, adjoining the more fashionable but less homey Hotel de Paris. She could barely remember what it was like to have a real home. Or even her own family, so she clung to intimacy wherever she could find it.

Finishing her juice, Romaine began to wonder what it would have been like to be a Princess Grace. Come right from Hollywood stardom, glide into your own little kingdom and become instant royalty.

Maybe I'll stay here, thought Romaine. Learn the language and get into French films. Become a sensation . . . L'Americaine! Why not? Thumb her nose at the studios back home. Home? Here with him is home.

Rhodes saw her standing by the newspaper stall on the street fronting the hotel. About to pull into the driveway, instead he eased over to the curb and rolled down the window.

She came over, a smile filling her face, looking laundry fresh in white dungarees, a blue shirt and a pink sweater draped casually over her shoulders.

Leaning through the window, a few curls of the red wig spilling across her cheeks, she asked: "Where'd you go?"

"Had to run an errand. Tell you about it later. How's the picnic?"

"Ready any time."

"You hungry?"

"So-so."

"I skipped breakfast so I'm half starved."

"You didn't eat last night either." She hopped in. "Can we go to the Casino again tonight?" And I'm starved, too, for you, she thought.

"Better not push your luck."

"But I'm lucky. I can feel it."

"How did it go last night?"

"8,200 francs on roulette and 10,600 on baccarat."

"Stay ahead . . . That's quite a lot," he said.

Rhodes had stayed at the bar when Romaine went in to

try her luck. A poker player, he didn't care for casino games; in none of them could you bluff, so you gave away too big of an edge to the house.

Pulling up to the front door, he asked the doorman to send in for the picnic hamper. Romaine wanted to drive to Cannes to see the Carlton Hotel. And visit the other places where they held the famous film festival, and then gander at those topless beaches she'd heard so much about.

After the doorman loaded the hamper into the Fiat's back seat, Rhodes threw the engine into gear. He swung around the driveway and cut into a side street.

They weren't going far. Nothing in all of Monaco was very far from wherever you sat or stood or slept. A mile away was all, up the Boulevard Du Larvotto, then a turn to the beach route, and head out for Cap de la Vielle, a jut of land sticking out into the sea. From its top you could see all three harbors and the entire coastline for miles when the air was right.

A blowy day. Clouds swam under a graying sky with the sun in hiding most of the time.

In the garden at de la Vielle, where they had walked yesterday afternoon, Romaine, delighting at the view, came up with the idea for a picnic. Rhodes decided it was as good a place as any to tell her what was best for her, for them, for everyone.

He parked near a small building and they made their way up a footpath. Rhodes lugged the wicker hamper and a plaid blanket borrowed from the hotel. A fist of wind, then another, swiped at them as they came out of the pines. Romaine ducked as the wind tossed her sweater, knotted around her neck, then kicked her way through palm fronds tumbling across the grass.

"Down there," Rhodes said, pointing to the lee side of some rocks. "Run on ahead."

"You want help?" she shouted from six feet away.

"Thanks, I can handle it."

"You sure?"

"Yes, go on." He laughed and the wind sent the laugh right back into his mouth.

She trotted down a glade, and he joined her shortly by a sheltering rise of rocks.

"Wrong day for a picnic, I guess."

"We'll be fine," he said.

"Let me have it."

He gave her the hamper. Rhodes spread the blanket on the ground as she lifted out a metal tin of sandwiches, a cellophane sack of fruit, a wedge of cheese, olives, and checkered blue and white napkins. Rhodes opened a bottle of claret, and dug into the hamper for plastic cups.

He sat on one side of the blanket eating a chicken sandwich as Romaine lay down across from him, nibbling on salted black olives. Her face was turned down and away, and he wanted to see her as he talked. He hoped she would somehow make it easy.

"Romaine?"

"Umm-hh." She turned her head his way.

"Been fun, hasn't it?"

"The greatest, Cliff. I could stay here forever."

"How 'bout a few months instead."

"With you? I'd love it."

"I've got to go back. But there's a place, a very nice place, you can stay. I saw it this morning."

"By myself? I don't know anyone here. Are you trying to get rid of me?"

"You know I've got to get back," he said. "You can stay on."

"A hotel?"

"A nice place anyway and they might be able to do a few things to help."

"Help who?"

"You. Me. It's a kind of a clinic but more like a country club and—"

"I don't need any clinic. A clinic for what?"

He evaded. "You've been under enormous stress. Months of it. Anyone would need some help coming off all that." Rhodes looked at her, imploring.

"I feel great. Just fine."

He toughened down. "I assume you know what you did at Fritzi's was pretty punk."

"She's lying to you. She's all dizzy about getting married. You're making a really dumb mistake, you know."

"That's my worry. She did you a favor, when other people didn't seem to care."

"Other people? Like the family I'm supposed to have, and you won't tell me about?"

"Those and others," he said blandly.

"I've plenty of friends."

"Who are they? Where were they?"

"They're private . . . Tommy Burke, he's one."

Rhodes drank some wine and chewed another bite from the sandwich. Damn, he thought. But then what could he expect?

"There are people who can help you," he tried again. "Right here in France. They're tops."

Her eyes stabbed at him, then she turned away. "You're sounding pretty shitty. We've had such a perfect time, and now you want to spoil everything."

"I want to remember it, Romaine. And mostly I want to help you. Believe me."

"Fuck off."

"Don't say that. I don't like that kind of talk."

"Fuck off two times."

He could feel it coming out. "Then there's the bracelet. I took it the night Fritzi and I packed you up," Rhodes said. "It was the genuine thing, wasn't it? And it never belonged to you."

Her head shot up. Romaine swept her hair back, and he could see the taut line of her jaw and chin.

"You can damn well give it back. It's mine! Marc gave it to me," she screamed at him.

"No, I don't think so."

"Well, you don't know!"

"I know you didn't pick it up at some charity bazaar."

"You're a bastard! A thief too. God, I hate you." Her face was hard as the craggy rocks a few feet away. "You're not even a man, you just look like one," she sneered, her mouth curling.

"At any rate, I'm not your man . . . And you better quit talking like a spoiled little bitch."

"Or what? I want my emeralds back, goddamn you. I'll sue you."

"I don't think so."

"Where are they anyway?"

"Where they belong. With Audrey—"

"She's a liar too. The biggest. Audrey Sterne is the worst one I ever met."

"But the bracelet is hers, Romaine," he said as softly as he could over the wind.

"Mine! Mine! How do you know, anyway?"

"I heard, let's say." He felt like a fool again, a collector's edition of a genuine jerk.

"So smart, aren't you? You make me sick. You're just like the rest. You want to control me, own me, stop me."

"Not at all."

"You're in with the Sternes, I know you are. You're all out to stop me one way or the other."

Wind slashed again on the other side of the rocks. He waited till it stopped. "I want more than anything for you to go on in life. Get a fresh start. For that you need help. Try to understand what I'm saying."

He kept reasoning and pleading with her, the best way he could, explaining what a struggle it is to come off a trial like the one she had gone through. Freed but tainted, hurt if not broken, bruised if still breathing.

Only dimly aware of what he was saying, and smoldering inside, Romaine had tripped off to her own past. The memory of it still vivid and so secret in her.

Marc had finally pushed me too far. Those photos did it. I saw them in my dreams, in the mirror when I washed, on the pages of scripts I memorized. I could see them passed around with all the snide jokes and my reputation in ruins . . . Just as that nude calendar pose had nearly ruined Marilyn Monroe . . .

I was going to go right to Julio Sterne. Beg him to get those pictures for me. If he scorned me, I would threaten to tell the police about his bastard of a son dealing in those drugs. I knew plenty. A fair trade. If I went down, they would fall with me, including that cunt Audrey, loving herself so much in the social columns.

I set them up. Even when they didn't want to see me anymore, I arranged it anyway. Called the house, faked it as a shopgirl at the florist, and Kardas took the call. "Would the Sternes be home that evening to receive a large horse-shoe of roses, a surprise from an admirer? Very perishable."

Yes.

Then another call to Marc's office, using Audrey Sterne's way of talking, which was easy. "Marc should come for dinner tonight, his father and I want to see him." Even simpler, because I knew Marc was out on location, and wouldn't be seeing his father at the studio.

They'd all be there. So would I. And we'd have it out for everyone to choke on.

But it didn't work that way. And when I went through the gate up to the house, only a few lights were on, and the house so strangely quiet.

Marc, at the door, sullen, asking me why I was there. I mumbled, nervous and so afraid, but telling him I wanted those photos and negatives: Please. He could keep my share of the money for the screenplay, but the photos and negs . . . Please.

He laughed in my face. Juiced up, and I could see he'd gone off to bongo-land again.

"Maybe," he said. "Come in, as long as you're here." As if I was some street girl.

Him smirking, and me begging. No other sound from anywhere. No one home. Why? I asked. He didn't know. He wanted sex again.

For the photos, yes. He didn't have them there. Later, he promised. As he always promised everything.

He fixed up a speed-ball, laughing and taunting me. He opened his fly. He was crazed, I played along, touching him there as he started injecting his arm, shouting his laughter until it rang off the ceilings.

Oh, God!

I calmed him, playing with him, undressing for him. Then undressing him all the way. We fixed another speedball for him, and I tripled everything. He kept touching me while I got his arm ready, twisting the hose, watching the vein go blue and putting it in him ever so gently. Pushing the plunger, wiping it, telling him to feed in the rest for himself, and he did. Then I pushed again but with my thumb on his.

After I left, with him babbling on the floor, he must've known he was done for. Wiped his print off the plunger.

Smart boy, always so clever. He almost got me with that one . . .

Dear Marc, you rotten sonofabitch, you tried to take me for a ride. Made me lie to everyone, about the abortion, about other things. But you're the one who fell down, never to get up again . . . I got you, didn't I.

"You can have everything, Romaine," she heard Rhodes say. "All the help in the world. But you have to want it first."

"I don't trust you."

"You have to trust someone. Otherwise, it'll get awful lonely out there."

"I trust only what I can see, smell, or put in the bank."

Jesus! he thought. What was the point? She seemed in a dream. He was practically crying dry, trying to get through to her. He had paid with his high court appointment, with Fahey, with a guilt that no soap ever invented would wash away.

Romaine's body went rigid, and then she leaped to her feet, livid, in a rage. She shouted at him, her eyes glassy.

Everything.

It all came out, exactly as she'd just been remembering that night in Malibu Pointe. Of how, out of her mind with cold anger, she nudged Marc Sterne into his grave.

So lucid and compelling. On stage again. She talked at Rhodes, around him, over and under him until she filled him with her presence.

Coming without any warning, a fear swept over him. He had wanted to grow a love for Romaine. Now the whole thing had become a cripple in only a few beats of time. It began to die on him. The hurt broke up his vision in a wave of dizziness . . . she'd become a painful shadow before his dimming sight.

"And the abortion?" he asked in a half daze when Romaine finished. "Did you make that up, too?"

"No. The baby would've made everything right. We could've married then." She lied so easily once more.

"And you'd be a Sterne with all your worries over."

"Some of them . . . But the bastard tricked me that day in Palm Springs. I lost the baby, but he lost everything," she lied again.

"If you'd told the jury the straight story, I think they'd have let you go," Rhodes said.

"You might take that chance with someone else's life. But not with mine."

"And now you're screwing it up something fierce."

"Uh-uh. You're not as sharp as you think . . . If I told everything and still got off, the Sternes would blacklist me forever in films."

"They might anyway."

"We'll see, won't we?" Romaine said flippantly.

"If it was so important to force a marriage with Marc Sterne, why did you abort the child?"

"You don't understand anything, do you?"

"Not that, anyway."

"The photos. He drugged me and had those photos taken. If I didn't go through with the abortion, he said he'd smear me . . . So I did, but he still wouldn't give them up." A third lie in less than three minutes.

"You killed him for that?"

"He was out to use me. Nobody uses me." She glared at Rhodes.

"I'll remember, Romaine."

"You'd better, because that's what you're trying to do, isn't it? With the Sternes. Put me away."

"God, no. Nothing like that at all."

Leaning against the rocks, Romaine laughed till the blood came to her face. Short, sharp breaths of laughter, with her eyes closed, and her hair whipping her cheeks. "They can't get me again. They can't try me twice for murder. You told me so . . . So there!"

She had killed. His daughter was a killer.

Rhodes stared. He didn't know at what, but he stared. A fire of agony charred his insides. She was confessing, but he was the wrong man, the wrong anything. Weeks ago, under the mist of a love he craved, he'd already made himself blind and deaf to everything but her. His hopes, for them both, went black as fast as if lights suddenly went off all over the world. A throb in his head, hurting, and he fought an urge to kick her lovely ass clear back to Paris.

"Why're you telling me this?" he asked, stung and in real pain now.

Romaine repeated, "You're all the same, that's why. Out to get me."

"And you believe everything you just said?"

"Believe? I know. I was there."

Was this some sort of act? A game? He didn't know whether to believe her or not. But then they sank into each other's eyes and found their lost souls. Somehow he had to keep her in Europe or she would destroy them all.

"You're going to stay here," he told her emphatically. "It's your only chance."

"I'll make my own chances. Not at any booby farm either," said Romain with remarkable calm.

"You go back and they'll skin you alive. Trial or no trial."

"How will they know anything? I'm free."

"I'll have to tell them. The police, anyway . . ." As well as his former colleagues on the Superior Court, he knew and failed to say.

"That's crazy. They'll obviously want to know how you found out."

"I know they will."

"But then they'll *know* we've been seeing one another."

"I'm already ahead of you there."

"You wouldn't! Then they'll skin you."

"Maybe, maybe not either."

"Big scandals and all. You won't do it." She sneered again.

"I have to, Romaine. A woman back there"—he'd almost said *your mother*—"is under some degree of suspicion."

"Audrey Sterne. Who gives a—"

"I do," he stopped her. "So should you."

"Well, I don't and I never will. I don't do guilt trips for anyone."

"It doesn't make any difference whether you do or not. It's got to be straightened out."

"Then they'll blame me again."

Rhodes made a strong effort to remain cool, but he was coming apart inside. "They might," he said. "Some people probably still do blame you. But they can't try you again on that count." His quiet dream of love for her began to melt away. He had made a living dream for himself and now he would have to work overtime to keep it from turning into a nightmare.

"You'll never do it," she taunted. "You'd have to tell them we were in France and everything."

"Maybe why we were here too."

"On a fling. Great headlines. Uh-uh. You won't."

"As a matter of fact, my dear little killer, I may head back to California tonight."

Romaine saw the obstinacy in his face. "I was only kidding," she said. "See what a good actress I am?"

"Do I ever . . . And, no, I don't think you are kidding. I bet on your side once and I made a helluva big mistake."

"Don't be silly."

"I'll see you at the car."

Rhodes got up and dumped the plates, cups, food tins and jars into the hamper. He looked over at the rocks and saw that Romaine had disappeared. He tidied up, chasing a few papers swirling off on the ground wind. He tried not thinking about any of it, but it kept coming at him, scraping away. Sometimes he stopped what he was doing, dizzy and feeling as if a quick punch had tagged him on the chin.

Romaine hadn't gone to the car. She walked around behind the rocks and out to a concrete ledge, a lookout point. The wet sea air mopped her face as she scolded herself; she had gone too far, telling him what she had kept locked away all these dragging months. Had acted too impulsively, and what if he talked now and told on her?

The wind shrieked. Romaine braced her knees against a low pipe railing that ran around the ledge. In a deep gorge of sheer rock down below, she saw the sea swelling up and smashing against the cliff. Swell and smash again. In the charging, frothy water she glimpsed a dull life ahead.

Wind whipped her again. She turned away, holding her wig. Her face took on a look of sudden elation. There was no one else there but him, twenty yards away, waving at her. She screamed suddenly. Throwing one hand to her forehead, covering her eyes, Romaine shouted and then furiously pointed down over the railing.

Confused, Rhodes dropped the blanket and hamper to

hurry over. He came up beside Romaine, pushing himself through the teeth of the wind.

"What is it?" he hollered.

"Down there." She pointed again. "A body. Look!"

He leaned over the rusty low railing that rattled in the heavy wind. "Where?"

"Look straight down."

She had her arm over his shoulder, and she brushed her lips against his neck. Rhodes leaned out again. She squatted behind him, low, her hands poised below and under his rear. Then she shoved up very fast and hard and with all her strength.

Air tickled his nose. Faster it came. His arms flailed wildly so that he looked to Romaine like a child learning how to swim. Rhodes had felt only the wet sensation by his ear, the final Judas kiss of betrayal. The air rushed harder, pulling his mouth apart, bending his back till it hurt, but a hurt that was lost on him. As he twirled, so easily, he sensed a kind of freedom. Once he tried to cry out, but his throat had already collapsed from fear. He spun toward the rocks, and they looked bright and red under the sun that seemed so high the last time he could see it. Almost as red as the explosion in his head two seconds later.

Wanting to appear frightened, out of breath, Romaine ran back through the pines, then down the path to the parking area. Making the gravel fly, she raced over to a small building near where they had parked the Fiat.

Bounding up the steps, flinging open a door, she screamed to a startled woman who was stacking tourist brochures behind a counter.

"Oh, help! Help me, please!" Romaine cried, her face streaked and wide-eyed with shock. "A man—m-my friend—w-went went over. Wind took him . . . Help me. Ohh . . ." She fell on the floor in hysterics, pounding on it with two weak hands.

Chapter Thirty-Nine

The wind quieted by the next morning. Till then it was impossible to get in close enough to retrieve the body off the sea rocks. A rescue team from the Monte Carlo police had sacked Rhodes in a canvas body bag and it lay next to the port gunwale of a harbormaster's launch.

A messy job, thought Paul Matin, who watched the wake churn off the stern as the launch sped back to the harbor. A deputy inspector, he had been assigned the task of tidying up after the accident. Matin had already notified the U.S. Consul in Nice that an American citizen had died in an accident at Cap de la Vielle. Now he would sign the broken and curled body into the morgue, and that would be the end of a grisly morning.

Stopping by the Hermitage Hotel last evening, he had inquired about the well-being of the young American woman. Sooner or later he would have to take her statement. She was asleep, or at least she wouldn't answer her phone; the hotel had even offered the services of a doctor to the shocked and red-eyed young woman, but she had refused the help. Matin had asked for both passports, a formality.

What struck him as slightly odd was the hotel manager's statement: "Mam'selle Pachmyer has asked the concierge to call Air France to arrange a seat to London."

"Nothing else, no other calls?" Matin had asked, almost absently.

"She requested a disconnect on all the phones in the suite," said the manager.

Later, Matin began to make guesses as to why the woman hadn't at least notified someone in the States. Family members? Friends? Someone to help with getting the body home, and for all the other depressing details of sudden death. Well, that was the job of the U.S. Consul and not the Monte Carlo police.

An illicit romance perhaps. Stolen days and nights in Monte Carlo, so famous as a lovers' oasis. Maybe that's why she hadn't called anyone.

Still.

Matin hoped the dead man strapped to the gunwale was a nobody. No wife, no special honors, no anything. There were all sorts of ways to roll a silk sheet over these small indiscretions, if the man had a family but was here with a paramour. It usually took some fancy footwork, though, and he hoped it would be unnecessary this time.

Chapter Forty

The next afternoon Matin knocked twice on the door. In his pocket he carried Edy Pachmyer's passport, having already sent Rhodes's to the U.S. Consul in Nice.

The door edged open.

"Mam'selle Pachmyer?"

"Yes, I am."

"I am Matin. Paul Matin from the Monte Carlo police."

"Yes. Hello."

"Would you be good enough to answer a few questions? Small details, then I shall quickly depart."

Romaine sized him up. A florid complexion, rimless glasses, and a belly. His bristly hair cut in military style.

"I'm very tired," she said.

"I will be brief. Only a few minutes, mam'selle." Matin

smiled. Romaine saw that he had very good teeth, pearly white.

"Come in."

Closing the door behind him, Matin followed her into the parlor. A fresh looking room done in pastels, with plushy stuffed chairs and two settees covered in a lime satin. A watermark showed in one corner of the ceiling, and it caught his eye immediately.

They sat across from each other. Behind Romaine the muslin sun curtains billowed from the doors opening to the balcony. For a moment, to Matin's startled eyes, she appeared to wear a huge bridal veil. She didn't seem to resemble her passport photo, and that bothered him. Honey-hued hair—not a redhead as described in her passport—though it was hard to see her face under those blue glasses she wore.

"We are deeply sorry," Matin began. "A lamentable incident."

"I'm sick over—sick from my nerves."

"Naturally."

"But what do you want from me?"

"Perhaps you can advise me of what happened. What you saw."

"I saw very little. It happened so quickly."

"Whatever you saw, then. Forgive me, mam'selle, I must make notes." Matin fumbled a small black book from his inside coat pocket, then unscrewed the top of a fountain pen.

Tersely Romaine described the picnic outing. The strong winds. They were there at de la Vielle for no more than an hour, maybe less. He'd been drinking most of a bottle of wine and was drowsy. When they were about to leave, he walked around to clear his head. After repacking the picnic basket, she went to look for him. He was out on the parapet, leaning over the rail there, and a terrific burst of wind took him . . . He might've been sick, she told Matin.

"Sick?"

"He hadn't been feeling well. Or from the wine. A whole bottle almost."

"You were nearby?" Matin asked.

"Twenty or thirty yards . . . Oh, it was so awful. He was the most wonderful man." Romaine's face trembled.

"You'd known him for some time then?" Matin asked idly.

"Yes, you see we were going to marry. We'd come here to think about it. Oh, I'll never get over—" Romaine looked away. Several fingers strayed nervously to her mouth.

"Such a terrible shock for you," Matin said sympathetically. "We'll do all we can to make it easier for you," he assured her.

"Oh, yes. Thank you. When can I go, leave here?"

"Very soon I should think. There is an autopsy underway," Matin explained.

"But why?"

"That is our way here in Monaco. Our regulations."

"Even in an accident?"

"Especially then, mam'selle."

"That's ghoulish. He should just be buried in a nice place." She paled.

"Is something the matter?"

"I get ill remembering it, that's all."

"Of course," said Matin with more sympathy. "Will you be accompanying the remains to America? Your U.S. Consul in Nice wishes to know."

Romaine hadn't counted on that one. "I'm unable to." She hesitated. "I'm due in London for rehearsals."

"Rehearsals?"

"A tryout for a stage play. It's all very uncertain, but I must be there," she said, thinking of Max Shapin's suggestion to try the theater in London.

"Ah! Mam'selle is an actress, then?"

"I've been in films," she said, suddenly feeling prickly. She could never fly back with the casket. The questions. Customs or whatever. Supposing they checked her passport? What if Fritzi Jagoda cornered her? She had to put everything behind her once and for all.

"You have not yet called anyone? Told his relatives or someone?"

"I couldn't. Just couldn't bring myself—"

Matin nodded dourly. "And, Mam'selle Pachmyer, you were born where?"

"California."

"You live there now?"

"I always have."

"I must visit there one day."

"The best of all places. But . . . well, so many memories. I don't think I want to go back there for now anyway."

Matin closed his notebook. "From your Consul in Nice, I have learned that M'sieu Rhodes was a judge. In California, no?"

Romaine nodded.

"A judge, yes," Matin said. "Too bad. Still a young man."

Romaine's nerves collided everywhere in her body. She didn't care for these questions, where they were headed or how the inspector asked them. She'd already had enough of the police to last three lifetimes.

Worried about her passport, she had discarded the pretense of being Edy Pachmyer. The wig, the fake mole on her cheek, and the makeup giving a fairer color to her complexion. She would tell Matin, throw herself at his mercy. Tell him things he could never verify; anymore than Pritter, that horrid toad, could check on her story at the trial.

"Inspector?" Romaine leaned forward.

"Yes?"

"There's something I should tell you. I hope you won't blame me too much."

"Please, yes."

Calm and slightly sniffy as she talked. Bold, too, about as bold as kneeling on nails and smiling about it. She had worked it all out, and would make it sound like a love sonnet . . .

. . . of how they had left California on the spur of the moment. There had been no time to get a passport, so she borrowed one from a friend.

Noticing how Matin's eyebrows came together, Romaine dug for his sympathy. She gave him her real name, who she really was, said she had been a defendant in a murder trial where Cliff Rhodes had presided as the judge. Many months she had spent in his courtroom.

After she was found innocent, he had taken a deep interest in her. Trying to help in every way. He even told her he knew she had never been guilty. They fell in love, unexpectedly and helplessly, and so they had come to Europe. To be alone, Inspector . . . and Cliff Rhodes was trying to escape the clutches of a woman who had chased him for years. A sort of hussy, a woman with a history to her.

As for herself—Romaine went on—she badly needed a change. The notoriety of the trial had tarnished her. An awful time, harrowing, had nearly broken her life up, till him who she loved so preciously.

"So you see, Inspector," Romaine looked at him, cool as a winter window, "we had to come over here. We could never marry in California or even live there together . . . the publicity would just ruin us."

Matin was uneasy. His mind had clicked, listening. A call had come in yesterday from the clinic in Gorbio. They had heard news of the accident on Radio Monte Carlo—was this the same Rhodes they'd been expecting? An American, they said, who was coming to place a Romaine Brook in their care.

What about it? Matin asked Romaine. His voice lowered anxiously.

"Oh, yes. That was his idea. He was always so right." Romaine snuffled again.

"Perhaps you'll explain."

She was ready for him. "We were going there together. Before we married we wanted to be sure. It was all so sudden, Inspector. I mean we were in love but he was older and everything, you know, and we were to have one of those tests. One of those compatibility tests, I think they're called. I'm not sure. He was taking care of it . . ." She broke again, beautifully, and the world had a new river today. "Oh dear God, Inspector, look what's happened. He's gone . . . he'll never be back. And he was so fabulous. The best thing that ever happened to anyone."

She slumped forward in her chair. Matin was undone.

Before him was an endearing young woman with tragedy stamped all over her. He had the cautious mind of a policeman, though, and hadn't liked the business about the passport. She told him she had stood trial for murder, and he didn't like that very much either. But he knew of the winds that day. Heavy enough to topple several small boats in the marina, damage homes, and take out the power for an hour or more. And what judge, even an American judge, would be seen openly with a defendant from his own court unless he really meant to be with her? It came to him as a little odd, her story, but he had known odder ones. Anyway, they were Americans, weren't they? A racc of children, liable to do anything. Yet she had been open, direct, and hadn't weaseled around about the false passport. Matin credited her on that one.

Going over to where Romaine sat, he waited until she looked up through tear streaked eyes. He had wanted to touch her shoulder reassuringly, but decided it was too familiar a gesture.

"Mam'selle?"

"I'm so sorry. I didn't mean to cry on you." She wiped her eyes slowly.

"I quite understand. You've been through a serious time." Matin hesitated for a monent. "Still, I must inform you that you will have to stay in Monte Carlo until this passport irregularity is put right."

"Am I in trouble?"

"We shall have to see. It's against the law what you've done. Much will depend on what the U.S. Consul says in Nice."

"Will I have to go see them?"

"No, you'll have to remain here in Monte Carlo. They'll no doubt come to see you . . . and I shall want your word you won't leave."

"Yes, Inspector, you have my word. I hope you'll help me. I had to get away. I had to."

"I'm rather surprised an American judge would allow you to do such a thing."

Romaine looked away as she said her first truthful thing that afternoon. She blushed becomingly. "He didn't really know until it was too late. It was my mistake, not his. We were so in love and, oh you know how that is."

Matin nodded dourly. "I'll let myself out, mam'selle. You'll be hearing from me in a day or two."

"Do I have to stay in my room?"

"You're free to go anywhere in Monaco. I warn you it will go hard on you if you violate your word."

"But I would never do that, Inspector." Her moist eyes widened innocently into mirrors of gratitude.

The door closed behind Matin and behind the baleful look he gave her as he left. She waited for a long moment, then let out a sigh of relief. A very contented sigh, like the one after good lovemaking.

Consuelo Ramirez was just finishing up her morning work in the kitchen when she heard the phone ring. She was lonely now that Rhodes was gone. This might be the call she expected from her sister, who lived down below the border in Aqua Caliente. She smiled at the thought of passing some time gabbing together.

Wiping her hands on her apron, she picked up the receiver. Several moments passed before she could untangle the identity of the caller from across the Atlantic. She thought it might be Rhodes at first. But the voice she heard was strange to her, a voice that kept asking even stranger questions.

Sensing trouble, confused, and not knowing what "next of kin" meant, she told the caller the number of Rhodes's chambers at court.

Hanging up, she went back to work, wondering what a consul was in France. Why the call anyway, and what did kin mean? Or was it the American name—Ken?

A wrong number perhaps.

Five minutes later, Macklin Price, sealing an envelope at her desk, took the same call. Everything dropped down inside of her as the news filtered through and slowly carved her up. She burst into a babble of tears.

From the outer office others scurried in to see what the howling was all about. They waited as Macklin tried to calm herself, but she could not, and after she gave them some of her shock, she called Fritzi.

And sobbed with her till she heard the phone drop to the floor at Fritzi's end.

Macklin left for the day. She was quite certain Rhodes had no next of kin. An only son of ranchers from a small Montana town, and they had passed away some years before, she couldn't remember when. Before departing, she called an officer at Wells Fargo, where his personal affairs were handled, to see if they knew anything more.

At Wells Fargo the officer who took Macklin Price's call did some checking of her own. She called the vault, asking for Rhodes's files to be sent up immediately. She remembered how he had made changes to his will only weeks before. But then she handled many trusts and estates, and amendments to them flurried in weekly.

Within the hour she read the file and opened his will, skimming through the key parts. She was aghast, all the way to the elevator and all the way upstairs to the legal department, where she carried this paper bomb about to explode in her hand.

• • •

Fritzi could hardly feel her heart beat. She had lain on her bed for hours. For keeping you alive, that heart, but she was certain hers had fled her body, was thousands of miles away in some corner of Europe beside his, and no longer beating any more.

Gone. So fast. How could it be?

She remembered Macklin Price calling, and remembered almost fainting. Hours later her mind seemed to have whited-out, become an empty blank. She shut herself off, then out from the whole world, her only world, her no more world.

Audrey had heard nothing at all about Rhodes. She answered the door that morning because the day help were off. The doorbell changed everything. She had greeted a nicely dressed woman who, smiling, asked Audrey to sign a receipt for an envelope.

From Julio's attorneys, she found. He was filing for a separation. His attorneys would be pleased to hear from hers so that temporary support could be arranged with as little fuss as possible.

So very goddamn polite, she thought, staring at the neatly margined page.

Audrey had sensed it coming. Even so, it was a chiller. She had seen precious little of Julio since the trial had ended. Whenever she succeeded in reaching him by phone, he sounded distantly cool: either out of town or too busy to see her when he wasn't.

Her attorneys could wait. They were busy enough with the Malibu sheriff who was still sniffing around, wanting quick answers for their stupid questions. Damn them all, she thought.

The phone rang. Three times it hooted at her before she elected to touch it. The Wells Fargo bank officer was on the line.

"Is Mrs. Sterne there?"

"Speaking."

"Mrs. Sterne"—and the woman introduced herself—"I have something rather urgent to discuss with you."

"Everyone has, it seems. I'm listening."

As the bank officer went on, Audrey felt her heart stop for a moment. "He's dead! Are you sure?"

"I'm afraid so. And you are named as a trustee under the terms of his will."

"You must be very mistaken there, I'm afraid."

"It's very clear, Mrs. Sterne. I checked it through with our legal department. Could you possibly come by here tomorrow? There may be a problem, and we'd very much like to take it up with all concerned."

"Who is *all*?"

"Yourself and a Miss Jagoda, at least. She's the—"

"I know who she is, thanks. Why so urgent? Don't these things take months?"

"Your husband's company, Mrs. Sterne. Parthenon Studios is a very important customer of Wells—"

"I guess I'm missing something here," Audrey broke in.

"There's a possible incident in the making, Mrs. Sterne," warned the trust officer. "We don't think Mr. Rhodes's death has been announced yet. And this might be the best time—"

"What incident, what do you mean?"

"I don't think we should go into it over the phone. It's too involved."

"I see." Baffled, Audrey's curiosity bloomed.

"We could send a car out for you."

"I'll make it on my own, thank you. What time?"

"Is ten all right? We're on the sixth floor and you can park . . ."

Audrey took notes.

Afterward she bent her head down, sighing as she shook it back and forth. My dear God, he's gone. Why didn't I hear before now?

She did hear it later on the afternoon news. Hardly more than a blurb. "A death by accident in Monte Carlo," said the newscaster.

She sat there with thoughts spinning in and out of every window she had opened with Cliff Rhodes over the past months. They might've made something together once. She remembered their arguments over Romaine. His stubborn belief of her innocence. How she herself had been vilified in his court. Where was Romaine now? What an awful mess.

Audrey thought of the bracelet he'd sent back. Good of him, even gallant. She started to weep softly and didn't know why.

Hours melted away, so slowly that Audrey thought time had actually frozen on her. In the wilderness of her huge glass house that was no longer a home, she tried steadying herself against the hard double bounce of the day.

Darkness fell, and she had two stiff gins. Julio nearly disappeared from her thoughts, but she couldn't quite seem to get Cliff Rhodes out of them. A jangle of the phone burst upon her again.

She heard the urgently frightened voice of Sister Marius. That good shepherdess herself, threatening then demanding the return of Romaine's file. Where was it? It seemed the news of Rhodes's death had also pierced the stone walls of Las Infantas.

There might be more trouble. Scold, scold.

"Sister," said Audrey at length, "if you get any hot inquiries, I'll get the papers back to you."

"You still have them, don't you? Those papers have been no end of trouble."

"No, Sister," Audrey said very sweetly now because the gin was working on her nicely. "It's not the papers that were the trouble. The trouble began— Oh, never mind."

"You'll send them back?"

"When you send me back the money," Audrey replied

stiffly. Fatigue hit her at last. Feeling a scream was about to gallop from her throat, she added: "G'night, Sister. I think I hear my plaster angel calling."

Closing one eye, she centered the receiver over its cradle and let it drop. It missed.

A miss of a day, she thought.

Chapter Forty-One

"I stayed out of it back there," Fritzi said, "but I'm still confused." Though tired and depressed, she still needed to talk.

"The bank isn't confused, I'm pretty sure of that." Audrey kicked off her shoes, tucking her legs under one hip as she leaned back in a couch. "I suppose that's why they hurried up with reading the will."

"I can understand how Cliff involved me. But why you?"

"That's a story with no end. Absolutely none."

Fritzi looked at her appraisingly. "You mind filling me in?"

They were not everyday friends. They were just two women who knew each other reasonably well, and who were now paired up by a tragedy. And the morning they had just spent together would ally them for a long time to come.

"You wouldn't have a spare martini around the house," she suggested to Fritzi. "I've got a slight hangover today and the bank didn't help it any. Don't spare the gin."

She watched Fritzi leave the room and thought she was seeing a suffering widow, who had never really been one. Sympathy grew and helped Audrey to forget her own troubles.

The reading of Rhodes's will at the bank had forced her to admit again she could never change what was already done. The past was going to cling like a barnacle, and she could never scrape it away.

A public record in the Probate Court. There were already too many records, Audrey thought despairingly. People were bound to hazard guesses. And those guesses would grow into rumors, and the rumors become suspicions. The worst of suspicions.

They had come to Fritzi's home after two maddening hours talking with the woman officer, a bank laywer at her side, from the trust and estates division at Wells Fargo.

A hand from the grave, Audrey had thought. The dead making a one-sided bargain with the living. Those droll passages in Rhodes's own writing. To her dismay he had finally made them into a family. Not much of one, but finally accounted for, however strangely.

Miffed that they were cut out of the trustee's fees, the bank showed even greater alarm at Audrey's role under the will. Why was she, they asked her, a trustee for Romaine Brook?

Fritzi's very same question of only a moment ago.

Audrey had brushed the bank off, telling them to mind their own business. She suspected they were far less worried over her than they were about their future with Parthenon Studios.

Cliff Rhodes had pinned her absolutely—and absolutely publicly—to the daughter she had denied for twenty-two years. Fritzi inherited half, outright, of a very considerable estate. The other half was to be held in a ten year trust for Romaine's benefit. Fritzi and herself were named as co-trustees.

There were other bequests, but Audrey had paid little attention to those. Suffering in fright now that she was shackled to Romaine as surely as if they were Siamese twins. Her thief, Marc's killer, she was sure of it. God, thought Audrey, I've never done enough sins in my life to keep on paying this way.

She could still hear Rhodes's written words: "I ask you to help me with Romaine and with her future and well-being. You will know why, both of you, and I am forever confident you will understand why I must turn to you. After longest thought this is the only way, I believe, for Romaine to be looked after . . . No one but the both of you could help . . . should I die or be incapacitated."

Fritzi had almost choked. The bank, she demanded to know, had called her for this? She neither wanted nor needed the money. Only him. Act as Romaine's guardian? There must be some other way, Fritzi had appealed to them.

"The courts could assume the task, or possibly even appoint us," advised the trust officer. "We are only informing you of Judge Rhodes's last wishes."

Hearing these words, and after a little more sparring, Fritzi's resistance softened. Audrey remembered her looking over and saying: "I'll act as trustee if you will. I hope you've got a good iron hand. Mine's already up by my ear."

Bewildered and upset, they had asked about the mysteries of estates and probate; how money would be handled; what was the tax catastrophe? Were there any other headaches?

Then they had come to Fritzi's house for woman-to-woman talk, catch their breath, absorb their shock, consider what to do next. Or not do, as they dwelled on their private worries and heartaches.

With an early afternoon drink in hand, a desperately needed painkiller, Fritzi was about to have her earlier guess confirmed.

Of how Audrey and Cliff Rhodes in slaphappy love had made a daughter. One that Audrey, for a hundred and nine reasons, had once wanted to find and help as an incognito-mother.

Fritzi had never linked him with Audrey Sterne. Casual acquaintances, her appearances in his courtroom, yes, but nothing else. Audrey, after all, had lived in London for nearly twenty years before marrying Julio Sterne.

"He said something one night at Chasen's," Fritzi said, stunned again as Audrey told her all.

"About me?" Audrey asked.

"Only that he was her father. God, I never heard anything like this. Not ever."

Audrey put her drink down. "It's been worse than a nightmare, believe me."

"For Cliff too," Fritzi said bleakly. "Why didn't you tell him, Audrey? Tell him a long time ago."

Audrey told Fritzi what she'd been telling herself all these months. Romaine had been an accident. What good would it do anyone to spade it up, years and years later? And when Marc Sterne died, it was too late to confide in anyone. "I was petrified," said Audrey, looking wanly at Fritzi. "You just don't know."

"But you told him halfway through the trial—"

"Yes," Audrey broke in. "Because of that subpoena threat. To get the records at Las Infantas . . . I was afraid for both of us, so I had to tell him. And he decided to stay in the trial anyway."

"I wonder why."

"One reason is all the commotion it would cause . . . And, well, me. Nice of him. He told me they'd find out somehow I was the mother if he withdrew from the trial."

"I wonder."

"I don't, Fritzi. It wasn't so hard for me to find Romaine. A little money is all it took."

"Was he named as the father?"

"Yes. That was a mistake. But my family insisted on it at the time. They damn near killed me as it was."

Thinking now of something else, Fritzi shivered up goose skin, shook her dark curls, and said: "Romaine stayed here for a while."

"You don't mean it?"

"I very damn sure do."

"She's trouble with wings on. No one seems to believe that but me."

"Now she's trouble who's worth more than three million bucks."

"It's just outrageous. How could he?"

"You suppose she's still in France or Monte Carlo?" asked Fritzi, almost to herself.

"Who? Romaine?"

"Cliff took her last week. To some clinic. This kind of clinic." Fritzi tapped her head with a finger.

"Why didn't you say so?"

"You've been doing all the talking."

"A clinic? For her?" Audrey hesitated. "He knew she was loco then?"

"Troubled, yes. Crazy? I don't think he thought that."

All the time she'd been talking, Fritzi could feel a stream of more pain flowing. She tried to block it off, but it roared on anyway. She fought the pain down because she might never get another chance to find out more. She thought of Fahey. He would have to know.

"Tell me something, Audrey. Do you think Romaine killed your stepson?"

"She beat the rap. People do. They just get away with it sometimes."

"But do you know, really know?"

"The jury screwed that one up," said Audrey. "But, no, I can't prove it. No one can."

Guided by intuition, and for her own moral support, Audrey explained about the stolen emerald bracelet, and how Rhodes had managed to return it to her.

"But you're still only guessing."

"I'm no lawyer, Fritzi, and I'm no murderer either as some might think... Romaine got him to do something. She had Marc around her finger."

"But no one will ever know, will they?"

"Not technically maybe, but I know," Audrey drew the words slowly as a frantic light shone in her eyes. "God, they really think I might've done it." She looked to see if Fritzi understood.

"I've heard. If I promise to never breathe a word, will you tell me something?"

"That all depends."

"Here goes anyway—did you have something going with your butler?"

"Fritzi!"

"I'll never say."

Fritzi had reasons for asking, and the biggest one was to learn if Audrey Sterne was truthful. She kept her eyes riveted to Audrey's.

"Supposing I said nothing. Would you be able to read me?"

"I'm not so sure."

"He was great in the feathers," Audrey said suddenly.

They smiled at each other, and Fritzi felt much better. She wasn't judging her. Half the people Fritzi knew were having affairs, or had had them, including herself. But if she were going to be dealing with Audrey for the next ten years over Romaine's trust, it was better to know who she was dealing with.

"Thanks for telling me," Fritzi said. "I swear it won't leave this room."

"Supposing I said I hadn't. Would you have believed me?"

"I would now."

"You were testing me?"

Fritzi nodded.

"And if I said I hadn't been with Ferenc Kardas and you didn't believe me, then you might doubt me about Romaine and Marc?"

"Something like that, yes," replied Fritzi. "How is Julio taking it? The trial?"

"He's in Hong Kong buying movies. Yesterday he served me with papers. He wants a separation."

"Oh, dear Lord, no! I'm sorry, Audrey. Oh, dear! And after all this—"

"It's sort've been in the works for a year now. At least that long. Like some dinner invitation you expected but took a long time in coming."

"Over the butler."

"He was really Julio's man. His valet. Everything . . . No, Julio knew about Ferenc." Audrey laughed. "I'll say he knew."

"Well, I'm sorry anyway."

"So am I. But it's for the best."

"Hope he'll be generous with you."

"Generosity isn't Julio's long suit when he wants out of something," Audrey said. "Fritzi, do you think we ought to call someone in Monte Carlo? Find out what's happening?"

"I've been thinking about it for two days." Fritzi's face clouded. "I only went to the bank *not* to think about it and now I'm thinking about it all over again." Her face widened and then part of it dropped from the mouth down. "We were going to marry and now it's a funeral." She began crying. "I-I can't bear to—to bury him."

Audrey sprang up fluidly. She went over and sat on an armrest, snugging Fritzi close, feeling the shudders and heaves Fritzi gave off. Someone had to do something and soon. Romaine had to be found and what about burial arrangements? There was a possible divorce to contend with, and those very unpleasant questions from the Malibu sheriff.

Fritzi mopped her swollen eyes.

"If you'll be all right," Audrey said, "I'll start doing some calling to Monte Carlo. What time is it there?"

"Night. Eleven or so."

"Well, I can call the State Department," said Audrey. "They can find things out."

"I know someone who can help . . . I think."

"Who?"

"Do you know Alonzo Fahey?"

Audrey dimly recalled that name from somewhere. "Should I?" she asked.

Fritzi explained who Fahey was; of how he had once worked for Cliff Rhodes, had even assisted in Romaine's defense.

"I'm not sure I want to know him," Audrey said. But now she recalled Fahey as the man Sister Marius had talked about.

"He's marvelous. Mostly. He was going to give me away at the wedding—"

"Oh, that's different then. How do I get a hold of him?"

"I'll do it."

"Fritzi, you can't tell him one word about me. That I'm Romaine's mother."

"I wouldn't."

"Won't he want to know why I'm here?"

"I'll think of something."

"You promise."

"Absolutely."

Fritzi went down the hall to her bedroom. Sitting at her dressing table, she dialed, and then spoke in hushed tones to Wanda Fahey.

Idly she stroked the strands of the thin gold chains hanging on a peg next to the mirror. One that Cliff Rhodes had given her, her favorite one with the enameled lion pendant, was gone. Recalling Audrey's story about the emerald bracelet, Fritzi's emotions shot from wet despair to dry anger.

Two hours later Fahey turned up. He looked as if he had come in from the hills somewhere with his faded dungarees, a blue and often patched sweater, and a livid red bandanna tied around his sturdy neck. Tousled dark hair fell everywhere across his forehead and a perfect line of beard shadowed his face.

"I meant to call when I heard," he said to Fritzi. "Never even said goodbye to him. Thought you'd be sore at me . . . And now look at you with all the sand in your eyes." Fahey came forward and swung his one good arm around her.

Audrey stood away, watching them hug. She tried to catalogue Fahey, and instinctively smelled a lean healthy male around, who was looking back at her now over Fritzi's bowed head. Deep warm eyes, Audrey saw, blue as a Swedish lake, and with thick lashes. An arm stiff as a toy soldier's. The Las Infantas interloper at last.

They broke apart, and Fritzi fluffed her hair. "Alonzo, this is Audrey Sterne. A friend of mine."

"You who I think you are?" Fahey said to Audrey. He came over, barely a foot away, surprising her.

"Probably."

"A looker, eh? You've a lovely pair there, too. Droolers, I'd say."

"Alonzo, stop," Fritzi scolded him. "God, don't you know when to behave?"

"But they're nice, aren't they, and she looks so gorgeous. They're like Mary Magdalene's in a painting I like," he said, and then to Audrey: "Hurt the feelings, did we?"

"Not at all," said Audrey, rubbing her neck lightly to cover a rising blush.

"Alonzo, I need some help," Fritzi said. "There's some things you ought to know. They absolutely must stay in this room. Not a word to anyone."

Fahey nodded.

It was his last nod for some time, as he slowly fell into the sump of disbelief. Fritzi gave him the bare bones at first, and then astounded him by revealing that Cliff Rhodes was Romaine's true father. Imagine the iron box Cliff had found himself in . . . and why at the end of the trial he could not lift so much as a finger to help Alonzo. Everything teetered on the edge: one misstep, one stray word, and disaster would mow him down for good. Trouble, and more to come, haunted him. Losing out on his appointment to the Supreme Court, he had taken Romaine to France for help and to get her out of Hollywood.

"He loved you, Alonzo, you know that," Fritzi went on. "And he worried so hard about you. I know because I saw him go through it."

Fahey wondered why all this news in front of a stranger like Audrey Sterne. A traffic jam filled his head. All of it was so beautifully cockeyed. With both ears ready for more, he loaded his glass again, halfway up, neat. Rhodesy-boy, the old dance-master, had pulled off a heist. The idea held a shape to it that appealed to Fahey's sense of irony.

Guilt nibbled away at him, though. It was he who had gone out to Las Infantas one fine day to help Tommy Burke find the real parents . . . ask them for money. The nun had run him off as surely as if he'd come to steal her praying virgins. To make shorter work of it, he'd thrown down the idle bluff of a subpoena.

And now he could see, starkly, that if he'd just shut up, Rhodes would probably never have known about Romaine. Who she really was. If he had never known, and never cared, he wouldn't have gone to Europe to die. Still be here, and Fritzi-girl would still be dishing out her good-natured laughs, a dozen at a time. Fahey knew he would be shadowboxing with his jumpy feelings for a long time.

Fahey was hungry. To maintain him, Fritzi left to make sandwiches. He turned his attention to Audrey who gazed back steadily. Why was she here, he asked through a smile that came at her with the force of a bullet.

"I came by to see Fritzi. See how she was holding up," Audrey replied blithely.

No mention of the bank meeting that morning, nor that she was Romaine's mother. Audrey wondered if the handsome lug sitting so near her would guess the truth. Not if she could help it. And she could.

"I guess you knew the girl pretty well?" Audrey heard Fahey ask, as if reading her thoughts.

"For a while I did. Or thought I did," Andrey answered. "What did you think of Romaine?"

"An invention, a lovely toy."

"That's all?"

"Only met her twice," he said. "An actress, of course, so an invention. We invent them so they can invent other worlds for us . . . I love them for it."

Audrey mused on his comments for a moment. "Maybe, but did you like her?"

"Which way?"

"I don't know." She hesitated. "Was she, did she sound right to you? Start pulling all her cute numbers on you?"

Fahey thought, then replied: "Flames of ice."

Audrey frowned. "Nice?"

"Ice-y. Has the talent, I'd say, for being of the many. Wet a man down though. Cold orgasms probably."

"That's an odd thing to say," said Audrey, feeling strangely intrigued. She smiled, hoping for more.

Fritzi returned. She carried a tray of drinks and a chicken sandwich for Fahey. But his hunger had flown on him. Trying to accept what he had done, so unintentionally, his mind, like his hunger, refused him.

Fritzi rescued him.

"Alonzo, you know how Cliff adored you. I want to bury him over there. I can't think of him here, so close by, in the ground. We would've married in a few weeks, and this isn't easy, Alonzo, because I know you were upset as all get-out before he left.

"Will you come and be with me . . . He loved you, Alonzo. Everything Cliff did he did for reasons of his own. He only told me the main one and I guess he felt he couldn't tell you any of them. You or anyone else, and it's not hard to figure out why.

"You have to forget now," she hurried on anxiously. "Bygones are bygones. He wanted the Supreme Court and he lost it all over that damn trial. He's lost his life now. But he shouldn't lose you or me, should he?"

Fritzi paused to catch her breath. "Please come. I know you will."

She sat only a few feet away, near Audrey, as Fahey was soaked up in new thoughts. He easily grasped why Rhodes had maneuvered at the end to show how Marc Sterne might have died in other ways. He looked at Audrey again. He knew she was under suspicion. He wanted to explore her mouth, with those finely chiseled Arabian lips. She looks like an orchid, he thought. An intelligent orchid.

Abruptly Fahey saw an exotic image of Monte Carlo: the sweep of the Riviera, the blue of those terraced hillsides at evening, the sunbathed shores. He saw something else, too. But that could come later if it ever came at all.

"Very short these days on French francs," he said, feeling his pride dip.

"I'll take care of everything," Fritzi answered. "Leave it all to me."

"Never borrow from women. Bad form, I say."

"You ought to start then. You know a ton of them," Fritzi shot back.

"A plate collection, you think? Pass the hat for old Fahey . . . On the curb there with his beggar's cup extended."

Fahey glowered. He held to a fast rule: never discuss money with women, they had so much of it these days. Should be sent out to weed the fields, all of them, for a month every year. Two months even. Good for slimming the thighs and keeping limber for the nights.

"What about me?" Audrey said. "I'm still on the outs with the sheriff, and I'd like to know what happened."

"You really want to come?" Fritzi asked Audrey.

"You mind?"

"Not at all." Fritzi gave her a knowing look. "That settles it . . . Alonzo?"

Fahey stood, his decision made. "You'll have to bail me out with a few thousand if I'm to go."

"No problem—"

"I can lend it to you," Audrey offered quickly. She was beginning to like this odd man.

"Jesus," said Fahey, enthused now. "Let's all get together more often if you're handing it out so easily."

"Thanks, Alonzo," Fritzi told him. "I mean it."

"I'll need your phone," he said. "What time is it? Fourish?"

"4:20," Audrey noted.

"Midnight or so in Monaco. Good hour to get them out of bed," said Fahey. "I might be a while."

"Use the one in the kitchen. On the table."

Placing a call to the Monte Carlo police, he worked his way up to the senior officer on night watch. In no time he had his parlay going. "A brother," he said into the phone. "And me the person charged with the estate . . . My hands full of wailing women . . . And what the hell is all this inefficiency about? Why did I have to be notified through the fucking newscasts?"

The police officer very politely agreed to call Matin on another line, no doubt asleep at this hour.

Fahey waited. His need for fresh action began to come alive. He had started something back there at Las Infantas. He thought of Cliff Rhodes. A debt to pay there, but how do you pay off the dead?

Back on the line again, the police officer gave a home number for Matin, who would be waiting for the call. Fahey signed off and a few minutes later made contact with Matin, who sounded relieved to hear from someone. Very soon the body could be released. Best to work through the U.S. Consul in Nice, who would gladly assist in every way.

"We'll be coming your way, Inspector. His fiancée wants him buried over there," Fahey said.

Matin seemed confused. "I believe his fiancée is here. She's made no mention of a burial in Monaco."

"Is the girl there? Romaine Brook?"

"Yes. She will be here for at least a few more days."

Again the wait, and it hung heavy on the line.

Fahey narrowed his eyes. "Keep that girl there and laughing," he advised Matin, "till we get over there. Can you?"

They agreed.

Fahey filled Fritzi and Audrey in. They talked it over, agreeing to leave the following night for France.

Audrey said her goodbyes first; she'd had enough for one day. As she drove off she mulled whether anyone could ever get the truth out of Romaine. Audrey knew she somehow needed to clear herself for good with the law.

But how?

She had tried to clear herself with Cliff Rhodes, but he saw right through her. That she had lied about Kardas and herself. She had been openly shamed, and he was the easiest target to vent anger upon. But she knew in her bones she was mostly angry at herself on three counts. Bringing Romaine back into her life, and all the grief that caused; getting herself bedded by Kardas; and now all the gossip.

She was being talked about around town. Snickering, low-down jokes she could do nothing about. It galled her but it wasn't nearly as bad as having the police pester you crazy.

She had to close the book on Romaine. But that seemed as impossible as the idea of Cliff Rhodes being dead.

Chapter Forty-Two

"Gin." Audrey discarded, fanning out her cards.

"That's very impure of you."

"Six games and that makes the set."

"You've a mirror behind me somewhere." Fahey smiled at her out of his new black beard. "Never heard of the luck," he added. "Like my gypsy."

"What gypsy?"

"Secret weapon. Going to sell her to the Russian Air Force one day."

Audrey stacked the cards. "Shall we finish this later?"

"Dropping out on me while you're ahead? Shame."

"I'll play if you want to . . . but I'd rather have more champagne."

He went over to the small galley in the 747's upstairs lounge. At 5:20 celestial time, they were still wide awake. Fritzi, exhausted, had grabbed a blanket and curled up on a row of seats down below in the half empty plane.

Audrey and he had come upstairs to be alone, to talk of

art and Fahey's recent discovery of the Tunisian poets—those forgotten and lost minstrels of the desert.

Fahey had talked of marriage and his theory that we are all the failures of someone else's hopes. "You drown in promises that even God couldn't keep," he explained. "And unlike time, marriage wounds all heals." But love itself, that was quite different. The most nourishing force, wasn't it? Best never to follow the directions on the label at all, but just drink it down when love came your way.

Audrey had pondered the point.

They had drifted into gin rummy, penny a point in view of Fahey's thin wallet.

Audrey wanted to drift into something else before they reached Monte Carlo. Other matters worried her. Fahey handed her a fresh glass of Pol Roget.

"After Monte Carlo," Audrey said, "I may go on to London. My sons are there. Twins."

"Nippers, eh? How old?"

She told him.

"Who would've guessed." Fahey leaned back, eyeing her. "A girl like you and hardly a wrinkle."

Audrey smiled majestically. "And I'm worried."

"Comes with life. Have to trounce the worries. Fall in love again, then you can worry."

"I'm serious."

Seeing that she was, Fahey let her go on. The lingering suspicions left by the trial were still waving a sword at her. Romaine? Who would ever know for certain? But Audrey knew, no matter how it appeared to anyone else, of her own innocence. She could not bear to have her sons wondering, for one day she meant to get them back, and any clouds hanging over her reputation could only cause problems.

"Will you help me, Alonzo? You know a lot of what happened."

"To my regret. Help you how?"

"Can I engage you? After we get back. Will you work for me and look into it?"

"A small problem looms," Fahey said. "My license may be lifted. Might beach me, the sodders." He explained his own predicament, tempted to tell Audrey that Rhodes was at fault. But that wouldn't do at all. Why blame the dead when they were safe and dry forever. He knew that he had pulled the real trigger one fine day at Las Infantas.

Rest him, thought Fahey. Give him peace and many girls for playing with on his own private star.

"Could I do something?" Audrey was asking.

"Many things." Fahey laughed. "But we'd better wait till Paris."

"C'mon . . . I meant about your license." She took a sip. "I've still got friends. I know the governor. I can try," she said, holding her glass precariously.

Fahey straightened her hand; for quite a time he straightened it. "Thanks, cherub, but there's another hitch. I represented Romaine Brook and so I can't do it for you if you're against each other."

"What do you owe her? That's over."

"Question of what they call ethics. Slim, but there swinging away all the same."

"Of course I'd pay you."

"Can't do. I'll find someone for you."

"I'd like to have you," said Audrey, disappointed.

Fahey barely heard her. His mind fastened on Romaine. Had she? Rhodes was in good physical shape. Took care of himself, a very agile boyo with fast reflexes. How had he fallen off a cliff?

"Are you asleep?"

Fahey opened his eyes. "Thinking of those Tunisian poets again. Vatican stole their best stuff. Ought to admit it and give it back."

"Oh, damn. You won't help?"

"Let's hear the tales of Monte Carlo first. Then we'll see," Fahey promised. A subtle sexual tension was pulling at them. He could feel it and wanted to turn this serious talk to the lighthearted variety.

"Alonzo, would you? Fritzi said you can do anything."

"She must've meant this," said Fahey, gently moving her face. A kiss became part of his life, to remember always as the first kiss of that minute at 34,000 feet over that precise place on the Atlantic.

Audrey quivered. She removed Fahey's hand from its high creep under her green woolen Givenchy suit.

"Somebody's going to come," she warned, pulling her hem down.

"But that's the whole idea." Fahey smiled thinly as the rest of him surged.

"You're silly. Im-poss-i-bblle."

"Listen, we can get one of those Air France medals... I'll call down to the skipper. Have a ceremony when we land."

"No thanks."

Fahey jumped. "Jesus, I forgot my other medal," he half shouted, startling Audrey. "Gypsy's probably hocked it by now... For funerals, you see. Honor the missing with it." And now he wished he knew even one Tunisian poet who would come to offer laments over his dead friend.

Audrey hadn't the faintest idea of what he was talking about. He looked so suddenly lost that she folded both his hands in hers, purring a nothing-everything in his ear. She could never recall kissing a man who kept a hankie tucked up his sleeve. Nor one who wore an orange ascot and a black beret.

Though the high season was over and the Hermitage had reduced its rates, Romaine worried about how she would pay the bill. The manager sympathized. The hotel would move her to smaller quarters, and credit her at the lower rate for the past three days.

"Couldn't you hurry things up with the police?" she implored. "I must leave here."

The manager shrugged, his mouth pursing. "The police are the police," he said. "Slow and often busy." He offered her the services of the public relations staff. "You've had a bad time," he said. "And here in Monte Carlo we pride ourselves on our guests enjoying themselves."

Shop or visit the palace. Lunch perhaps at the Restaurant du Port. Courtesy of the hotel, the manager offered affably. "You must," he insisted.

Romaine didn't have to think it over. She was bored. She began to see the Hermitage as another prison, a costly one. She thanked him with a rapturous look.

An hour's layover before the flight down to Nice. They waited in the VIP lounge of Air France, with Fritzi looking fresher but still grim and taut. No smiles.

Fahey paced around like a jaguar on the hunt. And almost looked it, too, as he claimed a chill from the low altitude of Paris and had Audrey's sable slung over his shoulders. Be a great winter coat, he thought, for the regiment, when they formed it up.

A fresh notion provoked him.

He wanted to call the Quai d'Orsay, tell the President they'd arrived. Could they assist in any way? How was the table fare this year? Like some guests? Was there a spare private plane to be had on loan?

An attempt to perk Fritzi up. She only frowned when he informed her of this newest idea.

Chastized, Fahey went to the lounge hostess, cajoling her into a free call to Monte Carlo. The police, he told her. Utmost urgency and could she pretend she was his traveling secretary when making the call.

Matin stood behind a glass partition on the upper level of the Nice airport. Twilight shaded the field, and the landing lights smoldered in the damp haze rolling in from the Mediterranean.

The Air France station manager would page the Americans, or at least the man Fahey, when the passengers filed into the terminal. Matin had already arranged it.

They came from all corners, Matin thought. Some for play, others on business, still others wealthy enough to live the year round on the Cote d'Azur. What would these new Americans be like? He turned away now for the short walk to the escalators.

"M'sieur Fah-hay . . . M'sieur Fah-hay, please come to Air France information desk," came an invisible and satiny voice.

Fahey beamed. He had just walked through the doors, sauntering between Fritzi and Audrey. "My celebrity . . . never leave you alone, do they? See you at the baggage."

He headed off for the Air France counters, his black beret perched rakishly over his eyes. Matin stepped forward. They shook hands, Fahey regarding the rotund inspector in delight.

"Inspector, I'm about to introduce you to the best women in all California. Sunkist as the oranges, tell you that for not a sou."

Matin made a very slight bow. "They're with you, yes?"

"My sentries. Never without them."

"I see. Should we find them?"

They engaged in a conference. Why not put them in their own taxi? "They know all about luggage," Fahey said. He would drive in separately with Matin. They could talk, clear up a few points . . .

Fahey liked Matin at first glance. He liked his pink jowls and the soup spots on his lapels. Matin was calm, the sort of man you could depend on to see the finer points of a problem.

Leaving Matin, he went to tell the women how lucky they were to be driven into Monte Carlo by themselves. The inspector needed softening up, seemed to have a temper, was drearily long-winded. He'd see them at the hotel, and waved them a cheery goodbye.

In Matin's Renault Fahey rolled down the window. He breathed in the night, testing it for flavor, and asked if Matin would kindly drive the coastal road into Monte Carlo. He wanted to see the sea villages again of Villefranche, Cap Roux, and further up, Cap d'Ail. Slower that way, but he needed to find out what Matin knew.

The inspector began describing the sparse details of Rhodes's accident—a plunge onto rocks far below. A strong wind that day, boats in the harbor were damaged, and Rhodes had been drinking wine apparently. Might even have taken ill.

"Do you know who he is, or was?"

"I do now," Matin said. "Your consul in Nice told me."

"What of the autopsy?"

"Nothing unusual at all from the chemical tests. Broken back and a fractured cranium. That's what killed him."

"Was he sick, did you say?"

"Dizziness perhaps. Nothing organic, though."

"Did you know, Inspector, she stood trial for murder in Cliff Rhodes's court?"

"Yes, M'sieur," said Matin softly. "She explained it all

to me. Quite openly. A very unusual relationship seemed to develop between them."

"Do you know anything about the young woman? Is she staying at the same hotel?"

"Next door. She is booked at Hermitage . . . No," Matin went on, "I know very little of her. I met with her once after the accident. We required her statement. We could find no other witnesses. She seemed very forthright. Though we didn't like the fact that she was traveling under someone else's passport."

"She was, was she? Anyone we know?"

Matin gave him the name.

"A stranger to me," Fahey observed. "When I first talked to you from California, you said the Brook girl was Cliff Rhodes's fiancée. Is that what she told you?"

"Yes. They were expecting to marry apparently, she advised me."

Not likely, thought Fahey. It was dark enough in the car so Matin couldn't notice the deep, sharp look on Fahey's face. His eyes bored into the night as if he were taking a bead on a dime a mile away.

Fahey said nothing, only thought.

Circling the small seaside village of Villefranche, they headed up to the higher crest of Monte Carlo. In the distance the lights glimmered pink and amber, and Fahey smelled a faint trace of brine on the night air. He wished for rain, thinking it might carry a different fragrance here. Like Chanel No. 5 perhaps.

They entered Monaco on the Avenue Prince Albert, rolling through a small park, and up several more blocks before swinging onto Avenue Kennedy. Almost every street in Monaco was named after some luminary or other: half of them, it seemed, for the royal family. Fahey designed a street sign for himself, in his other thoughts, as he played one more idea off Matin.

"Cliff Rhodes was my friend, Inspector."

"I assumed so."

"What if his death was no accident?"

"Ah, but we have no reason to think otherwise. An accident, M'sieur Fahey. A regrettable thing, but that is how we see it."

"But then, what if it wasn't? You're a cop, Inspector. I was a cop once. You have to think the worst sometimes. That's why I got out of it."

Matin failed to answer. They'd come to the Place du Casino, the cobbled street sleek and dampened under the pale burn of the streetlights. Ranks of Rolls and Daimlers everywhere, and across the way the Hotel de Paris in a splendor that doubled Fahey's heartbeat.

As Matin parked, Fahey opened his door. "Old gal looks grand, doesn't she?" he said.

Matin thought Fahey was referring to an elderly matron, silk-growned and fur-wrapped, being helped up the red carpet steps by a doorman. He shook his head.

"Can we meet tomorrow, Inspector? Say in the morning around ten. At our hotel."

"Very good, yes. And with Mam'selle Brook?"

"That'd be best."

"Is there something I should know?"

"Let's wait till tomorrow."

"M'sieur Fahey, why is it you want the young woman present tomorrow?"

"It's the Tunisians. They insist on it, Inspector."

Matin scowled into the windshield. Another befuddled American. He watched the "ex-cop" bound up the steps two at a time. Strange, he thought. The whole episode struck him as very odd, and he hadn't liked the more difficult subtleties of Fahey's questions.

He found them in their sitting room, a man's room paneled in richly polished walnut; in the middle of the room a round table holding a large silver bowl of red and white roses. He admired the sizes in this hotel. The room was large enough, he decided, to train a circus elephant.

"We ordered dinner sent up," said Fritzi. "All right with you?"

"What kept you?" Audrey asked before he answered Fritzi.

"Came the long way. Needed a moment with the inspector."

Fahey sat down. Already they were in their dressing gowns. How women could do it, undress so fast, but you could read a book while they were powdering up, was his constant mystery.

"Matin marks it down," he said, "as an accident. No witnesses. So there it is, and that's all he wants to hear." Fahey turned to Audrey. "I had to tell him you were under suspicion about Marc. That's a hand-washer for him. Solely a California matter . . ."

"Why did you say that?" Audrey complained.

Before he could answer, the dinner arrived of partridge stuffed with rice, a salad, two bottles of Batard-Montrachet. Fahey savored the wine, but ate little, telling them what he had learned from Matin. He said nothing about Romaine passing herself off as Cliff Rhodes's fiancée. He needed time to think on it, and he wouldn't upset Fritzi for anything.

Fahey yawned. Sleep yelled at him and he was losing tempo. Audrey was jet-lagged, too, and headed for bed. Caught in her own heavy thoughts, Fritzi found herself surprised. She had know Alonzo Fahey for years, but never seen him like this, so dead serious.

Fahey excused himself, needing time by himself. He'd shoot down to the American Bar off the lobby, and graze on a couple of Bushmills. Clear the head, then the sleep would come kiss him.

He woke in the gray of six the next morning, with the staying power of the drink turning into a bale of wool in his mouth. Shaking his fatigue away, he called Matin. He wanted to see the accident scene, could Matin arrange it?

An hour later a young police officer, who had picked Fahey up at the hotel, showed him the ledge at Cap de la Veille. The officer carried a diagram, a freehand drawing of the reconstructed accident scene, and then translated Romaine Brook's version of how it happened.

Fahey tramped the ground. He examined, then studied more, and asked until there was no more to ask. Not right at all, he thought. Rhodes could drink a horse to its knees.

Out on the ledge he leaned against the wobbly rail that reached only to his lower thighs. He asked the officer to get behind him, then push gently.

"I would not dare, M'sieur."

"Please. Do it while I hold on to this rail," Fahey urged.

The officer barely tapped him.

"Harder," Fahey shouted. "Give it some arm."

A grab at Fahey's belt, another push, the real thing this

time. Fahey ungripped the rail, but his reflexes, against the push, were quick enough. His knees buckled, but *under* and not over the rail.

A wind?

"Do it again," Fahey said. "Push me again but from underneath my ass. The derrière."

The push again, not so hard, but this time Fahey felt the sudden sensation of going over. His upper body suddenly bent forward as one move before he regained his balance. Down below, he saw white water foaming over the rocks, some of them sharp as steeples.

The young officer looked at him as if he were mad.

"Let's go, friend," said Fahey, and they returned to the path leading through the woods.

Fahey suspected Romaine for doing something so final and so terrible they would never straighten it out. A girl like her, one for making the light shake and jump, one of those rare ones. So hard to find even if you knew where to go looking.

And looking to his right now out at the roaming sea, so drastically blue, he knew Tunisia and those ancient poets lay somewhere across the nervous horizon. He could see everything with a hundred eyes, for two hundred straight miles, and he felt something come up in his throat.

"M'sieu is so quiet," said the officer before Fahey had finished planning his invasion of Tunisia.

"Truth," said Fahey, far away still in voice and thought. "I wonder what truth's address is these days."

A quizzical frown from the officer, and then: "Truth, m'sieu?" They rounded the corner to the Hotel de Paris.

"I was thinking truth must begin in places where they cook with garlic and wine... It frightened me so I had to be quiet for a time. Don't tell anyone."

He didn't elaborate. They pulled up in front of the hotel and Fahey got out, thanking the officer. Even though he felt drugged by depression, he took the steps quickly, wishing today were last year and already forgotten.

On the dot of ten they arrived. A double knock on the door, and Fahey, rolling his eyes and showing his palms, looked balefully at Fritzi and Audrey. Closing the bedroom door, he hurried out to the other one in the sitting room.

At first Romaine didn't recognize Fahey because of his beard. She hadn't expected to see him there, and her heart flipped when he greeted her.

"You!" she said.

"Me." Fahey winked.

"What's he doing here?" Romaine asked Matin, who quietly answered, "Perhaps he will tell us, mam'selle."

"How fun to see you again," she said to Fahey. "There's been an awful accident. I suppose you've heard."

Fahey said he had as he marveled at her. Romaine went over to the large round table in the middle of the room and plucked a white rose from a bouquet. She twirled it in her fingers, then sat on a divan near the windows.

"What brings you here?" she asked. "In all this?" Her hand swept out to emphasize the sumptuous room.

"Come to see my friend off," Fahey said. "Going to bury him here."

"Cliff, you mean?" Romaine looked at Matin.

"Yes," Fahey said. "Going to stage a proper wake for him."

Romaine smiled thinly. She signaled a warning to Fahey with her eyes.

"I asked the inspector to bring you by. I had a question or two."

"Do I have to?" Romaine asked Matin.

"What harm can there be, mam'selle? You are acquainted with M'sieur Fahey, is that not so?"

"Slightly, yes."

Fahey started in again, telling Romaine of his visit to the scene of the accident that morning. Wanted to get the feel of it, see where his friend had perished. It seemed strange that Cliff Rhodes—a man who had once been a highly trained soldier—would get taken off by the wind. At least any wind short of a tornado. Rhodes was a physically agile man, tough and fast.

"I don't really buy it . . . an accident," he said to Romaine, and then quickly added, looking at Matin: "No offense, Inspector, I'm sure you people are very thorough."

Romaine stood up. She looped an easy, sad smile at both

men. "If you'd only been with us that day you would have seen for yourself. But I'm so glad you're here, Alonzo. It's nice that a friend would come. Now I feel better."

She never missed a beat. Standing by the window, she touched the white rose to her cheek. A misty look crept through the Madonna smile lighting up her face.

"Why were you here with him, Romaine?" Fahey wanted to know.

"I told the inspector already."

"Tell me."

"Cliff and I were going to live here in Europe. Get married probably, though that's none of your business."

Fahey marveled at her again. Must be the fastest mind this side of Jerusalem, he thought. "That's not a nice thing to say. You know, Romaine, or maybe you don't know, I was going to give Fritzi Jagoda away at her wedding. She and Cliff were—"

"Oh, Inspector," Romaine gushed. "We've been all through this and it's such a bore. Cliff Rhodes wanted to get rid of that woman. I told you."

Matin opened his mouth, but said nothing. He wondered where those other women were, the two he had yet to meet. He wasn't long in finding out. He listened as Romaine rambled on, her back half turned, facing the window again.

Fahey felt a nightmare coming on as he went over to the bedroom door, pushing it open. He beckoned to Fritzi and Audrey. Romaine sensed their footfalls and wheeled around from the window.

Her face froze, going white as an ice carving, then becoming fragile and quivering. "God, what is this! What's happening here, Inspector?" The white rose fell from her fingers. She had no idea the three of them knew each other.

"Not a thing is happening, mam'selle," said Matin, rising to greet Fritzi and Audrey as Fahey introduced them.

Audrey sent Romaine a look laced with pity and scorn. They said nothing. But Audrey moved to a place where Romaine couldn't help but see the emerald bracelet around her wrist.

"Cliff sent it back, Romaine," she said evenly.

"Sent what back?"

"This." Audrey raised her hand.

"I don't know what you're talking about." Romaine's eyes, dark as gun muzzles now, swept them all. With one trembling finger she pointed at Fritzi, who had to force herself to look back. "See, Inspector, that's the woman I told you about. The one Cliff Rhodes wanted to dump. She's going to lie to you, so watch out."

Matin looked bewildered. It was as if he were witnessing a family argument with no idea of what would happen. He saw Fritzi Jagoda sag a little as Fahey put his hand on her shoulder. Matin cleared his throat and began to ask some questions of his own.

As he asked them, and Fritzi answered, and Romaine denied Fritzi's replies, Fahey observed everything closely. He saw Audrey's face go livid, flashing up to a bright pink. He didn't quite understand why . . . for he knew nothing of her real history with Romaine. He kept looking at Fritzi who seemed so drawn, thinner and beaten, and without her ever present smile for days now. That rankled him. But what could he do? It was just of those situations where the women would have to settle it, bite all the ice by themselves. Waiting for Fritzi to unload on Romaine, tell her what Cliff Rhodes was all about, he didn't notice Audrey slipping out of the room.

It wouldn't be easy, Audrey knew. Actually, it would be the hardest thing she'd ever done. She would have to live with it forever. But Cliff Rhodes was dead, and he probably died because she hadn't laid the truth on him a long time ago.

The hell with it, she thought. She couldn't shoulder that cross for even one more hour. What griped her even more was Romaine out there doing another fandango. Making fools of them, and brave Fritzi not smashing Romaine to bits, keeping her word not to reveal anything.

It had to stop. Now.

She rummaged around in her suitcase, and found what she was looking for. A moment later she was back in the other room, walking through the explosive blue air right up to Matin.

"Inspector," Audrey said. "If you'll just listen, I think we can put an end to all this." Passing the Las Infantas papers over, she told him: "Those are birth records and adoption papers . . . They prove, and I can prove, that I am this girl's real mother. She's never known it before this instant. What happened here in Monte Carlo, I don't know, but this daughter of mine is lying and—"

"Don't believe her, Inspector, it can't be true," Romaine blurted.

But Matin had already stopped Romaine with a policeman's look. He saw a dumbfounded stare widen Fahey's eyes before he urged Audrey: "Please go on, madame."

"When you go through those papers," Audrey went on, "you'll find out, Inspector, that Cliff Rhodes was this girl's father . . . your own father, Romaine," she nearly screamed at her daughter, "that's who died here. And now you want us all to believe he brought you here to marry him. You're the worst liar I ever met in my life, and I wish to God I'd never heard of you. Ever, ever, ever!"

Romaine began to reel. One by one the walls of the room seemed to cave in on her. She had lied to Matin, and now he would know it. The air around her became heavy with dread.

Fahey came quietly up beside Romaine. He knew it was all over now, but he had to ask anyway. "You finished them both off, didn't you, my darling? Both Cliff and the Sterne boy, eh? Tell me, I won't tell a soul," he coaxed her.

Another silence, this one like the day before the earth was ever created. Quick as a wildcat, Romaine clawed at him. He grabbed for her wrists but she slumped to the floor.

"Get away from me . . . You godawful people. You were—you were all in it together. Bastards! I hate you, hate you!" she yelled high at the ceiling. "Oh, Inspector, don't you see—I had to protect myself. My own mother. She's not my mother. She can't be! And that bitch"—pointing at Fritzi, then at Audrey, confused, her face streaming with tears—"they want you to think my fiancé was my, oh, the bastards, they were out to stop me. Put me away. Tell me I was crazy! I'm not crazy! I was going to be a star and everything . . . oh, oh, even Cliff. They got him to go after me. He was going to turn me in. I had to get rid of him."

Fritzi gasped.

Romaine stopped abruptly. But her words didn't stop. They cruised in and out of every ear in the room.

Matin's face knitted into a scowl. He spoke into the hush of the room slowly then angrily, looking directly at Romaine all the time.

"You have lied to us all, mam'selle. At least you have lied to me, and I must warn you you will answer for all of them."

Matin turned to the others. One by one he reminded them they were witnesses to Romaine's admission that she *had to get rid of him*. They would have to sign statements before leaving Monte Carlo.

Moving toward Fritzi, Fahey hung an arm around her. He was unable to take any more truth today. He began to think it was the truth that had somehow killed the Dance-Master, and the same truths would spell the end for Romaine now. The truth had been kicked around for twenty-two years until it finally lashed back in fury.

As Romaine sobbed again, Fahey thought of the opening line of the poem Cliff Rhodes had admired so much: *"Tiger, Tiger, burning bright."* She was one of them. One of those incendiary tigers purring in your ear, slashing at your heart.

He should've known it all along, for the gypsy had told him that truth is like a dazzling woman—it always takes you a hundred times to see her clearly.

While she blinds you.

About the Author

DAVID CUDLIP holds a master's degree in business administration from Dartmouth College and served in Europe with United States Army Intelligence before entering a business career with the New York banking firm, Brown Brothers Harriman & Co. There followed many years as senior vice-president and financial officer in the aviation industry. He is the founder and chairman of a privately held company developing an in-store couponing system, and lives in California. His first novel, *Comprador*, was published by E.P. Dutton in 1984.